Manisses

For Meredith —

Thank you...

I hope you enjoy my island !

a) novel

By

Steven R. Porter

Steven R. Porter

April 2016

Manisses
by Steven R. Porter

Print Edition
2012

Books and other works by Steven R. Porter can be obtained either through the author's official website: **www.StevenPorter.com**, Stillwater River Publications or through superior retailers.

Visit our website **at www.StillwaterPress.com** for more information.

ISBN-10: 1-47835-480-1
ISBN-13: 978-1-47835-480-2
2 3 4 5 6 7 8 9 10

Published by Stillwater River Publications, Glocester, RI, USA
Cover design by Wicked Smart Designs, Bellingham, Washington, USA

For Thomas and Susannah:

"Life can only be understood backwards; but it must be lived forwards."

-- Soren Kierkegaard

Chapter 1

Wequai was not aware of the significance of the moment, or her role as part of it. She was not aware that the violent battle that raged around her was to be a momentous turning point in the history of her people, an unrecorded but significant instant in time, and though it was a mere speck on a page of the infinite calendar, it was a moment that closed a millennia of peace and started her people on a decline after enjoying thousands of years of prosperity. And she was not aware of the plight of her brave young husband and brothers who were off defending their stout woodland village from a vicious enemy invasion. For Wequai was with child and she was determined with every force of her being to protect it -- and though there was expected be one more moon before her first child's birth, the uncompromising pain in her belly demanded otherwise. She feared that the child she would bring forth might arrive to a village that would no longer exist to welcome it.

Skirmishes among the coastal tribes were nothing new, and occasional raids to steal foodstuffs and weapons between rivals, and some occasional retribution, were an accepted part of everyday existence. But the sheer size of this attack was something different, much more forceful and vicious, and brought with it a current of doom and finality. The attack had been predicted by the elders, who watched the tension build for weeks. The warriors of Wequai's tribe had been sharpening their spears and crying out before the spirits, searching for the inner strength and skill they would need to defeat their great allies turned enemies and regain their village and way of life from the clutches of imminent annihilation.

Wequai burrowed into a pile of soft deerskins stored at the back of a wigwam in a remote corner of the compound where the tribe stored the bulk of their winter supplies. In the distance, the horrifying crashes and echoes of mortal combat crept closer and grew louder. The urgent sounds of men running past her along the dry, pounded earth at first calmed her fragile nerves, a welcoming sound that the warriors of her village were charging ahead to defend and protect. But the longer she laid still in her hiding place, the more anxious she became. She worried the village would not have enough brave men to fight off the attack, and the waves of pain in her belly were growing more intense, closer together, more jagged, and more urgent.

The battle raged through the afternoon, and as the sun retreated to the west, a moonless summer night fell over the stained battleground. Sweltering beneath the pelts, Wequai emerged and tore a small hole through the birch bark of the wigwam to examine what she could see of the scene. From her veiled corner, she could make out enormous fires glowing from the distant parts of her village, and she listened as the valiant songs of warriors were replaced by screams of pain, terror and death. She realized that the wails of the little children she was hearing in the distance were actually the cries of once brave men now dying -- some no more than 12 or 13 harvests old. She saw cragged old women and little children run by, terror welling in all their eyes, many stumbling and screaming. She saw hundreds of skirmishing warriors, as if dancing with their own shadows in the darkness, slowly moving toward her. Wequai began to chant and hum a peaceful song her grandmother, an honored medicine woman, taught her when she was just a little girl, to be applied like a salve to sooth her tattered nerves. The tip from an angry warrior's long, sharp spear slashed through the wall of her shelter, tearing a gash the length of a grown man, sending shards of wood and bark to rain down upon her. Though she remained unnoticed, she knew her time to move on, or die, had arrived.

Though the compound had surrendered to darkness, the terrible battle raged on. The pain in Wequai's abdomen was continuing to build, and she crawled through the entrance of her shelter and emerged into the chaos with one arm wrapped firmly under her belly. Ahead by the shore, there was a clump of sassafras trees and juniper shrubs where she believed she could remain unseen, or failing that, behind it was an old dugout canoe, stored by her fisherman uncle, that she thought she might be able to use to escape. The village smelled of a smoke that Wequai recognized, but it wasn't the sweet, comforting smell of cod stew or venison turning over the dinner fire -- it was the unmistakable, unforgettable, horrific odor of seared human flesh.

The fetid smoke helped shield and distract Wequai from the invaders who had now overtaken the village. All the buildings and wigwams had been set ablaze by enemy torches, and waves of intense heat were carried through the village by the cooling evening coastal breeze. Wequai dragged herself toward her new hiding place, and she leaned her exhausted, aching body against the side of the long canoe.

The vessel was more than the length of three grown men, and contained all her uncle's seafaring hand-made nets and tackle. As a child, she had been assigned the tedious duty of hollowing out the great log herself, using a bone hatchet and red-hot oak embers from the dinner fire to burn and smooth the vessel into shape. Standing up to her waist in the cool, salty water of the cove, she tried to push it out to sea, but did not have anywhere near the strength. For the first time since she had begun her labor, she screamed aloud from the pain of the impatient child inside searching for its own means of escape. Lifting one leg up over the side, she flopped into the front of the canoe on her back upon the netting, and surrendering to her hopeless predicament, her eyes welled with tears, and she sobbed.

Wequai was very small for her age of sixteen, but tough and wiry, and she wiggled and burrowed deep into the fishing nets. She braced her thin, spindly legs against the frame and did all she could to stay quiet between the sharp spasms of pain. She accepted that her child would be born here, in her family's canoe, as a gift from the gods, but without the aid or comfort of her husband or grandmother, sisters, or any of the trusted women of her village. Though the war raged around her, she tried not to think about the fate of her family. But now that darkness engulfed her, she was awash in fear and loneliness.

Before she could weep for herself or her family too long, the boat rocked. Wequai felt a sudden thud and looked up. Standing in the canoe above her was a warrior, as if dropped by the gods from the dark sky above. Through the glow of the fires burning in the distance, she could see enough of the war paint on his face to realize he was not of her village. Wequai opened her mouth to scream in terror, but was so paralyzed with fear, no sound would come out. Then she realized he did not see her -- it was too dark and she was too low in the vessel. She also saw, upon his sweaty, painted face, a look of terror she had not seen upon a man's face before -- it was clear he was afraid of something, and looked to be escaping it. Upon her bare feet, she felt the trickle of a liquid, the warrior's blood, painting and tickling her dusty ankles and toes. She closed her eyes tight, held her breath and remained still and silent.

The stranger grasped an oar, and straining with all his might, was able to push and detach the heavy canoe from its mooring, setting it afloat upon the tranquil cove. The hissing sound of invisible razor-sharp arrows sped by them both, a few embedding themselves in the solid, thick, oak walls of the canoe. Others splashed harmlessly into the water. The warrior paddled with fury, grunting and breathing deeply as the canoe picked up speed and headed into the shadows, toward the cove's narrow mouth and into the open sea.

An especially intense pain struck Wequai's belly without warning, and she was able to control her silence no longer. Her sudden, high-pitched cry startled the warrior, who let out his own intense, terror-laden scream. Together, the pair screamed for their lives into the blackened night, spinning the vessel around in a circle upon the ocean. The situation might almost have been comical, had both inhabitants of the boat not assumed they were about to be killed by the other.

The warrior reached out and grabbed Wequai by her clammy forearm and pulled her close. He clenched his teeth and peered into her eyes, trying to determine whether she was friend or foe. His breath was hot and rhythmic upon her face and he smelled of spice and tobacco smoke. He was much bigger and stronger and larger than any man in her village, and she thought the grip he had on her might snap her arm in half like a birch sapling. She gasped and trembled, and feared her heart might leap from her breast. She knew that with very little effort at all, if he chose to, the man could toss her into the sea to drown. His arm brushed her stomach and he realized she was heavy with child. He paused, then extended his enormous, weathered palm to stroke her swollen belly. With little effort, he pushed her back down to the floor of the canoe upon the nets and resumed rowing, uttering not a syllable, content that she would be no threat in her condition. Wequai sensed his compassion, took a deep breath, arched her back in the agony and relief of the moment and the pain, and escaped consciousness.

Chapter 2

The island was anything but flat, and featured several rolling and a few steep but majestic hills. At the point of the island along the shore there stood a curious outcropping of large, stunning black rocks, highlighted by a single tall black boulder that reached higher than, and as stately as a tree. Although it took millions of years of violent geological upheaval, millions of years of ice and snow, and millions of years of sharp, stone-carving winds to mold and create these rocks, the outcropping and boulders appeared to not belong, as if placed in that very position by the hand of a god with great care, much the way a whimsical child might place a beloved toy into a fanciful diorama.

Wequai leaned against the massive rock, her shoulder comforted by the colossal boulder, as she gazed across the sea toward the mainland, feeding her newborn son in the warmth of the morning summer sunshine. She could see smoke rising from the shore where she believed her village stood and only now did she appreciate how massive the battle must have been, as it appeared to her that the entire sky line was ablaze. The canoe that had delivered them to the island had been swept back out to sea by the incoming morning tide, and it bobbed in the waves in front of her, drifting away, taunting her, well out of her reach. She longed for her family, and wondered if any of them had survived, and if she would ever see them again. She longed for the love and wisdom of her husband who was a skilled and brave warrior, and she was confident he must have killed many of the wretched enemy. But most of all, she wanted to show them all the beautiful baby boy she had brought into the world -- the newest member of her proud tribe. Her son had been born in the early hours of the morning, all blue, skinny and messy, and silent, without a scream, near sunrise, behind the immense black rock which now gave her shelter from the cool morning sea breeze.

The great warrior who had saved her life, rowed her across the sea, and carried her up to the shelter of the great rock, was dead. He laid on his face in the matted beach grass by her feet with several arrows sticking straight up from his neck and back, dried blood bathing his ribs. She sat in awe of his strength and courage, and realized the warrior had achieved a level of heroism that Wequai had only heard in her grandmother's honored stories. She remembered nothing of their voyage across the sea that night, fading in and out of consciousness throughout the journey, now arriving at the conclusion that this warrior had been sent by the gods to save her so she could give birth to her son here on this island. Everything had a purpose. The chaos would someday make perfect sense.

As she stared at his stiff, lifeless body, she marveled at the size and tone of the muscles on his shoulders, arms and calves, and the perfection of his smooth, tanned skin. She reached over and stroked his cold shoulder, lovingly, to thank him. He was beautiful, and she believed he must have been a great husband — for a heathen. She pulled her baby from her breast and held him out to the dead warrior.

"Here, my son, look upon the brave warrior who sacrificed his life so that you could live. Do not forget him, for he was sent by the gods just for you." The baby opened his eyes for the first time, albeit briefly, revealing two pupils big, round and as black as the night sky under which he was born.

"Oh my, little god! Your eyes are so beautiful!" Wequai bubbled despite her dilemma, waves of joy bounding across her face. "We need to give you a name, so I will call you... Manisses! The little god."

Wequai held Manisses with both hands, naked, toward the sky, and bowed her head to thank the spirits for the gift they had bestowed upon her. She looked down at the body of the poor, dead warrior once more and wondered if he, too, had a wife and child. She assumed he did, and shared their sorrow.

"Well, Manisses, I believe his wife to be very beautiful, and that she was blessed with many children. A warrior this strong and powerful must have been a wise leader, too, and very well respected." Wequai paused and looked at him, troubled. "But I wonder what he was running away from, when he jumped in Uncle's canoe? A warrior with this much bravery and honor running through his veins would not run from a great battle. That's why I know he was sent to us by the gods to save you."

Wequai spent the morning pulling up the grasses from around the great rock, making a small bed for the newborn Manisses to lie upon, layering it with soft milkweed fluff. She removed what little clothes the warrior was wearing and swaddled Manisses in them. And in the warrior's beaver-skin belt, she found a knife.

"A gift for you, and for me," she said, tucking the little god into his cradle of fresh island grasses.

But her concern turned from her new child to the local island residents, and she wondered if she was alone. Tribal legend had taught her that both her tribe and people originated on this island, and being so isolated, they were able to grow and improve their culture without complication or fear of aggression. The island was just visible along the horizon from her village on shore, and was believed to be no longer inhabited. The fishermen knew to stay away from the island as it was a sacred and spiritual place -- a place where the gods came to play and rest. She decided it best to seek out the island people and try to tell them what had happened -- that is, if they existed at all.

Every muscle in her body was stiff and sore, and she found it difficult to stand and walk. But Wequai was born with the brawn of a small boy, and her wiry frame was built for climbing. In her youth, she had climbed every tree in her village faster than any of the boys. She pulled herself up on the rocks and began her ascent to the top. The rocks were slippery, smoothed by the island's constant winds and sprinkled at its edges with white sea salt, and although her aching back and legs argued, she climbed with great care, and was able to reach the top.

From the peak, she could see a great distance in all directions, and nearly the whole island. The ocean was calm, its waves small and blue, and the sun was hot on her back. The rocks themselves were already absorbing the heat of the day and warmed the soles of her feet. Wequai held her balance and scanned the horizon. There were signs of life everywhere -- gulls, ducks, plovers and birds of every kind -- even a few white-tailed deer bounded by off in the distance, no doubt once captured and brought to the island by those early ancestors. But there was no sign of recent human habitation. There were no settlements, no smoke fires, no field, no wigwams, and no moored canoes.

Manisses and Wequai were alone on the island.

Wequai stood on top of the great rock for a long time. She looked away toward her home in the distance, across the sea, and at the smoke that filled the skies and mingled overhead with the grey summer clouds. She was overcome with despair and wondered how she would ever get home. As a young girl, she had a beautiful voice and loved to sing, and her grandmother taught her more songs than any of the other girls in the village. Wequai inhaled, and the heavy, humid sea air filled her chest. With her arms raised and palms open, Wequai sang a song to the island that welcomed the morning, one of her father's favorites. And though she sang loud and with beauty, only Manisses, sleeping in his soft nest of grass and milkweed far below, and a perplexed cormorant pulling on a rotting clam, were on hand to enjoy her sweet, honest, soulful performance.

There was an abundance of crabs and lobsters crawling along the beach, so if her exile on this island would be long, Wequai knew she would not starve. She despised the salty, pungent flavor of shellfish, and accepted her fate as a punishment from the gods for all the complaining she did as a child whenever her mother served it at the communal meal. But it wasn't the sustenance of survival that worried Wequai the most, it was the corpse of her gallant hero, lying face down in the grass by the great rocks, already crawling with ants, that would not do well for long in the blazing summer sunshine.

Wequai strolled along the shore and gathered a few crabs for her lunch, and was delighted to see birds' nests nearby so easily accessible where she might happen upon a few eggs, as well. She also collected a few large quahog shells that she could use to chip into tools. But her priority was to first quench her raging appetite, and then to bury her savior.

The soil in front of the big rock was soft, sandy, and easy to move, but filled with small stones. Wequai cursed aloud each time she dug in and dragged her knuckles across one of the ragged little rocks, and she broke several useful shells. She remained tired and weak, still recovering from her traumatic ordeal, and it took her two days of periodic bouts of digging, napping, and feeding Manisses to create a pit round and deep enough for the warrior's heavy, lifeless body.

Wequai lined the pit with soft needles from the small pitch pine trees that grew near the shore, to provide the warrior a comfortable resting place. Although her enemy, his courageous acts proved him deserving of a burial fit for a sachem -- and she would do her best to provide it. Once the pit was prepared, she attempted to drag him into it, but he was too heavy. She struggled, groaned and cursed as she pulled on his arms and legs, but she was barely able to move him along at all. Sitting, she placed her feet on his hips and gave a great scream, pushing with all her might, and his body, after much effort, rolled over. It was the first time she had seen his face in daylight, now bloated and disfigured, and she was both struck by its beauty and reviled by its misfortune. She paused for awhile to examine it, so she would not forget it, and could describe it to Manisses once he was older.

The body fell into the pit at an awkward angle, arms and legs pointing in all different directions, and it took some time for Wequai to arrange the naked corpse into its appropriate, honorable pose, head facing toward his homeland.

As was custom, a warrior was to be buried with all his most important tools and possessions, but having arrived on the island with merely a breechcloth and a bone knife -- two items that Wequai and Manisses needed to survive -- the warrior would be buried naked and without a weapon. Wequai surmised that since the spirits sent him to save her, they would understand when he arrived in the afterlife unadorned. And if he was embarrassed when he got there, she thought, he was not of her village -- he was, after all, just a savage.

Once arranged in the pit, Wequai laid leaf upon leaf over the body, leafs she had painstakingly picked herself from the low growing red and green shrubs, chanting a song throughout the private ceremony. In her village, she carried no special title or responsibility, but had attended many burial ceremonies and could recreate most of it from memory. She did the best she could, improvised a bit, and sang her warrior many enchanting songs, wishing him a safe journey to the afterlife. When the burial ritual was complete, and all the soil was returned to the hole, she sat against the great rock and brought little Manisses back to her breast. Wequai sang to him and wept as she watched the sun set beyond the orange horizon, over her old village, blanketing them in a friendless darkness.

Chapter 3

Prissy poked the stiff squirrel with a pointed stick.

"Yup, he's dead." She proclaimed

"Are you sure?" Abby asked, stroking her chin.

"Yup, I'm sure." Prissy nodded, with all the cocksure confidence of a seasoned coroner.

"I don't want him to bite me." Abby crossed her arms and clutched her ribs, fearing the critter would burst back to life.

"He won't bite you if he's dead."

"Where did he come from?"

"I don't know. He looks gray like all the squirrels back at my old house where I used to live in Connecticut."

"How did he get here? We don't have any squirrels on Manisses."

"I dunno. Maybe he came over on the ferry. And stop asking so many questions!"

The two girls squatted over the unfortunate, dead animal in front of a great, large black boulder and continued probing, poking at it, and rolling it over. Its bushy tail fluttered like a flag in the stiff breeze. The girls had no way to know, that thousands of years earlier, a scared, lonely, young native girl named Wequai nursed her newborn son and sang to her gods on the very same spot.

Prissy was a curious and precocious little girl, with short dark hair and small, round wire-rimmed glasses, shrewd well beyond her ripe old age of nine. She was undersized but athletic, and preferred being outside running around across the rocks on the beach behind her parents' house, chasing gulls and searching for pirate treasure, than inside playing with toys, watching television or even reading a book. Although Prissy had cast off many of the traditional baubles of a more typical modern girl, her constant companion was her ragdoll, Otto. Otto's hands were filthy and his fabric worn through, a victim of months of constant attention, and his blue, marble-like eyes had been re-sewn and re-glued many times by Prissy's mother, and were now well out of alignment. Otto was the only person in the world Prissy would consult when she was in trouble, had a question, or needed advice. Otto was considered neither a toy nor a friend, but instead he was Prissy's spiritual advisor, mentor, and guide -- a cotton and canvas blended Dalai Lama held together with a few bits of thread, yarn and a silver safety pin.

"Do you think we should bury him, Otto?" Prissy asked.

Otto looked at Prissy and appeared to ponder the question, but as was often the case, he didn't respond.

"I think we should have a séance." Abby suggested. "Then we can ask the squirrel to tell us why he is here."

Abby was Prissy's neighbor, classmate and loyal friend, fair and feminine, always donned in the most stylish dress, never a blonde hair out of place, as one would expect from the daughter of such affluent, well-connected parents. Abby cherished all her material things, her salon appointments and the attention, but she reveled in Prissy's friendship, too, as she enjoyed living vicariously through Prissy's more eccentric activities and adventures. Abby knew she could often convince Prissy to try things she was too frightened, or unwilling, to try herself. In many ways, Prissy enjoyed the challenges and dash of hero worship, and though she had no interest in them for herself, she did enjoy listening to Abby brag on about her expensive new boots, the silver brooch her dad gave her, or the hours she spent in the island salon getting pedicures with her mom. Prissy and Abby, opposites in almost every way, held the same tribal instinct, were good friends and knew that they somehow needed each other.

"OK, then. Let's have a séance. We can ask the squirrel what he thinks he is doing being dead here on our island!"

To the casual passerby who might be eavesdropping on the girls' conversation, a request from one nine year-old to another for a séance might wrinkle an eyebrow. However, for Prissy, it was not at all unusual. In fact, it was a normal and integral part of her everyday existence.

Prissy's father, Clement Bradford, was a professional spiritual medium. Just off the docks, across the street from

Manisses' bustling ferry landing, Clement had opened a small practice where he could offer his clairvoyant services to the throngs of tourists who disembarked from one of six daily ferries sent overflowing with passengers eager to explore the island's rich splendor. Its convenience just over an hour from the mainland, made Manisses a perfect destination for summer day trippers, bike peddlers, hikers, and adventurers of all ages, including many who preferred to just sit in one of the countless upscale lounges, slurp raw oysters off the half shell, drink white wine, and enjoy the refreshing, cool summer breeze.

It was here Clement Bradford decided to scrape out a living and support his family.

Clement and his wife Jessica had moved to the island of Manisses just two years earlier after partaking in a weekend getaway themselves, and they fell in love with the never-ending, spectacular views and the friendly, no-nonsense Yankee islanders. It was a wholesome and beautiful place to raise their two smart and eccentric daughters -- sixteen year-old Lucretia and nine year-old Priscilla, Lucky and Prissy, who they worried about fiercely. Lucky had been performing poorly in school and had fallen in with a tough crowd of teens, making daily calls from the high school vice principal both dreaded and common place. Lucky had twice been escorted home in the back seat of a Hartford Police Department squad car, which had not gone unnoticed by her younger, observant and impressionable little sister.

So Clement and Jessica left their practice and apartment in the Hartford, Connecticut suburbs, liquidated their meager life savings, rented a small storefront on Water Street, and purchased a dilapidated farmhouse that they couldn't afford on a far point of the island that featured a large but unusual stone outcropping, to raise their children in a healthy New England storybook atmosphere -- and talk to the dead.

"Let's start." Prissy commanded. "Everyone hold hands."

So the three of them -- Prissy, Abby and Otto -- sat cross-legged in a circle around the dead squirrel, and held hands.

"Everybody close your eyes." Prissy commanded again, rocking the three of them side to side. Otto's grubby feet dragged back and forth in the sand on the ground, but he did not complain.

"Oh mister squirrel... speak to us. We ask for the spirit of mister squirrel to come to us now, on this island of Manisses, and tell us why he is dead." The girls continued to rock side to side, and the squirrel remained quiet. A large white seagull circled overhead, its screech piercing. Abby opened her eyes and looked up, squinting into the bright, hazy blue sky.

"If he poops on me, I'm going home."

"Shut up and concentrate. We must have total concentration at all times or we will scare the spirit world away. You stay quiet, too, Otto."

Otto remained stoic and obedient, and complied with Prissy's request. It was well within his nature to be supportive.

"Prissy? I have a question. When the squirrel talks to us, what is he going to say? I mean... is he going to speak English, or is he going to talk squirrel? I don't know how to talk squirrel."

"That's up to the spirit world. My dad says that sometimes, the spirits don't talk. They give you a sign, or a feeling. Sometimes, they communicate with a sound or a noise like a knock on the wall or a creak in the floor. And sometimes they will put a hand on your shoulder, or give you a hug, or even make you feel suddenly hot or cold."

"That's creepy."

"And sometimes, the spirit will call out your name or just put an idea right into your head out of nowhere so that even though you don't speak squirrel, the spirit squirrel will talk to you in your own brain."

"But Prissy, I don't want the squirrel in my brain!"

"You won't have a squirrel in your brain, you dummy! The squirrel's soul will talk to your soul inside your brain. Souls know how to talk to each other because they are both souls. Now be quiet, close your eyes and concentrate."

Prissy, Abby and Otto sat in their vigil for several more minutes without uttering a sound. Around them, the sea breeze raked through the tall spartina grasses causing a pleasant, rhythmic hum, and the seagulls shrieked and chattered, flying in perfect circles overhead. The surf had been building all morning, indicating a summer storm might be moving up the coast from the south, and the waves had become taller and crashed on shore with a bit more force and regularity than before, even showing off an occasional, fluttering white cap.

A single, sturdy gust of wind blew by them sending sand, salt and a few loose leaves into Abby's face. Abby shrieked and scrunched up her cheek muscles to keep the flying debris out of her eyes and mouth, but some of it did stick in her beautiful, flowing golden hair.

"Ewww!" She exclaimed. "I got dirt all over me!"

"Maybe it's the squirrel talking to us." Abby suggested. Otto chose not to share an opinion. "Maybe he's telling us he blew in here from the mainland on a big hurricane!"

"Why would the squirrel's soul throw dirt in my face? I don't want to do this anymore. I want to go home." Abby broke the circle and stood, brushing dirt and sand from her frilly new dress.

"You can't go home until we bury him. We have to give him a proper Christian burial like they would do at church."

Abby waited while Prissy jogged down to the beach, rooted around in the surf and returned with a large, empty quahog shell. She handed Otto off to Abby, dropped to her already dirty knees and began to dig a hole -- a much smaller hole than Wequai had dug for her hero warrior, but a burial pit sufficient for a squirrel none the less. And it didn't take Prissy long to finish. Using the stick she had been digging with to poke the little corpse, she flipped it into the hole and covered it up with the loose sandy, salty soil. The tip of its gray, fluffy tail protruded from the pile.

"There, now. Let's say a prayer."

The girls stood together, closed their eyes and bowed their heads, each praying for the lost soul of the anonymous squirrel, together, with a solemnity with which a pastor would have been proud. When the prayers were complete, Prissy took a deep breath and the girls turned toward town.

Abby paused.

"Prissy, wait. We forgot something. We need to make a cross to mark the grave. All the graves next to the church either have crosses, headstones, or both!"

Prissy sighed, considered the request, nodded her agreement, and returned to the diminutive grave site. She retrieved her stick and scratched around in the earth beneath the great boulder until she found another to make the cross. Once she located the second suitable stick, Otto offered one of his shoelaces so she could lash the two sticks together. Abby took the cross from Prissy and planted it firmly into the ground, with a seriousness not expected of such a little girl, at the head of the squirrel's shallow grave.

Neither girl would ever know that the sticks they used to create the squirrel's handmade cross were artifacts from the leg bones of a heroic, ancient native warrior.

"That was a waste of time. Nothing interesting ever happens on this boring old island." Abby complained.

Chapter 4

O tto escorted both Prissy and Abby on their daily afternoon summer stroll up Water Street. The sky was steel blue, the tourists were thick and sweaty, and all the local merchants agreed that the unseasonably hot weather was delivering them one of the most lucrative summer seasons in a decade. The girls first passed the fine art gallery, its walls plastered with paintings of badly drawn sailboats, then a jewelry store that featured multi-colored seashells and polished stones, then two different t-shirt shops each with a shocking selection of imprinted hackneyed sayings, and finally Manisses Liquors -- the busiest and most popular shop of all. Beyond that was Captain Kidd's Cafe where the girls sometimes were slipped free ice cream by the waiters if business was slow, but on this day, they were disappointed to find the waiters in the spastic throes of an early dinner hour. Next to the cafe was Prissy's father's office where he conducted his private and exclusive spiritual investigations, and then Island Convenience. On the well-worn sidewalk in front of the convenience store was a long pine bench under an aged, green awning where the three old men sat every day -- Guilfoyle, Sumner and Jude.

From their roost, the three old men could monitor the comings and goings of everyone on the island -- tourists, locals, visitors and scalawags alike. They were the true New England Brahmin, the elders from families who had inhabited and ruled the island for hundreds of years, holding court and passing judgment on anyone who would dare wear a skirt too short, smoke a cigarette, expose a tattoo, or throw a candy wrapper to the ground. And once they identified an assailant, they would each unleash their own individual scowl, wiggle their fingers, and then together, shake their heads in disgust, content they had identified further evidence the world had indeed gone to hell in a hand basket.

The three gruff old men who sat on the same bench, all day, every day, and had done so for many years -- through many a fall, winter, spring and summer -- had become as much a fixture on the isle as the wharf, seawall, docks and beach itself.

Prissy shuffled past her father's office so as not to be noticed, for fear she would be sent home early for dinner, and miss her daily visit with the three old men, which would be disappointing. Prissy enjoyed asking questions and feeding her natural intellectual curiosity. Abby didn't enjoy the chats much at all, but tolerated the daily act as Jude would always give them each a quarter for the gumball machine in the convenience store when they were through.

"Oh hello there, Miss Priscilla," Jude said as the girls approached. "And how are you on this fine day? And good afternoon to you, too, Miss Abigail."

"I'm fine, sir, thank you for asking." Prissy answered tilting her head to one side, knowing that the old men responded better to the etiquette and formality. Abby forced a smile and just nodded and shuffled back to stand in Prissy's shadow. "We came to the village for ice cream, but the cafe was too busy. It is very hot."

"Gotta be over ninety degrees today," Sumner answered, looking to the sky, squinting, and sucking on what was left of his front teeth. "And I'm thinking the humidity might be about ninety percent, too. In fact, this achin' old right knee of mine is tellin' me there be some big thunderstorms blowin' through later on tonight, and I'm thinking the barometric pressure might be down below twenty-nine inches of mercury right about now."

Sumner spent over fifty years working a fishing boat from a small dock in Jerusalem Harbor on the mainland, chasing cod in the warm gulfstream waters of George's Bank, and always talked in measurements. Prissy only understood half of what he was ever talking about but was intrigued, and smiled anyway.

"Yup, sure is a hot one." Jude agreed.

"Mr. Jude, why is Mr. Guilfoyle sitting way over there today?" Prissy asked. Guilfoyle was sitting all alone on another bench, in front of the candle store on the corner.

"It's because he's a stubborn old horseshoe crab!" Jude answered. Guilfoyle was close enough that even with poor hearing brought on by his advanced age, he could still understand every word of the conversation, and he tilted his head in their direction. Guilfoyle stared out into the harbor, arms crossed over his worn denim overalls covering his protruding stomach, and ignored them.

"He's only twenty yards away," Sumner added. "It's not like he's a half mile out in the harbor."

"But you are all friends. You always sit together. You are supposed to sit together, just like Abby and me at lunchtime at school." Prissy insisted, disturbed by the unnatural shift in the order of things.

"Old Guilfoyle has this fool idea in his head that the Dodge Family Barn should be razed. That old barn has stood in that very same lot for over four hundred years and now the fool wants to set a match to it like it's a barrel full of trash. What an idiot! It's the oldest building on Manisses. There is nothing wrong with it. We have to save our history, preserve our heritage and protect our way of life. Next thing you know, he'll be slitting old Sumner's throat, too, just to get rid of him." Jude said.

"No I won't! You're older than Sumner!" Guilfoyle shouted from his bench down the street.

"Oh, don't listen to him; his mind has gone all funny. My grandmother was a Dodge, and when I was a little tyke like you two, I would spend all of my summer afternoons playing in that barn. I used to spend hours digging in the old hay in the corner finding pieces of old bottles, arrowheads and all sorts of exciting hidden treasure. Once, I even found an old buckle that I'll bet belonged to Captain Kidd himself. Imagine that! No one is going to touch that old barn unless they go through me first."

Prissy was troubled by the discord, as the three old men just didn't look right not sitting together. She and Otto dashed down the sidewalk through the crowd of bustling tourists to reach Guilfoyle. Jude read the concern on her face and looked down at her through his Santa-like white beard and moustache and smiled to comfort her.

"Don't worry Priscilla; we'll get along again soon. They're just acting like a couple of nitwits today. The Dodge barn is rotted from the foundation and is falling down. The wind on this island is relentless, and it has taken its toll. Part of the roof caved in during that big snow last January... made one heck of an ugly mess. It will be very expensive to restore, and you know cheap old Jude won't be digging into his pockets to pay for it. The barn might be a historic structure and all, but the taxpayers won't want to pick up the tab on a useless, rotted death trap like that," Guilfoyle said.

"Oh no! Look!" Prissy cried out in dismay. One of Otto's eyes had come unglued again and was lying on the sidewalk between the laces of her untied sneakers.

"Poor Otto!" Guilfoyle exclaimed. "My third wife used to lose her eye like that."

"I need to take Otto home right away so my mom can fix him. Bye, Mr. Guilfoyle!"

"Goodbye, Priscilla."

As Prissy jogged back to Sumner and Jude, she collected Abby who rolled her eyes and exhaled in relief that it was time to go home. Jude extended a thick, wrinkled hand to stop them.

"Girls, listen to me. Make sure you both tell your folks to come to the town meeting this evening. The fate of that barn is on tonight's agenda, and we need all the support we can get to save it from the arsonists. And ladies.., you almost forgot, here, take these quarters and get yourself a gumball at the store." Jude extended his hand, in a much more jovial mood than he shared before.

"Thank you Mr. Jude." Prissy said.

"Would Otto like a couple of quarters, too?" Jude smiled and rubbed the coins together between his thumb and forefinger making a grating, scratchy sound.

"No, thank you, Mr. Jude. Otto doesn't like to chew. It gives him a headache."

With gumballs set tight against the insides of their cheeks, Abby and Prissy mounted their bicycles to begin their return trip home. A single-engine white plane, flying way too low, screeched overhead heading toward the island's tiny central airport landing strip. Live music and energy pulsed from each of the bustling restaurants and clubs as they rode past, every one radiating a different style and intensity of melodic sound, as the dinner hour had arrived and the island tourists were prepping themselves to feast upon the local summer seafood delights. The sweet smell of deep frying fish batter and bubbling clam chowder wafted past the hungry girls in playful, wispy waves as the pair turned north past the public beaches and onto the rolling hills of Corn Neck Road and peddled toward home.

The girls bicycled past throngs of sun worshippers departing the beaches, who were loading up the trunks of their cars, or merely dragging their lawn chairs and inflatable, brightly-colored playthings back toward their hotel or the ferry. Evading the multitude of vacationers was something of a game unto itself, and Prissy enjoyed darting around and through them like they were orange cones on a construction site, while Abby peddled with a fury to just keep pace, not hit anyone, and not lose sight of her friend who rode up ahead.

Without warning, Prissy veered left away from their expected route, and Abby followed along, shouting at Prissy to slow down, stop and explain where she was going. They drove alongside an old stone wall that seemed to ramble on forever, and they stopped at the entrance of an aged barn erected at the forefront of a vast, grassy open field. The barn was oversized and red -- or at least the parts that had not faded to a deathly gray were still red -- and Prissy dismounted her bike and stood before it with her arms folded across her chest, much the way Guilfoyle might do, as she pitched her head to one side and stared intently at the sad, sorry state of the historic dwelling.

"What are we doing here, Prissy? We're going to be late and you're going to get us in trouble again!"

"I just wanted to see what those old men were arguing about." Prissy answered, stroking her chin.

"It's just an old barn. There are a dozen old barns around here. What do you care?"

"It was important to them. So important that they wouldn't even sit together, which means it's pretty important. I wanted to see for myself if there was a good reason for them to be mad at each other."

"Hey Prissy," Abby began, in a tone Prissy knew all too well. She knew what was coming next, and welcomed it with a devilish smile.

"Do you think we should go in the barn?" Abby asked. "Old Jude did say there is buried treasure inside."

Prissy flew through the door of the historic Dodge Barn as if shot from an ancient warrior's bow, and Abby followed with an excited caution three steps behind. Inside, rotting debris from the roof cave-in was all over, and the smell of damp mold and decay offended their young nostrils. Where the roof fell, several wooden stalls had been crushed where it appeared pigs or cows had been raised decades before, and the remnants of worn and broken farm tools were scattered everywhere -- half a pitchfork, a rusted pail, and even the flat rubber tire from a very large tractor. There were also several beer cans and broken whisky bottles strewn about the dusty floor, evidence the dying barn had become a recent popular hangout for bored, local hooligans. The black, charcoal remains of burned shingles and seared trash were arranged like an altar in the center of the room in a neat circle, waiting to be re-lit by a secret high priest. Both girls picked through the artifacts looking for treasure, but found only garbage.

"If you were a pirate, where would you bury your treasure?" Prissy asked.

"I dunno." Abby answered, eyes wide, surveying the room. "I think I would bury my treasure in that corner next to the window. That way it would be easier to find later."

"Excellent thought!" Prissy responded.

The girls rushed toward the corner, fell to their knees, and started to scratch at the matted, rotting hay against the barn's shady wall with their short, stubby fingers. Prissy suffered a small cut on the tip of her finger on some rusty, abandoned chicken wire, but it didn't dissuade her from continuing to dig deeper. A family of daddy longlegs was disturbed, and scrambled to get away from the onslaught, as did a colony of termites feasting upon the leg of a discarded milk stool. Abby uncovered a rusty beer bottle cap and a corroded, bent nail.

"Here's something," Prissy announced, and held up a blackened coin, the size of the quarter Jude gave them for their gumballs. "Jude was right after all. We found real treasure!"

Prissy and Abby unbuttoned the front of Otto's trousers and inserted the coin, bottle cap and nail, then re-buttoned them for safe keeping.

"Otto knows more about these things than I do. I'll let him figure out if we found pirate treasure or just some garbage." Otto did not disagree, but was more concerned with his missing eyeball.

The Bradfords' home was an impressive, former beach house originally built to amuse a wealthy socialite, however in recent years, the home had fallen into profound disrepair. From afar, the uninformed might assume the Bradfords to be quite well off, because with the fresh coat of white paint just applied, the home glistened like new against the cloudless dark blue sky. However, up close it was obvious the house needed a lot of renovation and its state of dilapidation was the primary reason Clement and Jessica were able to afford it in the first place. Situated on a small hill, one could observe the majesty of the Atlantic Ocean in three directions, a view only interrupted by a large outcropping of boulders at one end -- where Prissy's squirrel and Wequai's hero both laid interred.

Prissy charged through the squeaky screen door and slid across the linoleum floor on the worn heels of her grubby sneakers. Always happy, but never punctual, Prissy was at least predictable. Jessica shot her a daily disapproving look, and ordered her to clean up for dinner.

"What's for dinner tonight, Mom?"

"Dad brought home some fresh steamers." Jessica said, holding up a bag of small white clams.

"Shellfish... again? Ewww. I'm sick of seafood." Prissy grumbled.

"Like I told you two years ago when we moved here, we're going to be living on an island, so you'd better get used to seafood."

Prissy scrunched up her face, and reached into her pocket.

"Mom... Otto needs his eye fixed again." Prissy held out a small blue stone with one hand, and Otto with the other.

"Oh my, look at him. Poor Otto! What has he done to himself now? He has seen better days, hasn't he?" Jessica held Otto up to the light and examined him from head to toe like a country doctor.

"How do you get him so filthy?"

"I told him he needs to stay clean, but he won't listen to me." Prissy insisted.

"I'll have a talk with Otto, later." Jessica said. "It looks like his right thumb is tearing, too. And what are these things in his trousers?"

"Pirate treasure."

"And what happened to his shoelace?"

Prissy sighed. "Otto gave it to the squirrel."

Jessica knew it was best not to ask follow-up questions, and walked to the antique hutch in the corner of the kitchen -- the only piece of furniture that came with the house and had not been brought with them from their old apartment in Connecticut. Jessica rustled through drawers stuffed with family mementos, photographs and dozens of faded receipts for items the family no longer owned. From beneath the rubble, Jessica produced a small sewing kit. She then placed Otto on his back on the family's pine kitchen table, and began to perform surgery on her small, indifferent patient.

"I remember the afternoon I made Otto for you," Jessica began, pinching a bit of dark thread between her lips. "We had to rush to finish unpacking because the weather service said a hurricane was moving up the coast and was going to hit the island with one hundred and fifty mile per hour winds. Your father and I worked like dogs all night long and weren't sure if the house we had just invested our life savings in would even survive the storm. You and your sister stayed with Grandma in Hartford. And at the last minute, despite the dire warnings, we chose not to evacuate and to stay here to try to protect and save what we could. Thank God the storm decided to miss us and blow out to sea."

"And that's when you made Otto?"

The rain and wind were still pretty fierce, so we were trapped inside all day. Your father fell asleep in his chair reading a book, and I took out my sewing kit and put Otto together. I thought it would be nice that when you got to the island for the first time to live, you had a friend waiting for you."

"Mommy, I love Otto. But sometimes I wish he would pay more attention to what I tell him."

More focused on his treatment, Otto ignored the slight.

"Otto is made entirely from things I found walking the island before the hurricane that weekend," Jessica explained. "I created his body from a material I found under a thicket of brush on the beach by the ferry landing -- I think it might have once been part of a boat's sail. His body is stuffed with the fluff of the native milkweed plants, which grow in bunches next to the cat o' nine tails down by the salt pond, and feels soft, a lot like cotton when you rub it. On the beach, I found an old piece of wire that was already in the shape of a doll, and I used that to develop his arms, legs and skeleton. The two blue stones I used for his eyes were in the sand by those big rocks you like to play on way out back. You see... Otto is a true, native Manissean. He's not part of the island -- in every physical way, he is the island."

Prissy stood with her hands folded, quietly concerned, as Otto's parts were once again made right. Jessica carefully placed his blue eye back into place with a small dollop of glue, and she set him aside on a shelf of the hutch to recuperate from his surgical ordeal.

"It is best we leave Otto here for the rest of the night, until he feels a bit better. And then tomorrow morning, you can have him back. And I would suggest you treat him with a little more care. I can make these little repairs for you now, but he won't last forever."

"I know. I know," Prissy nodded in agreement, then paused. "I wish Otto had a soul. Then Daddy could channel him for me after he dies."

Jessica's back stiffened at Prissy's offhand, innocent remark. Clement's little girl was growing up too fast and was bound to start asking more probing questions about her family's unconventional, if not flat out bizarre, profession. She knew kids often lived their lives through their parents' occupations --

fishermen, sailors, mechanics, lawyers, or shopkeepers -- it was part of their identity in school, who they were, and how they viewed their place, fair or not, in the unspoken social caste system of a modern society. Having a dad that talks to the dead was what drove the Bradford family out of Connecticut in the first place and onto this idyllic Atlantic isle. Prissy's older sister Lucretia did not handle that adjustment well as she grew older, and Jessica knew the disharmony in Lucretia's life was a direct result of Clement's abnormal career. Jessica felt that guilt every day.

"Mom, would you ask Dad to teach me how to talk to spirits?" Prissy asked. "Every time I ask him, he sends me out of the room to get something for him."

"Why in the world would you want to know about that? It's best to let your father just do his job and not worry too much about it."

"But Abby and I found a squirrel today -- down by the big boulders."

"A squirrel? I haven't seen a squirrel since we moved here. Might this be the same squirrel that stole Otto's shoelace?"

"He didn't steal it, Mom, Otto gave it to him. The squirrel was dead. Me and Abby wanted to know why he was laying there and where he came from. So, we had a séance..."

Clement had been standing by the door eavesdropping on the conversation, running a comb through his short, thinning hair. He wore a striped angora v-neck sweater and flawlessly pressed slacks with perfect cuffs which fell across his brown loafers. Had he added a pipe, he might have been mistaken for a 1950's TV sitcom character. His wardrobe portrayed exactly what the little old ladies expected to see in a professional spiritual medium.

"Hey, Priscilla... why don't you do me a favor and run down the driveway and check the mailbox for me?"

"See! What did I tell you!" Prissy frowned, stomped her sneaker and stormed out of the room. "Every time! Every time! Every time!"

Clement needed no special spiritual guidance to read Jessica's harsh expression and know that the rest of the evening was not going to be so pleasant. The couple had played out this argument, it felt, a hundred times, even though they always both agreed at its conclusion.

"We need to close the office, Clement," Jessica began, as she always did.

"And how do we pay the mortgage, Jess? Answer that one." Clement responded, as he always did. "We are barely paying it now."

"I can take a part-time job at Captain Kidd's Cafe. Brenda McMahon, you know her from the Preservation Commission, works full-time during the summer, and makes darned good money, too, and they are always looking for more help."

"We're going to pay for this big house on the salary of a waitress who only works part-time in the summer? And what will I do while you're bringing in all this dough."

"You always wanted to open a toy store and magic shop. Now, here's your big chance. You can set up your grandfather's old, classic train set around the perimeter of the shop, and all the happy children and their families will come in to see it. I'll bet people take the ferry over from Narragansett and Newport just to play with it and buy your toys. And then on rainy days, when everyone else is losing money, you'll have the most popular shop in the village. And just think about how busy you would be in the off season at Christmas time!"

Clement wanted to argue but couldn't help smiling. He took Jessica's hands in his own and brought them to his chest. The couple stood in their rundown kitchen alone and gazed into each other's eyes. A broken board beneath the floor creaked under their combined weight, and the scratches of a field mouse could be heard in the cracked, water-stained ceiling above them. Jessica glanced away at the peeling wallpaper behind their rattling refrigerator, and at the gaping hole in the screen door that was letting in an aggressive squadron of houseflies. Clement breathed deep and stroked Jessica's, thin, pretty face with the back of his hand, and then he buried his face into her long, light brown hair that rested upon her soft, dainty shoulder.

"Now that would be fun, wouldn't it... to run a toy store? This island could use a darned, good toy store. But my office on Water Street is too small, and I don't know of any vacancies in the village right now, they are one hundred percent leased. And what's your plan to fund this toy shop? There isn't a bank in their right mind willing to loan us the money for inventory or fixtures."

"We'll start small."

"Small? We don't even have the money in our checking account to buy a sign for the front door."

"We need to start somewhere, sometime... someday. Clement, this wasn't supposed to be your career forever. When you started channeling for these crazy people, it was just supposed to be to get us started, make ends meet, just so we could afford to get married and rent a little apartment near your parents' house. It wasn't supposed to be forever. It wasn't supposed to be like this."

"I know, Jess. You're right; it has been a long time. That was almost twenty years ago. But it hasn't been all bad either. My career has allowed us to buy this house on Manisses, for example, with this breathtaking view, near all these nice people. But If I can deliver one solid business season here, on this island, with all these rich tourists, we might just be able to pull it off and open that toy store after all."

"But didn't you say that last season, too? Didn't you say that once we got settled here, you'd give it up and do something else?"

"Last year, it rained almost every weekend. This year, the weather has been near perfect... so far. I've been able to catch-up all our bills and the season isn't even half over. If it stays this busy, and we keep tightening our belts, and if we can just get a little farther ahead..."

"Clement, I'm worried about Priscilla."

"I know. So am I."

"One more season, and that's it."

"Yes, one more season and that's it. I promise."

In the doorway behind them, a bony girl of sixteen stood motionless, her hands cupped firmly over her hips. Her frilly tan dress and lace stockings were something snatched out of a Dickensian saga, and her thin lips were tinted brown, while her skin was pale and sepia-toned. Upon her head she wore a miniature black top hat adorned with a single ostrich feather, and on her forehead, she sported a set of brown leather airmen's goggles. An oversize, round pocket watch with a long gold band swung from her waist, ticking loudly, announcing her arrival.

"Mom... are you gonna make out, or are you gonna make dinner? I'm hungry."

"Dinner will be ready in a few minutes, Lucretia, my dearest love." Jessica mocked.

Lucretia glanced over at the hutch where Otto was staring back at her with grave contempt.

"Is that thing going to watch us eat? He creeps me out."

Chapter 5

The young boy squatted atop the large, black boulder and squinted into the bright horizon to the south. The chilly autumn westerly winds were creating an army of tiny goose bumps along his forearms, as did the anticipation of what he hoped he was about to witness, and he pulled his elbows in close to conserve his dwindling body heat. And though the muscles in his legs had started to ache, he held his balance and his focus, and did not dare blink.

The news had spread up the coast by runners and messengers, sharing the incredible communiqué from tribe to tribe, that an astonishing seafaring vessel – the likes of which no one in the Manissean tribe had ever witnessed – was heading toward them. The excitement had been bubbling through the people of the island villages for days, the only topic of meaningful conversation, and the tribe's elders asked the spirits to indulge their request and deliver the strange ship to their island.

The elders' interest was more than mere curiosity, but was fueled by news that the unusual strangers were very eager to trade, and they knew that the mirrors, bells and shiny metals the strangers carried could be worth several seasons of fresh corn and many beaver to the mainland tribes. And according to the messengers, all that the strangers wanted were a few clay pots and some fresh water -- the transaction would be a steal.

The young boy had been fooled by a family of seals playing in the waves in the distance along the horizon once, and would not be subjected to the ridicule of his friends again for issuing a false alarm. This time, he waited. And even though he saw what would be the tip of the mainmast from the ship, *La Dauphine*, emerge above the dark blue line of the horizon; he dared not call out until he was sure, until it came a bit closer. A smile hurried across his face when he realized at that moment that he was the first of his people to see the glorious sight – a heroic moment he would recount for his children and grandchildren for the rest of his life.

A flush of warmth galloped through him from head to toe, and he stiffened. He cupped his hands around his mouth in a cone, and let out an ear-piercing screech at the runners and villagers behind him. Young boys darted in all directions like startled rabbits, and the villagers who were close enough to hear the boy's proclamation, dropped whatever they were doing and sprinted toward the shore.

The first handful of Manisseans to arrive at the shoreline scampered to collect driftwood, seaweed and bundles of dried grasses to start massive fires. They did not want the strangers aboard the ship to believe their island to be uninhabited and deliver their cache of treasure to the mainland tribes instead. Burning the damp seaweed produced a thick, dark smoke that the strangers would be able to see from a good distance, and would serve as a beacon to steer them toward their beach. By the time the great ship sailed close enough for the sailors to make out the reddish, sandy beaches of the island for themselves, a mass of over two thousand native Manisseans had assembled to welcome them, smiling, arms flailing over their heads, anticipating the exciting, historic moment of first contact. It was a surreal scene, one that the lonely Wequai and her infant son Manisses, sitting alone watching the sun set, could not have fathomed hundreds of years earlier.

Wequai and Manisses did not encounter another human being for several weeks after the terrible battle and arrival on the island. Shellfish and berries were plentiful, and the summer winds continued to draw warmth up the coast from the south, so the island climate remained warm and agreeable. Wequai was able to provide quite nicely for the two of them during their unintended exile. In her childhood, she had helped lash together many bark and grass-woven shelters, and the island's saplings, vines and tall grasses were abundant. It took her only a few days to create a small comfortable accommodation to shelter them from the occasional summer showers and the ever-present, searing wind. Caring for her newborn son and establishing their new residence monopolized most of her time, and she refused to allow thoughts of loneliness and home to distract her from the critical task of fundamental survival. Manisses only opened his eyes a few times each day, as newborns were apt to do, and it was only then that Wequai would see and feel the caring soul of her missing husband in her son's deep, dark, innocent eyes.

Back on the mainland, the devastation from the war was eerie and profound. Thousands had died in the fury and rage of battle, including over half the residents of Wequai's village, and every shelter and wigwam was burned, crushed or destroyed. Yet, despite the vast destruction, the savage invaders had retreated, beaten back by the bravery and immeasurable inner strength of the village's warriors, and the villagers who had survived claimed victory and vowed to stay, rebuild and press on. In the aftermath, their most immediate task at hand was to collect, honor and bury the dead before disease could set in. Corpses were stacked like bundles of reed grass, and graves quickly dug in the charred brown earth still moist with the rich blood of the victims; tasks assigned to all except the injured and those committed to nursing them. There was no time for mourning. Survivors from Wequai's family knew nothing of her whereabouts, and as chaos limped back to order, her grandmother comforted herself with the belief that Wequai would appear from her hiding place in the woodlands at any moment, newborn cradled in her arms. And as days passed and her return became less likely, others surmised she had been kidnapped by the raiders – a pretty, young squaw heavy with child could be of great value to some of the diverse tribes of the woodlands. No one would guess that their beloved young maiden and infant son stood alone, just out of reach, bathed in song, on a deserted island across the tranquil sound.

The village fisherman knew the island to be deserted. The elders spoke of civilizations out there that had thrived many generations before, but it was said that those early ancestors abandoned their settlement and moved ashore following a powerful hurricane, leaving the island abandoned as a private play area for the spirits – and it was now honored and respected as a sacred, mysterious place. Fishermen in their long, dugout canoes would report seeing the spirits dance in the twilight or morning fog, or they would claim to hear sounds of wailing and singing, and out of fear and respect, gave the island wide berth. Whether the reports were true or the figments of active imaginations did not matter, as the villagers respected the rights of the spirits to dwell wherever they chose.

It was Wequai's uncle, Mowashuck, who weeks later, fishing with his children from a distance in the abandoned canoe of a slaughtered neighbor, first saw the thin, wispy trail of smoke from Wequai's campfire in front of the great boulders rise into the red morning sky. The unwelcome news of a fresh encampment on the deserted island sheered through the community like a warrior's hickory spear. Their nerves still frayed and raw from battle, they feared the settlement could be evidence of another and perhaps stronger invasion yet to come.

The village's newly appointed sachem called an urgent meeting of the surviving elders, and around a campfire near the shore where Wequai had fled, they debated their concerns and strengthened their collective paranoia and resolve. From within their huts, the villagers recognized the intensifying chants and shouts of the elders echoing into the night, and knew the village would once again be preparing for war.

All the remaining able-bodied men of the village, many still nursing the wounds of their previous victory, some barely able to walk, assembled at dawn by the seashore. The fishermen gathered together all the fishing canoes that remained undamaged or had not been sunk, and the broken, reluctant warriors piled in -- the largest of the canoes long enough to carry fifty men. The Sachem raised a quartz tipped spear in his clenched fist and shrieked his battle cry into the dew of the heavy morning air. Altogether, dozens of boats pushed away from the shore, warriors paddling with a frenzy of rhythmic splashes, and the army moved forward to attack and remove this new threat from their existence.

Wequai was picking raspberries and collecting hickory nuts at the edge of a field behind her encampment, storing them in a basket she had finished weaving just the night before from the sticky bark of the pines that grew by the beach. In the distance, the flock of canoes would have looked like ducks along the horizon and even if she had seen them, she would have ignored them anyway. By the time she glanced up and realized her island was being invaded, it was too late to flee. She buried herself in the painful mounds of briars and brush, clutching her son to her chest, and strained to see if her guests would be friend or foe.

The canoes pulled up onto the rocky beach, and the warriors disembarked, weapons raised high, some refusing to leave the ankle-high surf for fear of angering the gods by setting foot upon their island without permission. Hundreds of warriors were now present, tripping over the slippery stones along the beach.

There was no immediate sign of life.

The sachem and a few scouts crouched, and carefully walked up the embankment toward the great boulders, eyes darting from side to side expecting an ambush, feet calculating every step, until they reached Wequai's modest campsite. They examined the smoldering coals, the small shelter, and Manisses' tiny bed and confirmed their fears and suspicions that the island was indeed inhabited. A scout scampered up to the top of the boulders and scanned the horizon. He shook his head, reporting that he could see no other activity.

As the sachem was trying to decide if he was relieved that there was no great enemy or perturbed that he had brought his warriors across the sea to attack a single campsite, the warriors all at once crouched in fear at a piercing scream coming from the field in the distance. Dozens of spears and arrows were raised to defend, and fixed upon the silhouette of a single, small young woman running toward them. Wequai recognized the distinctive blue war paint on the faces of the warriors from her hiding place, and she knew the men had been dispatched from her village. With Manisses clutched to her chest, she charged forward with endless joy to gladly surrender herself to her hapless invaders.

Mowashuck recognized her, dropped his weapons, and ran in her direction. The two embraced by the great rocks, nearly squishing poor, little Manisses in their wash of enthusiasm and joy. As they embraced, the invasion force stood confused, some still refusing to set foot on the island, others remaining poised, ready to attack, and all the while the Sachem was slowly losing his patience with the sum of the operation. It took the rest of the afternoon to convince the brash, new leader that the invasion had been a success, the enemy repelled, and he could return to the village with his warriors an honored champion of his first-ever crusade -- a tale he would embellish and retell to his own unborn grandchildren.

As the last of the warriors boarded their canoes and sailed back home, Wequai and her uncle sat together by the campfire.

"Look at you, Wequai, you are so skinny. We must get you home and feed you. Next time, the north winds won't be able to blow you so far away."

Wequai smiled, but her Uncle Mowashuck looked down to the earth.

"Your husband fought bravely, Wequai. He killed many of the enemy. He killed so many that the spirits honored him and called him to them. You should be proud. He now defends the spirit world."

Wequai frowned and nodded, did not cry, said nothing, and showed no other emotion.

"Your mother and grandmother both survived the battle unharmed, and together, set up a camp to nurse our wounded. Your grandmother is strong in the powers of herbs and healing and has saved many of our villagers from death. It is a blessing that she was not taken from us in the battle. I believe it is a message from the spirits that they want us to survive as a people."

Wequai sighed and nodded again, then looked away toward the horizon, toward home.

"Tomorrow, I will return you to your mother and grandmother. They will be so happy to see you. And they will be joyful to see your child, too. They have had little to celebrate. Wequai, it has been a time of great sorrow. A time of death. You and Manisses have changed our fate. You have returned to us from the dead. You are a blessing for all our tribe."

"Uncle," Wequai began, looking at her feet, swirling the soft sand with her toes. "I cannot leave this island."

"What are you saying, girl? Of course you will both come with me... at sunrise. After we arrive home, I will slaughter a deer and we will have a feast. We will honor your bravery and cunning, and we will welcome your child."

"I dreamed every night of our village, these last few weeks. My husband, my love, came to me in my sleep many times, so I would never feel alone or abandoned. And he would comfort me through the eyes of my child. I knew he had not survived the battle. He wanted to meet his only son before he traveled to the spirit world, and he wanted to make sure we would be cared for. He told me he prepared this island for the two of us. I believe he sent us that enemy warrior as a guide to deliver us safely here, for a reason. For Uncle, this is the only land that Manisses knows. This is his home, not our village on the mainland. No one else in our village, or anyone else alive in the world, has been born here. On this island, Manisses is sachem -- he rules over the red beaches, the fields of berries, and all the hickory trees and shrubs. He is master of the crabs and quahogs, the ducks and all the seabirds, the trees and rocks on the shore. The great stones behind us are his throne where he can oversee and rule his rich empire. I am sorry, Uncle, but we cannot go home if we are already home."

Verrazano stood on the deck of his ship and stared across the waves at the island as the wind pushed his ship closer, the weather had taken a turn for the worse and storms appeared to be brewing. His black matted hair and thick curly beard fluttered in the chilly Atlantic breeze. He placed his boot upon a bundle of rope and rubbed his furry chin with nervous anticipation, squinting at the column of smoke to the north. Contact with natives was his least favorite duty as captain of *La Dauphine*, but a necessary evil, as the local heathens possessed both the provisions and intelligence he needed to continue his quest, on behalf of King Frances I of France, to successfully locate the trade routes to Cathay, ensuring his fame and Francis' fortune.

"Captain, sir," Dufour asked, begging his pardon." Can I tell the crew that we intend to lay anchor and rest here on this island?"

"Aye, Dufour, but first, we must make certain these natives will not eat us." Verrazano proclaimed.

Verrazano's men were desperate for both rest and supplies. Many of the crew were weak and falling ill from malnutrition, and their captain's continued refusal to either tend to their needs or turn back for France had some of them whispering of mutiny. Several opportunities to lay anchor had passed, and now this small island presented itself as a safe and harmless solution. But as the ship crept closer, the sight of thousands of screaming, waving natives gave them all pause. No one on the ship could know for sure if these islanders would be welcoming or savage, and the modest crew of fifty could easily be overwhelmed if their captain made the wrong choice.

"Dufour... fetch me the cabin boy, Bissette." Verrazano demanded.

"Bissette? Why Bissette?" Dufour asked, openly questioning his captain's simplest request.

"Why must every command I issue be met with a question!" Verrazano barked. "Did that dog Magellan even once endure such insolence? I think not! It is my burden before my creator to have a crew of rude Frenchmen. I would sell you all to these savages for a single, half-witted Italian sailor."

Within moments, Bissette appeared before Verrazano, standing at attention. The boy of thirteen years shuddered in fear at what order might be coming next. Verrazano paced back and forth in front of the boy, his arms latched behind his waist, appearing pensive. Several of the crew had gathered to hear what fate their indecisive, paranoid captain had planned for the poor child.

"We have already located two passages from here to Cathay in the south, and I predict we shall find two more to our north..."

"But sir!" Dufour interrupted. "We cannot be sure those two bays you found go anywhere. You did not wish to explore them."

"That is enough, Dufour. I know a passage to Cathay when I see one. And apparently, you do not. I suppose you would have our small crew sail into unknown waters to be plundered by the Spanish? I think not. The Spaniards have never ventured this far north, and if I intend to locate all the passages for your king, we need the supplies of these savages now. Therefore, Bissette, here is what I want you to do. In this bag, I have collected a few beads, shiny stones and other worthless trinkets that should amuse them. I want you to swim from here to the shore and present them to their leader as a gesture of peace and goodwill from the King of France. We shall see how friendly they are, and determine if they want more."

It was not the first time in their voyage that Verrazano employed a swimmer to be dispatched to shore, en lieu of anchoring and sending a skiff. Unfortunately for the swimmer, the results were not always good.

"Sir! Bissette will never make it; we are too far from shore! And the water is too cold for such a swim!"

"I demand your silence!" Verrazano roared, and Bissette swallowed hard.

"You have heard my orders, and I will not repeat them. Bissette here is the best swimmer remaining among us all. The waters along this island are very shallow, and we must know if there is any value in laying our anchor here at all. A storm is approaching, so we must act now. If I hear one more word of complaint, I predict we will have many more swimmers among us."

The crew stood in concerned silence and watched Bissette balance barefoot along the edge of the ship's rail, clutching the bag of beads to his side, trying to find the nerve to leap. Verrazano placed his hand on the small of the lad's back and with a quick shove, sent him plunging head first into the cold, gray sea, to what the rest of the crew assumed would be his inevitable death.

"May God show mercy on his soul," Dufour prayed.

From the deck, Verrazano and his crew watched the boy swim valiantly and with great energy. The waters were cold and the boy knew he only had a limited amount of time before his muscles would tighten and he would sink. Stroke after stroke, Bissette's arms waved overhead and dug through the heavy waves, feet kicking in rhythm as he struggled and the crew began chanting and cheering him on, inch by inch, stroke for stroke.

From the shore, the Sachem and his villagers watched the puzzling scene unfold, unsure what to make of it all, listening to the shouts and cheers coming from the ship. At first they guessed the crew had thrown something overboard, and it took a few moments for them to realize it was a crewman, and he was swimming toward them. The sachem knew that unless the stranger was some sort of a god, he would drown in the violent waters as he approached the sharp rocks and eddies near the beach, at the very moment he would be reaching physical exhaustion. Concerned, the sachem waved an order, and a canoe filled with the island's best fisherman pushed off into the surf to attempt a rescue.

The men of *La Dauphine* saw the canoe and its crew of warriors paddling toward Bissette and fell silent. The boy had made great progress, and had almost reached the rocky shore when the native's canoe came into his view. Eyes widening in terror, the boy held the bag of beads high overhead and threw them toward the beach with all his might. The bag hit the top of a sharp black rock and burst open, sending a brief shower of shiny stones and trinkets into the air and surf. A few natives standing nearby dove into the water to try to recover the tiny treasures. Bissette had now turned, and with energy no one could have imagined he had left in reserve, began swimming feverishly back toward the ship, in a panicked attempt to evade the cannibals, and preserve his own life.

But as predicted, Bissette's arms were growing tired and heavy, and he could no longer fill his lungs with the air he needed to continue his heroic effort. Near exhaustion, he sunk beneath a white cap and did not re-emerge. The crew held their breath, praying the poor boy would bob back up to the surface unharmed and continue his ordeal.

The natives' canoe reached the point at which Bissette had last been seen going under, and a fisherman leaned over the edge of his canoe, extended a long, muscular arm into the sea, and snatched up the boy by the back of his shirt. Bissette's lifeless body, arms and legs appearing unhinged like those of a ragdoll, was pulled into the canoe as it turned around and headed for the now cheering throngs on shore.

The crew stood silent, not sure if poor Bissette had already died or was now being transported to his death. Once on shore, the native fisherman handed Bissette's body to a group of women who had assembled near one of the fires. A crowd gathered around him, eager to see for themselves what a white skinned man would look like up close, each taking turns poking, pulling and prodding him -- not unlike a precocious child might do to a dead squirrel. Bissette coughed and gagged, and realizing the predicament he was in, let out a terrifying scream so horrific, the men of *La Dauphine* wondered if Bissette had arrived at the gates of hell. The women on the shore held him down next to the fire and began to undress the flailing, frantic boy.

"Dear merciful God in heaven," Verrazano screamed at the shore. "They are going to eat him... cook him alive! They are preparing Bissette to be their dinner! Savages! Cannibals!" The crew shrieked and fell to their knees in prayer. Dufour and a few of the others plotted how they might attempt a rescue, but abandoned the idea for fear of being captured and served as breakfast themselves.

The native women finished undressing the boy and hung his clothing to dry on spears that were perched around the fire. Others massaged his back and arms to help warm his body and relieve his cramped muscles, and he sat on a mat of dried grasses, warming his hands. Yet another pretty maiden bowed and presented the boy with a platter of food and drink, and the natives cheered when he sipped and swallowed a gulp of fresh berry juice, then held the cup overhead to salute and thank them. The crew watched agape, in stunned silence.

"Captain?" Dufour asked. "Do you need another swimmer?"

"Dufour... drop a skiff into the sea and go rescue Bissette from those savages this instant. A storm is brewing, and in this wind, this coast is too rocky and the water too shallow to drop anchor. I cannot afford to swamp another of his majesty's ships. We will sail to the north and seek safe harbor there."

"But sir! These savages are friendly. They could give us everything we need."

"Then we will honor their good humor by naming this savage place after the queen mother, Louise. Put it on the map, Dufour. I name this island, Luisa. Perhaps that will impress your greedy French king."

"I will fetch your journal, sir, so you may record your first contact with this tribe while the details lay fresh upon your mind."

"No, Dufour, do not waste your time. I see nothing in our visit here as worthy of the effort. This island is too small, and its shores too rocky to ever be useful. I doubt anything of interest will ever happen here."

Following Bissette's reluctant rescue, *La Dauphine* sailed north into what is now Narragansett Bay where it anchored for two weeks, allowing the crew to enjoy a much needed rest, trade with the more northern Wampanoag tribes and re-stock its dwindling cache of critical supplies. No one told the Manisseans their island now belonged within the realm of France, named for the mother of a king who lived thousands of miles away, whom they would never meet, nor want to. And no one told them that the captain of that great ship carried with him a particular phobia of being eaten by savages, and that he would meet his ultimate fate four years later -- in what the Manisseans might have considered a perverse sentence of spiritual justice -- when exploring the Bahamas, Verrazano rowed out to meet the native Caribs, and was killed, cooked and eaten.

Stories of the first meeting between the Manisseans and Europeans, near the great rock by the shore, were soon forgotten after the ship sailed north, a pinpoint on a history map discarded by all parties who considered the moment disappointing, unimportant and irrelevant.

The small collection of beads the Manisseans recovered that day, thrown at them by a terrified cabin boy, were unremarkable. A few of the trinkets were later traded to the Pequots for corn, and a few others were affixed as decoration to the sachem's headdress. Most of the rest disappeared, lost to antiquity. However, two piercing blue beads would be discovered one day washed up on the beach hundreds of years later, unearthed from their sandy tomb by the pounding waves of an approaching Atlantic hurricane, snatched up from among the pebbles by a caring mother worried for Prissy's loneliness, helping them begin a new existence as the empathetic eyes of a beloved ragdoll named Otto.

Chapter 6

The Bradford family was among the first to arrive and took their seats near the middle of the town council chambers. Clement sat near the aisle next to Jessica, Prissy and Otto beside her. Lucky sat across the aisle as far away from her family as she could get in the soon-to-be crowded meeting room, grabbing a wooden chair alongside someone who Clement considered to be one of the island's least desirable young suitors, Vance Asher.

Clement leaned in close and whispered into Jessica's ear.

"I will not approve of any boyfriend who wears nicer earrings than my own daughter does," he said.

"I think he looks like a vampire." Prissy whispered back.

The town hall was a new structure, built just a few years prior, and featured all the modern amenities any bustling upper-crust township could hope for -- including solar panels, wireless computer technology, and a state of the art, digital sound system. The building stood in stark contrast to many of the historic, well-preserved, salt-stained structures that attracted so much business to the community, as if it existed to remind the residents that the Draconian zoning laws were in place to preserve not the island history, but the high-wire economic carnival act they perform from May to September each year.

But the building stood as more than a cathedral to the stench of stagnant, fermenting small-town political squabbles. It existed as the island's official meeting place for the few hundred residents who called the rocky island home for all twelve months of the year. Entering its doors and sitting among its congregation was a time honored activity, defining the participants as exceptional, the ruling class, a caste above the rank and file tourists in their baggy Bermuda shorts who strolled with ice cream cones past the structure in the sunset. Present in the room were representatives from founding families whose roots went back generations, while others were more recent landowners -- like the Bradfords -- who might take a decade or more to become fully trusted and established. All together, on a good day, they were the village's most respected warriors assembled to echo the war cry of their sachems. Or on a bad day, they could be a mutinous crew prepared to throw their indecisive captains into the violent sea.

Jessica hated these meetings, considering them no more than chest-pounding and a waste of a fine summer's evening, and would spend her time sitting quietly, thumbing the pages of a new romance novel. The girls tolerated the interruption of their lives a bit better. Lucky saw it as a chance to socialize with Vance -- a black leather, earring-wearing teen son of an investment banker fond of pasty-white make-up and dark eye shadow, while Prissy followed the debates with the eagerness of a future head of state. Following each meeting, Prissy would pepper her father with questions, feeding her fascination with the drama of the human political interaction.

When the last of the townspeople had taken their seats, and the councilmen had finished whispering and plotting and had also found their places, the sergeant-at-arms sealed the door and all the room fell quiet in anticipation. A muffled *boosh boosh boosh boosh* rhythm emanating from the nightclub across the street annoyed everyone.

"How many million did you spend on this building, and not one of you thought of sound proofing?" An anonymous voice shouted from the crowd. The room shared a broken, uncomfortable chuckle.

"Maybe somebody ought to enforce the island sound ordinance!" Shouted another. The usual wave of campy discontent was building among the masses.

"That's enough," Mr. Smyth, the grizzled elderly council president interrupted, squelching the grumbles with a sharp crack of his gavel. With all the elegance of an army drill sergeant, he ordered the attendees to stand. "Now everyone shut up and honor our country with the *Pledge of Allegiance.*"

The room stood as one, in patriotic unity, young and old, liberal and conservative, rich and poor alike, and recited the pledge in perfect cadence, accompanied by the artistic stylings of the offending neighboring nightclub.

"I pledge allegiance..."

Boosh Boosh

"...to the flag..."

Boosh Boosh

"...of the United States..."

Boosh Boosh

"...of America..."

Boosh Boosh

"...and to the republic..."

Boosh Boosh

"...for which it stands..."

Boosh Boosh

"...one nation..."

Boosh Boosh

"...under God..."

Boosh Boosh

"...indivisible..."

Boosh Boosh

"...with liberty..."

Boosh Boosh

"...and justice..."

Boosh Boosh

"...for all."

Boosh Boosh Boosh Boosh

Smyth's gavel pounded the council table again.

"Captain Honeywell, I demand you go next door and tell the fool that owns that club to shut that music down this instant!" Smyth waved the gavel over his head, wielding it like a cavalry officer's saber. "I don't give a damn if he violates an ordinance or not! He will not disrupt my meeting, or I'll have his liquor license!" The crowd cheered its approval.

"Now let's get this meeting to order. Madam Secretary, please read the roll..."

"Hey Clement," Skip Payne, Abby's interminably annoying father, leaned across the aisle. "What do you think is going to happen tonight?"

"Your guess is as good as mine, Skip. The folks I have talked to seem split. Half of them want to raze the old Dodge barn, the other half want to preserve it. The council is split, too. The town budget is already in the red. The only way they are going to be able to pay for it is to come up with another fee. And I, for one, don't need to start paying another tax. I'm barely making ends meet as it is."

"You can see into the future, Clement... why don't you just tell me what is going to happen so I can go home early and watch the ballgame." Skip flashed a well-maintained, toothy-white grin, trying to provoke him.

Clement didn't take ribbing about his vocation lightly, and responded with an even tone through his clenched teeth. "I can't see into the future, Skip. I am a medium... a spiritualist. I provide a pathway into the spirit world, I can't see the future."

"Aww, come on Clem, relax. You know I'm just joking around." Skip's smile widened. "Then why don't you ask one of those ghost friends of yours to sneak up behind Smyth and check his notes for us. I'm dying to know what deal they got worked out for this." Skip laughed out loud amused at his own humor.

"You're a laugh a minute, Skip." Clement responded, sighing, while Abby and Prissy made silly faces at each other back and forth across the aisle.

"What about tea leaves, can you read tea leaves? What about coffee grounds? I don't drink tea, so all I got left here are some leftover coffee grounds in the bottom of my cup. See? This coffee cost me five bucks at that new fancy cafe on Spring Street, so there's got to be some extra-sensory value in it, don't you think? Hey Clem... the coffee grounds are predicting the future. Can you hear them? They are saying I'm going to throw them in that trash can on my way out of the building!" Skip laughed out loud again, wallowing in his usual smugness. Clement sat back and sighed, doing his best to ignore the childish banter.

"Alright, folks," Smyth's gravelly voice announced. "We have voted to move the issue of the old Dodge Barn to the top of the agenda. We know there's a Yankees-Red Sox game is on TV tonight and everyone wants to get home."

Boosh Boosh Boo...

The annoying sound stopped cold, and everyone cheered.

"Smyth for president!" Someone shouted, and everyone laughed. Smyth ignored him.

"We have a proposal before the council sponsored by Councilman Dorry.

Dorry cleared his throat and rose to speak.

"Since the barn on the Dodge estate is in such a sad state of disrepair, and has become a public eyesore as well as a danger, I propose the council order it razed as defined in zoning ordinance 11B and bill the Dodge estate the cost of its removal."

The chamber vibrated with muffled chatter.

Old Guilfoyle sat in the front row and rose first, hooking his thumbs in the straps that held up his denim overalls. Smyth nodded in his direction and instructed him to begin to speak.

"I've lived seventy years on this island, and I ain't never seen an issue debated so long by so many intelligent people in my life. It's just a barn folks, just an ugly old wooden barn. When I was a kid, the Dodge family threw their trash in it before they got around to burning it. Then later, they put their old goats out there and used it to store extra hay, then much of it rotted in place. Now I've been told that barn has stood there for four hundred years in that same spot. Four hundred years, eh? Well let me tell you this. In my lifetime, I saw that barn painted five times that I know of. I saw the roof replaced twice, too. And I'll bet half the boards that make up those walls have rotted and been swapped out. So when all the parts of the barn have been replaced and updated, one after the other over the course of centuries, at what point is it no longer the barn that was built there in the first place? What are you people trying to preserve? That barn is already just a memory. This ground ain't any more sacred than any other inch of earth on this floating rock we all live on. There ain't never been a president or leader born anywhere on Manisses! Just last week, they chased a pack of kids who had started a campfire out in that barn. They hang around out there drinking, fornicating and smoking mother nature to all hours of the night. Is that the sacred ground you want to preserve? Nothing good has ever happened out there... nothing. I say tear the damn thing down!"

The chamber filled with a divided chorus of cheers and boos.

"Old Jude raised his arm next to speak, and was recognized by Smyth. He shot a nasty look at Guilfoyle who sat with his arms folded, staring straight ahead.

"We have a responsibility to our children, and to our ancestors, to preserve our history, our heritage and our way of life. That barn has stood the test of time, and all manner of blizzard, hurricane and flood. It has stood in the same place for centuries, housing the animals that gave us sustenance and storing the critical supplies that allowed our society to develop in this wondrous place that we all love and call home. That barn is not only our past, but also our future. I am of the Dodge family -- my grandmother was a Dodge and she worked in that barn her whole life raising chickens, milking cows and tending to the family farm. The history and culture of this island grew from that structure, and now we want to tear it down? Raze it? Set a match to it? It has given us so much, and has so much more to give our children. What is wrong with you people! Is it merely a question of dollars and cents? A few dollars among otherwise generous citizens?"

Smyth interrupted. "Councilman Dorry, do you have the estimate from the Preservation Commission on what it would cost to restore the barn?"

"Yes, I do, sir... it comes in at about a half million dollars."

The crowd again erupted into random jeers and shouts.

"The simple fact," Dorry shouted over the noise, "is that the town does not have the money anyway without levying a new fee."

The debate over the fate of the Dodge family barn wore on for an hour as resident after resident chimed in with their own take on the issue, each punctuated by their own emotional chorus of cheers and boos. Abby was now sitting on the same folding chair as Prissy, squished together, and both felt part of the lively debate. This was the first meeting they had attended where they understood what was going on. They had visited that barn and knew it well, and also knew how much the issue meant to old friends Guilfoyle, Sumner and Jude. The girls watched and listened carefully as volleys of opinions, both for and against, were hurled from one side of the room to the other, some exploding, others falling to the floor with embarrassing thuds. As the debate wore on, the room had begun to grow very warm, the state-of-the-art air conditioning was not keeping pace with the hot air generated by the debaters, and folks were fidgeting and becoming irritable. Smyth had removed his jacket and tie, and sweat dripped from his gray, wrinkled eyebrows. His patience worn thin, he decided he had heard and seen enough, and slammed his gavel on the table with a ferocious crash.

"We're not going to change any more minds. Let's put this to a formal vote. Though, I think it's clear what the council will decide." Smyth said, and the members nodded in agreement. No one was happy the barn was to be razed, but they felt they had little choice. "We'll select a contractor for the razing at our next meeting."

"Madam Secretary, please record the votes..."

"Prissy! They're going to burn down the barn!" Abby was upset. Tears were welling in the corners of her little blue eyes. Even Prissy, who had hoped the barn would be saved also, was surprised by the depth of emotion in Abby's heartfelt response.

"They can't burn it down! They can't do that! They can't! Prissy... quick... do something!" Abby exclaimed, hoping Prissy would act on her behalf, as she always seemed to do.

But this time, Prissy's back stiffened, and she felt powerless. She squeezed Otto close to her chest and pulled away, shaking her head, enduring a sudden rush of guilt, accepting that she did not have the first idea what to do or say next that could help her friend.

Abby shot up, lunged forward, and charged down the center aisle at full gallop toward the councilmen. Even her father was caught by surprise, fumbling his empty coffee cup and newspaper in an ungraceful attempt to follow his hysterical daughter down the aisle and apprehend her before she reached the councilmen.

"Mr. Smyth, please don't burn the barn!" Abby pleaded. Smyth breathed deep, then exhaled.

"Somebody shut that girl up!" An anonymous voice hollered from the back of the room. Smyth, who was annoyed at the girl's interruption, too, was more annoyed by the profound rudeness exhibited by the onlookers.

"Hey, you hold your tongue back there! You hear me?" Smyth said as he wiped his brow. "I'm sorry Abby, but there isn't much more we can do. But I am glad you are taking such an active interest in this topic."

"You don't understand! Tell him Mr. Jude! Tell him!"

"I've said my piece, Abby. I agree with you. But I don't know what more I can say." Jude added.

"Tell them about the buried treasure! Captain Kidd's treasure!"

The crowd giggled. A few were so bold as to laugh out loud. A bit embarrassed, Jude smiled, bent over and squeezed her dainty hands together.

"Sweetheart, I don't think there is any real treasure in that barn. I am sorry I told you that story. That was just a game I used to play when I was a little boy. I had a lot of fun growing up and playing in that barn. It breaks my heart just to think that they plan to destroy it. Thank you, though for caring, you are a very sweet girl. Now I think maybe you should go back to your seat with your dad here." Skip reached out to take her hand, but Abby defiantly pulled it away.

"No! There is treasure! Real pirate treasure... show them Prissy, show them!"

"Oh God... how did I know Prissy would be caught up in this!" Jessica declared as Clement's chin fell to his chest. Both parents emitted a choreographed sigh.

Prissy approached the councilmen and placed Otto on the table before Smyth and Dorry. She reached into Otto's trousers and removed a rusty nail.

"Impressive!" Smyth declared. "That is some treasure! Is there anything else?" Prissy then reached in and produced the cap to a beer bottle.

"Ooooh, fascinating!" Smyth said, feigning interest and patronizing the girl, prolonging the hot crowd's agony.

"Oh, come on Smyth! The Sox are already down three runs! Let's do this!" Someone shouted. Half the room cheered the score, the rest booed. Otto wanted to roll his eyes, but considering they had been recently re-glued, he reconsidered, fearing they might fall off again.

"Everybody just pipe down. These two girls have been sitting in here all night showing more patience than all of you have combined, so let's let them have their say, too. It won't kill you to wait two more minutes. Now ladies, do you have any more treasure to show this council?"

"Just this, sir." And Abby handed over the coin.

"A quarter?" Dorry inquired. "I say we seize it and add it to the town treasury. We could use it right now." The crowd laughed again.

"It's not a quarter, it's... it's... well, I'm not sure what it is." Smyth scratched off the heavy black discoloring with his thumbnails, and held it up to the light, squinting at it with one eye. Brenda, come over here, what do you make of this?"

Brenda McMahon was the Preservation Commission president, part-time waitress at Captain Kidd's Cafe, and town know-it-all. With all the panache of a true swamp Yankee, she spit on the coin and rubbed it hard into her white apron, leaving a large black circle. She held the coin up to the light again.

"Well, I'll be," Brenda declared. "Young lady, where did you find this coin?"

"In the corner of the barn ma'am!" Abby announced with a renewed, I-told-you-so pride.

"What are you thinking, Brenda?" Smyth inquired.

Brenda continued her careful examination. "I am not going to tell you whether it is from Captain Kidd's buried treasure or not, but I do know two things. First, this coin is very, very old, and second, it is, without a doubt, solid gold. We are going to need to get this checked out and evaluated. Mr. Smyth, on the chance that this coin came from inside the Dodge barn, I recommend you table a decision on that property until next month."

The room exploded like someone had tossed a lit match into a can of gasoline. Jude threw his hands to the sky in victory, and Guilfoyle threw his hands to the sky in disgust. Smyth pounded the gavel on his table again and again, frantically trying to bring the chaos back to order. After the tenth or twelfth strike, the handle of the gavel cracked and the crowd quieted.

"Now..." Smyth began.

Boosh Boosh Boosh Boosh

The crowd groaned and erupted into pandemonium yet again.

"Hey Bradford," an anonymous voice shouted from behind, "did Captain Kid's ghost tell your girl where he hid the treasure?"

Clement possessed a docile character, and had never been nor wanted to be a fighter. Though when he spun in anger, he accidentally knocked two old women from their folding chairs to the floor. Jessica instinctively grasped Clement around the waist to hold him back from getting hurt himself, and a stranger believing Clement was being attacked, grabbed Jessica. The mass mayhem rolled past the sergeant-at-arms and through the council doors where the loud, rambunctious, argumentative crowd spilled into the street. The owner of the nightclub next-door watched the madness unfold, shook his head, and considered how he might file a noise complaint against the city council.

Lucretia and Vance gathered up the two little girls from the front of the room and walked them out toward the parking lot where the arguments were in full bloom. Both teens had trouble walking along the cobblestones in their black stiletto heeled boots. A white patch of makeup was visible on Lucretia's cheek, where earlier in the night, Vance had tenderly kissed her.

"I'm sorry, Lucky you were right. I can't believe your family acts like this in public." Vance said.

"It happens all the time." Lucretia added.

Chapter 7

C lement's best customers were always the ones waiting at the door when he opened for business each morning. They were consistently the most motivated, the most revealing, and the most open and more important than any of that -- the most affluent customers he had. These were the customers who sought him out the moment the ferry docked, or their private plane landed on the narrow island airstrip. They were the customers who had spent months planning their vacation to Manisses not just for the breathtaking views, gourmet seafood and pristine beaches, but for the rare and exciting opportunity to sit with the island's leading spiritualist and visit with the ghosts of their deceased loved ones.

Just before 9 a.m., Jessica saw the wide eyes of a woman peering at her through the curtains of the front door of the office. She knew this to be a good sign, and shouted out to Clement that they may have a customer. Jessica welcomed the woman and her husband into the parlor, and invited them to relax and take a seat.

The room was adorned with an impressive collection of Victorian-era antiques, and well-made reproductions. Red velvet drapes decorated the walls from ceiling to floor, fastened with gold-tasseled ties. A red and bronze flowered throw rug lay beneath a small mahogany coffee table, scuffed just enough for a guest to believe it authentic. A heart-shaped love seat with a hand-carved scroll of fruit and nuts along its edge sat in the room's corner, accompanied by a Tiffany-styled reading lamp. The shelves and fireplace were over-stuffed with iron picture frames and candelabras, while the soft music from an obscure operetta danced in the background. It was clear to Jessica that their new customers enjoyed the enigmatic surroundings as the couple stood in the center of the room and soaked in the atmosphere.

"Clement, my dear. We have visitors!" Jessica announced, her floor length gown whispering along the polished wooden floor boards.

Clement entered the room and walked toward them with a calm and deliberate gait. The first rule of landing a successful mark was to provide a credible atmosphere. He needed to transport his quarry back to another more uncomplicated time, help them forget the modern constrictions of science and technology, and become comfortable in a simple, more open-minded, non-judgmental era. The second rule was personal believability. Once they had been entranced by the atmosphere, Clement would approach his customer with a tender but determined look, always approaching and greeting the husband first with respect, and then flattering his wife immediately thereafter, acting as if he had laid his eyes upon some delightful mystical goddess. Clement knew that nine out of ten times, it was the wife who was dragging her husband into the reading and not the other way around. He was able to "cold read" the subtle muscular movements of his clients' faces within moments after their initial contact, and he knew right away if he had captured their interest and achieved an acceptable level of believability, or if they remained skeptical. If they believed him, from that moment on, the rest was easy.

"My name is Imelda Fabrizi. I am so excited to meet you." Imelda held out her hand, bent at the wrist, an invitation for Clement to kiss it, and he obliged. Her hand was thin and bony, her jewelry gold and authentic, and her nails polished and glimmering. "And this is my husband Edward," she said.

Edward Fabrizi was an intimidating, square-jawed man in his early fifties who wore a gold ring on each hand and had a pair of expensive sunglasses that may have cost more than Clement and Jessica's house perched atop his salt and pepper hair. His thick black eyebrows formed a V in the middle, pointing down at the bridge of his nose, and both Jessica and Clement saw no signs of obedience in him. Edward was uncomfortable, shifting his weight from foot to foot, and glancing around the room as if waiting for someone to jump out in ambush -- perhaps a ghost.

"What's this gonna cost me? That's all I want to know." Edward asked, his eyes refusing to focus on any one person or thing.

"A full one hour session is four hundred." Jessica responded. Negative news was always easier to take coming from an assistant. It should never come from The Medium.

Imelda didn't flinch and smiled, and Edward shook his head in defeat. He reached into the vest pocket of his jacket and flipped a credit card onto the coffee table like it was the ace of spades in a poker tournament.

"I'll take this in back and get you a receipt," Jessica offered. "Mr. Fabrizi, you are welcome to stay and watch the session, but we ask that you remain quiet so as to not disrupt the room's unique metaphysical energy."

"No, no... if you're going to be talkin' to spirits in here, I want no part of it. This place gives me the creeps. The people I know who are dead, I want them to stay dead. I'll go for a walk. I saw a deli on the next street over. Looks like they had some fresh pecorino and provolone in the window."

"Oh Edward, we just had breakfast!" Imelda nagged.

"I'll decide when I eat, and when I don't cat. You just worry about talkin' to four hundred dollars worth of ghosts."

Edward walked out the door and Jessica left to ring up the sale in the back room, leaving Clement and Imelda to sit in the high backed Victorian chairs and begin the session.

"So what brings you to the island?" Clement asked, knowing that answers to a few soft-spoken, open-ended questions would reveal much about his client, and served to put her at ease.

"We're here for the week. We're staying at that quaint little bed and breakfast on Mosquito Beach. My girlfriend told me all about how restful this island is, and how incredible you are at these readings. Oh, I couldn't wait to get here. She said you're not like those terrible phonies on television... you're real."

"Thank you, Mrs. Fabrizi. But it doesn't sound like your husband is as open minded."

"Edward? Oh, don't worry about him. I know he comes off difficult sometimes, but he is a very loving and generous man."

"I'm sure he is. I could tell just by looking at him," Clement agreed, respecting that even in an alternative business, the customer is always right.

"Take my hand now, Imelda. Tell me what you feel."

"Honestly, I feel a little nervous."

"Excellent, That's a very normal response. We're about to communicate with a spiritual dimension that may be uncomfortable for you. Nervousness helps sharpen your senses and will keep you focused. If at any time this becomes too much and you want me to stop the session, just say so. It's OK. Do you understand?"

"Yes..yes, I understand. I am so excited!" Clement could feel Imelda's pulse quicken and her grip on his fingers had become stronger. This was a good sign, as she was nibbling at the bait. He closed his eyes and feigned concentration, reeling her closer.

"Oh my dear, Imelda. You have a very strong aura, one of the strongest I have felt in some time. Understand that I am a medium. My body acts as a conduit, or a channel, that can guide messages from one existence to another. Sometimes, customers come to see me who have no aura at all. For them, there is little I can do. Many of the messages I will deliver I may not fully understand and you may need to help me interpret them. The language of the spirit world is complicated, my dear. Messages come to me in many forms, such as colors or feelings or senses, and they don't always follow our mortal logic. Do you understand so far?"

"Of course! Of course!"

Jessica burst through the door carrying an antique, polished silver tea set, steaming from the top, and set it upon the table. Imelda was startled and pulled her hand back from Clement, appearing angry. Clement, too, shot Jessica a disapproving look and chastised her for the poorly-timed interruption.

"Dear, please make sure we will not be disturbed again. Imelda's aura is quite strong this morning. I do not want to risk damaging the connection. I cannot predict with any certainty the damage we could cause if we are interrupted again. Could you please do that for us?" Clement folded his arms.

"Yes. I will hold all calls for the next hour and will not disturb you again. I am so, so sorry. I just wanted to be hospitable and offer our new guest a cup of tea. It is a standard English blend, but it is seasoned with herbs grown right here on the island, and quite delicious."

"Oh, how lovely!" Imelda responded, and she sipped at her silver cup, soaking in the extra special pampering. Jessica handed them each their own napkin as a good servant would, lowered the lights, and politely bowed and excused herself from the room.

The interruption was no accident, but all part of the well-choreographed performance. On the back of the napkin in Clement's hand was the quick research Jessica was able to gather in the few minutes she was alone in the backroom with Edward's credit card. An adept typist, and experienced at quick online research with three computers simultaneously searching for different facts, she was able to find records concerning the Fabrizi's tax records, home ownership, family obituaries, society page mentions and even some concerning information regarding Edward's alleged mob connections and arrest records. The results of the research were scribbled on the back of Clement's napkin in a shorthand only they understood in case it fell into the wrong hands. Clement sipped his tea, dabbed at his lips, and devised a strategy based on Jessica's research in a matter of just a few seconds.

"Take my hand Imelda, close your eyes, and let's concentrate together. I am starting to see the color blue, all around you. Why blue? Do you like the color blue?"

"Yes, I do. But my favorite color is purple."

"Yes, yes... I can see that, too. The colors are still coming into focus. I do see purple now... the hues are changing. Lots of purple. Wow, you really do like the color purple."

"That's amazing!"

"I feel from your aura that you are a sensitive person... you're very emotional."

"Yes that's true! I am!"

"You care for everything, sometimes too much."

"Yes. Edward tells me that all the time, he says... *I don't give a crap, why should you?*"

Clement paused. "Well that's strange... now I see... animals? That doesn't make sense. I see the sensation of all kinds of animals... lions, elephants, tigers... exotic animals. These must be animals that have passed into the spirit world but for some reason think they have a connection to you. I don't understand."

"I know! I know!' Imelda nearly jumped out of her seat. It's my wildlife fund. I operate a foundation and raise money to help save endangered species!"

"Wow, Imelda. This is incredible. This is beyond anything I have ever experienced in all my years. The message I am receiving from these animals is so strong. They must know what you do for them. They appreciate that. Their spirits must follow you and protect you wherever you go." Jessica's research was paying off especially well this day.

"But I see a pink hue around your aura, too. You've been hurt. The pink hue tells me this, but I can't tell what... yet."

"Oh please, go on!"

"I am feeling a sense of agitation from someone, a feeling of worry. There is a spirit who is trying to contact you. I see the letter C. Does the letter C mean anything to you? I'm sorry that's vague... but wait, I see more. I see a phrase a word CAR... maybe something to do with automobiles or travel? CARLOT..."

"It's my mother! Oh my God it's my mother!" Imelda was near hysterical. "Her name was Carlotta!" It was another hit for Jessica's adept research.

"Carlotta? Are you there Carlotta? Is there something you want to say to Imelda?" Clement reached out into the darkened room with both arms.

Imelda was hyperventilating. She no longer held Clement's hand nor was she keeping her eyes closed. Her head pivoted back and forth searching around the room for a visible sign her mother was present.

"I feel she worries for you. I feel her energy, it is gray."

"Why does she worry about me?"

"It has something to do with your husband."

"You know, she hated him when we got married."

"Could it have something to do with your husband's friends?"

Imelda stiffened, and Clement realized he had tread on dangerous waters and would need to back off a bit. If Imelda were to be convinced her deceased mother knew about whatever trouble her husband was getting in, it could become too unsettling. He had to be careful, especially if something illegal was involved. Clement needed to regain control of Imelda's emotions and direct her where he wanted her to go.

"Your mother has a message for you. It's a message of understanding. She worries about you every day, but I feel she understands."

"She does? She understands? What does she understand?"

"She is communicating to me a powerful feeling of acceptance. It is very strong. I believe she now accepts your husband and your relationship with him."

"That's all I ever wanted."

"She knows you worry about him so much, and she knows there has been trouble, but she wants to be there to help both you and your husband no matter what the problem may be. She wants you to rely on her for guidance, like you did when you were a little girl. I can feel the warmth of her smile in this room, and it is potent. I feel her hand extending out to hold yours. Imelda, reach your hand to the air. Close your eyes tight. Sometimes, if your aura is strong enough, you might be able to feel the spirit's presence without my help."

Imelda trembled and did as instructed and Clement exhaled hard yet silently in her direction across the table, and at the same time, pressed firm upon the loose floorboards under his left shoe without allowing them to creak.

"Oh! Oh! I felt something. I felt my mother!"

Throughout the session, Jessica performed additional research in the next room in case it was needed. She monitored the situation through a peephole in the curtain. Clement had developed a series of hand signals he would use to communicate with his wife throughout the sessions in case he needed assistance or an unexpected, sudden interruption. Through the years, they had experienced all sorts of reactions to Clement's startling abilities, including clients who ran out the door screaming and others who would collapse and fall on the floor unconscious. The talented EMT's of the Manisses Fire Department would visit about once a month during the busy season to revive the fallen believers. The extreme reactions annoyed the authorities but were good for business.

Imelda's session lasted for the full hour, and the two weaved back and forth between idle chat and profound spiritual discoveries, and Clement remained on top of his game as he guided her on a rollercoaster of emotions -- never too high and never too low -- ensuring her experience was intense and satisfying. Once the hour had expired, and Clement believed he had fulfilled his end of the bargain, he would slump forward onto the table in exhaustion. The session would be concluded. He would apologize that he had offered all the spiritual energy within his being, and now needed to rest, and then tell the client that he felt there was so much more out there yet to be revealed.

"I will come back tomorrow." Imelda insisted. "We can't let this end here! I want to know more!"

I will need time to rest, Imelda. But the same time tomorrow should be fine."

Clement could see the silhouette of Edward standing on the porch eating something, and hustled Imelda out to join him before he came inside. The diminutive Imelda gave her large husband a big bear hug, and Jessica and Clement watched as the two walked away together like newlyweds, toward the harbor and dock. Imelda's arms were waving about, her jaw flapping a mile a minute, as the pair disappeared together around the corner.

"She was sweet, but he scares me." Jessica confided.

"She will be back tomorrow at nine. If we're lucky, we might see her every morning this week. She is a perfect fit to the profile."

"I'll put it on the calendar."

"What is Lucretia doing in the morning?"

"Why do you ask?"

"I'd like to put her in the attic again... rattle the chandelier... work the lights."

"You know she hates it when we make her do that."

"Maybe she wants to earn a few dollars this summer and not just mooch off Vance."

"Why don't we have Vance bring out the tea set? He looks like a ghost."

"Hmmm. That's funny. I'll have to think about that."

As the two watched the morning tourists shuffle past the office with their designer coffee and newspapers, Councilman Smyth jogged up the sidewalk to their door, taking both Clement and Jessica by surprise. His expression was strained -- even more so than normal -- and it was clear something was amiss.

"Good morning, Mr. Smyth. Come on in. Is everything OK?"

Smyth stopped short of the door looking spooked, reluctant to enter, poking only his head in and looking around the interior.

"I normally don't like coming over here," Smyth said, "but I just wanted to stop by and let you know, since it was your daughter that found that coin... It turns out it is authentic. Solid gold. Brenda had it cleaned up and has it stored away for safe keeping in the town hall safe. They date the coin to about sixteen-ninety."

"Wow! How about that! Prissy actually found real treasure. She will be thrilled." Jessica exclaimed, beaming on the success of her brilliant daughter.

"Oh, but that's not all. Right now, the Dodge estate is under siege. It's crazy down there. You might want to come over and take a look for yourself. That is... umm, if you can get away from your... umm, work."

Chapter 8

The tall stranger pulled his leaky row boat ashore and buried it among the abundant weeds and thicket along the beach. He considered it a miracle that he and the boat had not sunk beneath the pre-dawn surf. His black leather boots were soaked, his feet were cold, and the tails of his overcoat were wet too, adding to the raging discomfort in his aching back. The morning sun was beginning its rise in the east, but as he had rowed in the dark with haste from the sloop anchored far offshore, he was unsure which part of Manisses he had the pleasure to land upon. He climbed up the outcropping of unusual large, black rocks and scanned the circular horizon. The June sun felt warm upon his face, and he could see smoke rising from dozens of small shacks and cottages to the south. The air was still, as was the sea, and he removed each piece of the wet, offensive clothing, his wide-brimmed capotain and cutlass among them, and laid them around him on the large stones, then he laid down himself, long legs splayed like the hands of his gold pocket watch, and he took a nap in the morning sunshine.

The stranger was awakened a while later by the screeching of an angry cormorant, and he instinctively reached for his sword, which fell from his perch, clanking all the way to the sandy beach below. He reassembled his clothing, still damp, but more suitable now for socializing, and climbed down to retrieve the leather sacks he had stowed beneath the seat in his boat. The sacks were wet, and heavy with his belongings, but they lacked food, and he regretted not pinching a square of cornbread from the ship's galley before he made his hasty exit. As a child back in his hometown in Dundee, he would pilfer seagull eggs from the nests along the River Tay that his mother would fry into his favorite breakfast. He looked up at the swarm of gulls circling overhead, making their own breakfast by dropping unfortunate clams upon the stones, and believed that if he could not secure proper accommodations before sunset, he still might at least enjoy a tasty dinner.

His leather bags were overstuffed with cargo and difficult to carry, and he dared not drag them for fear the tattered leather would tear and burst open. His broad shoulders ached from their weight, and he stopped often to rest, wiping the sweat from beneath the black curls that hung along his furrowed brow. It was becoming obvious that before he could complete the critical business he had come to Manisses to conduct, he would have to locate a safe hiding place for his baggage as dragging it about in this manner was sure to kill him.

Ahead he spied a barn -- a new construction, as shards of boards and wood lay strewn around the grass in the field on which it had been erected. The sweet fragrance of fresh pine board filled the warming air. The owner's cows had already taken up a comfortable residence inside, and being anything but curious beasts, the stranger knew they would not bother his belongings. He expected only to hide them here a day or two, out of the weather, until his business was concluded, and he could gather them up and sail on toward home.

He arrived on the sandy main street of the small village late in the afternoon, and entered the one and only general store. The street appeared abandoned. Inside, the shopkeeper was stacking crates by the door and recoiled at the sudden sight of the tall, thin stranger, who removed his hat and bowed with all the grace and confidence of a member of the king's own court.

"Your name sir. What is your name?" The shopkeeper demanded, clutching beneath his counter as if scrambling to locate a weapon.

"I do beg your pardon, sir. My name is William," the stranger responded, his unusual accent bouncing off the walls of the little shop.

"Your accent... you are from Scotland? You are a Scot? What manner of vessel brought you here!" The shopkeeper peered through the window of his store, wide-eyed, looking to see if there were any more of his kind lurking about on the main street.

"I am alone sir, I swear to you." He said, holding his hat at his belt. "I am here for only a day or two, as I am employed in the king's service, and have urgent business to attend to."

The king's service? And which king might that be? The King of England, or the King of France?"

"I am sworn to serve and protect my namesake, his royal majesty King William. May God save the King." William smiled and placed his hat over his heart.

"Do you believe I am a fool? Am I to believe that you have just fallen from the sky and wandered into my shop out of chance, and you are not here to rob and ransack me?"

"I swear to you, I come to you sir in peace, unarmed."

"Unarmed? How do you explain the cutlass hanging from your belt?"

William smiled. "Oh, this? This little thing? A mere bauble! Would you deny a loyal subject of his majesty the right to carry a blade as harmless a thing as this? I swear to you sir, I barely know how to use it. Look here, my good man, from you, I only demand a referral. I require a hearty meal and a place to stay, for just a few nights. Nothing more. And I am committed to pay you handsomely for your advice, kindness and troubles." William continued to smile.

"Show me your purse, sir. How much will you pay?"

"You may set your own price, my friend, but I stand before you penniless. When my companion arrives tomorrow, I promise, you will be reimbursed handsomely."

"So now I am expected to extend you credit? You are no better than a guttersnipe out to steal my apples. It would be best for you, my Scottish friend, to turn tail and find the ship, wherever it is, that brought you here." The shopkeeper pointed a crooked finger and waved it toward the door.

A young woman had appeared behind the shopkeeper, emerging from a backroom carrying a hand-woven reed basket. The shopkeeper had momentarily forgotten she was in the building, and he spun on his heels.

"Stay back Mrs. Raymond. I am unsure of this man's intentions," the shopkeeper warned.

"I heard every word of your conversation, Mr. Faxon," she said, tilting her head to one side. "I believe you said your name is William? You may stay at my inn for the next few days. I have plenty of room and could use the revenue from even a temporary boarder."

"Mrs. Raymond, have you lost your mind! Think of what you are saying. Look at him, this man is a danger and a scoundrel. His clothes are filthy, and he is penniless." William stood silent, communicating to the pretty, dark-haired woman and encouraging her with his dark eyes and the warmest of smiles.

"Yes, his clothes are a mess. But I am schooled in the best of European fashion. Those britches he wears were hand made for an aristocrat, from the finest cotton, as was his coat... very nice craftsmanship, even with the stains of mud and tobacco juice on his sleeves."

"And you expect this companion of his to show himself and pay you?"

"I do not know. However, look at his vest pocket, Mr. Faxon. I see the brilliance of a gold chain just peeking out above the button hole. That chain I am certain, is attached to a gold pocket watch which shall serve as his security for his room and board..."

"...and warm meal?" William interrupted coyly, raising a finger to his nose.

"Aye sir, and a warm meal," Mrs. Raymond nodded and affirmed.

William removed the watch from his pocket and handed it to the lady. "This watch was presented to me by my one and only true love on this earth. And I only concede to your request as your hands are soft and delicate like hers, and I can tell by your eyes you are an honest woman, and shrewd in the manners of business. I offer this watch to you as down payment on my account, and know you will return it to me upon the payment of my debt." William said, smiling.

"I do not approve! I do not!" Mr. Faxon shouted, slamming the palm of his hand on his counter. "Mr. Raymond will be furious."

"No, sir. I believe Mr. Raymond will be delighted that his enterprising wife has found a way to keep the accounts of the inn current in his absence," Mrs. Raymond answered.

"It is unacceptable! It is improper." Faxon continued, growing louder.

"If you are so concerned for my honor and economy, Mr. Faxon, I suggest you lower your prices and forgive my balance here from your shop, then I will let this stranger find other accommodations that you will find more suitable!" Mrs. Raymond demanded.

Faxon grumbled, but added nothing.

With his hat placed firmly back upon his flowing mass of hair, William extended his elbow to the young lady and the two exited the shop like a proper English couple. As they walked by the few town folk out that afternoon, William would smile, remove his hat, bow his head, and offer his most humble greetings in his foreign but warming Scottish brogue. The islanders were such a close knit community, the site of any stranger brought cautious pause, but the site of a statuesque and handsome Scot, on the arm of the young bride of the prominent innkeeper, would be nothing short of scandalous -- perhaps even seditious.

"Will you honor me with your name, my dear, or shall I just call you Mrs.?"

"My name is Mercy," she answered. "And yours?"

"But I have told you. My name is William."

"So that is your God-given name is it? Well, William, you are the most charming pirate I have ever met."

"No madam. I am no pirate. Some may call me a privateer perhaps, in the honorable and dangerous business of protecting his majesty's empire from the scurrilous French. But madam, I am not, nor have ever been, a pirate."

"I see. Though I must admit not seeing much of a difference between the two.

"Aye, Mercy, my dear. That I do understand. I regret that even the most powerful and sovereign nations of Europe often share your confusion. Now... if you presumed I was a lecherous pirate, why would you consent to bring me back to your inn?"

"Because nothing ever happens here. This island is the center of boredom. Ships come and go every day, bringing with them stories of the wars in Europe, the Indian adventures in and around Boston and New York, and tales of exotic places in the Caribbean... stories from places all over the world. They come with beautiful but expensive clothes and goods that I can never hope to afford. Instead, I bide my time alone in an inn where no one wants to stay, looking out my window, staring across an ocean at the ships, loaded with adventure, that pass on by -- day after day. You, William, are now my adventure." Mercy smiled and her eyes sparkled.

"And you do not fear I will slit your pale throat as you sleep in the night?" William joked.

"Better I die tonight at the rugged hands of a gallant pirate grasping at my throat than die like a shriveled grape hanging in an abandoned vineyard."

"I am confident, my dear Mercy, you will live a long life, and that your wine will be forever sweet."

"You, Sir William, are quite the rogue. Such a charmer! But I knew from reading your eyes and the movements in the muscles of your face you were honest and a proper gentleman. I know I have nothing to fear from you. I have made it my career to read people's intentions in this manner."

"As have I, my dear. The high seas are a dangerous and unpredictable place, where laws are drafted and broken on the whim of a captain's momentary disposition. Liars, pretenders and frauds are everywhere, and one's survival is dependent upon reading within the captain's eyes if the flag that flies above their ship is authentic, or only a ruse to draw in the gullible and unsuspecting to their death. In your eyes, I read innocence and wonder. Perhaps, my dear Mercy, fate brought us together, as you and I are more alike than we realize."

"Perhaps that is true."

"I hope that as your first pirate, I will live up to your expectations for adventure."

"Oh, how sweet it is for you to say that. And how naive it is for you to think.... that you are my first pirate!"

Through its history, Manisses had a notorious reputation for harboring pirates. It's central location in the rich shipping lanes between New York and New England, too small to become a center of significant commerce and warrant protection, yet too big to be ignored, meant that for centuries pirates, troublemakers and cons would use the island as a convenient, central location to re-stock and re-supply. Ten years before William's arrival and his stay at the Raymond family inn, French privateers stormed the island and stripped it of everything of value. After gaining the confidence of the locals by posing as English, they slaughtered all the livestock, smashed the weaponry, and then stole grain, corn and even the clothing off the very backs of the settlers. Mercy's father, a prominent fisherman, had his boat and nets taken, and even had his farmhouse gutted and seized to be used as a prison for any resident who did not offer complete submission to the plundering forces. The end result of the siege was that many residents left for the mainland in fear and financial ruin, abandoning their property, and dreams, never to return. The stout islanders who remained lived in constant suspicion of strangers.

For five days, Mercy and William lived alone together at the inn, sharing stories. Mercy laundered and mended all William's clothing returning to him the look of a dashing European aristocrat. William adored Mercy's roast duckling and a Portuguese egg pudding she learned to make from a previous tenant of the inn. William told her the details of his adventures off the coast of Africa and around the exotic island of Madagascar, as well as of his voyages in the Caribbean. Each afternoon, the pair would stroll like newlyweds through the dusty streets of the island's little village, Mercy relishing in the turned heads and scandal she was bringing upon herself, William even enjoyed portraying the role of upstanding citizen.

On the fifth day, as they reached Mr. Faxon's shop, William stopped cold in his tracks. Standing before them in the street was a small, beautiful, blonde-haired woman. William rushed to her and fell to his knees, burying his face in the ruffles that adorned her chest, his long arms and wide hands placed firmly upon her back. She cried and stroked his hair, and the two stood as still as a statue, as one.

Mercy was stunned, and stood speechless.

"My dear, Mercy, allow me the pleasure to introduce you to my wife, Sarah."

Mercy remained silent.

"It is a pleasure to meet you dear," Sarah extended her hand.

Mercy did not move.

"My dear husband, I have missed you so," Sarah said, stroking his cheek with her thin, pale hand.

"And I have longed for you every moment I have been away," William responded. "But we must make haste. Does anyone know you are here?"

Manisses

"Only Mr. Paine, your reseller, who arranged my passage here knows where I am. I must not stay on this island more than a day or two, as my absence from New York will be questioned if I take leave for too long. Your safety is in question too, my love. I pray the privateers do not locate you first, there is quite the bounty upon your head."

"But did you bring with you the good news that I so badly hope to hear?" William's eyes widened, and he held his breath like that of a child expecting a present.

"Yes. I do. Your old partner, Bellomont, has arranged for your clemency. You must get to Boston as soon you can arrange passage and turn yourself in to the magistrate. I must assume someone on this dusty rock of an island has an old sloop you could hire."

"Bellomont, that dog! I had him pegged as a scoundrel! Oh my dear, you are an angel."

"I have been widowed twice my love, and I have not yet reached my thirtieth birthday. I will not be widowed a third time. The die has been cast. I think it best that we gather together your things and go quickly."

William turned to Mercy, still smarting from what she perceived as a slight.

"Mercy, my dear, do you know of a ship I might hire to get me to Boston quickly?"

"First, sir" Mercy began slowly, "there is the matter of your debt to the inn."

William had been blind to Mercy's raging jealousy, and now realized he was in trouble. Her eyes were searing through him. Even the trusting, honorable Sarah began to wonder what the depth of their brief relationship had been.

"Sarah, my dear, would you kindly pay this innkeeper for my stay?" William asked, reaching deep for a last ounce of charm to see him through the moment.

"And for the mending, and the laundering.... and the warm meals!" Mercy demanded.

Sarah looked up at William with a gaze of concern.

"My dear, I have but a few shillings upon my person. The dirty villainous captain who guaranteed my safe passage took everything I had, that villian." Sarah confessed.

"My dear, Mercy," William began, removing his hat and dropping to one knee, "my wife Sarah is one of the wealthiest socialites in the city of New York. And I too, as a result of my voyages, am quite well-known and independently wealthy myself. Upon my return home, I will forward to you all that I owe and more."

Mercy was not impressed. "I have your watch stowed away as collateral, and I know you want that back. But I think the prize on your head might be worth ten times the value of that watch. I think my husband might be quite impressed that I captured a real pirate, the legendary Captain Kidd. What will the privateers pay for a renegade like you?"

"Fine! I will pay you now! I want you both to meet me back at the inn in one hour. Do not speak to anyone, and by God's grace, do not let anyone know we are here."

William left his coat and hat with the women, and ran as fast as his legs could carry him up the road and toward the new barn, holding the sword at his side so it would not carve open his own leg. Once he arrived, and after he moved two uncooperative cows out of the way, he located the two leather sacks he had hidden days before. He drew his sword and plunged it into the manure and soft earth, and dug quickly. One of the bags he decided he would leave here and retrieve after his name was cleared, while the other bag he decided to bring back to the inn and use its contents to pay his debt and his voyage to Boston. The jog back to the inn, down the stony lane, was arduous with a sack so heavy across his back, and upon his arrival an hour later, he fell to the steps in a heap of exhaustion. The women waited for him by the door having spent the previous hour avoiding conversation and politely ignoring each other.

William untied the latch and opened the sack, exposing a stunning array of hundreds of pieces of gold, silver, coins, jewels and other trinkets. He reached in and withdrew a handful of the bright, shiny coins and handed then to Mercy.

"There you are, my dear, there is enough gold and silver in your hand to pay for the room and a hundred of those roast ducks" William said, still breathing heavy from his ordeal. "You wouldn't mind sharing with my wife how you prepared that duck, would you?"

Mercy considered the silver and gold in her hands, and glanced into William's leather bag.

"Do you believe your freedom to be worth just this? A handful of coins and trinkets?" Mercy asked, determined to extract her revenge.

"Then, what is it you want?" William asked, short on time, and running shorter on patience.

Rather than answering directly, Mercy reached down and held out her apron.

"This should about do it," she demanded.

William and Sarah exchanged glances, then William lifted the bag and dumped its contents into Sarah's open apron. Coins and jewels spilled off the cotton apron and onto the wooden stairs. Mercy beamed, then laughed aloud.

"This treasure comes from the Quedagh Merchant, an Armenian ship my crew and I seized that sailed for the French," William said. "Many are looking for it with earnest, so I advise you to care for your treasure and spend it with discretion. There should be enough gold and silver here to buy half of Connecticut."

For over 300 years, stories of Captain Kidd's buried treasure were told all over Manisses, but no one had any luck finding it. Expedition after expedition searched the island, overturning stone walls and digging into the caves along the bluffs, all experiencing and sharing in the same rotten luck. When Captain William Kidd reached Boston to clear his name in 1699, as had been pre-arranged, he was seized and returned to face trial in London for piracy and other crimes. It seems Bellomont, his former friend and business partner, had tricked William into turning himself in to deflect attention away from accusations of his own piracy. In London, William was found guilty and hanged, his body left on display in a steel cage for three years, as a gruesome warning to anyone considering piracy as their own future vocation. William's wealthy wife Sarah, imprisoned herself for a time, returned home and took her fourth husband.

And following her own husband's death, Mercy Raymond used the contents of her apron to purchase a large parcel of land for her and her family north of New London, Connecticut.

Until Prissy and Abby uncovered a single gold coin in the

earthy debris in the back of the Dodge family barn, the locals conceded that the fanciful tales of Captain Kidd's buried treasure were simply that -- just tales.

And now, they had proved otherwise, and everything began to change.

Chapter 9

Smyth led Clement and Jessica up the twisting road toward the Dodge farm and the controversial old barn, his penny loafers treading along in the ghostly footprints Captain Kidd had laid down over three hundred years before in the scramble to retrieve his own buried treasure.

The tall June spartina grass that populated the field around the marsh near the farm had been trampled flat. Yellow police emergency tape was strung from one end of the field to the other, and back again, in both directions, and fluttered in the persistent summer breeze, in the shape of a large, shimmering chessboard grid. In each of the squares was one, two and sometimes three or more of the island's most distinguished citizens – friends, relatives, shopkeepers and a few anonymous yet enterprising tourists – digging and quarrying with fury at the earth within their own pre-assigned square. Altogether, it appeared that over one hundred people were digging with shovels, rakes, picks, and even their bare hands, clumps of sod flying every which way, intent upon uncovering the once thought imaginary treasure hiding beneath the ancient, rich, sandy island dirt.

"What in blue blazes!" Jessica exclaimed.

"The culprit is over there!" Smyth pointed his skinny, crooked finger at a tall and overweight blonde woman in a tan polyester suit stumbling in their direction. The clumps of grass in the uneven field caused the heels of her shoes to twist and buckle, and neither Jessica nor Clement were sure she would make it to them without falling flat on her face. Somehow maintaining her balance, she extended a sweaty palm out to greet them with one hand and adjusted her ill-fitting eyeglasses with the other.

"Hi folks, so glad you could make it. Each square will cost you just one hundred dollars. Either cash or check will be fine." The woman removed a ragged steno book held together with thick green elastic bands from under her armpit and waited, with an eager smile, for an answer. Jessica and Clement were too confused to respond.

"This is Mr. and Mrs. Bradford, Winnie. Prissy's parents." Smyth said, recognizing their confusion and breaking the awkward silence by introducing the confused couple.

"Oh my! It's a pleasure! Such a pleasure! I'm Winsome Hunter, the attorney for the Dodge family. But you can call me Winnie."

"It's nice to meet you, Winnie." Jessica responded, shaking Winnie's sweaty hand, growing more confused and suspicious by the moment. "But I must ask... why and how do you know our daughter?"

"Oh! Prissy! Such a smart little girl... I'm sure you're very proud of her. Without her, we wouldn't have achieved any of this!"

Behind her, what was once a peaceful, majestic field was now submerged in a bath of chaos. Though the Bradfords didn't know all the names of the diggers, they recognized most of their faces. In one square, was the high-strung woman who managed the canoe rental agency by the library; in the square next to her was Jack, the retiree with the pilot's license who shuttled the impatient rich people back to the mainland ahead of the ferry; next to him was the lady with the bad breath who worked Saturday mornings at the post office; beyond her was the ever-pompous Skip Payne and his wife Kitty, their matching tan cargo shorts uncharacteristically stained in filth; near the stone wall was Old Sumner, the fisherman; and next to him was Lucky and Vance dressed as if they were burying a corpse, in a surreal scene that could have been ripped from the pages of an Edgar Allen Poe short story; and so many others. And in the broken window of the barn, chins perched upon the dry-rotted wooden frame, were the dirty beaming faces of Abby and Prissy smiling back at them.

"Ahhh! Ahhh! Ahhh!" Sumner screamed, hopping up and down in his square. "I found something!"

All heads turned toward Sumner who was waving some sort of metal artifact over his head. Many of the excavators stopped and rushed toward him hoping for official confirmation that pirate treasure had been once again discovered.

"What is it?" Someone asked.

"I dunno. Looks to be about a foot and a half long, though." Sumner answered.

"Looks like a coat hanger to me," said another.

"Maybe it's a pirate coat hanger!" Someone else barked, and the whole group laughed. Sumner slipped the find into his canvas shoulder bag with a sheepish thrust, and turned his back. The gaggle of giggling treasure hunters then returned to their quarries.

"Here! I have something here!" Skip called out next, cradling his find against his stomach with care, brushing chunks of black, caked earth onto his boat shoes. "Hey, it's an old horseshoe!"

"Not surprised to see one of those," Guilfoyle shouted from his own square beyond the barn. "I used to ride a horse back there when I was just a boy, back in the Forties, during the war."

"Mr. Bradford, please pardon my boldness, but your daughter's wonderful find inspired the Dodge family heirs to contract me as their official agent of record, and I'm offering these folks a chance to find the treasure." Winnie said.

"Why wouldn't the family just excavate the property and keep the treasure for themselves?" Clement asked, unable to repress his suspicious nature.

"Because," Smyth interrupted, sarcasm thick in his raspy voice, "the heirs don't believe for a second that there is anything out here. They're about to lose this property to the town for unpaid back taxes, and lose use of their barn either to restoration or razing. This is the last chance they have to make a profit off this old place -- or maybe even save it. Every square inch of this field has been turned over, trampled, plowed and dug through for generations, and the only things they have found so far are beer bottles, some old rusty nails and a few Manissean arrowheads. They are not worried about losing their pirate treasure. In fact, they are glad to give it up and put these foolish rumors to rest."

Across the field, Lucky was inserting her latest pirate artifact into a pre-drilled hole on the side of Vance's tattooed nose. When she was done, he kissed her on top of the head.

"Please tell me," Jessica pleaded, arms folded high across her chest, "that you did not take Prissy's money and sell her a square in that barn."

"Oh goodness, no." Winnie responded. The girls were invited to dig and play wherever they want! They are having a fabulous time searching for the pirate treasure. We appreciate and recognize that if it had not been for their natural curiosity in the first place, we would not have had this opportunity."

A terror-filled shriek interrupted the conversation and startled a flock of curious seagulls perched on a nearby rooftop, sending a chorus of sharp squawks cart wheeling across the field. Abby's mother Kitty was screaming, and hopping about in her square as if her feet had been lit on fire, shaking her wrists. She reached down into the rich earth, picked up an object and hurled it away toward the street, and then ran off screaming in the other direction toward the beach with her hands flailing over her head. While Skip chased his hysterical wife across the field, begging her to calm herself and return, the other treasure hunters dropped their tools and dashed toward the mysterious, new artifact now lying unclaimed in the gravel by the side of the road.

"What is it?" Someone asked, kicking it over with their toe.

"Wow... it looks like part of a jawbone. I think those are teeth."

"Well, would you look at that." Smyth dropped to one knee and removed his eyeglasses.

"Did we find a body? A corpse perhaps? Is this a murder scene?" Vance asked, eyes widening and showing an unprecedented level of interest. Clement wondered if it was the first time he had ever heard Vance speak.

"I am honestly not sure what we are looking at here." Smyth answered, rubbing his chin.

Just then, Jude, who had been standing by the barn and observing the scene with disgust, removed a toothpick from between his front teeth, flicked it into the summer air, and waddled over to the group.

"Yup... I had a suspicion," Jude said, nodding his head. "Looks like you folks found Grandmother Dodge's old dentures."

But just as the group began to enjoy a hearty laugh, they realized that while their backs had been turned, Jack the pilot and one of the tourists had become clenched in mortal combat. Jack had grasped the unlucky stranger by the throat. The tourist's face was red and his bloodshot eyes were bugging from his sunscreen-lathered forehead, and the tourist had two fists full of Jack's golf shirt. The two fell with an uneasy thud onto a pile of overturned loam in the damp field. The group abandoned the dentures and scrambled over to the two combatants, grasping at their swinging limbs, attempting to end the fight before one of the men got hurt.

"He was on my claim! He was digging on my side of the tape!"

"That's my side, you idiot! You moved that tape back to give yourself more room!"

And while the disruption had captured everyone's attention, Lucky picked up Grandma Dodge's dentures and slipped them into her pocket.

Prissy and Abby ignored the chaos erupting around the farm and continued to play inside the barn, out of the scorching sun and away from the adult craziness. Otto was sitting upright on a gray mound that had once been a hay bale, wearing a crown fashioned from a remnant of chicken wire that Abby had found and twisted into a small circle. A ring of well-placed clamshells decorated his throne. The girls had been conducting their own treasure hunt and were taking turns presenting their discoveries, like Verrazano in a French court, to their benevolent new king.

Though a bit embarrassed by the attention, Otto was cooperative and appreciated that the girls had offered him a role that recognized his stature and importance.

Otto's treasures were impressive. On top of the dry, decomposed hay at his feet were several pieces of broken white and blue pottery, a button, a handful of pins melded together by years of rust, the cap from a bottle of 7-Up, and the bottom of a corroded iron skeleton key. Otto was pleased with the offerings but was careful not to let on, sensing that there may be more valuable treasure yet to be found.

Prissy sorted through a pile of old paint cans that had fallen years before from a broken shelf. Beneath the pile was a locked tin box, wrapped with a cowhide tie. Abby took great care to brush the dirt and corrosion from the relic, and though still latched, the metal lock had long rusted away. Prissy pried the box open with her dirty fingernails and after some effort it obliged, popping free. Inside, was a leather bound book, several inches square, and over an inch thick, tied with a pretty maroon ribbon. The rich smell of fresh mustiness startled Prissy's nostrils.

"So what's inside?" Abby asked.

"It's just a stinky book." Prissy answered.

"What's it about?"

"I dunno. The words are hard to read." The pages were thick and dry, and crinkled as she turned each one.

"Maybe it will tell us where the rest of the treasure is buried."

Outside the barn, the adults again erupted into a raucous cheer. The treasure hunters had gathered around old Sumner this time and in his hand, he held a rusted pistol.

"That looks to be a .38 caliber double-action revolver. Or at least, it used to be." Sumner bragged to the crowd, squinting through one eye and pointing the rusty relic at the horizon as if to take aim at an invisible invader. "Mighty nice piece of history here! I'll be cleaning this one up. It's gonna make a fine looking trophy for the mantle of my fireplace."

Jealous and disappointed, Skip opened his palm and looked down at the small, twisted piece of metal he had found at the same time as Sumner. He careened it off the nearest trash barrel with disgust, angering a swarm of yellow jackets. Had he known it had been an authentic piece of the buckle from Captain Kidd's leather bag, he might have acted with much less haste.

"Excuse me, Mrs. Bradford? There is someone here who would like a word with you." Winnie said, waving an older woman toward them.

Bernice Cowan was a tall, round mass of a woman with a mess of gray hair that stood straight up and shot in all directions like the spokes of a wagon wheel. Jessica had never seen her wearing anything other than a blue denim tent dress that made her look even larger than she already was, covering her from the base of her thick neck to the swelled, pale ankles that drooped out over the edges of her orthopedic shoes. Though they had never formally met, Jessica was well aware of who she was and was careful to avoid her whenever their paths threatened to cross around town. The island was too small not to know all the year-round residents even if you didn't like them or want to talk to them.

Bernice wore the reputation of being a troublemaker like an army veteran might wear a purple heart. Beneath her coarse, intimidating exterior was an even more self-centered, acidic personality. If Bernice decided she wanted something, she would complain, whine, threaten and manipulate until she achieved her outcome, at any cost -- and be ready to brag about her conquest to anyone within earshot. Her henpecked husband Luther, who owned an unassuming hardware store behind the post office was pleasant enough when alone, but served as her willing accomplice -- the Clyde to her Bonnie -- whenever called upon. On this day, as Bernice hunted her latest prey, Luther was selling metal detectors from the back of his pick-up truck to desperate treasure hunters at twice the price of retail -- an idea no doubt forged by Bernice.

"My dear Mrs. Bradford! Oh what a pleasure it is to finally talk to you in person!" Bernice's smile and big teeth were displayed across her Halloween pumpkin face as if carved.

"Yes, it is a wonder we haven't chatted before, isn't it?" Jessica responded, slowly backing away, searching for an exit to the conversation that had not yet started. "It is such a small island."

"Well, Mrs. Bradford, I had an idea... may I call you Jessica? Because that is your name now, isn't it? Well, Jessica, what do you think of this..." Bernice bowed her head, and began to speak in a quiet pitch so no one else could hear. With her back against a stone wall, Jessica had no choice but to concede.

"Now... your husband has an amazing reputation, Jessica, you do know that, don't you?"

"He is a very hard-working businessman, just like all the other shopkeepers in the village." Jessica answered, choosing each word with great care, knowing they would no doubt be used against her.

"Yes, I suppose he is that, isn't he. Myself, well, I don't believe in all that hocus-pocus nonsense he sells. I mean talking to spirits? That's just silly. Yet the folks who come into Luther's store who have endured one of his sessions rave about what he's able to do. Now I was thinking, that if your husband can truly talk to the spirit world, we need to do a session ourselves. Maybe out here, maybe at night. Maybe he can get some insight from those spirits as to where that treasure might be hidden."

"I'm sorry, Bernice, but..."

"You can call me Mrs. Cowan."

"Of course.., I'm sorry, Mrs. Cowan, but didn't you just say you didn't believe in this yourself? That talking to spirits was silly?" Bernice placed a flabby arm across Jessica's shrinking shoulders.

"And I don't believe. This would be just for fun, of course. Just for a laugh. But then I was thinking... What if there was a tiny, little bit of truth to it? Just a little. It can't hurt to hedge your bet now, can it? What if we could find a clue about the location of more hidden coins, or gold. Now wouldn't that be something to talk about."

"The problem, Mrs. Cowan, is that spirits don't always talk to Clement with words. They communicate the way they choose to communicate -- with feelings, or colors, moods and senses."

"I didn't expect them to draw up a treasure map, my dear. But they could point their bony, ghostly little fingers, couldn't they?"

"I'm sorry; it just doesn't work that way. And don't you think that if we could use Clement's abilities to find priceless, historic treasure, we would just do it ourselves?"

Bernice smiled. It appeared her pudgy cheeks were being inflated. "I'm not one to believe in coincidence either, my dear. It was your daughter who found the coin now, wasn't it?" Bernice paused. "There are some people on this island, my dear, who view what you and your husband do as improper -- even un-Christian. It wouldn't hurt to have a couple of upstanding citizens, like Luther and me, on your side."

"I'm sorry, but I don't see how this is going to work."

"I understand. I understand." Bernice smiled again. "Sometimes, I just get these crazy ideas. Don't mind me. I think I'm just caught up in the excitement of the moment."

Jessica sensed she hadn't heard the last of the conversation. Bernice had given up far too easily.

"Mom! Mom! Look what we found!"

Prissy and Abby stood before them as if contrived in an instant from the salty air, and both Bernice and Jessica were startled by their sudden appearance. With two fingers, like a seasoned optician, Prissy plucked a pair of old eyeglasses from Otto's face and handed them to her mother.

"Look! Aren't they neat?" Prissy asked.

"Why yes, they are!" Jessica said, inspecting them. "They look to be very old. Maybe one hundred years or more. That's a wonderful find, Prissy. I am thinking you two may have careers as archaeologists ahead of you!"

"Oh my stars, that thing is absolutely hideous!" Bernice shrieked, stepping back. "Oh how can you stand it!"

"Mrs. Cowan, are you alright?" Jessica asked. Bernice had turned pale, and her thick, sausage-like fingers were laid flat across her chest.

"That doll is the creepiest thing I have ever seen. What a sight! Oh, it isn't right."

Otto thought Bernice was creepy, too, but was too polite to say so.

"Oh, that's just Otto. I made him myself from..."

"I don't think I would go around telling people you made him if I were you, my dear. That thing is the most vile doll I have encountered in all my years. Just look at those blue eyes. They look right through you, like they are peering into your soul. They're almost evil. I don't like that one bit. That's just not normal."

"Oh, it's just a child's doll, Mrs. Cowan. It won't do anyone any harm." Jessica pleaded.

"Little girl, you'd be smart to toss that thing into the next fire pit you see, that's what I think."

Prissy clenched Otto close and frowned, and Jessica stood up straight, looking for an escape from Bernice's threatening presence.

"Prissy, why don't we walk back down to the village and I will get you both something nice for lunch?" Jessica said, taking both girls by the hands.

"I can see now," Bernice added, nose in the air, "that I was right. It wasn't any coincidence that it was your daughter who found that gold piece in the first place!"

"Oh Jessica, there you are!" Clement shouted, jogging over to the group. "I was wondering where you had gotten off to. Look at this awesome metal detector I just bought from Luther Cowan."

Jessica looked with a deep concern into her husband's eyes.

"Oh Clement, it's happening again."

Chapter 10

Clement and Jessica eloped when they were eighteen. They believed it was the only choice they had to stay together. Clement's parents were opposed to the marriage of their immature, awkward little boy to the carnival performer he had met just weeks before. And Jessica's father was furious that his talented daughter would threaten the family legacy to marry a talentless, introverted, underachiever.

Clement was raised as an only child in a modest, middle class, raised ranch in Hartford, Connecticut. Clement's father Hank Bradford was a burly, blue-collar career driver for the St. Johnsbury Trucking Company, spending his days hauling freight up and down the Eastern seaboard. The best money was made collecting overtime, so Hank was on the road more days than he was home, often weeks at a time. To help pay the bills, Clement's mother Edith, who fancied herself an amateur historian, took a job as a part-time docent and gave tours at Hartford's famed Mark Twain Museum. So in love with history and literature, she named her son and only child in honor of her favorite, greatest American writer, borrowing from the Twain's original surname of Clemens. Throughout Clement's childhood, the three members of the family spent more time apart than together, and Clement surrounded himself with thick books and long movies to fill the time and the emptiness in his life.

In school, Clement was an awful student. It wasn't that he was not intelligent, in fact, it was quite the contrary -- he was very smart. It was embedded in Clement's nature to be practical -- and he just didn't see the point of working to accumulate meaningless grades for their own sake. As long as he was passing, his parents left him alone, so his academic goals in school became focused on achieving C's. He made the conscious decision to spend more time on those things he enjoyed doing, rather than those things his teachers told him he was required to enjoy.

When he was twelve, His mother gave him a magic set as a Christmas gift. He had always been fascinated with the illustrious magicians he watched on television -- Doug Henning, Harry Blackstone, and David Copperfield to name just a few -- and fantasized he would someday become one of them, performing spectacular and wondrous illusions for huge, adoring audiences on the Las Vegas strip, and then be whisked off to headline his own million-dollar world tour. And once he developed his gift for sleight of hand tricks, he would routinely make his classmates' pencils disappear to their wonder and amazement. Each night after dinner, alone in his room, standing before his dusty mirror, waving his hands and arms back at himself in his reflection, he would practice his intricate, choreographed gestures into the wee hours of each morning. What intrigued him most was how people reacted to his clever little illusions. While most would smile, and sometimes even applaud, others would back away in fear, as if concerned that the disappearing pencils were the work of some inner, darker, unspeakable -- perhaps even evil force. Clement learned early that there was great power in these reactions, though he didn't consider that the reactions could be harnessed, manipulated or used to his advantage.

Clement's future bride-to-be Jessica had been born into a large family of acrobats and performers somewhere in the Midwest, and though her birth certificate listed Chicago, even Jessica wasn't positive in which town she was truly born. Before Jessica arrived, her family had achieved some local fame and notoriety as the "Flying Zelenkos" -- a name her grandfather created because it sounded dangerous, Eastern European, and much more exotic than the family's given name, which would have made them the "Flying Johnsons." The family played to small community theaters, festivals and county fairs across the Midwest and South, continually on tour and living out of trailers like drifters, earning just enough to feed the many mouths in their growing, extended family. Her mother died young in a tragic practice fall when Jessica was just an infant. Her broken-hearted father then immersed himself in non-stop rehearsals and the day-to-day duties of running the family business, leaving her to be raised communally by a gentle troupe of aunts, uncles and countless cousins.

Jessica would often joke that she had learned to jump from a trapeze before she had learned to use the potty. Small, lithe and quick, Jessica was born with an overabundance of the family's God given talent -- genetics she would later pass on to her spry and artful daughter Prissy -- and she wowed audiences from state to state walking a tightrope with elegance and style at the tender age of just four. Jessica's father Carl (spelled with a K on the carnival posters) viewed his clever, young and talented progeny as the troupe's central star and heir apparent to the Flying Zelenkos' future empire.

Despite her large extended family, Jessica suffered from chronic loneliness, and life on the road -- travelling from one gig to the next, week after week -- did not lend itself to creating many friendships outside her family, and her close-knit inner circle taught her to breed a broad distrust of strangers.

One month after his high school graduation, with a future no more exciting than September classes at the local community college, assuming he couldn't find permanent menial employment, Clement took a temporary job at the fairgrounds when the summer carnival rolled into Hartford. Local kids were drafted and used as fill-ins for any travelling sub-contractor, better known as a carnie, who might have run off, disappeared or was sleeping one off in the city drink tank. Working as a carnie for a few days, he thought, sounded like fun and beat lying around his bedroom watching stale summer re-runs on television.

When the head carnie asked the new recruits if any of them had experience performing in front of people, Clement foolishly raised his hand and said he did. His assignment was therefore to staff the "Guess Your Weight" booth where he was instructed to charge patrons five dollars for the privilege of having him guess their height, weight or age. If Clement's guess happened to be correct, Clement would earn one dollar and the patron would walk away empty handed. If the guess was wrong, the patron would win and select a cheap stuffed animal prize and

Clement would receive nothing. He was told, however, he could keep any tips he was able to collect.

Who in their right mind, he thought, would tip him for making a mistake?

Clement arrived nervous for his first night on the job, and it turned out to be a disaster even worse than he feared. He earned a total of seven dollars for ten hours work. He smiled a lot and nodded, but mostly stood quiet next to the booth and watched the happy crowds pass by -- but no one would stop. Before his shift began on the second night, the manager pulled him aside just before he took his place in front of the booth.

"Kid, I thought you told me you were a performer."

"Well, I do magic tricks."

"Magic tricks? You're kidding." The man sighed and ran his fingers through the greasy, gray hair that dangled like wires from his head. "Well, look, if you want to make this work, here's what you need to do."

The manager jumped out in front of the booth and began shouting and waving his arms, creating a spectacle.

"Come on over folks, five dollars to guess your weight. Win a prize!"

The wily old carnie started to dance, pirouetted, then reached out and grabbed the first passerby by the arm.

"You sir look like you want to win a prize for your lovely girlfriend, here." He said. The girl giggled, and the young man conceded and reached into his pocket for a handful of cash. As the carnie played and toyed with his prey, a small crowd started to gather. The carnie made a production out of coming up with a number and the assembled group now hung on the answer. But before the man stood on the scale, the carnie threw his hat to the ground and broke into song. Before long, the hat was filled with about ten dollars in singles and coins. And by the time the young man stood up onto the scale, it didn't matter if the weight guess was right or wrong -- the carnie had made his money, and five other people were waiting in line, clamoring for their own turn.

"The secret, kid, is in the volume. Guessing the weight isn't where you'll make your money -- and you will get better at that part as time goes on. Earning money here is about the showmanship and the tips. Entertain them. Put on a show for the folks and they will reward you. Do you think you can do that?"

Clement knew he had no chance.

"Yes, sir. I can." He responded anyway.

Clement knew he could neither dance nor sing, but for the remainder of the warm summer night, he did the best he could and flopped around the booth feeling like a fool. By the end of the night, he had done much better.

He had earned fifteen dollars.

In bed later in the evening, staring up at the swirling patterns of shadows in the paint on his ceiling, he accepted failure, and decided to tell the carnie manager the next day that he was going to quit -- or maybe he wouldn't even show up. He was exhausted, his back ached from standing and dancing for ten hours, and what he had earned didn't even cover the corn dogs or the purple slush he had consumed for dinner. His disappointment ran deep, and he glanced at the pieces of his magic set laid across his dresser in front of his mirror. It was then that it occurred to him -- what if... instead of making a spectacle of himself singing and dancing, he might perform magic tricks instead. Why not? He knew a hundred of them, and it was more within his nature. He did tell the manager he was a performer, after all, and if there was any chance for that Las Vegas gig or future world tour, he needed to be able to at least handle the local carnival. If it didn't work out, he could still quit later. If asked, he was sure David Copperfield could do it.

The next afternoon, Clement arrived at the carnival loaded -- that is to say, his body was pre-set with the hidden pieces, props and parts needed for an extensive performance of magic. He didn't know what to expect, and in the late afternoon sun, he could feel the straps and wires in his outfit chafing his sweaty flesh. He took off his cap and threw it to the dusty earth in front of him. All sorts of folks walked by, mostly ignoring him. He inhaled a lung full of warm, dusty summer air, then began waving his arms about making quarters appear and disappear as he had done for his friends and in front of his mirror at home dozens of times before.

It took only a few moments before a small group had gathered to see what on earth his gyrations were all about. When

Clement grew tired of playing with the coins, he pulled out pencils and showed some impressive tricks he had perfected in high school that he was sure even the great Blackstone himself did not know about. He performed with enthusiasm and vigor for a half hour straight, and when he looked down, he had almost fifty dollars in his hat, and the crowd was waving five dollar bills at him, begging him to use his magical powers to guess their weight.

By the end of the week, Clement had the act perfected and was starting to make some decent money. He was fast becoming a showman, and had even added a boom box with disco music to his developing repertoire. His most popular trick was to conjure a stuffed rabbit from thin air, then hang it on the prize wall as if he was re-stocking the display. The little kids loved it and they would cheer and clap, over and over again, for every rabbit he could produce. He convinced the most naive children that he was responsible for creating every stuffed animal in the carnival. They adored him. And they believed him.

It was then that he started to notice a thin, pretty girl in the crowd. There were many scantily clad, pretty young women in the crowds at the carnival, most with a dashing young man on their arm, but Jessica caught his eye because Clement thought it odd anyone would come to the carnival in the ninety degree summer heat wearing a long robe. Jessica was intrigued by Clement and his tricks, and she would return to watch his shows over and over again, between her own scheduled performances with her family in the bull ring nearby. Jessica had performed at dozens of carnivals and circuses in her lifetime, and the sudden appearance of a new performer on tour was always an exciting development. By the time the first week of the carnival was over, Jessica figured she had watched Clement perform his magic routine at least thirty times.

But Clement was not a seasoned performer. Though his talent and magical aptitude were admirable and improving, and his ability to collect spare change impressive, he wasn't prepared or trained to deal with every problem that might arise.

Early one afternoon, Clement began his shift as usual, tossed down his hat, then began to grab random coins out of the humid, dusty Connecticut air. The crowd was thicker than normal, and the expected pleasant and curious patrons began to assemble. A brutish looking man and his friends stationed themselves square in front of Clement's act. Clement could tell they were looking for trouble.

"This guy sucks," the man exclaimed, swallowing the last mouthful of liquid from his beer can. His friends, and a few others in the crowd giggled. Sensing the uncomfortable aura of the moment, others began to back away and leave.

Clement panicked and froze stiff, and a single quarter slipped from his sleeve, and bounced off the laces of his black shoe. Had Clement ignored the man and continued with the act he might have been alright, but once the man saw he had taken control of the scene, and had inserted himself under Clement's skin, there was no turning back. He continued to pepper the poor performer with a barrage of nasty insults. Clement blushed and stood quiet, his mind racing, not knowing what he was supposed to do. When he bent down to pick up his wayward coin, the man stepped on it.

"Lets' see some magic, Mr. Magician. Let's see you make that coin re-appear from under my shoe. Because I think you're a fraud." With his other foot, the man kicked Clement's hat aside, sending it and the first few coins of the day tumbling into the dust. When Clement stood up to face him, the man blew a lung full of cigarette smoke into his face and laughed. The situation was not good and getting worse, fast.

"These carnies are all con artists," the man declared, seeking approval from the gathering crowd. "They're only here to steal your money."

Clement's heart pounded in terror and he shrunk in embarrassment. He had never been much of a fighter, and avoided conflict whenever and wherever it arose. Was he supposed to swing at the beast? Or run away? Seconds passed like minutes as his eyes darted around the midway as his racing mind fumbled through his limited options.

To Clement's surprise, someone had snuck up behind him and turned on his disco music. Off to the side, Jessica was dancing, drawing the attention of the crowd toward her. Jessica was an accomplished and graceful dancer, trained in both ballet and folk steps since the day she could first walk, and combined with her sensational acrobatic and gymnastic skill, she was an elegant delight to watch.

Clement remained still. Although he recognized her immediately as that pretty girl with the strange, long robe from the crowd, he at first assumed she was working with the bully to further humiliate him. Jessica spun herself like a Spanish matador in circles around the confused Clement, her robe now a cape swirling high in the air as if taunting an invisible bull, in a near hypnotic blend to the music. After dancing and spinning a few circles around Clement, the thug and his friends took a few steps back -- there was no sport in heckling a talented and pretty girl. The crowd began to clap to the rhythm and her dance, and she stopped for a second in front of Clement, her nose so close to his he could feel her warm breath on his cheek. She blinked once and her green eyes peered deep into his.

"Don't stop. Continue with your act." She said with a soft whisper, and danced away.

He did not dare question her. Hands shaking, and with no other option, Clement reached into his vest and produced a handful of colorful handkerchiefs, that he began to spin and swirl overhead. Jessica knew the routine almost as well as Clement now, and she was able to improvise her dance steps and moves around the natural dramatic moments of Clement's clever illusions. The crowd was now twice as large and energetic as it had ever been before, and Clement found himself matching Jessica moment for moment, and movement for movement, as if they had performed the routine on the Vegas strip for years. When Clement divined his first cheap, stuffed rabbit of the day, he dropped to one knee and presented it as a heartfelt gift to his beautiful, new assistant. The crowd let loose with a spontaneous *awww* and without hesitation, she spun, dropped to one knee, and presented the rabbit to the bully with sarcastic tilt of her head, a wink and a smile. The crowd roared and the thug and his friends sulked away.

Jessica's best friend in the world Lucretia, the carnival's old Gypsy fortune teller, often said Clement and Jessica were a match made in heaven. But the truth was that it was a match made on a hot, dusty carnival midway in Connecticut.

And had the two not believed their love for each other was destined, and their future careers could be as spiritualists, they would never have allowed themselves to succumb to their egos, risk their family, and be forced to relocate to Manisses in the first place.

Chapter 11

C lement and Jessica snuggled together on the top step of their deck, sipping lemonade, and gazing to the west at the calm, gentle sea. The orange summer sun was retreating over the rock outcropping at the outskirts of their property near the shore, casting a long, restful shadow across the spot where Wequai had once slept, and where Captain Kidd had dragged his bulky treasure ashore. Comfortable New England days were precious -- a respite from the contrasts of blazing summer heat and painful winter cold. Jessica pulled her bony knees up under her chin and leaned into Clement's shoulder.

"Why..." she asked, squinting into the purple and red clouds that zigzagged across the sky, "...can't life be simple?"

"Maybe life isn't supposed to be simple," Clement answered. Deep, philosophical discussions were not his strong suit and made him squirm and he would often go to extremes to avoid them. But next to Jessica, he felt a calm and balance that he felt nowhere else in the world, and with her by his side, deep discussions didn't only feel comfortable, they felt natural.

"Maybe that's the point of all this, it's about the struggle. If you stop and think about it, our generation -- in this so-called modern era -- has it pretty darned easy. We have electricity, communications, running water, indoor plumbing and benefit from an evolved economic system that fills our local shops with all the food, water and provisions we could ever hope for. I can only imagine what it must have been like for the first settlers to set foot on this island and try to survive off it -- to sustain their lives off this big, desolate rock in the ocean in the middle of nowhere."

"Settlers? What about the Indians? They were here first. Think about it. For thousands of years, this island was inhabited only by Indians who survived off this land. Come on now

Clement, can't you feel it in the air? Their spirit? Their very essence? Every time the wind blows, I can feel their warm breath on the back of my neck. I can almost hear them talking, I think, sometimes singing. If I look over to the beach, then close my eyes, I can see the shadow of an Indian girl wading in the surf collecting clams and crabs to roast for dinner... maybe even sitting next to those very rocks, over there, by the shore."

"I know what you mean. I once had that same feeling walking across the battlefield at Gettysburg. The sense of terror and pain, human emotion so thick it made the air hard to breathe. I think it is one reason people so enjoy visiting historic sites, many over and over again, not to learn about dry, historical facts and details -- you can get all that stuff from books. They go to absorb the energy and residue of human thought and emotion that still hangs in the air from those distant times."

"Like ghosts?"

"There are no such things as ghosts."

"I know. I was just checking to see if you were paying attention."

"Take that old Dodge barn everyone is arguing about... look at all that junk they dug up in there. There is evidence at every turn of the toil and struggles of daily life. Maybe that is the real treasure."

"But I wonder if they knew they were even struggling, after all. The first Indians to live here may have looked at the natural abundance of plants and fish and thought they had it all -- a paradise -- just like we do now. They could not have imagined that there was anything more in this world than what was here. They had everything they needed. There were plenty of fish and berries for food, plants and trees to make shelters, and fresh-water ponds to collect drinking water. And then the settlers came along and wondered how the savages had been able to survive in this barren wasteland without the help of their modern conveniences like axes and guns. I believe future generations will look back on us, here today, and wonder, by what miracle, we were able to survive within the confines of our own primitive culture."

Clement stretched out his legs and laid back on the stairs, gazing up at the darkening sky. Summer peepers in the marsh behind the house had started their evening song, right on schedule as their peeper ancestors had done for thousands of years, timed in perfect rhythm to the gentle beating of the waves lapping at the beach, and a swarm of frantic but determined black flies laid claim to Clement's lemonade.

"I wonder sometimes." Clement began. Jessica knew to pay attention when Clement was being philosophical. He chose his words with care, and hated conjecture. She turned her head and looked into his eyes, hanging on every word, almost worried about what he might say next.

"Sometimes I wonder what would have happened if we never had left the carnival."

"You hate my father," she said.

"I know I do. But your father hates me more."

"Oh, that's not fair. You never gave each other a chance."

"Maybe we did, maybe we didn't. I don't know, but it wasn't ever going to work out. When two men love the same woman -- even it's for totally different reasons -- one will win and one will lose. The end is never pretty."

"Oh really! And so Don Juan, you know this how? From the hundreds of women you have seduced through the years? From the throngs of angry lovers who have hunted you down, demanding duels for the hands of the scores of beautiful maidens you defiled?"

"Why go through all that drama? I read it in a book."

"Such a smart husband I have."

"Do you think, that if we had stayed in the show, things would have worked out for the better?"

"That's a ridiculous question. If we hadn't left, we wouldn't have been exiled to this bucolic island in this beautiful run-down house caring for two eccentric children, talking to ghosts now, would we?"

"But I don't want to re-live Eastbury, either Jess. I don't want to go through all that again. What you told me Bernice Cowan said got to me today. It got into my head, and she got me thinking. I know she's a rotten old wind bag, but she isn't afraid to say what other people are already thinking. She believes we are drawing upon some dark, evil force to conduct our lives -- and she doesn't like Otto much, either. It's not just Bernice though; many families on this island are suspicious of our business. They are suspicious of us. Ever since we got here, we have been treated like outsiders."

"But there are families on Manisses who have been here for a hundred years and are still treated like outsiders."

"You know what I mean. Your senses were on high alert. I know her comments hurt you, too. You even told me so yourself."

Clement looked up at the ginger glow of light coming through Lucky's upstairs bedroom window. He couldn't see the peculiar daughter he loved so much, but he looked with love upon Lucky's shadow as it meandered back and forth across the room with a purpose. In a sudden bright flash of orange, Lucky's shadow disappeared.

"She just loves that welding torch you picked up for her birthday," Jessica said.

Chapter 12

L ife as part of a travelling carnival act was not easy, often
bizarre, and as foreign a landscape to the sheltered, young
Clement as if he had found himself strolling on the rocky
landscape of Mars. What made the situation even more difficult
was the reaction of his parents to the news that he had eloped
with a carnival performer and was running off to tour with her
troupe. His blue-collar, truck driving father Hank at first refused
to let him go, pounding his fist so hard on the Formica coffee
table that he snapped off the corner. Clement's mother Edith
wept, was inconsolable, and said nothing for days on end,
refusing to even cast her eyes upon her son's pretty and talented
young bride.

Clement and Jessica's new life together was off to an
auspicious start.

For the remainder of that first summer, Clement
performed and perfected his clever little magic act in a record-
breaking heat wave that blanketed the Northeast, and then the
upper Midwest. The prickly hair from the cheap, fake fur of the
stuffed rabbits, artfully hidden around his sweaty torso, gave
him such a severe and painful rash that he could barely walk or
sleep. And draped in his wool magician's costume, necessary to
conceal the tools of his trade, he would lose as much as five to
six pounds every day, returning to the trailer drenched,
dehydrated and exhausted. But the value to his career from the
non-stop activity and practice as a working magician was
priceless, and he was able to not only perfect his craft, but was
also able to accurately guess his customers' age, weight and
height ninety percent of the time, to the amazement and
amusement of the ever-growing crowds.

After hours, and between acts, Clement would spend his
free time watching Jessica, her father, and her cousins practice
their routines. At first he was swept up in a sense of the wonder

of it all, much like a wide-eyed visitor at any performance. But as he watched the high-wire routines again and again, he developed a deeper understanding and respect for the concentration required to pull off such daring tricks, and was horrified by the very real danger that hung on Jessica's talented yet dainty finger tips. Clement's admiration for his wife's abilities turned quickly to anxiety, and a lump would rise in his throat when he began to consider that in the blink of an eye, her ultimate fate could end up the same as that of her late mother's.

Clement, Jessica, her father Carl, her aunt, uncle and four cousins all lived in a turquoise aluminum Winnebago camper built and designed for use by a family of four. A black and red "Flying Zelenkos" logo was emblazoned across the back, but was faded and peeling. The table where the family would squeeze together to eat their meals doubled as Jessica and Clement's bed at night, and with such a large group, the cousins preferred to stand naked outside dumping buckets of water over each other's heads rather than wait for their more private indoor morning shower. Privacy, as Clement was forced to accept, was better maintained as a state of mind.

Despite the close and uncomfortable quarters, Clement for the most part enjoyed the steady presence of Jessica's family. Following news of their elopement, he was unconditionally accepted by the troupe, and was included in all the activities as one of the clan. When time permitted, between chores, and practices, the Flying Zelenkos would form a makeshift, out of tune country music band, and the other carnies would circle around to sing, dance and empty a few cases of beer. Although Clement was no musician, he was a respectable harmonica player, and slipped into the fabric of the ragtag group with a comfortable ease. Clement had grown up alone with no siblings, and with parents who worked around the clock, so he found the daily familial activity both entertaining and intoxicating. Had it not been for Jessica's father's continual, icy stares of contempt, their life on the road would have been oddly idyllic.

Carl Johnson was a burly man with thick forearms and a rock hard chest, giving him more the look of the carnival strongman than a carnival acrobat. He would routinely dye his curly hair, arm hair and handlebar mustache jet black for marketing purposes, and to hide both his advancing grey and his true Irish ancestry. The sudden loss of his wife years before had nearly killed him. Jessica was his only child, and heir to the Flying Zelenkos name and empire, so Clement's sudden appearance not only threatened his business and family realm, but it threatened the tender threads that held together the frayed remnants of his broken heart.

When Carl first heard news of the elopement, he flew into a violent rage, smashing the windshield of the Winnebago with his fist. He was by nature a peaceful man, and Jessica couldn't recall him ever raising his hand or acting with any kind of aggression before. His reaction scared her -- and mortally terrified Clement -- setting the stage for years of quiet resentment and hatred between the two men she loved the most. Jessica adored her father but knew he could be thick-headed and stubborn -- traits that on one hand intimidated young Clement, but on the other hand, kept the family act successful and together.

Jessica grew up without a mother. Yet what many perceived to be a deep and tragic loss in her life didn't bother her one bit. In those moments when her aunt and cousins couldn't offer the quality of feminine advice she needed, she turned to her best friend and surrogate mother Lucretia, whom she and Clement would later honor by naming their first born daughter in her memory.

Lucretia was Jessica's guiding light -- her mom, her friend, her physician, her psychologist, her ally and her conscience. It was Lucretia who became the first to know the shocking news about her sudden new boyfriend Clement, and their planned elopement. In fact, it was Lucretia who found a judge, filed the paperwork and ensured it would all be official, legal and binding -- and then conducted the private ceremony herself on a romantic moonless night under a black sky filled with stars behind a greasy corndog trailer.

And it would come as no surprise to anyone that Lucretia and Carl did not get along.

Lucretia made her living as the carnival's popular Gypsy fortune teller and plied her trade from a bright red and yellow tent set-up at the farthest end of each compound. (Many of the regular carnies found her creepy and wanted her as far away as possible.) Lucretia was older than most of them, and was never seen without her long flowing purple and red robes, gold hoop earrings and an array of scarves that dangled off her in a rainbow of vivid colors, whether on or off duty. She spoke with a strained Eastern European accent, and Clement was convinced that despite what she told everyone about her mysterious Romanian ancestry, he could hear a distinct New Jersey inflection embedded deep in her voice. With Lucretia, it was difficult to tell where the Gypsy fortune teller act began and ended, or if it was all one and the same.

Lucretia's tent was filled with all the supplies one would expect a state-of-the-art, ancient fortune teller to have at her disposal. There were multiple crystal balls, each with a distinct size and hue; an oversized deck of tarot cards carefully wrapped in an ornate silk handkerchief; a tattered and yellowed paperback copy of the *I-Ching*; an iron rack holding an impressive array of candles and incense; and even a small kitchenette with a variety of traditional, green and herbal teas.

In the absence of a travelling doctor, or proper health care provider, even the most squeamish and doubting of the carnics would visit Lucretia when they were in sufficient discomfort. Depending on the affliction, and the patient's belief system or lack thereof, "Doctor" Lucretia might prescribe a green tea, an herbal ointment, an incantation or even a prayer -- and sometimes an artful combination of several of them. She believed that the connection between healing, spirituality and medicine was an integral part of the natural world and needed, at all times, to stay in proper balance.

So when Clement could no longer stand the itching and pain from his rashes, and Jessica could no longer stand the complaining, she brought him to Lucretia's tent for treatment. Clement stood on display in the middle of the tent before Lucretia as she circled around him, Clement's arms extended to each side. The Gypsy paused behind him, closed her eyes, laid her wrinkled fingers on his shoulders, and stood very still.

"Don't you want to see my back?" Clement asked, cracking the nervous silence.

"Patience, my young friend. You must have patience. I must absorb your aura. I must not only see your pain, but I must understand it. I must believe it."

"There's not much to understand. I had some sort of allergic reaction. Those stupid stuffed rabbits gave me a rash," Clement explained, and Lucretia sighed.

"Very well. Let's go outside in the better light and take a look."

Jessica led Clement out through a hole in the back of the tent into the bright sunshine. Clement stopped, turned and rolled his shirt up to his neck to expose his raw, painful back. The rash and sores were red and oozing and Jessica felt sorry for Clement, and winced at their ugliness.

"Oh my, you poor boy! Lucretia exclaimed. "Why don't you bend over and let me get a closer look."

No sooner had Clement placed his hands on the empty cart in front of him, Lucretia grasped his trousers at each hip and with one sturdy, determined tug, pulled Clement's pants down to his ankles, exposing his naked, red, sore rear end to anyone who happened to pass by.

"Hey!" Clement screamed.

"Oh those bad, bad bunnies. Look what they have done to your bottom." Lucretia said with a blunt, matter-of-fact tone. "Those awful bunnies."

Blushing and humiliated, Clement instinctively reached down and tried to pull his pants back up, but Lucretia grabbed his wrists to stop him.

"No, no, no.... your wounds, they must breathe. The evil must dry and be absorbed by the gods and goddesses who heal within the sunshine and air. You stand still, right there, while I retrieve an herbal salve for those terrible bunny wounds. Don't you dare move one muscle!" Lucretia breezed back into the tent and Jessica stood with her hand over her mouth, using every ounce of her energy to refrain from laughing, as the first carnival goers of the day had entered the compound and were heading in their direction.

"Jessica, please! Get me out of here!"

"I swear to you, Clement, she knows what she's doing. Please, just wait a minute."

Clement scrunched his eyes and tensed his arms as the seconds slowed to what felt like hours, until Lucretia emerged from the tent stirring a mortar and pestle. She knelt behind him and began to chant and sing in an ancient language Clement did not recognize, then she began to pat his sore behind.

"Oh, what a terrible thing to happen to such a nice round, young bottom." She said as she smeared a foul smelling, olive colored ointment onto Clements back and rear. "I tell you what... I know someone. I will find you some real bunnies to hide in your pants. No more of these fake bunnies. Fake bunnies are bad karma."

"Oh my God!" Clement screamed, arching his back. "That feels incredible! Whatever you do, please don't stop!"

Once his back was covered in a thin film of greasy, cool salve, a grateful Clement fixed up his clothing and the three returned back into the sanctuary of the tent. Lucretia went to work at her small stove preparing a soothing, sweet tea for her best friend and her newest patient. The pain was now gone, and a relaxed Clement was amazed at how good he felt.

"That was amazing, Lucretia. Simply amazing. I can't wait to go to bed tonight. It will be the best night's sleep I've had in weeks. Thank you. Do I owe you any money?"

"Money? Goodness, no." Lucretia giggled. "I must prepare for the customers in a few minutes. I will take their money, not yours. You are the husband of my best friend in this realm. You are now my family. Family takes care of each other. I will take care of you, and you will take care of me."

"Well you let me know what you need. I will help you anyway I can. That is a promise."

Lucretia paused and exchanged knowing glances with Jessica. It was then that Clement realized he was the victim of some sort of a small conspiracy.

"Now that you mention it," Lucretia began, "I do need someone. I am getting old, and divining fortunes for people takes too much energy. The people who come to the carnival all seem to like you, Clement. You have an agreeable face and a nice way of talking to them."

"So what do you want me to do?"

"Serve as my assistant. Just in between your own acts, of course. I need someone to visit with and warm-up my customers, get them thinking, open and prepare their minds to the wonders and mysteries of my practice."

"Do you plan to guess people's weights for the rest of your life? You know you can't do that magic act forever," Jessica chimed in. "You should learn a more sophisticated bit... a trade, even. You could be Lucretia's apprentice, and have a chance to learn the ins and outs of the business from one of the greatest anywhere."

"You want me to become a Gypsy fortune teller?" Clement asked.

"Fortune tellers, psychics, mediums, spiritualists -- even magicians and illusionists -- on the surface they may appear to be different, but they are all of the same organic origins and use the same technique to distract, engage and manipulate attention to entertain their followers." Jessica told him.

"I will teach you to read the ways and workings of the spirit world. It is a very powerful skill to have, my young friend. In the right hands, you can do much good with it."

Clement paused. He loved performing magic tricks and aspired for more. Maybe this was the avenue he needed to take to bring him to that next level and even someday forge an independent life for himself and his new bride.

"Alright, then. I will do it, Lucretia. I will come by early tomorrow and we can talk about what exactly you expect of me. But right now, I need to go get changed. It looks like there's already a big crowd coming through the gate this morning, and I don't want to miss out on the early rush. But no bunnies today." Clement smiled and darted through the front of the tent, and headed back to the trailer to change for his act. The women watched him rush away and sipped from their tea cups until Lucretia's first customer of the day happened by.

"Oh, Lucretia... thank you so much for helping him. I haven't seen him this happy in weeks."

"I'm sure that salve helped quite a bit, too. His back looked terribly uncomfortable, the poor boy." Lucretia shuddered.

"But was it necessary to stand him outside naked like that? He wasn't very happy about that part of the treatment."

"Oh heavens, no. It was just a benefit of being the only person in the compound that people think is a doctor. I could have sent you both back with a tube of that stuff I picked up at the pharmacy, but that wouldn't have been as much fun."

Clement studied under the loving, detailed tutelage of Lucretia for two years and absorbed every tip, trick and tried and true technique like a sponge. Her talents and abilities were more similar to his own tricks than he realized and they became very close. He was fascinated at how she could control her customer's senses -- their sense of smell with her candles and incense; their sense of taste with an herb or cup of tea; their sense of hearing with her strange accent and occasional unexpected moan; their sense of sight with the ambience of her clothes and her tent; and their sense of touch as she instructed them to feel the vibrations and auras swirling around them in the room. At the right moment, her customer was then immersed, ready and willing to accept anything she told them. It was no different than distracting someone with the wave of one hand while producing a stuffed rabbit from seemingly thin air with the other, only this was far more intriguing. And Lucretia would be proven right -- it was far more powerful.

Clement studied with Lucretia every moment of every day he was with her, right up until the day she died in his arms. The suddenness of her passing and the severity of her illness was a shock to almost everyone including her distraught best friend Jessica and her dutiful assistant Clement -- neither of whom knew there was anything even remotely wrong. A few others in the compound did know that Lucretia had cancer and was treating it herself they only way she knew how -- relying on the herbs, teas, meditation and the spirituality that she had spent her life learning and dispensing upon her faithful patrons. She was such a master in the art of deception and misdirection that she was able to conceal the truth from the two closest to her, but she also believed deeply in the power that these ancient medicines brought her. If she had been able to speak from the grave, she would have explained that her treatments were proven and had extended her life years beyond any modern treatment she would have received from a conventional doctor. But there was no way to prove it, either way.

Now trained and prepared, Clement took over Lucretia's tent and business with a sad and efficient enthusiasm, and dispensed his own brand of spiritualism more in league with his own personality. He changed the decor of the tent from that of an old gypsy fortune teller into that of a Victorian mesmerist, replaced her colors and draperies with faux antiques and an iron chandelier, retooled the message from fortune-telling to channeling, and re-opened for business within a week of her funeral. Both Jessica and Clement knew she would have been proud that they were committed to carrying on and advancing her life's work.

And when Jessica discovered and announced to her family she was pregnant just days later, those who believed in reincarnation were quick to point to the obvious spiritual connection. Whether it was a random, happy coincidence or a deliberate memorandum from the nether world didn't matter. Jessica and Clement agreed that if the child was born a girl, she would be named Lucretia in honor of their dearest friend.

But as Clement's popularity and success on the midway soared, the rest of the carnival struggled. Months later, mere days before Lucretia was born, the Flying Zelenkos disbanded. Having not been paid for a month by the cash-starved carnival owners, fresh out of food and supplies, and living in an unsafe trailer held together with electrical wire and duct tape, the troupe voted to just give up. Jessica had been unable to perform due to her pregnancy, and two of her cousins had been offered more lucrative gigs with a large, well-known circus. The time had come. It was over. Carl was beside himself with inconsolable grief.

Jessica and Clement had to make a difficult decision. Lucretia had left Jessica a small inheritance in her will, and Jessica felt it most appropriate to bank it for little Lucretia's future -- maybe even for a college education. It wasn't much, certainly not enough to pay for college now, but it would be enough to rent an apartment and maybe start a small practice of their own somewhere. Or, they could turn the money over to Carl and see if it would be enough to keep the troupe together another season and roll into the next town.

They decided to move on, thinking it the best option for their unborn child's future. And with few choices in front of them, they settled on a community that at least one of them knew well. So with Jessica expecting any day, and stained cardboard boxes filled with candles and crystal balls, they arrived on the steps of Hank and Edith Bradfords' small, sleepy Hartford, Connecticut home.

Chapter 13

C lement's fork scratched across the enamel of his melamine breakfast plate and the silence-piercing sound bounded and echoed around the Bradford's small kitchen. Edith, Hank and Jessica flinched at the noise, but were all secretly thrilled there was something to distract them from the suffocating silence that had hung in the room like the crossbar of a guillotine since they had first sat for breakfast. Clement ignored the sound and twirled the bright yellow scrambled eggs in circles on the mint-green plate, and joined by some charred hash browns, he created an unappetizing, sublime mess. Every few moments, Edith would clear her throat, look up, and begin to say something, but would then reconsider her comment and retreat back into her eggs. Hank ate two fisted and angry; gorging on what was a rare, warm morning meal in the Bradford household without letting go of his well-groomed grudge. Jessica was feeling out of sorts, a bit woozy, just days away from delivery, and didn't fit between her chair and the broken Formica table, but did her best to chew, smile and swallow each inedible bite. The Bradford's French poodle emitted never-ending, annoying yaps from the next room.

"What's your dog's name?" Jessica asked with care, selecting a simple, unobtrusive question designed to cause no harm.

"Bartles." Edith responded with an uneven smile.

"What a cute name for a dog." Jessica answered, seizing on an opportunity for at least non-descript conversation.

"Made more sense before James was hit by that delivery truck." Hank said without looking up.

Friendly conversations between the two couples were few and far between, and the house was too small to avoid each other for long. When the tension became too much to bear, the young couple would take refuge in Clement's old bedroom, barely large enough for one person, now straining from the unexpected presence of its young inhabitants and their bulky belongings. Jessica and Clement would talk for hours about their future – how to start a business, how to raise a child, the kind of house they wanted to buy – rich discussions filled with hope, fantasy, excitement and naiveté. Jessica even attempted her hand at interior design, reorganizing the confined room into a more functional, pleasant, albeit temporary, living space complete with a hand-sewn frilly curtain and fresh-cut flowers she picked from a vacant lot across the street. Compared to the Flying Zalenkos' diminutive Winnebago, Jessica believed the room felt more like that of an English manor.

While Jessica tried her hand at playing house, Clement would immerse himself in and play with his grandfather's old train set.

The set was an original, 1930's Lionel Hiawatha locomotive, still in its original packaging. The faded orange and blue boxes that housed each of the cars were tattered and moldy, victims of years of neglect and damp basement storage, but as a testament to their superior design, the trains still worked like the day they first came off the assembly line. Clement would spend hours snapping the track segments together, meticulously polishing each metal contact, then weaving the track segments in, around, under and through the couple's personal effects strewn about their bedroom. Empty shoe boxes made ideal tunnels, discarded soda bottles and cans doubled as trees and buildings, and a dead, petrified June bug retrieved from between the window panes, sat upright atop the lead car, retained and contracted to serve as the railroad's dutiful engineer.

Clement had been fascinated as a child by the freight trains that ran back and forth between New Haven, Connecticut and Worcester Massachusetts, passing over the Connecticut River near his home. The warm smell of oil, grease and burning coal always seemed to ignite a spark deep in his soul. Each time the great engine would pass, the ground would tremble and the steel bridge would creak, and each time Clement's eyes would widen and his pulse would quicken, standing in awe of the sheer size and power of the great steel dragon.

And then alone back in his room, he would recreate the scene with the his models, borrow from his magic tricks to create wisps of smoke, blow his train whistle, and lose himself in a secret domain where he could execute complete control, direct the action, and rule the empire as his own robber baron.

"So Jess, what do you think? It's beautiful, isn't it!?"

"Yes, it's very pretty." Jessica answered, reaching deep to find some encouraging remark that wouldn't insult him.

"Pretty? I don't know if I would ever call it pretty." Clement answered, insulted by the implication his hobby could be anything less than macho and virile. "The Hiawatha is sleek and stylish – a classic of its era -- but not pretty."

"I'm sorry. You're toys are not pretty. I meant to say that they are..."

"And they are certainly *not* toys! They are models. Icons. I don't think you understand."

Clement was right. Jessica did not understand. To her they were just little toys–fun and fanciful perhaps to a child, but juvenile, frivolous and unbecoming of an adult with responsibilities and a child on the way. It took less than a minute for the train to traverse the small loop on the bedroom floor and shove a dirty sock aside, only to start the exact same journey all over again once the route was complete. The amount of time Clement would indulge himself watching the train repeat its cycle without purpose, again and again, baffled Jessica -- she was far more practical and efficient with her time. If there was no formal purpose or reason for doing something, she would simply not do it. Time, and the effort she would choose to put forth, were always calculated and budgeted. Jessica would get out of bed within three minutes of the same time every morning without the aid of any alarm, and return to bed at night the same way. Each moment of her day was planned, executed and analyzed much the way an actuary would scrutinize a profitable, new business venture. And if an investment of her time and energy did not work out to her complete satisfaction, the activity would be abandoned and her time reinvested on a new, more productive activity the next day.

The contrast of Clement's whimsy against Jessica's obsessive-compulsive practicality created a magical yin and yang between the two young lovers that neither would ever appreciate, but both would cherish – a distinction which would also serve to drive their friends and parents crazy.

And it was that same distinction that made finding a place to live and an office in which to conduct business arduous, painful and on the brink of impossible.

So when Clement and Jessica weren't sparring with Hank and Edith, or hiding in their bedroom fantasizing about their future, they would borrow Edith's crumpled gold Chevy Vega and drive it along with its rumbling muffler to visit storefronts around the Greater Hartford area, searching for the perfect place to open their exciting, new family business. The money they received from Lucretia's inheritance was shrinking, plundered to cover their day-to-day living expenses, and they knew it wouldn't last forever. They needed to act fast, before it was gone and they were both bagging groceries at the 7-Eleven to pay the bills. But every shop or office they visited was either too expensive and impractical for Jessica's tastes, or too small and plain for Clement's vision of their legacy. Day after day, week after week, they would empty the noisy Vega's thirsty gas tank and debate -- each presenting the utmost respect to the other's opinion, but neither willing to budge even a millimeter from the relative safety of their own.

"I love it." Clement would say.

"It's too expensive." Jessica would respond.

"This is what we need," Jessica would say.

"But it's small, old and falling apart," Clement would answer.

When they rolled into the town of Eastbury for the first time, they both agreed. They both hated the neighborhood.

Eastbury was a rusty old New England mill town, one of dozens of such villages that either decorated, or littered, the northeast landscape, depending on one's perspective. One hundred years earlier, the town was a vibrant, bustling center of commerce and activity. It was a place where one would visit the coffee shop for a homemade doughnut each morning, have one's hair cut at the barbershop, buy a hat at the five and dime, enjoy a leisurely BLT at the luncheonette, and if the kids behaved, take them to the Majestic Theatre on the corner for the fifty-cent

Friday evening show. But now, with the mills long ago massacred and shuttered by a changing, depressed economy, the mile long Main Street presented a sad array of vacant storefronts, secondhand shops, social service agencies and antique stores. Each building was dirty-red brick and two stories tall, most with bent or missing gutters and impressive plumes of crabgrass shooting up around the edges of the crumbled sidewalks. Each building came with its own set of angled parking spaces out front, the white lines long worn away or covered in oil secreted from the tired engines of older model cars. Each parking space featured the stub of a rusty parking meter protruding from the sidewalk, each sheared in half by years of visits from sleep deprived snowplow drivers. Remnants and wrappings from so many fast food meals, purchased at the restaurants built on the outskirts of the village intended to draw customers away from the downtown area, were visible everywhere, left to blow back and forth across the street like lonely urban tumbleweeds until thcy would fade and decay where they landed. Pedestrians were few and far between, excepting for an occasional ruffian on a skateboard, or for three old men who sat together on an iron park bench under an awning in front of a dry cleaner.

"This neighborhood is depressing." Clement said as the Vega shook and rumbled to a stop.

"And it smells like the exhaust from the cotton candy trailer back at the carnival -- burning sugar and diesel fuel." Jessica added. "Dad used to always try to park behind the food trailers to have the first crack at the leftovers when they closed. I used to go to sleep at night with a pillow over my face just so I didn't have to smell it."

Their doors creaked in harmony with the broken suspension, and they exited the car and walked up to one of the many vacant storefronts. The windows were cloudy with the dried salt that the town used to treat the icy roads, and a red and white "for rent" sign further obscured their view. The old men on the bench next door stared at them, and whispering among themselves, their wrinkled brows wrinkled even more by their collective nosiness. One of the old men pointed an accusing, worn cane in their direction. Clement felt uneasy.

"Maybe we should just go." Clement urged.

"We told Mr. Knicely we would meet him here at two o'clock. We are fifteen minutes early."

"This place is a mess. I don't see how this dump is ever going to work out. Look inside, if you can... I think I see water damage on that back wall, probably a leak in the air conditioning unit on the roof. And in the corner, over there, do you see those exposed wires?"

"Clement..? Did I just see something move?"

"Yup. I think that was a rat."

"Hi, folks!" A friendly, booming voice interrupted their conversation from behind. "Are you Jessica? I'm Al Knicely. I believe you said you were interested in renting this property?"

Jessica believed Al Knicely to be a very handsome man, almost. He was tall, thin and dark, and wore an expensive suit. Though he was middle aged, he was also young and athletic looking, and the sweet wisps from his cologne was a welcome respite from the fetid air in the village. But the expensive suit he wore was twisted around him at an awkward angle, and didn't quite fit, one of his wing-tipped shoes was untied, his hair needed to be combed, and the stubble of his beard was peppered with gray and at least three days old. He wore a large gold wedding band on the wrong hand, and Jessica wondered what his wife might be like, and what was so wrong with her that she could have let him out of the house looking this way.

"This is the best unit on this strip," Al said. "I've had three successful businesses use this place in the last two years alone." He said, tucking in the tail of his wrinkled blue dress shirt.

Al fumbled with a steel ring of what looked like thirty dangling keys to locate the one that would release the latch of the bulky door and let them inside. The door creaked open, and Al reached in and flipped on the light switch. The room brightened, and the presence of the three humans caused something rodent-like to scamper in the ceiling above them. Acting on instinct, both Clement and Jessica ducked.

"Atmosphere." Jessica whispered.

"I think I smell something electrical burning." Clement whispered back.

"Are you kids from around here?" Al asked, initiating small talk, attempting to warm up to his prospective clients.

"Clement grew up in Hartford, but I'm new to the area." Jessica said.

"Well then," Al began, clearing his throat, "let me tell you about this little village. It's a special place. Do you see outside that window, there?"

Clement squinted through the cobwebs and dirt streaks. "No, actually I can't see anything."

"Well, just outside the window, on the traffic island, next to the orange construction barrel and yield sign, there is a large stone with a plaque."

"I see it now," Clement said, "next to the chain link fence."

"No, no... that's the plaque commemorating our high school football state championship. I'm talking about the smaller one, on the rock. The town council had it installed years ago in a fancy ceremony with a parade, the high school band... you get the picture. It commemorates an historic Indian battle that took place here over three hundred years ago in that very same spot. You see, the Connecticut militia hid down the river bank and snuck up on an enemy Indian encampment and shot over a hundred of them in their wigwams while they slept -- killed every last one of them too. It was the most important moment of those old New England Indian wars, and was the turning point that helped our ancestors peacefully settle this part of Connecticut, establish this town, and start America. And across the street, there is a river. The barn that was on the banks of that river forged all the bullets that they used to kill those Indians. It was the forge in that barn that put this town on the map, and years later, attracted all the mills and business into this valley. So by renting this shop, you are renting historic property, renting your own piece of history and carrying on the storied traditions of this fine community. I can't help feeling all patriotic just thinking about it."

Neither Clement nor Jessica were listening, but instead, wandered around the room immersed in their own thoughts, examining what little there was to see. The room was larger than it looked from the outside, and had private cubicle spaces, a bathroom and a tiny kitchen in back that was just big enough for an office-sized refrigerator, toaster oven and maybe a coffee maker. The floor was littered with brochures and pamphlets left behind by the previous tenant, who appeared to have been in the business of buying jewelry from people having financial difficulties, and then re-selling it at a profit, only to purchase it back again later. Clement picked up one of the colorful brochures from the floor and casually thumbed through it. The top half of a dead cockroach was stuck to the back and it peered at him.

"That guy did a bang-up business in here. He was always busy. Always a crowd, always a line and he always paid his rent on time... up until they arrested him. And then the sheriffs came and took all his inventory and fixtures away. Heckuva nice guy, too, terribly sorry to see him go down like that. I'd rent to that guy again in a second, but he won't be out for five years. So, what kind of business are you folks planning to open here?" Al asked.

"My husband here is a professional medium." Jessica answered, pride thick and apparent in her voice.

Al paused. For an uncomfortable moment, the only sound they could hear was the hum of the dry cleaning machines running in the shop next door.

"Aww, what the heck. Why should I have an objection? I'm all for an honest, family business. Good luck to you, both. You seem like a couple of real nice kids. But.., I will require two months' rent at the time you sign the lease." Al insisted.

"So, how much is that going to be?" Jessica inquired.

"It's just two thousand a month, not including utilities." Al answered.

"Wow. Two thousand dollars! For this? We could never pay that, Jess, and still afford to find a place for us to live, too." Clement said, impatient and somewhat relieved the offer was well out of their price range. "Come on honey, let's get out of here."

"Did I just hear you say you were looking for a place to live?" Al asked, sensing his sale was walking out the door.

"Yes, we are also looking for an apartment." Jessica answered.

"I'll tell you what I'll do. Upstairs, there is a two-bedroom, unfurnished apartment. It has a separate entrance through the alley in back, if you don't mind the tight squeeze back there, that is... and the trash cans. I'll throw the apartment in for free. But, I have to warn you, it's nowhere near as nice as this shop. It's going to need some work."

"Oh God, no, but thanks, Mr. Knicely. I don't think it will work out. I think we'll be on our way." Clement reached out for Jessica's hand, but she yanked it away.

"We'll take it!" Jessica announced.

"Wait! No! What?" Clement was stunned.

"How could it be any worse," Jessica explained, "than living in your little bedroom with your parents hovering over us all the time? Clement, please, I am suffocating in there. I feel like a sparrow trapped in a cage, trying to fly around and get out. I need to get out, and I don't care if we live in a tent on the sidewalk. Here, we'll be on our own -- just you and me and our new family. It might not be the penthouse we were hoping for, but it will be something we can make special. It will be something we can make our own." Jessica's eyes widened and she flashed a quick, blushing smile.

"Holy Cow, Jessica, you're supposed to be the practical one. You're supposed to be talking me out of doing insane things. Do you know how much it's going to cost to renovate this shop before we can ever hope to welcome our first reading? And I don't even want to think about what that apartment looks like up there, never mind sleep in it. I don't even know how to hammer a nail, never mind renovate a whole building. And there's no way we can afford to hire a contractor."

"I think..." Jessica paused. "I think I know someone who will do the work for us for free."

"Who do you know in Hartford?" Clement felt a sudden, inexplicable twinge of adrenaline scuttle through his veins when the realization struck him that he had been set-up.

"Clement, I didn't have a chance to tell you. My father called last night."

Chapter 14

Wequai spent the rest of her days on the island. Once her Uncle Mowashuck had exhausted his pleas to return her to her family on the mainland, he surrendered, threw up his hands, stomped back to his canoe, and pushed off for home leaving Manisses and Wequai behind. News of Wequai's miraculous journey, improbable survival and newfound motherhood were met back home with exuberant joy and elation -- the incredible story flashing through the village like a spider web of lightening across the summer night sky. Everyone wanted to hear the juicy details, and Wequai's poor, beleaguered uncle became a reluctant folk hero. He was forced to recount the tale to group after group at the shore of the cove, over and over again, pointing out at the island in the distance to the south with a finger twisted crooked by years of throwing his heavy fishing nets, each version of the tale more embellished and wondrous than his last.

After a few weeks, the women of the village began to bribe the fishermen to drop by the island and deliver Wequai personal supplies -- blankets, food, bowls, herbs -- anything they believed she might need to make her self-imposed exile more comfortable. After several weeks, when the curiosity became too much for the women to bare, they persuaded the fishermen to carry them as passengers so they could visit and speak with Wequai in person, and have their chance to fuss over brave, adorable, little Manisses. The women had unknowingly become the island's first tourists, and the fishermen the first ferries, to be replaced hundreds of years later by large, noisy, ungraceful ships from the mainland that would slice through the choppy waves in around an hour, weighed down by trucks, automobiles, cargo, hundreds of t-shirt wearing day-trippers, fortune seekers, and the occasional renegade squirrel.

Each afternoon, Wequai would be greeted by different canoes carrying family and friends bearing gifts that they would lay at the foot of Manisses' makeshift grass-filled manger. Manisses would utter not a word, but like a perceptive ragdoll, he would silently communicate his approval. And Wequai would sit with her back to the great, tall stones, bony, tanned knees pulled up under her chin, and tell her own version of the tale to her captive, and captivated, audiences. After a time, some of the villagers -- many who were orphaned children or widows who had lost whole families to the terrible battle, asked to remain -- won over by the peacefulness, the isolation and the indescribable majesty the tiny island offered. It provided an opportunity for these early tourists to begin anew -- to shake off the pain, loss and memories of those dearly departed at the point of their enemies spears, and forge a new life in a serene, uncompromised new land.

It only took a year for the island to populate itself with dozens of former villagers -- the first tribe of Manisseans -- ruled by the perceptive hand of an infant monarch, whose unconventional entry into this new world was accepted as a sign that his people would be guaranteed thousands of years of peace.

"Uncle," Wequai began. "I am troubled." She laid her head on her uncle's shoulder.

"What worries you, my dear?" Mowashuck asked. Wequai had become increasingly quiet over the months the island was being populated, visibly pensive, retreating deep into a jungle of her own thoughts. The women of the old village now considered Wequai a seer – a modern day spiritual medium – whose survival from her ordeal only proved her importance, vision and unearthly powers.

"Why do I no longer see lightning in the night sky?" she asked. "Or hear the thunder rolling like war drums in the distance? Since our villagers have come here, the sky has been quiet. At least once a week in the warm months, the sky would dance with light and drum – and sometimes it would last for days. Why does it now rest?"

"This is what troubles you? The spirits who bring us rain, and wind, and lightning can be devils. They often tease us and just as our wilted crops are ready to perish, they bless us with a rain shower just heavy enough to dampen their roots. We take our canoes to fish when the waters have been calm all day and a single gust of wind pitches me headfirst into the sea. Manisses was born under a dark, moonless night sky, and he delivered us peace. He brought an end to the great battle. And now, I believe, the heavens are pleased, content and at rest. This is good, Wequai, all good, you have no need to fill your mind with such tangled thinking."

"But it isn't just that. Last week, just after sunrise, I saw something. It was at a moment when I was not yet awake, but no longer asleep, the sky offered me a vision. Warriors. I saw warriors within the clouds."

"You had a vision of warriors?" Mowashuck sounded concerned. It was long understood and accepted that visions of soldiers could be a bad omen.

"They were not of our people, Uncle. It is difficult to describe them, but there were many, and they looked strong. I did not recognize them from any other tribe I have ever seen. What if the quiet sky means the gods are away, or at rest, or have abandoned us? I fear another great battle may be coming."

"Then, it will be so. But if there is another war to come, you and Manisses are now on this island, and your family and friends have joined you. There is food and plenty of fresh water. You are all safe here and there is much to celebrate. Our enemies cannot easily bother us when we are here. I say it would be easier to carry water in one of your aunt's braided sweetgrass baskets than invade and conquer this island." Mowashuck joked, and kissed the top of Wequai's head. Two old women prayed behind them at the base of the great rocks, while a gaggle of orphaned boys climbed and played upon them.

As a military foothold in the indigenous world, the geography of the island was ideal. Its multiple hills offered lookouts the opportunity to see toward all horizons making sneak attacks impossible, and its shallow surf made landings by larger vessels both dangerous and problematic. Warring tribes from the mainland, especially those to the west on what would later be known as Long Island, New York, would send war parties from time to time, but they would be easily identified and repelled, lucky survivors of each ill-advised assault then sent paddling home in embarrassment and defeat.

And if the invaders were successful in sneaking on shore under the cover of darkness, guided only by moonlight, as did one notorious Mohegan raiding party intent upon pillaging and stealing from the peaceful native islanders, their fate was destined to be far more ghastly. The invading Mohegans were deterred and driven to the southernmost point of the isle where they were backed up against the top of a stately, two hundred foot cliff – in an area known on the island as "The Bluffs." Here the Manissean warriors pinned them in, offering no hope of escape, and presented their terrified intruders a horrific choice -- face the reality of slow starvation and a certain death or take their chances by jumping from the top of the cliffs, being careful not to splatter themselves on the picturesque, rocky shore, two hundred feet below.

Though invasion was wrought with certain peril, communication and trade between these same violent tribes and the Manisseans was relatively easy. The island was isolated, yet still a central maritime location which for centuries allowed its inhabitants to expand its villages, grow its economy, cultivate corn and other crops, and eventually even open the land-locked salt pond in the heart of the island to the ocean, providing their fleet of dugout canoes safe harbor and easier access to the rich and abundant variety of fishes, and a chance to hide from the fickle winds, that the ocean gods presented to them.

And as would be the fate of all the indigenous peoples of the North American continent, as their culture thrived, unbeknownst to them all, it had also reached its peak. Exciting, chance encounters with ships such as Verrazano's *La Dauphine* had served to alert the European empires of their existence -- and of the greedy promise of their abundant wealth -- puncturing the fragile bubble of their cultural isolation with a leak that could never be patched. News of other ships and more white men would arrive at the shores of Manisses with more frequency and unbelievable news many years later of permanent settlements of Europeans on the Niantic mainland, or farther to the north in

Wampanoag territory, at what is present-day Plymouth, Massachusetts, would shake the Manisseans' confidence to their core. Wequai's vision in the clouds would prove true.

Despite who would inhabit or conquer it, the island was an ideal place to hide: to hide from the pain of war, to hide plundered treasure, or to hide from the drudgery of daily routines and picnic below The Bluffs upon the ancient dust of once great Mohegan warriors. Or to hide from the guilt of a terrible mistake.

And as Clement would learn, you could hide but no amount of magic, no matter how hard you try, can make the past disappear.

Chapter 15

etective Forrest Mayweather sat with his legs crossed in Clement's high backed Victorian chair in the Bradfords' parlor, sipping at a cup of tea that Jessica had rushed to prepare. A heavy snowstorm was forecast for the central Connecticut area, the radio had just announced that school had closed early, and both Lucky and Prissy were expected to bound through the Bradford's front door at any moment. Mayweather was uncomfortable sitting in a seat usually reserved for one of Clement's most typical customers, an older widow looking to channel and reach a dear departed loved one. The pupils of his eyes were wide, and he shifted them from side to side, squirming in his seat, scanning the well-placed shadows of the room as if he expected a dangerous criminal to lunge out at any moment and attack him.

"I don't usually come into a place... like this, I have to confess." Mayweather admitted, his hairy, sausage-like fingers fumbling to hold the dainty, hand-painted Victorian teacup. "I don't think Father Duffy over at St. Mary's would approve. Nothing personal, Mr. Bradford. I hope you understand."

Mayweather was a large man, tall and square-jawed. His buzz-cut hair was beginning to grow out, but was leaving a round bald spot just behind the top of his square head. He was Eastbury's top cop, well-known and liked by everyone in the neighborhood, and he had ridden his commendable twenty year career on the force walking a downtown beat to a desk job, where now he could pick and choose for himself the most interesting and meaningful cases.

About a year earlier, a talented and pretty girl named Hannah Griswold disappeared while walking home from school. It was assumed from the start that she was abducted, but there were no witnesses. To some, she simply vanished into thin air.

Detective Mayweather, Eastbury's most upstanding citizen, became the primary face of the investigation, and he pledged in multiple newspaper and television interviews, that he and the Eastbury Police Department would not rest until they found the poor girl and returned her safely to her mother's loving arms. When the news story first broke, the high school and the neighborhood fell into pandemonium as a deluge of reporters flooded the typically deserted downtown neighborhood, and frightened parents refused to let their children out of their sight for even an instant. For weeks, the town resembled a war zone placed under martial law, with an impressive militia of armed police officers and wooden barricades at every intersection. Buildings -- including the Bradfords' -- were searched, sometimes more than once, without finding even the hint or strand of a clue. A team of trained search dogs sniffed their way up Main Street every day for a week trying to pick up the girl's scent. There would be none to find.

Hannah was a pleasant and popular girl, had been in all of Lucky's classes at school, and was considered a personal friend. The two had shared a particular interest and talent in the visual arts -- sculpting had been their favorite -- and the pair worked together on many different and interesting projects. The shocking news of Hannah's probable abduction struck Lucky hard, as one might expect, and for a time Jessica couldn't even convince her to leave the safety of her bedroom, never mind go to school. Lucky's response to the crisis was to retreat inside herself, refuse to eat, and explode into erratic spouts of unexpected, inconsolable weeping. Jessica worried for her daughter, as Lucky's adolescent mind throbbed in pain, and it wrestled and struggled to wrap itself around the reality and horror of what had happened, and make sense of it.

"Mr. Bradford, I'm here today because I need your help." Mayweather abandoned his teacup and set it on the end table.

"Of course, Detective, I'll do anything I can. Is this about Hannah?" For a brief moment, Clement's irrational paranoid side wondered if he was a suspect. His heart pounded, his breathing stopped, and he sat upright.

"It is about Hannah, I'm afraid. But before we begin, I need you to swear to me that our conversation will remain between just us -- you and me. It is critical that you tell no one about this conversation. Repeating any of this could compromise our investigation. Am I making myself clear?"

"Yes sir. Very clear."

"Good. Since you are willing to help, I want to share some sensitive information with you about the case." Mayweather produced a thick manila file of paper from his shoulder bag and let it fall to the table in front of them with a soft thud. He pulled a large color photo from out of the folder and handed it to Clement. Clement held the photo up close to his face to examine it, and his fingers trembled.

"Mr. Bradford, this is a photo of the river across the street from this building. You should recognize the old stone walls around the old mill, and notice all the feral cats that are everywhere back there. In those tree branches, near the river bank, you will see a pink and blue jacket. We believe that to be the same jacket Hannah was wearing on the afternoon of her disappearance."

"So you think she fell in the river?"

"Yes, sadly we do. Now this next page here is a statement from a security guard at the rail station a few miles downstream. He claims to have seen something resembling a body -- the general size of a teenage girl's body -- float by the station a few days after Hannah's mother reported her missing. Of course, we dispatched officers to investigate but there had been some heavy rain and the river currents were strong, and they weren't able to substantiate the guard's story or find a body."

"Such a tragedy. My God." Clement sat back in his oversized chair and thought of his own two girls, how much he loved them, and how grateful he was that no tragedy like this had ever afflicted his own family. He also thought of Lucky and wondered if this news of Hannah's death would help bring her closure and heal her wounds, or send her deeper into her dark, psychological tailspin.

"There is a lot more here in this file, too. With your permission, Mr. Bradford, I'd like to leave this file with you and ask you to review it, read it through, and become familiar with the details of the case. I will send an officer to retrieve it in the morning."

Clement was confused. "Of course, detective, I would be glad to read it. But what does any of this have to do with me?"

"What we need you to do... what I'm asking you to do... is to review the case file and then talk to Mrs. Griswold."

"Why Mrs. Griswold? I don't understand."

"I meet with Mrs. Griswold almost every day, and I have done so since the day Hannah disappeared. She is a smart woman, and a proud woman. And she is also a woman of profound faith and conscience."

"So what do you want me to say to her?"

"Well... unfortunately, she is also a stubborn woman. The biggest hurdle we must overcome in this investigation is Mrs. Griswold. Despite the clear evidence, she will not accept that her daughter has died. She insists she can hear Hannah's voice calling to her for help every morning, just before she wakes. She says that when she looks to the sky, she sees the images of police officers in the clouds -- many of them marching like soldiers -- searching for her daughter, and because of this vision, knows we will find her. She is someone who believes, very deeply, in the power of mysticism and spirituality to find a solution to her problems."

"So you want me to tell Mrs. Griswold that her daughter has died. Is that it?"

"No sir. We want Hannah to tell her, herself."

Clement could not believe what he was hearing. The Eastbury police were sitting in his parlor placing an order for a channeler, much the same way someone would hire a carpenter, plumber or a pastry chef. He sat speechless, thumbing through the thick pile of papers in his lap, considering his options. It was a bizarre and uncomfortable decision to make.

Mayweather continued. "I will be blunt with you, Mr. Bradford. I don't believe in any of this spirituality mumbo jumbo, but I do know it still makes me uncomfortable, so there must be something to it. I'm not here because I believe it; I'm here because I think it might help Mrs. Griswold. We are talking about a woman who had a husband walk out on her years ago, worked two jobs to raise a wonderful daughter alone, and is now on the brink of losing not only her home, but her sanity and her life. This crisis is literally killing her. It has become an obsession. She is a good person and deserves peace. She deserves closure, Mr. Bradford."

"I 'm not sure. My daughter Lucretia was a good friend of Hannah's. This feels like it is hitting very close to home. I don't know if it's a good idea for me to become involved, for Lucretia's sake."

"All the more reason you would be perfect. Not only are you a spiritualist, and a medium, you are also a trusted neighbor and family friend. How could she not believe you?"

"Let me think about this, Detective. There is something about this that makes me very uneasy."

"I understand. We are all uncomfortable. But look at it this way. Don't think of me as a police officer, think of me as a customer. What if I was just a stranger passing through town that walked in off the street and asked for your services? You wouldn't turn me away, would you? The Eastbury Police Department is not asking for a handout, here. Police departments all over the country hire spiritualists, mediums and psychics all the time to help them re-fire cold leads, uncover hidden clues and locate victims. In some departments, it is standard practice, and they might even keep a psychic on staff. I would not be doing my due diligence as an officer of the law if I refused to even consider this an option in this unique case. Plus, as you know, our little town's budget is being slashed every year, including the finances for the police force. We can't continue to invest resources we don't have into a case where we already know the outcome. It's becoming an issue of public safety as well. Please, Mr. Bradford. We need your help."

"Maybe I misunderstood. Did you say you want to hire me? I wouldn't be conducting this session for free?"

"I'm sorry, Mr. Bradford, for not making that clear when I first arrived. I received a budget allocation from our Chief of Police early this morning to spend as much as twenty thousand dollars to resolve this case favorably. If you...um, or Hannah.., can convince Mrs. Griswold to allow us to close it and move on, the money is all yours."

"I will do it." Clement answered without hesitation. He could not refuse that kind of money. Business was business after all.

"Thank you, sir. Thank you. I think it best if you call Mrs. Griswold yourself -- maybe tell her you had a vision or something and it's important that you see her right away. And remember, do not let her know under any circumstances that we have had this discussion. If by chance this doesn't work, I hesitate to think of her condition if she were to realize we are conspiring against her."

As the two men talked, a snowball struck the shop's front window with a slushy thump and an already edgy Mayweather leaped up from his chair. On the sidewalk, a small regiment of children, armed with well-forged, round snowballs were beating a hasty retreat as what appeared to be a huge child, well bundled and six feet tall was firing volley after volley of cannonball sized snowballs at them, and they all scrambled for cover. As the last of the children ran past, the door of the shop sprang open and Prissy and Lucky rolled inside. Behind them, the bigger kid followed, dropping his arsenal of snow by the door and stomping the slush from his oversized leather boots. Prissy and Lucky fell onto the Persian rug red-faced, engulfed in hysterical laughter, trying to grasp at each other with mittened hands. The large child removed his floppy fur hat, locking eyes with Detective Mayweather. An alert and wide-eyed Clement snatched the files from off the table top and cradled them to his chest.

Carl Johnson immediately recognized Mayweather. Drips of cold melted snow puddled around his boots on the wooden floor.

"My son-in-law and his wife earn an honest living here, Forrest. What business do you have with them?" Carl Johnson asked, throwing back his shoulders with machismo, as if trying to pick a fight. The girls both looked up from the floor, recognized the detective right away, stilled themselves, and stopped laughing.

"Relax, Carl." Mayweather assured him. "There's nothing unusual going on here. I simply dropped in today to inquire about a personal matter with our neighborhood's top spiritual medium."

"I see." It was clear from his drawn expression that Carl did not believe him.

"And I was about to leave, anyway. I'll guess the roads are beginning to get slippery, and the calls are starting to come into the station. It's amazing to me that year after year, people forget how to drive in these storms. I need to go. Thank you, Clement. And it has been a pleasure to see you all." Mayweather put on his coat and backed toward the door in one sweeping motion, making a graceful exit from the room, stepping into the raging storm.

"Don't trust him, Clement. I have never met a cop I could trust. If he's a good cop, then he's up to something sneaky. And if he's a bad cop, well... then you will be in real trouble."

"Policemen help people, don't they?" Prissy asked, her voice high pitched and oozing with innocence. "Aren't we supposed to trust policemen?"

"He was here about Hannah, wasn't he?" the more cynical Lucky asked, eyeing Clement's folder and rising to her knees. "Why did he want to talk to you about Hannah? What's going on?"

Clement searched for all the right words, and didn't know who to answer first, but was saved from his dilemma by Jessica who swooped into the room from the back office just in time.

"Well look at all of you, you're soaked to the bone. Strip off all those wet clothes, head upstairs and find something warm to wear," she insisted, stomping her feet like a mother goose intimidating her goslings. All three obeyed, and scampered away, peeling off multiple layers of outerwear, leaving a soggy trail behind them. Jessica folded her arms across her chest.

"Did you hear any of that conversation, Jess?" Clement asked, wondering what he had got himself into. "That was the strangest thing."

"Yes, I heard every word."

"So.., what do you think?"

"I suppose what I think doesn't matter now. What matters is that you now need to channel the most believable spirit of your career."

Chapter 16

L ike any small town entrepreneur running a family business in a depressed village during a down-turned economy, Clement viewed twenty thousand dollars as a godsend. For fourteen years, the Bradfords worked around the clock to ensure their strange business venture would succeed. There had been no time for socializing with neighbors, little time for fun, and there was a need for painful, personal sacrifices to be made at every turn. The family had never been on a true vacation, never purchased a new car, rarely even went out to dinner together, and scrimped and squeezed each penny just enough to keep Mr. Knicely's rent payments arriving in his mailbox on time at the end of each month. Paychecks were erratic, and the family became used to surviving during lean, and leaner, times -- falling into debt, pulling out, then falling back into debt again. Any unexpected financial windfall that found its way into the family coffers went to support the well-being, wardrobe and expense requirements of two young, clever girls learning the ways of the world -- and to support the girls come again, go again, irascible grandfather Carl.

It took the better part of a decade before Clement had developed a reputation grand enough to convince people to travel out of their way to visit him in Eastbury, and allowed him to raise his fees to the respectable level he would need to support a family. After a busy day, he would often continue to work into the wee hours of the morning writing articles on spiritualism and conducting psychic telephone sessions, dispensing his good name, powers and abilities to whoever's mind would be open to his message. On weekends, Clement even tried to ply his wares on the children's birthday party circuit performing magic tricks dressed as a clown -- a harrowing experience that caused him to store away his magic kit and swear off magic and magic shows forever. So to make ends meet and keep decent food on the table, Jessica accepted all manner of dismal part-time jobs, from delivering pizzas to bagging groceries and eventually landed a convenient gig as a seamstress for the dry cleaner next door. During her days as a performer with the Flying Zalenkos, Jessica had been responsible for creating and mending the troupe's costumes and developed a knack for the sewing, darning, mending and stitching needed to keep the troupe outfitted, sharp and professional. Though the dry cleaner only paid a few dollars per item, Jessica had been bred and trained to be frugal, possessing the magical ability to create something from nothing whenever the family needed it, like a carnival performer might divine a stuffed bunny from thin air, or a loving mom might create a rag doll from a collection of random artifacts found on a beach.

Jessica and Clement agreed later that if they had declined Mayweather's offer, they would have continued to muddle along with the scant family finances just as they always had, and might never have left Eastbury. They saw the cash as a way to pay off a few bills, make a couple of much needed home repairs, and even engage in some frivolity and escape for a romantic week on one of the nearby, idyllic coastal islands. They didn't need the money to survive, but they wanted it. And in many ways, they believed they were entitled to it.

Carl, on the other hand, was a financial liability and profound disappointment to his devoted daughter. After the break-up of the troupe, Carl hooked-up with the Ringling Brothers, Barnum and Bailey Circus for a season as a coach and trainer, instructing their trapeze act how to perform a few of the Zalenkos' most memorable tricks. But the pay at this new job was poor, and having spent decades in charge of his own gig, he was no longer psychologically suited to take orders from kids half his age for very long. When he turned up on the front stoop of the Bradfords' decrepit new rental in Eastbury shortly after they rented it, he was already showing the stress of his new lifestyle, and Jessica's offer to take him in as a boarder and handyman was met with an odd mix of both embarrassment and relief -- uncomfortable emotions that Jessica, Carl and Clement all shared for very different reasons.

Carl and Clement went to work refurbishing the new apartment and shop right away, side by side, all the while despising the other. Despite his talents with magic and his nimble, sleight of hand tricks, Clement was barely able to swing a hammer without hitting his thumb, or sometimes Carl's thumb, to Carl's continual frustration, contempt and fury. The more able and handy Jessica would sit on the sidelines and watch the two men she loved most in life, nurse her newborn Lucretia, and serve as an umpire to their frequent squabbles and petty disputes. In Clement, Carl saw an inept, weak, self-centered little boy incapable of supporting himself never mind the burgeoning needs of his daughter and granddaughter. In Carl, Clement saw a bitter, mean, unreliable has-been using up what little resources the family needed for little Lucretia's future. Yet despite their differences and the disrespect they shared for one another, they were joined together not only by their love for Jessica and Lucretia, but by the fact their individual hopes for the future could not survive very long without the help of the other.

Given enough time, the two may have eventually reconciled had it not been for Carl's nomadic lifestyle. Never having been one to stay in one place for very long, after a month of carpentry, cleaning and painting, Carl would start to feel trapped and confined, then drive off for parts unknown in his rusty Winnebago without warning, leaving all the projects half done. Clement would then find himself alone trying to figure out how to complete each half finished task, inevitably screwing them up, only to have Carl reappear a few weeks later to chew him out for being brainless and inept.

"How can you be that stupid! Does this look like three-quarter inch plywood to you? Does it?"

And Clement knew he could never hope to tell one sheet of plywood from another.

Jessica pitched in when she could, but it was the intermittent visits from her roaming, vagabond troupe of cousins who would save the day, and rescue Clement's fledgling career. The band would appear in the night like happy, magic elves, unannounced, weighed down with pizza boxes and a few cases of beer, throw a party, sing a few songs, paint a room, then disappear off on another whimsical adventure. As part of their contribution to family tranquility, they converted one of the small office cubicles into a rudimentary little bedroom -- just long and wide enough for a six foot tall man to squeeze into and sleep -- and to also get his sleeping bag and camp gear off the middle of the parlor floor. Carl's little bedroom just off the main parlor was an imperfect compromise, but allowed the family some semblance of privacy upstairs in their already cramped apartment.

As annoying and unpredictable as Jessica's family could be, they were deeply loyal and committed to helping one another, almost to a fault. Clement both envied and hated them for it. He never felt any such devotion from within his own family. Hank and Edith would make less than one visit per year to see him, his wife and his granddaughter, and they lived just a few miles away.

It took several days for Clement to work up the courage to call Mrs. Griswold. For days after his meeting with Mayweather, he would pick up the telephone receiver, stare at it, pace around the room, but not be able to bring himself to actually press the little numbers. The first time he amassed the courage to dial, he dialed the wrong number -- his trembling hands had pressed all the wrong buttons. After another attempt, when Mrs. Griswold finally answered, he worried that his voice would waver too much and she would suspect something was amiss. It turned out that the authentic uneasiness that rumbled through his voice helped convince her that his motives were genuine, and she agreed that she should drop everything and come to see him right away.

Clement's thoughts and stomach pitched and rolled like a ferry coming through the breakwater. He knew he had only minutes to regain his composure and present the most believable experience possible for Mrs. Griswold. By the time she arrived, he was prepared, cold-faced and professional, taking her coat and guiding her to the parlor for her special, personal session.

"You have news, Clement?" she asked, perched forward on the edge of the very same seat where Mayweather had suggested the ruse. "What is it?"

Maria Griswold was a small, thin Italian-looking woman in her mid-forties, with long, coarse black hair that flowed down her back collected into a frizzy ponytail with a bow. Mayweather was right in his observation that the trauma of her missing daughter had taken a terrible toll. Clement and Jessica knew her as Hannah's mom -- petite, dark and modestly cute -- whenever they happened to make her acquaintance in passing, around town or at school. But now she was a mere shadow of her former self, and appeared to have aged twelve years in just the last twelve months. Her large, dark eyes had sunk into her skull leaving dark loops the size of silver dollars, and her cheek bones protruded from her emaciated, pale face, threatening to break through her skin. Her wrists were so thin they looked like they would snap if someone pulled on her arms too hard, and even the faded blue jeans she wore, which appeared to be a child's size, were baggy around her pencil-thin waist.

"Yes, Maria, I do have news. Thank you for coming so quickly." Clement swallowed hard, and did his best to remain in character.

"You know, when Hannah first disappeared, I thought of coming to you to ask for help. But you and Jess seemed like such nice folks. I didn't think it was fair to drag you both into this. I owe so much to everyone in this neighborhood. I don't know how I'll every repay them." Maria smiled.

"I've found the people of Eastbury to always be willing to help one of their own, much like an extended family." Clement said.

"Exactly. It's inspiring, don't you think? It's what keeps me going. Knowing that Hannah is out there, and everyone here loves her so, and are searching. If only the police could be as caring."

"I thought the police were working around the clock on this case."

"The police say they are, but they're not. I believe they simply gave up. They want me to believe that Hannah is dead. But I know better. I won't. Did you know that I suggested to the police that they call you months ago, but they refused? They said you didn't fit into their protocol -- whatever that's supposed to mean. They didn't contact you, did they?"

Clement bristled at the question. "The police? No, of course they didn't call me. I never heard from them."

"I know. It's so sad, isn't it? Sad that so many people don't respect the inner radiance of the soul and the spiritual light that guides us. But I don't have to tell you that, do I?"

"Maria, the reason I called you here tonight. I had a premonition. A sense. I felt a slight quiver of energy waft through me from the spiritual realm and it called your name. I believe it may have something to do with your daughter. Please understand that I am only a conduit, I can't do any more than relay the messages and feelings that I receive. Sometimes, the feelings I have can't be explained and require interpretation. That's why I need you here. Your presence will help to amplify those senses, and if this does involve Hannah in any way, only you would know."

"I understand how this works."

"First, drink this tea. Does it taste bitter or sweet?'

"Ooh, that's quite bitter."

"Good. That means it is cleansing your palette to prepare your senses. I would have been concerned if you found it sweet. Now, light this candle. The candle is made from a special paraffin wax with an additive from Tibet. This paraffin retains a higher level of heat than most waxes, and the additive is an herb grown only in the Himalayas. Both help attract and enhance spiritual development and provide clarity of thought."

"I can feel the heat already. It's all around me."

"It's has a soothing warmth, you should find it quite comfortable and relaxing, too. Now, close your eyes and take ten even, deep breaths, and concentrate on nothing except the sound of my voice."

"OK, I am ready."

"Did you bring Hannah's things as I asked?"

"Yes, of course. They are here in this bag."

Clement reached into Maria's duffle bag and pulled out a few random articles of clothing, a pair of tap shoes, a school history book and a teddy bear. He placed the bear on the table next to the candle. Knowing what had happened to Hannah, combined with the presence of her beloved teddy bear on the table in front of him, was a sight almost too emotional to endure. His heart throbbed. He took a few deep gulps of air to re-focus himself and locate his composure, retrieve his game face, and continue with the session.

"The bear and that candle are a powerful combination, they work together like magnets. I am starting to feel the same presence I felt last night, this time only stronger. Do you feel anything yet?"

"Yes. The air in the room feels like it is moving, like there is a gentle, warm breeze."

Jessica, alone in the kitchenette behind them, was working dutifully on her responsibilities to the production, as well.

"Maria, I am sensing something. It is coming into focus. But it is not a human soul. It has an aura more like that of an animal, like a cat."

"A cat? We don't have a cat. Hannah always wanted a pet. She loved animals. But our landlord wouldn't allow it."

"I am sensing this animal is in distress. It needs help. It's very afraid."

"I don't understand." Maria was confused, but continued to concentrate.

"Now there is another presence here. The one I felt last night. I sense the colors blue and pink. Would Hannah and the colors blue and pink make any sense to you?"

"Her bicycle was blue and pink. And so was the coat she wore on the day she was abducted."

I feel blue and pink from one aura, and fear from the sense of the small animal in the other. Now I sense something else. I sense water... lots of running water. Maybe it's a pool, a river, or a lake? Did Hannah like to swim?"

"Hannah loved to swim. She would spend half her summer in that municipal pool on Valley Street. But it was winter time when she disappeared. The pool was closed." Maria sat upright, her eyes welled with tears. Clement was bringing Maria down the path he had prepared, and he could see she was putting the pieces together faster than Clement expected.

"Maria, are you, OK?"

"Detective Mayweather asked me many times if Hannah ever went down to that river across the street. I wouldn't listen to him. You don't think..."

"That is not for me to presume. I can only present the essence of these feelings. Remember, I am just a messenger. What I do know is that there is an unusually strong, forceful spirit trying to communicate through me right now, to you. I think I sense Hannah's presence in that spirit, but that's something for you to decide, not I." The floors began to creek seemingly on their own, and the chandelier was now rocking, gently, side to side. The lights flickered.

"I believe you, Clement. I do. But why a cat? A cat in the water? I know my daughter. If she saw an animal in distress, maybe falling into the river, she would not hesitate to go and try to help it." Maria's hands trembled and her voice quivered. She began to cry. Clement worked to soften the mood.

"The presence in this room is changing now. It is a happier feeling, a feeling of great accomplishment. The essence of the animal spirit is now at peace, too."

"Hannah drowned in the river, didn't she!" Maria's tone had turned angry and accusing. "Tell me, Clement; please tell me my daughter is still alive!" Maria fell to her knees, knocking the bear from the table.

Clement tried to swallow, but his throat was so dry that it closed up and nothing would go down.

"I don't know Maria, I swear. But I do know the spirit I am feeling is one of love and reassurance. It's a feeling that everything is alright. Wherever this spirit resides now, it is full of joy, and it loves you a great deal."

"My God, Hannah! Please, not Hannah" Maria rolled into a ball on the floor, hugging the teddy bear. Clement sat in his chair unmoving, every muscle in his body tensed.

"I love you, Hannah! I love you!"

Clement fell to the floor and placed his consoling arm around Maria. Jessica, hiding in back, couldn't bear to cry alone, and bolted out to soothe them both. The three hugged, rocked and cried for a good long time in the center of the parlor, mourning poor Hannah's passing. Then when they were able to gather Maria's attention, Jessica placed a loving arm across her shoulder and escorted her in back to freshen up and have a cool drink, while Clement stared out the window into the near vacant street to calm himself. A thin blanket of freshly fallen snow had whitened the drab stores along Main Street, giving the false impression that the storefronts were cleaner and newer than they truly were.

"Well Clement, I have to hand it to you. That was quite a performance." Carl was now standing behind him, a silent witness to the session from his room behind the parlor where he had been taking a nap. Clement refused to turn and look at him. "It sounds to me like you've graduated from pulling rabbits to little girl's souls from the sleeve of your coat. Congratulations. But you'll have to help me decide. Are you the most masterful spiritualist in history, or the world's biggest horse's ass?"

Days passed, and neither Clement, Jessica nor Carl would consent to discuss Maria's session again. They did their best to resume their daily routines without thinking about Hannah, Maria or anything that occurred or was said that day. Even when the local news reported that the police were dropping their investigation on the presumption that the little girl had drowned, and that the family had filed papers with the court to declare Hannah legally dead, no one in the Bradford household did any more than nod acceptance. Clement tried to convince himself that Maria already knew the answer, but wouldn't admit it, and his role had been to merely speed up the inevitable. The city council voted a day later to install a memorial for Hannah between the plaques for the Indian massacre and the high school football team, only much larger than the other two. Clement's session had not only effectively killed Hannah, achieving Mayweather's assigned goal, but it had also served to place Clement's name and address dead-center of the front page of the Sunday newspaper.

Only Lucretia exhibited any reaction at all to the new developments, retreating for a few days into her room to cry and mourn in her own way for her dear friend. She was fully aware of her parents' role in the case, and it crushed her. Since Hannah's initial disappearance, only Lucky's artwork brought her any solace, and she channeled that abundance of energy into creating sculpted things new, expressive and amazing. Lucretia was experimenting with metal materials, and she learned to release and control her personal tension by twisting, turning and shaping the soft sheet metal with her bare hands, allowing the metals to tear at the flesh of her fingers, smearing and fusing permanent bits of blood and skin into her works with a gruesome precision.

Sessions with the famous Clement Bradford of Eastbury were now the hottest ticket in town. Appointments were booked from eight o'clock in the morning until ten o'clock at night, six days every week. Believers were driving in from as far as one hundred miles away just for the chance to spend an hour with the brilliant and insightful medium.

At first, Jessica and Clement didn't know how to react to the attention and growth in their business and reputation. But it didn't take long for them to become accustomed and enjoy both the fame and the money. Local television news crews all clamored for interviews and Clement was happy to oblige at each opportunity. But not once did he break his vow to Detective Mayweather and confess that the police department had hired him to channel for Maria. And despite the desperate pleas from other families of missing persons throughout the state, looking to make use of Clement's miraculous and rare ability, he vowed never again to work on another police matter -- for any reason.

It was six o'clock on a Sunday morning when the Bradford family first realized something was amiss, and that some sort of elemental shift had occurred in the cosmos. It was at that moment that a common red brick crashed through the front window of their shop, scaring the hell out of poor Carl who was sleeping in his cubicle, covering the room with a layer of tiny, shiny glass shards.

The initial response from the police dispatcher to Clement's initial frantic phone call was perplexing.

"So Mr. Bradford, what did you expect would happen?"

Hannah Griswold, they would learn, had been found alive.

The Bradfords were told that the police had scheduled a ten o'clock press conference, and Jessica and Clement paced around their small apartment running their hands through their hair waiting for it to show up on TV. Although they were all genuinely relieved to hear that Hannah was OK, they were mystified as to what could have happened, as was everyone else in the community. An Eastbury police cruiser was parked just outside their front door on Main Street, assigned to deter anyone else inspired to unleash similar acts of vandalism on the building or upon the bewildered family inside.

Detective Mayweather opened the press conference with a statement. Maria Griswold stood beside him at the podium exhibiting a wide, teary smile that seemed to stretch well off the sides of her emaciated face.

"Late last night, "Mayweather began, "officers from the Eastbury Police Department located and secured Hannah Griswold, age thirteen, who had been reported as a missing person last February. Hannah is healthy, appears to be unharmed, and is currently being evaluated and observed at Hartford Community Hospital. At about ten p.m. last evening, officers from the Stamford PD and the Eastbury PD conducted a joint raid on a home in Stamford, near the New York state line, as a result of ongoing surveillance that was part of our investigation. In that home we located and safely removed Hannah. At that time, we also arrested her estranged father, Terence Allan Griswold, age 49, who will be questioned later today and is currently being held by the Stamford PD. Before we begin, please understand that this is an ongoing investigation, so I may not be able to answer all your questions. I'd also like to acknowledge a lot of fine police work put in by many officers from both departments, too numerous to mention here right now. Their persistence and hard work may have saved a little girl's life."

"Mrs. Griswold, can you tell us how Hannah is feeling?"

"She's fine. And happy. I am so happy to have my baby girl back. It is a blessing."

"Mrs. Griswold, could you tell us Hannah's reaction to being rescued?"

"It's overwhelming -- for her, and for all of her friends and family. She couldn't stop crying. I know she was just happy to be back in her mother's arms."

"Mrs. Griswold, did Hannah have anything to say?"

"She had a lot to say! And she asked for ice cream! And for her teddy bear." The room released a friendly, collective chuckle.

"Detective, can you speculate as to the motive of Hannah's father?"

"I can't speculate at this time, however, her father had walked out on the family many years ago, and I believe, simply decided it was time he had his daughter back."

"Detective, why did the department announce several weeks ago that it had closed the case?"

"The case was closed at the request of the family, who received inaccurate advice from a local psychic. It is shameful how some people try to elicit fame and fortune from such a tragedy. However, our department had no direct evidence she had died, and took no stock in the psychic's findings, and we continued to exhaust our leads even while the file was in the process of being closed."

"Detective, can you confirm or deny the rumors that you are planning a run for public office, particularly for Connecticut Attorney General?"

Mayweather looked at the camera's big lenses and smiled a tooth-filled grin at the audience.

"I have no comment on that," he laughed. "Today, I'm just a police officer doing my job."

"I can't believe it. He set us up! We've been made the fool in this!" Clement fumed, hands cupped tight over the back of his neck. Jessica said nothing, and could only stare at the television and frown.

"I'll bet that rat bastard never paid you, did he?" Carl added.

"Yes. And he paid cash," were the only words Clement could bring himself to say without screaming. His eyes scanned the room at the things he had bought for his family, all conveniences they had gone so many years without. His head pounded with guilt and remorse.

"I told you, and you wouldn't listen to me. Never trust a cop. They are all good for nothing."

The reality was that Clement had been played the fool, but without his involvement, the police might never have found Hannah alive. Clement's exceptional ability at convincing Maria that her daughter was dead had caused Hannah's estranged and dangerous father to relax, drop his guard, and act just careless enough to provide the police an opportunity to find them. It had been Detective Mayweather's strategy all along, as Terence Allan

Griswold was both a suspect in Hannah's disappearance and her possible murder, from the moment she went missing.

Sadly, the community of Eastbury would never hear that part of the story. The media fell in love with the tale of the gallant police hero who rescued the innocent child from a deranged madman, and the presence of an evil psychic only added to the legend and jacked up newspaper sales. Clement tried to tell his side of the story many times, but his appeals either fell on deaf ears or were interpreted as pathetic attempts at damage control, portraying him as an even more despicable con artist than people already thought he was. As expected, Detective Mayweather, and the police department, denied all accusations and refused comment.

But the lion's share of Jessica's worries were reserved for Prissy and Lucky. Prissy was not only much younger than her sister, but was also born with a much thicker skin and a natural resilience that would get her far in life. She accepted and easily dismissed the teasing and cruel comments at school, not understanding many of them anyway, and forged ahead with her usual daily agenda of friends and interests with glee, as if nothing unusual had ever happened. Lucky, however, struggled. Hannah was a friend and celebrity to everyone Lucky's age, and had once been her friend and art partner. The same girls who rallied around Hannah the day she returned to school, attaching themselves to Hannah's celebrity, also identified and rejected Lucky as a creep and an outcast. Adolescent girls already carry the reputation of being evil and cruel under the best of conditions, but when armed with a purpose and alacrity, they possessed the ability to make Lucky's life an agonizing hell of incessant teasing, pranks and abuse. And the first time she was able to get Hannah alone, intent on telling her how much she missed her and how glad she was that she was OK, Maria Griswold slapped the entire Bradford family with a restraining order.

Clement was convinced his career would be over, and wondered if it was time to retrieve the magic supplies from the top shelf of the broom closet and get back on the dreadful birthday party circuit. But what shocked Clement and Jessica the most about the aftermath of the incident was how it had no effect on business. In fact, the appointments and bookings seemed to pick up. Clement was as busy as he had ever been.

All of their new customers were well aware of the controversy that surrounded Clement and the Griswold case, but came for sessions anyway. Some of them were forgiving and would say that the outcome of the case didn't matter to them -- after all, no one was perfect. Some others believed that all spiritualists were persecuted because of their special abilities, and they didn't believe what they read in the biased newspapers anyway. And still others wanted their sessions conducted by a notorious spiritualist, not just a run of the mill psychic, as it was somehow darker, more exciting, and dangerous, that way.

Over time, the vandalism and attacks to their storefront became less frequent, and the barbs and nasty comments aimed at Clement and Jessica when they went out into the community became less forceful, replaced by more mundane cold shoulders and occasional icy stares. The collective attention of the community had been re-directed to other more newsworthy gossip and scandals, as the Bradford family's painful wounds healed into ugly scars.

But there were two wounds that refused to heal. The first was the blame and guilt Clement harbored for the way he had treated Maria Griswold. He had conspired to tell her that her daughter had died, breaking her heart, hope and dutiful spirit, all while Hannah was very much alive and in desperate trouble and desperate need. Clement and Jessica tried to contact Maria many times, to explain what had happened, and offer their deepest apologies. Maria refused every olive branch the Bradfords could think to extend, and after a time, faced with a restraining order anyway, they decided there was nothing more they could do except to just let the issue pass. The second wound, infected and still festering, was the cavernous hole blasted through Lucky's already fragile teenage psyche. Neighbors had become accustomed to the sight of squad cars pulling up in front of the apartment with a scowling Lucky squirming in the back seat. The first time it happened she had been caught trying to sneak into a nightclub in downtown Hartford. The second time, she was apprehended trying to break into a convenience store with a group of local delinquents on the outskirts of the village. The third time, she was arrested driving a car that belonged to her boyfriend -- five years her senior -- at the tender age of just fourteen.

While at home, Lucky seemed to be able to isolate her center and focus her spastic energy on her artwork. Out in the presence of her peers, though, she began to accept her place in the high school caste system as a loser and a criminal. The most upsetting thing Clement and Jessica learned about losers and criminals was how accepting and welcoming they were to additions to their not-so exclusive fraternity.

Clement had based a career and good fortune on his uncanny ability to read the minds and faces of people, yet he was powerless to read the spirit within his own daughter.

If he could find a location more accepting of outcasts, a place they could hide, a place where his sins could be forgotten and forgiven, then he thought, perhaps he could forge a new start for the sake of his children and their future.

Chapter 17

The planks that made up the wooden floor of the *Princess Augusta* were soaked and stained with the bodily fluids of human despair. Eva Ulrich sat against a wall in the lower hull, squeezing her little boy close to her hip as he slept. The great ship rocked and pitched backward and forward as it punched a hole through each wave with a violent, persistent rhythm. With every thunderous strike, the great old wooden ship would creak, and with each creak, Eva would gasp a breath that she expected to be her last.

The *Princess Augusta* had left Rotterdam at the end of a warm summer, packed to its masts with promise and hope for the future, intent upon reaching its destination of Philadelphia before the harsh northern winter would take root. Its cargo of over three hundred and forty passengers, all who paid the captain a hefty fee for their exclusive place on the promised three month journey, were either dying or had already succumbed to a ghastly pestilence that had infected the occupants of the vessel from the moment it left port. The passengers lucky enough to die were unceremoniously discarded overboard by a godless and lawless crew, their costly fare having purchased nothing more than a permanent resting place at the bottom of a cold Atlantic sea.

Eva's husband Hans had died early in the journey, one of the first to yield to the sickness. No one expected such a strong and fit young man to die so easily, especially not his young wife. Hans was a strong, muscular farmer, tall and square-jawed, intent upon providing a better life for his wife and son in a prosperous new world. Here, they would free themselves from not only the chains of poor harvests and famine that had plagued their beloved Palatine home country, but also from the constant fear of religious persecution and war that robbed the peace from their everyday existence.

Eva had lost track of the days and weeks they had been at sea, it was far more than had been expected, each day and night of excruciating hell blending with frightful ease into the next. No sooner had they left, than the good winds turned bad, and the ship stalled for days making no noticeable progress in any direction. And if that had not been enough, its fate took another turn for the worse, and the ship was pummeled by brutal storm after storm, adding to its delay and pulling it well off its course. The ship meandered across the sea for months at the random whims of the violent winds and its inept crew. When one of the other passengers suggested that it might be Christmas Day, Eva openly laughed, breaking free, for a moment, from her oppressive, glossy-eyed, depressive trance. Had it not been for her duty to the safety of her little boy, she knew she would have leaped overboard herself into the comforting arms of death to join her husband beneath the icy waves.

The dashing Captain Brook, who had welcomed the passengers aboard months before, extracting their life savings with his kind eyes and warm smile, was dead, unable to escape the same sickness that had taken so many of his passengers. To make matters worse, the captain was replaced by a first mate more interested in plundering what was left of their passengers' wealth than delivering them safely to their destination. (It was rumored by some that Captain Brook may have even been murdered.) As food stocks aboard the *Princess Augusta* either rotted or ran out, the pirate-like crew would threaten their passengers with starvation, unless they turned over what was left of their meager possessions. Those with means would part with hundred year-old family heirlooms and pieces of gold in exchange for stale crusts of bread, while those without would just go hungry. Eva had not eaten in three days, choosing to turn over her few scraps to her starving boy, subsisting only on the putrid, brown water collected in community barrels during the all too frequent rainstorms.

Eva stroked the boy's forehead often to search for signs of the ship fever. By some miracle of God, he had not yet been afflicted. Perhaps it had been the extra bits of stale biscuit Eva was able to find for him that maintained his strength. But for Eva, she could feel the sickness growing inside her. Her eyes were dry and they burned when she blinked, and her stomach, sore from the constant pangs of hunger, now flinched with different spasms of a sharper pain. Even her knees and ankles were swelling, throbbing with her every movement. If the ship did not reach shore soon, she knew, she would be done for, and her young son would be left alone to fend for himself to survive in a foreign, new world.

"Mother, do you think we will make land today?" Her son asked, with a calm and innocence in his voice that soothed Eva's soul.

"If God be willing, we will make land today, Otto." She said, brushing the sandy brown hair from Otto's round, cherubic face. "We must maintain our faith, no matter what ordeal our Lord chooses for us to endure. Do not worry. Remember that God will always provide for those who honor him."

"Mother?" Otto asked. "How long does it take to grow carrots? I would very much like some carrots. Father showed me how to plant them last season, and I know with those seeds..."

"Hush now, Otto. Let us not talk of food." Eva quieted her son. Though talking and dreaming of food was unwise, if not unavoidable, what concerned Eva more was mention of her husband's heirloom seeds. Hans was not only a farmer, but a good one. His impressive collection of vegetable seeds, carefully bred, harvested, dried and stored was the only possession Eva had not turned over to the crew in exchange for rancid scraps. The seeds were almost as valuable as her own life, and she held them close beneath her arm in a shoulder bag that rarely left her side, even sleeping with them beneath her pillow at night. If the crew were to learn she had the seeds, they would be confiscated, and probably eaten.

The ship lurched forward with a sudden jolt, and the passengers in the hull all moaned and cried out in a hellish chorale of despair. Otto wrapped his short arms around his doll and squeezed it, trying to extract and absorb whatever comfort the little doll might possess. It was clear that a new storm was brewing outside and that the temperature in the ship was dropping. Otto shivered, and his mother draped a tiny frayed blanket over them.

"It was very nice of that little girl to give you her doll." Eva said.

"Anneke made me promise that I would keep him safe forever. She told me he was very important."

"Beware the sin of vanity, Otto. Material things such as tools, and fancy clothing or even dolls such as this, are never important. They do not have a human soul. She was a very sweet and thoughtful child to think you so important to bless you with a gift that once gave her meaning. Let us return her gift and say a prayer for her immortal soul together tonight, before we sleep."

Otto dared not tell his mother that his new doll had told him that his name was Didier.

Anneke, who had given Didier to Otto was Dutch, and was, like Otto and his family, hoping to forge a new, prosperous life on the other side of the ocean. Otto had developed a friendship with the girl, and while on the ship, they had become inseparable. Otto hoped that her family could settle near them once they arrived at their destination outside the city of Philadelphia where Otto's aunts and uncles had settled after a previous voyage. But the disease aboard the ship was blind to age and innocence and took the poor girl's life to the horror of her grieving, hysterical mother, who had already become a widow at the hands of the same disease just days before. Anneke's last conscious act was selfless, asking Otto to care for her most beloved friend, Didier.

"We see lights! There are lights!" Someone shouted from above, and the passengers who were able to still stand, scrambled to get up to the top deck.

Above the hold, a fierce blizzard had materialized, and wind driven sleet and snow stung the faces of the passengers who peered out toward the horizon. In the distance, they could see two lights waving in the dark skies, between the rushes of falling snow, as if rescuers were directing them into a safe harbor.

But by now the wind and waves had increased, knocking the passengers from their feet, and the first mate and helmsman struggled to maintain control of the ship as it rocked and twisted in the heavy seas. A large wave crashed into the vessel and sent a shower of sea water over the cold, shivering passengers.

"Head for shore! Head for shore!" The passengers begged and wailed. But the crew ignored them, following the first mate's orders to lay anchor instead.

"Are they mad? It's an island! We are saved! Why does the crew forsake us? What are they doing! They are killing us!" Panicked and desperate voices shouted from all corners of the vessel.

Skirmishes were breaking out between the crew and passengers for control of the ship as Eva and Otto reached the deck. The cold wind took Otto's breath away and the sharp sleet pricked at his cheeks, causing him to burrow his face into his mother's side. Fists and arms flailed wildly in the air, amidst the chaos of the panic and anger. Behind them, the ship's only skiff had been lowered into the raging sea, its frantic occupants now rowing for shore, carrying the first mate and a handful of his most loyal and most vicious crewmen. The passengers on the ship were beginning to realize they were being abandoned, perhaps even to sink, just off the shore, perhaps to cover-up the treachery and abuse they had endured for weeks, allowing any evidence that might indict the deceitful crew to sink or drift away.

The passengers felt a moan, then an unexpected crack and rumble, almost like that of an earthquake, causing many of them to slip on the icy deck, and the realization that their ship's hull had been breached sent them to scatter in a collective frenzy of horror. The ship pitched to one side, and the most desperate passengers began to jump into the stormy seas in a decided attempt to swim to shore to try and save their lives. Lanterns near the captain's quarters had tipped over in the disorder, spilling their flammable oils, setting the deck ablaze with a sudden, fast moving inferno. Cries of terror filled the darkness as passengers swam for their lives, bobbing heads disappearing one by one beneath the tall, powerful waves.

Eva clutched Otto close, grabbing at a nearby barrel to keep them from being washed into the sea. It was then that Eva realized she had left the heirloom seeds behind, in the hull, beneath her bedroll. It was the one worldly item she could not leave behind. The seeds represented the only remaining connection to Otto's future from their past, a legacy from his father Hans, and could not be abandoned at any cost.

"Wait here, Otto! Please don't move! I will be right back! Eva screamed and retreated back down the stairs. The flames on the deck had climbed their way up into the masts, lighting what was left of the frayed sails. Someone had reached the anchor and cut through the cable, setting the ship spinning, floating it ever closer to the perilous, jagged rocks along the shore. Men from the island had now made their way out to the wrecking ship, and it appeared some were risking their own lives, fishing the drowning passengers from the sea, while others appeared to be looting and offloading abandoned supplies and cargo. Otto was obedient and did what he was told, and in the face of such profound pandemonium, he found bravery by closing his eyes and allowing Didier to comfort him.

The ship was breaking up on the rocks, each snapping plank sounding like its own singular clap of thunder. Otto felt two hands come to rest upon his back, and thinking it was his mother returning for him, he turned.

The hands reached under his armpits and lifted him off the deck, hurling him over the ship's railing headfirst into the sea. Beneath the cold waves, Otto heard nothing. It was an eerie silence that contrasted with the clamor and chaos above. When he bobbed back up to the surface, his head struck Didier who was floating atop a wave. Otto snatched him, acting on the purest of instincts, and vowed to the doll that he would not let him go again.

Otto was a good swimmer for such a young boy, having spent many a summer day lapping the oversized cows' pond on his family's farm, but ocean swimming was different, and though he could keep himself afloat, his short flapping arms and legs, struggling in the heavy waves, were sending him whirling in circles. Throughout his ordeal, he swam with only one arm, using the other to hold Didier above the surface. Behind him the ship had all but sunk, crashing into the rocks, sending violent plumes of debris, fire and water into the snow-filled night sky. What was left of the ship was now fully engulfed, every inch of its once majestic hull now adorned with tall, orange flames, a spectacle visible to all the residents of the island who watched in helpless horror from shore. The dangerous ship had now been abandoned by all but one woman, who unwilling to give up her most important possession, now searched for her boy in vain, screaming his name at the top of her lungs as she perished, disappearing into the growing flames.

However Otto could not hear her calls, focused instead on battling through his own life or death struggle, and he was tiring. The fierce cold of the water was slowing and numbing his muscles, and he was losing both the ability, and will, to swim on. Two hundred years earlier, Verrazano's young cabin boy tired and was rescued in the same sandy cove by a tribe of kind-hearted Manissean natives. But for Otto, there would be no heroic rescue. With one final gulp of air and a glance to the heavens, Otto slipped beneath a breaking wave and was not seen again.

Along the shore, the ship's survivors were stumbling along the beach in the slush and surf, moments from their own death. The compassionate residents of Manisses brought them blankets, nursing their injuries along the beach, some choosing to take the poor dying souls back to their own homes for personal attention and care. The Island had just endured and survived a disappointing and devastating growing season, leaving the islanders themselves with little to eat. Several islanders not involved in the rescue used the opportunity to loot what they could out of the debris that was floating ashore, battling the vicious winds and heavy snow, exploiting the mishap for a chance at finding their own treasure.

One islander, an unassuming Black slave named Hubbard, did both.

From his perch atop the great rocks, a revered place where Wequai had once sung a hymn to her burning village, and where a young Manissean brave first saw the sail of Verrazano's ship, Hubbard squatted in the blizzard bundled head to toe, feet wrapped in rags, and watched the *Princess Augusta* burn and sink along the rocky shore. He climbed down in time to assist and rescue a tall, Dutch woman named Katherine, and bring her back to his shack, and along the way, he used the opportunity to collect lost clothing, some rope and to pick-up a waterlogged doll

-- a curious child's toy named Didier who had been saved from destruction by a selfless, brave, loyal, little boy, drowned and forever lost beneath the cold waves of a sadistic sea.

Chapter 18

"M om! Otto's stuck on the roof again!"

Prissy stood with her fists planted firmly on her hips and stared up into the hazy, gray sky, shaking her head from side to side in disgust. Otto was laying on the shingled roof of the Bradfords' home, one arm dangling over a rusty gutter waving at her in the gentle breeze. Abby stood alongside her good friend, striking the same disapproving pose, as if in an audition to become Prissy's shadow.

"Oh, Prissy. You are impossible!" Jessica shouted, storming through the rickety screen door of the house and stomping across the porch. "Why won't you take better care of your things!"

"But mom, I keep telling him not to go up there anymore. And he won't listen to me. You heard me tell him, didn't you Abby?"

Abby nodded a hesitant agreement.

"Well, Prissy, this had better be the last time Otto ends up on the roof. If it happens again, I will be putting Otto away in the dining room hutch for a good long rest. Do you understand?"

"Yes, Mom. I understand." Prissy tilted her head downward toward the earth, conceding the point with the appropriate respect. Otto thought that a good long rest might be something to consider. He had been exceedingly busy as of late.

Jessica slipped out of her flip flops, walked barefoot through the coarse summer grass and approached the wide red brick chimney attached to the side of the house. She reached out with one hand grasping at a brick above her head with the tips of her fingers, and she placed the side of her bare foot into a crevice. With the nimbleness of a chimpanzee, Jessica scaled two stories up to the aging shingled roof in just a few agile movements. Despite her age, Jessica had kept herself in fine shape, and had never forgotten the acrobatic skills she learned growing up with her father and the Flying Zalenkos. Jessica scampered on all fours like a squirrel to the roof's edge where she snatched up Otto with one hand and tossed him down to Prissy's waiting, outstretched arms. Prissy squeezed her doll and grinned, and then planted a kiss in the middle of Otto's dusty forehead.

"Now you heard what Mom said, Otto. You stay off that roof! Do you understand?" Prissy scolded, mocking her mother's tone and wiggling an index finger in Otto's face.

"Your mom is wicked cool," Abby said. "I wish my mom could climb houses."

Jessica looked down at the girls and flaunted a wicked little smile.

"Oh, so you liked that, did you?" Jessica asked with a mischievous tone, scampering back to the peak of the roof. From the very top, Jessica could see much of the island. It was cloudy, and to the south, she could see a fog bank rolling their way. Cars snaked by in the near distance out on the main road; a few pulled off to the side to park and dodge the slower tourists on assorted bicycles and mopeds. She filled her lungs with thick, humid air and arched her back as if in performance on a high wire above the three rings of a grand circus. She stepped up onto the top of the chimney, and with one graceful motion, did a full leap and mid-air summersault landing with perfect balance on both feet back upon the peak, in triumph. Tiny bits of grit from the weather-worn shingles bounced their way down the roof, rattling into the aluminum gutters as they fell.

The girls squealed and clapped in tribute to her stunt.

Next, like a seasoned Olympic gymnast, Jessica ran across the peak and executed a perfect forward handspring. Then when she reached the edge, she did three faultless reverse handsprings that brought her back to the precise point where she had begun. The roof creaked and moaned, and again Jessica raised her hands high in victory. The girls continued to hop up and down, cheering and applauding with enthusiasm.

Jessica then placed one hand in the center of the roof's peak and pulled her skinny legs up over her head, her second hand and arm out to one side, performing a flawless one-handed handstand. Jessica held the pose for several seconds, and the girls laughed and rooted for a passing gull to land on one of her outstretched limbs. Jessica's small athletic body, silhouetted against the billowing gray clouds, being circled by a seagull, was a curious sight to behold.

"Sweet Jesus!" Clement screamed dropping his bicycle in the driveway and running toward the house, hands and arms flapping over his head. "Jessica! Jessica!" He shouted.

Jessica released her pose and flopped down upon the peak to sit, wiping wisps of hair from her sweaty face and revealing a wide, impish smile. The sight of Jessica in peril on the roof of the house caused Clement to flashback to their days at the carnival when he would sit and watch his wife practice on thin wires and trapeze bars high above the earth, hour after hour, wondering if her next move would bring glory or send her plunging helplessly to the unforgiving ground. The color in Clement's face had drained from pink to white, and the corners of his mouth had turned down as if he expected to vomit.

"My God, Jess! What do you think you're doing up there?!" Clement shouted with one hand kneading his stomach.

"That's exactly what I asked Otto," Prissy whispered to Abby, who nodded her mutual disapproval. "And he wouldn't answer me, either!"

"Oh, loosen up, will ya?" Jessica demanded, basking in the attention. "I was only having a little fun with the kids." Jessica had been raised to be the center of attention, and it took years of effort before she was comfortable letting Clement take the lead in the family business and allowed herself to withdraw into the background. But once in a while, she enjoyed the rush of reliving her glorious moments in the now dimmed spotlight.

"You're giving me a heart attack down here, Jess, I mean really!"

Jessica scooted down the chimney in the same manner that she had climbed it, skipped barefoot over to Clement, pirouetted, and planted a wet kiss on his now cold, clammy cheek. The two embraced on the lawn, Clement stroking Jessica's hair, as a few spritzes of drizzle began to drop around them.

"Let's go, Abby." Prissy commanded. "They're gonna go in the house and argue then smooch. We don't need to see that."

"Don't stray far girls, the weathermen all say we're getting a big rain this afternoon. Don't you be coming home all wet." Jessica warned.

Prissy and Abby walked away from the house and shore and into a meadow of thickets several acres wide, decorated by an aged, craggy stone wall that some said was built by the island's first farmers, though others believed they were built by more ancient civilizations. The waist high walls had stood for centuries, and were a remarkable feat of antique engineering skill, thousands of round stones placed by design and care for both permanence and purpose. Paths only wide enough for a child zigzagged around and through the thickets and briars, sassafras and arrow-wood, pokeweed and bayberry, and perilous waterfalls of poison ivy with vines as thick and hairy as an old pirate's leg. Along the ground, fluffy green tufts from the tops of what locals called wild onions and carrots tickled the girls shins, though not indigenous to the island, their seeds were perhaps carried over in the droppings of birds or perhaps washed ashore from a long forgotten shipwreck. The girls jogged and skipped along the paths worn bare by centuries of white tailed deer, rabbits, pirates, Indian maidens, colonial farmers, slaves, tourists, refugees and precocious children.

In some places, the wild brush resembled more of a lush, primordial forest, vines reaching up several feet in all directions, and the girls would disappear then reappear around and under the path's frequent twists and turns. It was an exotic wonderland for the two Alices to explore, hide and play.

"I wish my parents were cool like yours, Prissy." Abby said.

"My parents are not cool." Prissy objected.

"Your parents are, too. They talk to ghosts and climb up houses. My mom and dad don't do anything interesting. They just argue about money."

"My mom says there's no need to argue about money if you don't have any." Prissy added with a know-it-all tone.

"Well, my mom says this island is too expensive and she wants to move away. But my dad wants us to stay here forever. They fight about it all the time."

"You're going to move away?" Prissy stopped dead in her tracks. Otto tensed. "But Abby, you can't move away. You belong here."

"I don't want to move away either, Prissy! But my dad has been acting all funny lately. He spends all his time talking about treasure hunting over at the barn. He goes over there every night to dig in the grass, and he keeps buying more and more of those stupid squares. He says he's going to be the one to find the pirate's treasure and then we'll be rich. Hey Prissy... let's go over there now and look for more treasure." Abby's eyes widened, hoping to entice her friend.

"No, I'm sick of looking for treasure. All the adults came and it wasn't fun anymore. They were always arguing and fighting with each other. It was stupid." Prissy frowned and kicked at the ground.

"But we have to!" Abby was restless. "You're the best one at finding stuff. You have to come and help me."

"I don't think there is anything else left to find. Just lots of trash and garbage. And I keep getting boo boos on my fingers."

"But you have to help me, Prissy! You have to or they'll make me move away!" Abby was now angry, unable to convince Prissy to act on what she perceived to be a simple yet important request. She folded her arms and tapped the ground with the toe of her patent leather shoe.

A sudden wind interrupted the calm, dead air, and Abby's hair and dress billowed around her as the bits of sprinkles had become more frequent, now dampening their shoulders. The leaves on a nearby maple tree fluttered at them, as if relaying a warning.

"I think we should go home now, Abby." Prissy said. "My dad says that when the maple trees decide to turn their leaves upside down and they look all silver like that, the tree is telling him that a big storm is coming."

"The trees talk to your dad, too?"

"No, stupid. It's just a sign of Mother Nature. Old Mr. Sumner says that he knows how much snow we're going to get in the winter by looking at a caterpillar. He said old farmers and Indians could read the signs in nature to tell the weather before there were TV's."

"That doesn't make any sense. Caterpillars can't talk."

"The caterpillar in *Alice in Wonderland* could talk!"

"That's just a story, dummy. And I don't like caterpillars. They're itchy."

"Do what you want. I'm going home. I don't want Otto to get wet or my mom won't let me play with him outside anymore."

"Well I'm going treasure hunting for my dad." Abby paused. "Hey! Why is Otto looking at me like that?" Abby tensed and took a big step backward. Otto said nothing, but continued to stare at her.

"Like what? He looks at you like this all the time."

"He looks like he's mad at me."

Prissy brought Otto up to her nose and examined him with care, squinting into his blue eyes and scanning his pudgy, round face, now damp from the light summer shower. Otto said nothing, but stared back at Prissy with a confident defiance.

"Otto thinks you're being stubborn." Prissy said. "He's not mad at you, it's just that he doesn't want you to go treasure hunting. He thinks it would be better for you to go home."

"I didn't hear him say any of that!" Abby demanded. "You made that up! And Otto is a stupid name for a doll. Why did you name him Otto, anyway?"

Prissy paused, but wasn't sure how to answer the question. When Jessica first surprised Prissy with the doll, and she held him in her arms for the very first time, she somehow sensed his name was Otto. He looked like an Otto, acted like an Otto and had the personality traits of an Otto. It had never occurred to her that she could have selected the name to begin with, or considered he would have another, it just sort of came along with the whole package. When Jessica later asked Prissy what her doll's name was, she said Otto. It made perfect sense. It was a logical and natural fit.

"It's because that's what his name is." Prissy finally answered after careful thought.

"Well, I would have dressed him like a girl and called him Patsy."

Otto bristled.

"His name is Otto!" Prissy insisted, insulted by Abby's harsh and disrespectful tone. "You can go ahead and go off looking for pirate treasure if you want to, but I'm going home."

Abby spun on her heels and stomped away, heading down the winding path and disappearing into the thicket. Prissy and Otto stood alone for a while and watched her go, then turned and headed back to the house. It was late afternoon, near sunset, and the thickening clouds made it feel as if night was approaching much quicker than it should. Where Prissy could see through the overgrowth out to the sea, to the south, the long horizon had disappeared behind an oncoming bank of rolling fog. Except for the distant sound of the waves lapping at the shore, all was quiet -- even the peepers and crickets, it seemed, had hopped on home, heeding to the many warnings that nature was providing. Prissy and Otto walked along until they reached an undersized, round freshwater pond, not much larger than a swimming pool, once used by colonial farmers to water cows, and they stopped to watch the raindrops decorate the surface with little circles around the lime green lily pads.

"You don't think Abby will really move away, do you Otto?" she asked. Otto couldn't be certain.

"You know, Otto, Abby is my best friend.., after you of course. I would really, really miss her. I remember what it was like when we moved away from our house in Connecticut. I left a lot of friends behind Otto, and I missed all of them so much. Abby would be very lonely if she had to move off the island."

Prissy carried Otto around the little pond thinking about her friend. She plucked a dandelion from the grass between her feet, puffed up her cheeks, and gave it a hearty blow, sending the small, white, fluffy seeds spiraling up into the air, carried by the increasing sea breeze, and then landing on the surface of the pond like a flotilla.

"And there aren't that many kids here on Manisses, either. At least, not like back in Eastbury. Most of the people who come to the island in the summer are old. And the kids who come here just to stay for the summer are different. It's hard to make friends with them, they just want to make friends with each other. Some of them are pretty nice, I guess, but not as nice as Abby."

Prissy walked a little farther through the tall grass and flipped over a flat stone, sending a large black beetle and a family of little red ants to scuttle around her feet in a life or death frenzy.

"I know, Otto. I know what you are trying to tell me. I would make more friends. And I'm glad that you think I am such a nice person. That's what Mom always says to me, too. She says that I'm smart and nice and I should try and make more friends and not hang around with just Abby. I don't think she likes Abby very much. Or, she doesn't like Abby's mom and dad. I dunno. She says if I talk to different kids, I would make lots more friends."

Prissy squatted down under the branches of a pine tree and examined pieces of broken powder blue egg shells that had fallen from a robin's nest hidden within the thick branches above them. She squeezed the dry, fragile shell pieces between her fingers and they crumbled to dust.

"Lucky? No, she's never any help. All she wants to do is play smoochy face with Vance and hide in her room and build weird things. She doesn't even talk to me anymore. Ever since her friend Hannah died, and then came back to life, she has been really sad... and weird. You didn't know Lucky when Hannah was around. She was really cool back in those days, and she had lots of friends. She and her girlfriends would always play with me when I was little. She doesn't play with me much now that I'm a big kid."

Otto escorted Prissy across the property and back to the beach. Prissy kicked off her shoes and waded into the cool surf. The sea foam from the small waves massaged and tickled her ankles and shins, and she wiggled her toes in the coarse beach sand. The clouds had broken to the west over the bluffs revealing a spectacular bouquet of color for the evening's sunset, as all the purples and oranges of the spectrum had arrived in time to perform an intimate waltz around a dance floor of charcoal gray clouds.

Prissy thought she heard the faint sound of a woman's scream, and then something along the horizon caught her eye. First she thought it was a bright light, perhaps shining from the deck of an expensive yacht cruising by out in the distance. But the light was too wide, odd and orange. Then she thought that maybe a single ray from the setting sun was reflecting off a sailboat's deck or sail, but there wasn't much bright sunshine to be seen. To Prissy, the orange light looked like a big fire -- as if some grand wooden ship had been set ablaze and was drifting helplessly toward the island. She squinted into the distance again until her forehead hurt, trying to make some rational sense of what she was looking at, when just as suddenly as the light appeared, Prissy blinked, and the image was gone.

Prissy swore that it looked like a burning ship. Otto was quite sure that he knew what it was, and he was not happy about it.

Chapter 19

H ubbard carried Katherine back to his shack, just a few hundred yards away from the beach where the debris, cargo and corpses of the *Princess Augusta* were still washing ashore and just a few feet from, where forty years earlier, the privateer William Kidd walked on shore. As he dragged her near lifeless body through the thicket, he could hear the screams of other passengers drowning, begging to their gods for mercy, in languages he had never before heard but in a chilling, ghastly tone that required no translation. The snow was now falling at a furious rate, and was piling up on the shoulders of his torn coat as he trudged along the path that led to his home. Katherine was slumped over his shoulder, conscious but unresponsive, and the fresh, sticky snow had frosted her hair, eyebrows and eyelashes white giving her the look of a wise and ancient sage. Katherine was a big boned woman, tall and solid, and Hubbard was having a difficult time traversing the path, the hem of her long, tattered dress slowing them as it was being clutched and further shredded by the fierceness of the island's native bull briars.

Once inside his shack, Hubbard laid her with tenderness upon the dirt floor in front of the warm fireplace and exhaled a sigh of relief. Katherine moaned and cried out in Dutch, but Hubbard couldn't understand a word of what it was she was trying to say. Whenever he would reach out to touch her, in any attempt to remove her wet, freezing clothing, Katherine would lash out at him with two beefy swinging fists, one that even struck him square on the jaw, breaking a tooth and knocking him into a wall. For the balance of the first evening the two spent together, Hubbard brought her food, water and blankets, most of which was thrown in a violent rage, crashing against the thin wooden walls of the room.

Hubbard was a slave, the property of a Mr. Balthazar Littlefield, the respectable, elderly owner of the land that the ill-fated ship wrecked upon, and title-holder to the whole southern quadrant of the island. Mr. Littlefield lived alone, and as his one and only slave, Hubbard, was responsible for tending to his horse, cows and the basic needs of his modest farm. Mr. Littlefield treated him better than most owners might, and in the winter, as long as Mr. Littlefield was properly fed and his animals were tended to, Hubbard was left alone to do as he saw fit with his time.

Manisses had just endured the worst harvest in its history, plagued by a summer of never-ending cold rain that rotted vegetable roots and turned most stored supplies to mold. Many had abandoned their property on the island and headed for the mainland before winter set in; some succumbed to a nasty pestilence, but most chose to tough it out and pray to God for a mild winter and to lay mercy upon their wretched souls.

No one prayed for a shipwreck. But some were convinced it was a sign that God could and would provide when they needed it most.

Katherine pitched and shivered, falling in and out of a high fever and consciousness for many days. Hubbard did what he could to feed her and keep her warm, but assumed that God would eventually take this woman away from him, the most curious bit of salvage that he had ever found along the island's long shoreline. On a mantle above the fireplace sat Didier, himself soaked to the durable wire frame that held his parts together, drying in the warmth of the dry December fire. Hubbard would alternate between staring down at Katherine, and staring up at Didier. There was something amusing and compelling about the doll that he just couldn't place and Hubbard would scratch at the white whiskers on his chin and laugh, swearing Didier was making silly faces at him whenever he turned his back.

Hubbard was old for a slave, just past forty years, and with each passing season, his back would scream in pain, and his bones would ache just a bit more, and he found it more and more difficult to meet his obligations to Mr. Littlefield and get his work done. Since he had arrived on the island, willed to old Balthazar by his late brother a decade before, Hubbard lived a lonely existence, tending to his chores then watching the sun set squatting upon his perch atop the great rocks. Hubbard had never taken a wife, the Massachusetts farm where he previously toiled held no women, and he had accepted his fate that he would live a solitary, celibate life. On Manisses, there were only a handful of other slaves and most didn't ever wander far from their homes. Hubbard had once nursed an abandoned plover chick to adulthood, and then raised an orphaned fawn he found trapped in the thicket. Katherine's unexpected appearance was a message, to Hubbard, that after so many years, now that he had proven he was ready, God had answered his prayers and sent him a wife to look after.

It took many weeks for Katherine to fully recover. At first, she was too weak to object to much of Hubbard's fussing, deciding that submission to his annoying persistence took less energy than fighting him off. The thin fish stew that Hubbard prepared each night for their supper was sour and vile, but Katherine accepted that, too, as an acceptable alternative to starvation. And though with time, she would learn that Hubbard had a kind and gentle soul and meant her no physical harm, she still slept huddled alone in the corner of the shed with her back to the wall and a fireplace log grasped in each hand, just in case.

Katherine was raised in the great economic center of Amsterdam, and had been exposed to several simple words and phrases in many foreign languages throughout her life, including fragments of English. Her father was a well-known cooper who conducted business with captains and shipbuilders from all over Europe, and when in his shop, she would be captivated by the stories of adventure and excitement from across the seas. Katherine's mother had died giving birth to the youngest of her twelve siblings, and as the oldest child, she assumed all the household responsibilities and raised her brothers and sisters for her father, who never remarried. Katherine was smart and resourceful, and though her father was considered successful and a suitable provider for his family, with so many of them, there was a never-ending need for more clothing, food and medicine. Katherine could read and write, was taught to keep her father's ledgers and accounts, and enjoyed absorbing the diverse bits of culture and information that her beloved Amsterdam offered, applying them for practical use within her own family as was needed. She learned of many herbal and natural remedies for illness, experimented with new and exotic cooking spices and techniques, and even dabbled with mysticism and pagan religions introduced to the city by merchants returning from the far east.

Had Katherine been born male, she would have dutifully inherited her father's business and advanced the rich family legacy -- but that honor would fall to the family's oldest son. For Katherine, after her youngest siblings had come of age, she had become simply an old maid at age twenty-eight. Her father lobbied tirelessly among his colleagues to find someone willing to marry her. She was big and not attractive, and eventually found a pastor and evangelist who was leading a flock of pilgrims to the New World -- a place called Philadelphia -- to free themselves from the strains of European religious persecution. The old pastor was in need of a resourceful, strong-willed woman to marry and become the matriarch of his fledgling congregation. Not much of a religious man himself, Katherine's father saw it as an honorable transaction for both he and the family, and betrothed his daughter to the old man without a moment's hesitation.

Leaving her family and beloved Amsterdam home broke Katherine's heart, but she also saw an opportunity to travel across the seas and explore a new world, and become part of one of the grand stories she always heard discussed in her father's shop. As she boarded the *Princess Augusta*, all her belongings tucked under her arm and strapped to her back, she daydreamed of lush landscapes and abundant wealth, friendly natives and exotic foods, and wondrous sights and thrilling adventures.

But now, each night before sleep, huddled in the drafty corner of Hubbard's shack, she would weep -- cursing at Providence for delivering this wretched fate, longing to be returned to the comfort of her family, her father and her native home.

Early on, Katherine considered leaving, but there was just nowhere to go. She had been shipwrecked on a small, foreign New England island in the dead of a brutal winter, with limited access to the transport of ships and no money, all her personal possessions lost to looters and the sea. Whatever her eventual fate may be, she realized her immediate well-being was dependent solely upon Hubbard's charity and good graces.

Language was the first barrier they needed to overcome. Hubbard was uneducated, illiterate, and spoke in broken phrases and frequent mispronunciations. Katherine spoke native Dutch, but possessed just enough English vocabulary to get by. Each evening after Hubbard completed his chores for Mr. Littlefield, the two would sit across the room from one another and try to have a meaningful conversation, together agreeing upon certain phrases to describe the most critical things in their household -- firewood, cooking pots, snow, crabs, and so forth. Together, they forged what many would consider to be a whole new language that only the two of them would ever fully understand -- part English, part Dutch and part necessity. In fact, as long as the pair were together, Hubbard never once knew her real name, calling her and introducing her to others as simply, "Kattern."

As the winter months waned and an early spring rose over Manisses, Katherine spent more and more time outdoors, exploring the abundance that the little island offered. Within just feet of Hubbard's shack she found many roots and herbs that looked familiar, and experimented with others she found intriguing. The first responsibility she accepted within the new household was that of the cook, no longer able to choke down the inedible gruel and swill Hubbard had become accustomed to feeding the two of them. Then Katherine went to work cleaning and repairing Hubbard's shack. Having lived alone his entire adult life, he didn't keep the tidiest of residences. Katherine went about sorting and organizing his meager possessions, repairing holes in the drafty walls, cleaning the caked mud from his tools, and mending his worn blankets and shoes. When Hubbard would walk in the door, boots covered in manure from Balthazar's horse, Katherine would curse at him in Dutch and strike him in the shins with a broom handle until he retreated outside to remove them.

And when the sun shone bright and the wind was calm, Katherine would disappear alone into the fields and sit for hours, her back nestled against the stone wall where years later Prissy and Abby would often play, eyes closed, in a silent, soulful meditation. When Hubbard would ask where she had gone off to, she would tell him she had traveled home to see her father in Holland, and that he was well, and that he missed her.

Had all the islanders been as kindhearted as Hubbard, Katherine's life on Manisses might have been at least tolerable. But most of the islanders were distrustful of strangers, and even more so of foreigners. It was well known that Katherine was one of the few survivors from the *Princess Augusta* tragedy, and the only one who made a permanent residence on the island. The bodies of the victims who had washed ashore that night or died from the ordeal later -- including Otto and Katherine's new husband and parishioners -- had been tossed into a massive hole and buried on the far side of the island, with nothing but a single, lichen-covered stone to mark their lives and their memory. Back in Amsterdam, Katherine was well known, the daughter of a popular craftsman, and new wife of a prominent pastor. Here in Manisses, she was an outcast -- no more than a low-bred concubine of a Negro slave, banned from even setting her unclean foot in any one of the few shops on Water Street.

The islanders feared and avoided her. Stories of her silent meditations and her mystical journeys back to Holland spread among the gossiping superstitious islanders, her activities whispered to be both dangerous and blasphemous. Her ability at creating broths and medicines from the island vegetation was considered blatant witchcraft. Some even accused her of being an opium-eater, attributing her long meditations and bizarre trances to the affects of the powerful, illicit drug. Some advocated running her off the island, or even throwing her in jail. Katherine grew to hate the residents of Manisses as much as they hated her.

Trying to exist off the land and the paltry scraps collected by a slave were not sufficient for the two of them to maintain their health or existence. Katherine knew she needed to do something to pay her keep, and she found her vocation trading medicines to the town's women folk. At first, they were reluctant to even speak to her, but it only took one of them to reap the soothing benefits from one of her magic salves spread across the ravages of poison ivy, for word to spread of her brilliance. Once proud Katherine was able to trade her medicines for vegetable seed, food, clothes and other much needed supplies, all the while enduring their insults, threats, verbal abuse and humiliation of abject prejudice.

When they came to Hubbard's door at all hours, they would knock and demand to see the witch. Katherine would not argue, and would keep her head and eyes glancing downward.

"Ja, I am dat witch, Kattern." She would tell them. "What is da remedy dat you ask?"

Most would want ointments for rashes or burns, and many would ask for herbs and teas for the persistent coughs that seemed to plague everyone on the island. Some even looked to acquire the secret recipes themselves. And every once in a while, they would inquire, with the utmost discretion, if her powers as a witch allowed her to divine the future from within her exotic brews and potions.

"Nee," she would say. "No fortunes. So sorry."

Over time, her annoyance and frustration with the residents deepened. Not only did she see herself as their equal, in social status, she believed she was above them, and her continued treatment as an outcast infuriated her.

One sunny afternoon, when she was in need of a single needle and a remnant of cloth, she asked Hubbard to accompany her on a visit to town. She required Hubbard's presence on such visits as he was welcome inside the shopkeepers' stores, a well-known slave from an established, respectable family. Katherine, on the other hand, was forced to wait outside in the street, passersby taking a wide birth, some even mocking her under their breath. Katherine's physical appearance and hygiene had also deteriorated from her days in Amsterdam, now rarely able to wash or even comb her hair, her only dress stained and tattered, she inadvertently portrayed the very image of the witch they all imagined her to be. As the sea breeze rustled through the ends of her matted hair, she boiled in her anger, and she noticed a man seated on the bench on the corner. The cloak he wore was thick and black, of German design and production, and she recognized it right away.

"*Mijn God*! Dat cloak, where did it come from?" She demanded of the stranger.

"What matter is it to you, witch!" He shot back, surprised she had the gall to even speak to him.

"I know dat cloak. Dat cloak is of my husband!" She accused, her hands rolling into formidable fists.

"You are clearly mad and mistaken, Madame." The stranger mocked back. "I advise you to hold your tongue."

"You steal dat cloak from my husband's grave! Ja are the thief!"

Katherine had never loved her husband, though she had accepted their marriage as an arranged and appropriate business transaction. After meeting him for the first time, and traveling across the seas, she still wasn't even sure if she even liked him all that much. But the cloak the stranger wore represented many things to her -- the shipwreck, the looting of the cargo, the excruciating death of her future, and the constant insults and injustice that it was now her destiny to endure.

A small crowd began to gather around the two as the man stood from his bench and confronted Katherine.

"I do not owe you an explanation, Madame." He said, pacing around her. "Look at you. What a mess you are. You arrive on our island uninvited, like a piece of driftwood. We take you in and save your wretched, pathetic life, out of the goodness and kindness of our hearts. And how do you repay us? With witchcraft? With insults? You, my dear are an insolent witch, nothing more. Know your place. It is a shame you didn't drown or burn with the rest of the rats on that festering ship!"

"Ja give to me dat cloak now!" She demanded. "Or I rip it off you body."

"Now you threaten me?" The stranger laughed. "Oh my! Perhaps you prefer the comfort of the jailhouse to that shack where you currently reside. And I promise you, my dear, it will be arranged."

"I said, give to me dat cloak!"

"Oh, perhaps I misunderstood. Is it just a cloak you want? Sure, then! And why not his boots as well? Or his pocket watch? Or how about his Bible? That shipwreck was the most lucrative event to happen on this island in decades. A stroke of brilliance. I take my hat off to whoever thought to hang the lights over that beach and draw those idiots into the rocks. Brilliant.., don't you think?"

Katherine was larger and sturdier than the stranger, and now out of her mind with rage, she grabbed him by his chest, wrinkling his shirt and lifted him straight up off the ground. And had it not been for Hubbard's sudden interference, most believed she might have snapped his neck on the spot. With effort, Hubbard was able to separate the two, and he dragged Katherine into the street, her arms thrashing as she swore out in Dutch. *Mijn hemel!* The crowd surrounded them and stared at her with a cautious fascination.

"Ja all think me a witch, eh? Then, I will be a witch for ja. I curse ja! I curse ja all! Hear me words! I curse ja! I curse ja for each soul lost on dat ship. Ja all deserve no peace. As long as dis island floats on de sea, it shall be cursed. Each time ja hear da cry of a woman, remember dose souls and dis curse. Whenever ja see a spirit ship in flames on da horizon, know dat it brings with it great evil. I curse ja, all of ja, all who live here, your children and all your descendents. Like the *Princess Augusta*, may ja all burn in hell!"

Hubbard and Katherine returned to the shack and said nothing to one another for a long while. Katherine sat on the floor and stared into the crackling fire and sobbed, while Hubbard sat behind her carving a mortar and pestle he had created from a wooden scrap of the *Princess Augusta's* hull. Hubbard had been careful to always avoid mentioning the shipwreck, as he could sense it brought Katherine great pain.

"Kattern, it was not good to make the town folk angry. Not good."

"I know dat, Hubbard. I am sorry."

"They didn't mean nothin, Kattern. They are good people, here on the island."

"Some of dem be good. Some not." She said, eyes welling with tears." Dat man wear my husband's cloak like nuttin happened. It's not right."

"But it's just a coat."

"I know. I not tell ja before, but each night when I sleep, when my head strikes dat pillow, I hear da screams of da people on dat ship. I want to save dem, Hubbard, I want to help dem. But me, I am drowning. I cannot help dem."

"Oh, Kattern. The ship is gone now, and that's just a dream. Ain't no point thinkin' about bad dreams. You have a new life now."

"Ja don't understand. It was not a dream, Hubbard, it happened to me. I live it again and again every night. My husband and I jumped from da rail of dat ship together, in each other's arms, and when we hit da water, he just disappeared. Da water was so cold, it would not let me breathe. I never saw my husband again. I could hear da woman on deck screaming her little boy's name, and I could see fire all around her. I wanted to go to her. I could not."

Katherine looked up at Didier sitting on the mantle. Didier appeared to look down at her with compassion.

"How did you know to save that doll?" Katherine asked.

"I dunno. There was lots of stuff all over the beach. I picked up stuff I thought I could use here in the cabin. For some reason, I thought I could use that doll for somethin'. I duno what."

"Dat doll belonged to a little boy. I saw him on the deck. He was very brave, more brave dan me. It is good you saved dat doll."

Hubbard nodded. Didier appreciated it, too.

Six months later, a passing Dutch merchant who had heard horrific tales of the shipwreck, offered Katherine safe passage off Manisses to New York. There, he told her, she could make contact with other survivors of the disaster, and then might be able to either continue her journey to Philadelphia or arrange passage back to her home in Amsterdam.

Katherine refused.

As much as the island and its people repulsed her, the thought of leaving Hubbard behind repulsed her more. She was the island's only witch and its first fortune-teller. And whether the curse she levied upon the inhabitants was real or imagined, she knew they all feared it, which kept her safe and relevant. And she felt she owed staying not only to Hubbard for saving her life, but to the bodies of her fellow passengers whose corpses lay rotting at the bottom of a shallow grave, and at the bottom of a remorseless shallow sea. For all of them, she would stay, her mere existence bearing their witness, and she resolved that for as long as she remained alive, and could take a salt-filled breath, their memories and the final voyage of the *Princess Augusta* would be honored and not be forgotten.

When Katherine and Hubbard died many years later, they passed their meager belongings on to Mary, one of their three children, which included a few farm tools, a goat, a diary, a mortar and pestle, and an appreciative little doll.

Chapter 20

C lement, we still can't find Abby anywhere. Are you sure you haven't heard anything new?"

Skip Payne stood in the doorway of the Bradford's residence shifting uncomfortably from one foot to the other, soaked through to the skin by the sudden sporadic downpours. His face was pale and cold, and water dripped from his elbows onto the Bradford's welcome mat. His usual smart-alecky attitude had been replaced by reserved panic and a profound worry.

"Come on inside, Skip, and warm up. Let me get you a towel." Jessica offered.

"No, I should get back home. Just thought I would check one more time. I thought maybe..."

"I swear, Skip, we will call if we hear or see anything. I promise."

" I know. But Kitty's going crazy back at the house, and I have to keep doing something." Clement placed a reassuring hand on Skip's wet shoulder. Skip thanked them both and jogged through the rain, back to his car.

"Jess, I think I should go out and help him. It's dark, and if Abby is still out there, she will be getting pretty miserable right about now."

"OK, go ahead. I'll call you if she turns up here."

Prissy stood behind them frowning, squeezing her fingernails into Otto's chest. Her mind raced. She knew something had gone terribly wrong, and the appearance of what she believed to be a burning ship along the western horizon convinced her there was even more going on that she didn't understand. Clement grabbed his raincoat and looked down once again at his confused and upset daughter.

"Don't worry, dear, I'm sure Abby is just fine." Clement said as he forced a comforting smile and pulled on his bright yellow slicker. Prissy frowned again and nodded. "Is there anything else you can tell us about what Abby said or where you think she might have gone?" he asked.

"I told you a bazillion times, she wanted to go to the barn and dig for more treasure. That's all she told me. I'm sorry that I didn't go with her." Prissy was becoming angry sensing that they didn't fully believe her. She was convinced they never believed her.

"There's nothing to feel sorry about, dear. You didn't do anything wrong." Jessica said, surprising her with a hug from behind. "Abby will turn up very soon, and everything will be fine. You'll see."

No sooner had Clement closed the door behind him, and drifted out into the windswept rain, than Jessica recognized a distinctive, dull thumping noise echoing in the room behind her."

"Oh, crap."

Jessica turned and sprinted into the kitchen, grabbing an empty trash pail and placing it under a leak that was now dripping with vigor from the ceiling in the center of the room. A puddle had formed on the checkerboard-tiled kitchen floor, and she scrambled to find a towel to clean up the mess as the trail of water was advancing toward the dining room at a disturbing rate.

"Oh crap."

A fresh leak had now sprung in the dining room, and when Jessica looked up, she could see new trails of liquid running like pulsing veins across the ceiling, racing down the faded yellow wallpaper, curling it at its corners. Prissy and Otto ran to the garage to retrieve more empty buckets and pans as Jessica scampered to contain the burgeoning mess. Before the evening was over, Jessica and Prissy would contain a dozen such leaks, some large, and some small. It was another warning of the horrid physical condition of their home, and a reminder that the roof needed to be replaced much sooner than later, before everything they owned was ruined and succumbed to mold. Jessica had no idea how they would ever be able to pay for the renovation. It was a large, unbudgeted expense the family just couldn't begin to handle.

Between rounds of mopping and bucket emptying, Jessica stared out the window at the driveway, hoping to see headlights turn up to the house heralding Clement's return bearing happy news. It would be several hours before she saw those headlights, dimmed by sheets of cascading rain, and they would not bring the news she longed for.

"No luck?"

Clement shook his head. Dejection and exhaustion visible in his expression. He removed his wet raincoat and shook it with one hand outside the door. The steady gale was pushing the driving rain sideways, and Clement was relieved to be back inside.

"It is miserable out there tonight, Jess. Just awful. I can't believe it was eighty-five degrees and sunny just yesterday. There had to have been a thousand people on the town beach," he said.

"Wasn't it your namesake who said, *If you don't like the New England weather, wait a minute?*" Jessica inquired, reaching, trying to remain positive.

"Now that's what most people think. But Mark Twain never actually said that. My mother will torture you with a twenty-minute lecture if you ever say that with her in the room."

"I really hope Abby is inside and safe."

By dawn, the rain had not ceased and Abby had still not been found. The weather forecasters all agreed that a powerful nor'easter had stalled off the New England coast, churning up the sea, and islanders were told to expect several days of cold, windswept rains. With the weather so foul, Clement didn't expect to see many customers -- half-empty ferries were not good for business or for financing leaking roofs. Tall waves along the shore crashed with vicious anger onto the beach every few seconds, sending walls of spray and foam into the shrubs and pines along the water's edge. The well traveled tourist road that encircled the island appeared abandoned, and even the lunatic surfers who only materialized during bad weather didn't dare venture out on this day. The only activity visible from the porch of the Bradford's home were the three cars owned by the Manisses Police Department that traveled back and forth in front of their house, searching for some sign of poor Abby.

Clement did not sleep that night, and had barely sipped his first coffee of the day when the Manisses Police rang his doorbell. Captain Honeywell stood peering through the screen door, his hat, covered in clear plastic to protect it from the rain, was tucked up snug under his arm.

Honeywell was captain of the police force and a true leader of the community, arguably the most recognizable person on the island. His round, pink face was a fixture on the cover of the weekly *Manisses Times* newspaper, he handled traffic control details at all the island events himself, and never missed a public meeting or the opportunity to shake a hand. Honeywell hated to do real police work, and the sleepy island atmosphere suited his tastes just fine -- most criminal activity confined to traffic incidents, petty theft, public drunkenness, and chasing young lovers off the beach under the bluffs. Honeywell was one of the few islanders who openly welcomed Clement and Jessica when they first arrived to open their shop -- Clement believing he was an authentic nice guy and solid citizen, while Jessica, borrowing a page from her father's script, believing he was only nice because he didn't trust them.

"Clement, can we talk to you and Jessica for a minute?" Honeywell requested appearing uncomfortable.

"Of course, come in. Please."

Honeywell sat at the Bradford's long, pine dining room table, circled by buckets collecting rainwater. Jessica poured him a fresh cup of coffee, just after Honeywell had emptied the last drop of milk into the bottom of his mug.

"I swear we buy milk every day. I don't know where it all goes." Jessica said, wrapped in an old housecoat, more embarrassed by the dripping rainwater than the absence of milk, or her wardrobe and not happy to be entertaining so early in the morning.

"My brother Earl is a contractor. He brings materials to the island on his own boat. He could get you a fair price on this roof," Honeywell offered, looking up at what appeared to be a fresh leak forming right above his head. He put his police hat back on. "I'll call him for you a little later."

"That would be great," Clement answered, fairly certain he wouldn't be able to afford it anyway.

"Folks, I'll cut to the chase. Abby Payne is still missing this morning, and she was last seen on your property, in the company of your daughter. I have pulled together all the officers and resources of the department, and in about fifteen minutes, we will be conducting a ground search and sweep of the property starting by those big rocks by the shore, and moving past your house and into the fields and bushes back to the east." Honeywell's arms were extended and his fingers pointed like a ground general about to launch an offensive.

"Of course," Clement said. "Is there any way we can help?"

"Yes. There are two things you can do. First, I would like your permission to talk to your daughter Prissy myself."

"Sure, but I don't think she will be much help. We quizzed her for hours last night, and I don't think she knows anything."

"I see." Honeywell had pulled out a small pocket sized notepad and began writing, glancing around the dining room. To Clement, his notes looked like a child's random, unintelligible scribbles. A drip of water struck the bill of his Honeywell's cap, exploding into smaller particles of water that sprayed across his notebook. Honeywell looked back up at the ceiling as if the ceiling had assaulted him on purpose.

"And I have another request." Honeywell said, sliding his chair back, away from the annoying dripping. "I'd like permission to search your house."

Jessica and Clement froze and swapped glances. A million words and questions were transmitted, received and understood between the couple in that single instance, faster than the speed of light. The couple worried deeply for Abby -- they cared and adored her like one of the family -- and they were committed to do whatever they could to help find her. But, they thought, did this mean they were now suspects in her disappearance? Should they decline the request and find a lawyer? Or should they open their doors and allow Honeywell and his men to rifle through their personal belongings?

"Clement? Jessica?" The two said nothing, as if waiting for the other to respond first. Honeywell waited. "Of course, I could get a warrant, but that would take some time, and I don't want to delay things. I understand if you don't want us poking around, I wouldn't want my house searched either. But I'm thinking you will want to be cleared of any suspicion in this matter as soon as possible. It would be a big help to our department."

"Of course, go ahead and search. Just give me a moment to go upstairs and wake Lucky and Prissy, explain what's happening, and let them get dressed. Of course we want to help any way we can," Jessica said, taking the lead and breaking the painful silence.

"Yes, go ahead." Clement said, unhappy with Jessica's decision. "Jessica's right, we want to do whatever we can." Honeywell grasped the two-way radio attached to his shoulder and mumbled a garbled order into it, something only the police could understand.

The three were startled by the sound of the squeaky front door swinging open, and the sudden appearance of Lucky shuttling in from the storm. Clement and Honeywell sprung to their feet. Lucky's hair was matted down, soaked by the rain, and she wore a thigh-high black leather skirt hemmed with purple lace, and calf high boots each with three-inch heels and six silver buckles. Her black eye make-up was running down her cheeks and over her rose lipstick, giving her the appearance of a mad, Victorian clown.

"Lucky!" Jessica exclaimed. "Where did you come from?"

"Didn't you just tell me your daughters were upstairs?" Honeywell asked Clement.

"I thought they were." Clement blushed, and Honeywell scribbled more notes.

"Is everything alright? Why is there a police car in the yard?" Lucky asked, makeup swirling into the rainwater now puddling around her heels.

"Abby Payne is missing. You wouldn't by chance know where she is?" Jessica asked. Lucky sighed, exhaling a deep breath of relief, secretly pleased that the police visit had nothing to do with her.

"No. I haven't seen her." She answered.

"And by the way... where on earth have you been?!" Clement demanded, crossing his arms and tapping his toe upon the wet wood floor. Clement thought it might be an excellent time to show Honeywell what a responsible disciplinarian he was, and try to save some face. He was furious at Lucky, but thought it best not to lash out at her in Honeywell's presence as he didn't want to appear violent, either.

"I was with Vance." She answered.

"All night?" "Clement asked, eyes widening.

"I didn't want to walk home in the rain last night, so I waited. Besides, if I hadn't seen the police car in the driveway, I would have climbed up the chimney like mom does, and just gone back in my bedroom window. You never would have known I was out."

"Mom, did the police find Abby?" Prissy interrupted at the perfect moment, stopping Clement from lashing out, standing at the bottom of the staircase with Otto.

"Not yet, Prissy. But we will." Honeywell promised. "But to do it, we will need your help. Prissy, if it's OK with you, I would like to invite you out onto the porch and ask you a few questions about Abby. Your mom and dad already told me it would be OK."

"Can Otto come with me?" Prissy asked.

"Who is Otto?" Honeywell asked, eyes darting around expecting another child to magically appear from the shadows. Prissy extended both arms and held her doll out in front of her.

Though Otto and Honeywell had never been formally introduced, Otto was insulted and felt Honeywell should have known who he was.

"Of course Otto can come. Maybe he can help us solve this mystery."

Otto was sure he could.

Jessica handed Prissy a bagel, and she and Honeywell strolled out onto the porch. The rain was still falling but on the covered porch swing, the two were shielded from the torrent except for mist carried in by an occasional wind gust. A group of officers, sheriffs and a number of volunteers, wrapped and bundled in plastic, gathered down near the great rocks where the island's native women once nursed Verrazano's cabin boy. From the porch, Prissy could hear them shouting instructions at each other, but they were too far off to make out what was being said. The volunteers formed a long single, straight line, starting at the spot where Prissy buried her squirrel, and extending along the coast to the place where Hubbard had found Didier in the snow. All at once, the line slowly advanced forward in a sweep, the volunteers' heads dashing side to side, searching for any small bit of evidence that might lead them to learn the whereabouts of the lost child.

"So Prissy, tell me." Honeywell began, as the two swung back and forth." What do you think happened to Abby?"

"I don't know, sir. She said she wanted to hunt treasure and I didn't want to go. We had a big argument." Abby said, nibbling little bites from her breakfast.

"You know, Prissy. It's OK to argue with your friends sometimes. Everyone argues. All it means is that you and your friend share different opinions, and you both believe strongly about stuff. Those are good things. You shouldn't worry about that."

"That's what my mom said... that I shouldn't worry. But I can't help it. I want Abby to come back real bad."

"So do I, Prissy. Abby's mom and dad are very worried about her, too. That's why they need me to do everything I can to find her as fast as possible. We all want to make sure she is OK."

"What if she isn't OK? What if something bad happened?"

"Something bad? Like what?"

"What if she got herself kidnapped. Maybe by pirates."

"Hmmm, let me write that down. That's a great lead, Prissy, I'll look into that. But I don't think there have been pirates in these waters for hundreds of years. But that makes me think of another question. Have you seen anyone hanging around lately... like pirates? Or any other strangers?"

"No, I haven't seen any pirates or strangers. But I did see an old ship yesterday."

"Wow a pirate ship! I've never seen a real pirate ship. That must have been exciting."

"Honestly, it was kind of scary. And I don't think it was a pirate ship, anyway. Otto and I were on the beach when we saw it. It was all orange and on fire. It was far away on the horizon."

"On fire? Hmmm, Is that a fact. We haven't had any reports of any boat fires lately. Well, I don't think it had anything to do with Abby."

"But the witch said that it was a cursed ship. She said that when you see the burning ship, it means something bad is going to happen."

Otto agreed, and felt the investigation had taken an important and productive turn.

Honeywell paused and stopped the swing from swaying. He crumpled up his eyebrows and looked down at Prissy and Otto.

"A witch? Who is this witch?" he asked.

"The witch that cursed the island. She said that as long as people live on this island, and they see that ship, bad things will happen to them. That's why I think that something bad has happened to Abby."

"What else did this witch tell you? Did she say where Abby might be?"

"No. But I was thinking... what if Abby fell into the witch's well?"

"Your witch has a well?"

"Yes, sir. She said that one of her goats fell into the well and died, so she made her husband cover it over. What if something like that happened to Abby? What if she's in the well?" A single tear exited her left eye and dribbled down her face. Honeywell could tell that Prissy believed her own story.

"Where is this well?"

"It's out back in the field behind the frog pond."

Honeywell's heart ached for Prissy, but he was starting to think that this conversation might be causing her more harm than good. Prissy was a bright and creative child, and she was upset, and Honeywell didn't want his serious investigation to become distracted by Prissy's imagination and whimsy. He glanced down at his watch and decided it might be time to conduct the search of the Bradfords' house itself, before it grew too late. One of the department's officers had been standing by with a cardboard box filled with empty evidence bags, just in case, as Honeywell had reserved this duty for himself, in a kind-hearted effort to preserve the Bradfords' dignity, and stay out of the rain.

"Thank you, Prissy, you have been a big help." Honeywell gave her a reassuring hug across her shoulders.

Inside, Honeywell and his assistant began the embarrassing task of searching through the Bradfords' home and personal items. Each of Clement and Jessica's threadbare furnishings were lifted and looked under, each cupboard and drawer was opened and rummaged through, and each closet was unbolted and the contents quickly yet carefully inspected. All went well until Honeywell's assistant let out a blood-curdling, ear-piercing scream from the hallway. After opening the hallway closet, a human forearm -- complete with curly hair, a birthmark, and a wedding ring -- had rolled off the closet's top shelf and landed across his boots.

Everyone in the house came running.

"It's a prop! It's a prop! I keep all my magic supplies in that closet," Clement pleaded. "It looks just like my forearm, see?" Clement waved his own bare arm over his head. "Just pick it up and squeeze it, it's just made out of rubber! I swear it!"

But the officer's shock was nothing like his reaction when he opened Lucky's bedroom door.

"Oh, my!" Honeywell exclaimed.

Honeywell and his assistant stood in the doorway, almost afraid to step inside. Lucky's room was the largest in the house, once considered the house's master bedroom, that Clement and Jessica gave to Lucky to provide enough space for both herself and her growing collection of artwork. Half the room looked like a construction site, complete with welding torches, soldering guns, tools, metal scraps and as many as a dozen half completed modern sculptures. The other half of the room could have been a snapshot cut from the pages of a Jules Verne novel. On one wall was an oversized flat clock, with Roman numerals each a foot tall. Around the clock were dozens of brass switches, dials and levers, each that logic would dictate controlled nothing, but could have been salvaged from the wall of Verne's own *Nautilus* submarine. The two chairs in the room were both black leather, upholstered with small silver buttons, and between them sat an oversized sepia-toned globe featuring a 19th century nautical map. Against the back wall was Lucky's mahogany desk, furnished with an hourglass and an 18th century gold telescope that pointed out her window to the sea. From the ceiling hung a gold chandelier that held white candles, and a large, shiny brass periscope. And in the middle of the room sat Lucky, thumbing through the pages of an old book, plopped into the center of her round bed, surrounded by a dozen brown, frilly overstuffed pillows. The officers weren't sure if they were stepping back in time, or forward into the future.

"So go ahead and look around," she said. "I really don't care what you do."

Outside, the search team had reached the end of the property, fences and impassable terrain stopping them from searching any further, their only evidence from their morning's effort was a few discarded candy wrappers. From here, they decided to break into smaller teams to more efficiently search through neighboring properties.

The family stood with Honeywell in the driveway as the search party began to return and reassemble, disappointed, but enjoying a temporary respite from the swirling rainstorm. Low, gray clouds whisked by them, and the sound of the waves pounding the shore was as loud as any of them could remember.

"We are through here, Captain." One of the officers told Honeywell. "This heavy rain probably washed away any trail there might have been. We didn't find a trace of her. It's like the ground opened up and the girl just dropped right in."

Honeywell stroked the back of his neck and stared down at Prissy.

"A couple of you boys come with me; the rest of you can head back to the station. Clement, I was told there is an old well on your property out behind the pond; can you take me over there, please? I'd like to take a look around myself."

Clement looked puzzled. "There isn't any old well back there. I'm sure of it. And I know every inch of this property." He said.

"We didn't see any well back there, either," one of the volunteers from the search party added.

"Yes there is, Dad! There is!" Prissy piped in, using Otto to point in the correct direction. "The witch says it's back in the corner where the two longest stone walls meet."

"A witch?" Jessica asked. "Prissy, this is a very bad time for games. Captain Honeywell is very busy trying to find Abby."

"See Otto, I told you they wouldn't believe us! They never believe us!" Prissy stomped her feet and dashed back to the house.

"This is stupid," Lucky exclaimed, and followed Prissy inside.

"I'm sorry, Captain, for wasting your time. We're all struggling with this, especially our daughters." Jessica said.

"If it's all the same to you, I'm going to take a walk back there anyway."

The group trotted down the same path Abby and Prissy had the day before, past the same poison ivy and the same poke-weed bushes. They each took turns catching their clothing on the briars, and all soaked their feet as the heavy rains had caused the frog pond to flood out of its soft banks. The group arrived near the corner of the stone walls, as Prissy's mysterious witch had instructed, but there was no well to be found. They all scratched at the earth around the thick plant life, and kicked over stones, but found nothing more than a few irritated scampering salamanders.

"Prissy told us it was in the corner," Jessica said, alone in defending her daughter's honor. "But all that I see is that old dogwood."

At the point where the stone walls came together, as Prissy had described, there was a large, thick dogwood tree, over one hundred years old, overgrown and dying. Honeywell inspected the base of the tree, and the stone walls, and shook his head. He kicked at the dirt under the tree pushing leaves and dead branches aside from around its knotty roots, then paused.

"Hmmm." He muttered.

Honeywell dropped to one knee and pounded the damp ground with the back of his flashlight, and they all heard a distinctive hollow echo. Perhaps, they considered, there was something here after all.

The searchers all dropped to the ground together and scratched at the muddy, wet earth with their fingertips. The cold rain had returned with a vengeance, and it pounded the back of their necks as they crawled around on their hands and knees in the mud. Beneath a few inches of thick sticky, black loam and rotting leaves, they discovered a flat stone slab, and it took all of them to pry it up and flip it over, exposing a round dark hole. Honeywell spun his flashlight around and shined the beam down into the opening. It truly was a very old well. At the bottom, they could all see water, a few rocks and natural debris -- but no sign of Abby.

"Well, your daughter was right. There is an old well here, how about that." Honeywell said. "But there's no sign of Abby."

Jessica was mystified, and looked at Clement for guidance. "How could Prissy possibly know that this well was even here? It was completely hidden under all those leaves and dirt. Am I supposed to believe she is communicating with some kind of witch, or some kind of ghost?"

A disturbance from a nearby property caught their attention. It was the sound of a scuffle within the thicket, the sound of grown men fighting. Someone shouted, and someone else swore, others could be heard scampering and struggling.

"Captain!" An anonymous voice shouted from somewhere out of sight.

"Do you have Abby?" He shouted back.

From between the tall shrubs his volunteers appeared with a stranger in custody, battling to restrain his greasy hands behind his back. The man appeared old and thin, his hair and beard were long and greasy, and his clothes were dirty and tattered. The man smelled horribly of urine and mold and he expelled a violent cough as he was dragged from the thicket, spitting a mouthful of lime-green phlegm at Honeywell's feet. Clement and Jessica were startled and jumped back as the struggle moved toward them, and Jessica was able to make brief contact with the old man's bloodshot eyes.

"Daddy?"

Chapter 21

O
n an island with so many secrets, it is surprising that no one ever seemed able to keep one.

News of Abby's disappearance and the subsequent arrest of a suspect in the case moved across the island faster than a flock of migrating Canadian geese. But what made the gossip so juicy was that the heinous, unkempt suspect just happened to be a relative of the island's oddest family. Attendance at Sunday church services always seemed to increase during summer rainstorms, and the news spread from pew to pew with the vigor of a 19th century pestilence: from the Episcopalians to the Catholics; the Catholics to the Baptists; the Baptists to the Methodists; and from the Methodists back to the Episcopalians all within a single, pious, simultaneous Sunday morning hour of worship.

And with a chilly rainstorm still ravaging the island, and with nothing else to do on a rainy summer's day, families were expected and trained to leave service and walk directly to the Manisses Free Library in search of the day's entertainment. Here, the island's center of the universe, storm-weary islanders could sign out books, play chess, rent movies, or just mingle in and out of the tall stacks and compare notes on the hottest, most shocking, and tastiest morsels of gossip.

I heard that family knows what happened to the little girl and isn't telling.

Well, I heard that vagabond killed her but the police can't find a body. He's a Gypsy, you know.

I think they sacrificed the poor girl to their Satanic cult, that's what I think.

I heard they found severed body parts in that house.

I knew from the first day they showed up on this island there was something wrong with them.

The police had cleared Clement and Jessica of all wrong doing, for now, and although Honeywell still didn't know what had happened to Abby, his professional police senses told him the Bradfords had nothing to do with it. While Prissy's otherworldly prediction was concerning and had caused a number of wrinkled eyebrows, the curiosity didn't seem relative to the investigation, and was set aside.

For Honeywell, however, the arrest of Carl Johnson was a key moment in the investigation. He believed the vagrant knew something about Abby's disappearance, and vowed not to rest until he found out what it was.

Jessica paced around the cramped waiting room of the Manisses police station alone, arms crossed and hands placed firmly under her armpits, her mind fluttering in worry. Serious crime on the island was rare, and the island's only jail cell looked more like a locked, empty white room in a cheap hotel, usually occupied by a tourist unable to handle his alcohol intake. Jessica waited as an officer unlocked the thick door to escort her inside.

Carl was thin and emaciated, but with the assistance of the local Seamen's Church charity, he was allowed to shower and shave, provided a set of clean clothes, and fed a hot meal. He looked better than he had when Jessica saw him dragged out of the thicket the day before, but he still looked tired and sick, a shell of the man she had looked up to her whole life and loved so dearly. Carl sat on a wooden chair against the wall with his hands nervously rubbing his knees as the door closed and locked behind his daughter.

"Are you alright, Dad? Do you need anything?" Jessica asked, not sure if her father would lash out at her, or burst into tears.

"I'm OK." He answered, rubbing his knees with even more energy. "Really, I'm OK."

"What were you doing out there? Why didn't you come to the house?"

Carl paused. His dry, cracked lips moved but no sound came out. He struggled to find the right words.

"What do you want me to say, Jess? That I was right to be hiding from you in your bushes? I have been camping back in that thicket for a couple of weeks now, trying to find the right time to come see you. But you saw what I looked like yesterday. I couldn't come to you for help in that sorry condition."

"Of course you should have come to us! What's wrong with you. You know we would have helped you."

"If nothing else, I have my pride."

"Pride? You raised me to believe in family. You raised me believing that we needed to watch out for each other, and you taught me that it was what family is for."

"You have your family, Jess. I don't have anything, or anyone, anymore. I ran out of money, then sold the Winnebago just so I could eat. I stowed away on the ferry a couple of weeks ago and made my way over here. I had to see you, I had to know you were OK, but couldn't bring myself to talk to you."

"What? You've been camping out there for two weeks? How? What were you eating?"

Carl paused and looked away. He didn't want to answer.

"Don't be too hard on her, Jess."

"What are you talking about?" Jessica asked, her concern slowly being replaced by anger, confused by his answer.

"Lucky stumbled over me the day after I landed here. I was sleeping down by the frog pond behind the tall grass. I scared the daylights out of her. Once she calmed down, I begged her not to tell anyone, especially you, that I was here. I made her swear to it and told her I planned to come forward myself in a few days, once I got settled. She took me back to your garage and she gave me Clement's old green pup tent, along with some matches and a few other handy supplies. Each morning, just after dawn, she brought me a little something to drink and eat. She would leave it on top of the stone wall for me to find. Please, don't blame her for this. She was a sweetheart."

Jessica realized Lucky hadn't spent the night with Vance after all. She had been sneaking out to feed her vagabond grandfather. It also explained where all the missing groceries had been going. When she got back home, Jessica wasn't sure if she should kiss Lucky or strangle her.

"I love you, Dad."

"I love you too, Jess. I really do. You don't deserve a father like me."

"Oh, Dad... of course I do. Now you're being ridiculous."

"I've watched the way you have raised your daughters, with nothing but love. They are both smart, funny, and beautiful kids. You are ten times the parent I ever was to you. While Lucky brought me food, Prissy entertained me with a daily floor show. I would spy on her from behind the stone wall and smile as she danced around that pond with that doll of hers. The depth of conversations they shared blew my mind. The doll, of course, never actually said anything... anything that I could hear. But Prissy could hear it, and they chatted for hours about all sorts of crazy things. You'd think that doll was a living, breathing being. They almost had me believing it, too."

"When we get home..." Jess began, but Carl interrupted her.

"I don't think I'm going anywhere for a long time, Jess. They think I am responsible for the missing girl. These walls are thin, and from what I can hear through them, they want to ship me to the state prison on the mainland for a while, until they sort this all out."

"For what? You didn't do anything!" Jessica paused. "Did you?"

Of course I didn't do anything!" Carl shot back. "What the hell do you think I am? I saw the girl run by me and disappear into the thicket. It was raining, so I went back to my tent to stay dry. That's it. Nothing more. But what does that matter now? These cops are no better than the idiots back in that town of Eastbury where you used to live. They are a bunch of sneaky, back-stabbing, con-artists out to make their reputation at our expense. They'll pin this on me any way they can just to make a name for themselves. They can all go to hell, as far as I'm concerned."

Carl was fuming, up from his seat and now pacing around the small white room. Without warning, the door opened, and

Honeywell poked his head inside.

"Mrs. Bradford, I am sorry to interrupt, but could I have a moment of your time... right now?" Honeywell requested with urgency.

"I'll come see you later."

Jessica hugged her father, kissed him on the cheek, then followed Honeywell back to his undersized office. The room was as small as Carl's jail cell, except stacked with volumes of thick law books and littered with random pieces of paper. There was only enough space in the room for Honeywell's desk and two, stately, tall-backed, black wooden chairs. One of the two chairs in the room was empty, while the other was occupied and strained under the weight of its irascible occupant, Bernice Cowan.

"What's going on here?" Jessica asked Honeywell, surprised by Bernice's unexpected presence and sensing a problem.

"This is a travesty," Bernice shot back. "I demand to be released this minute!"

"Bernice, you're not being held." Honeywell answered, rolling his eyes and massaging his own forehead. "You came in here to see me. Remember?"

"I expect that a good police officer will handle all police matters and NOT drag their most important witness into an ambush."

"Bernice, you are the one dragging me into this ambush, now pipe down!" Honeywell ordered. "Jessica, please, have a seat."

Jessica sat as instructed, and she fidgeted as Bernice's chair was uncomfortably close to her own, and the scent of Bernice's cheap lavender perfume was choking her throat. As was her practice, Jessica took great care to avoid Bernice anywhere she went on the island. Bernice was like a black cat, brimming with bad luck, and Jessica had not crossed her path since they last happened to meet at the treasure field next to the Dodge barn. Honeywell leaned back in his chair and examined them both.

"What is this all about?" Jessica asked a second time, becoming angry, waiting for any sort of intelligent response.

"Mrs. Bradford," he began, "Mrs. Cowan here believes she has evidence proving that your family is responsible for Abby Payne's disappearance." Honeywell held out a bulky stack of photographs and dropped them in the middle of his desk. "I'm not sure what these all mean, but I am trying to find a missing child right now. I don't have time for foolishness. I am telling you both, all this ends here and now, is that understood?"

"That's absolutely ridiculous!" Jessica was baffled. She had no idea what Honeywell could be talking about.

"Well, if you are too chicken to call a spade a spade, Captain, then I will." Bernice began, clearing the gurgle from her own throat. "The Bradford family is evil. And I have indisputable evidence in these pictures that proves you are responsible for the disappearance of that poor, innocent girl." Bernice talked to Honeywell as if Jessica was invisible, ignoring her uncomfortable presence.

"Look... here!"

Bernice lifted the first picture from the stack and laid it out flat for them to see. Jessica squinted at the photo, which appeared to be a picture of the Bradfords' home, taken early in the morning, with a shadowy figure in a black cape scaling the side of the building like a superhero.

"It's a devil. It comes out at night and returns at dawn," Bernice insisted. "And it looks like a gigantic vampire bat."

"That's just a picture of my daughter, Lucky," Jessica answered, the pitch of her voice starting to rise. "She sneaks out sometimes at night to visit her boyfriend, and then she climbs back up to her bedroom window. And she owns a lot of black clothing."

"No, it's a demon! If you look closely, you can see its claws."

"No, it's a manicure... and she's wearing stilettos."

"And look over here, there's a vampire in the shadows."

"That's just Vance Asher. People have seen Vance and Lucky together many times, all over the island. Come on, now. I'm guessing he was just dropping her off."

Bernice pulled another photo from her stack and threw it down on the desk like an ace in a game of blackjack.

"Then how do you explain this?"

Jessica's heart sank to the pit of her already acidic stomach and her mouth gaped open. It was another photograph of their house, but this time it focused on the roofline. Above it was Jessica, her lithe body spread gracefully in midair, arms spread apart wide as if in flight. Even to Jessica, the picture looked quite shocking and bizarre.

"Only witches can fly, isn't that true Captain?" Bernice insisted. Honeywell said nothing, but shook his head and looked to Jessica to offer some sort of logical answer.

"Of course there is a simple explanation," Jessica began. "We were having a little bit of fun. You see, I was raised as part of a troupe of acrobats and aerial performers. We would travel all over the country performing at carnivals and other special events." Though she knew what she was saying was one hundred percent true, she had to admit to herself that the words coming from her mouth sounded contrived and hard to swallow. As she struggled to better explain herself, Bernice pulled picture after picture from the stack, each showing Jessica in a different pose, in flight high across the island sky.

"So you expect us to believe that you had the sudden urge to climb on the roof and do acrobatic tricks? Why not just do them from the ground where it's safe."

"I climbed on the roof to retrieve my daughter's doll..."

"Oh! That doll!" Bernice's fat, stubby arms were now sticking straight up in the air, the flab under each flapping against her own head. She wiggled her short fingers like little birds wings. "Does the doll fly, too?"

"That's ludicrous!" Jessica fired back.

"I haven't been able to figure out why, but I know that doll is at the root of all this evil, I can sense it. You can feel it when you get next to it. It radiates evil... like heat. Captain, you should seize that doll as police evidence in the name of public safety, and destroy it."

"For goodness sake, Bernice, get a grip. It's a little girl's doll. Why are you so afraid of a toy?"

Bernice tossed down another picture of the house. This time, in the upper window, was a clear image of Otto, his blue eyes staring down at the camera. Otto appeared angry.

"I took this picture myself. Just look at the expression on

that wicked, little face. You can just tell he is the embodiment of evil."

"Bernice, it's just a doll. That's all!"

Bernice didn't respond, but instead, threw down another picture, and then another, and then yet another. Altogether Bernice had a photograph of each window of the Bradford's house, and in each one, there was a picture of Otto staring back out at her.

"You're stalking us? You're stalking my family?" Jessica was becoming incensed.

"I knocked on your door and it was obvious no one was home. Then I looked up and saw that doll looking back down at me. As I walked around your house -- merely to confirm that you were not perhaps in your backyard out of range of your doorbell of course -- I noticed that creature following me from window to window, threatening me with those evil, horrible little eyes of his. Whenever I looked to a different window, the doll would magically appear. It followed me everywhere I went. So I know that doll can fly, too. It flies around the inside of that house when no one is at home. It's possessed. I saw it myself, and I have the evidence here to prove it."

"This is absurd. I made that doll myself. Otto does not fly."

"Oh, I'll bet you did!"

"Bernice, It sounds to me like Prissy was home, and you were the victim of a little girl's harmless prank."

"You have an answer for everything, don't you, missy. Then where is Abby? Why won't you answer that! What did you people, and that doll, do to that poor girl!"

"Alright, ladies, I have heard enough. As I said before, there's a little girl out there who is in trouble and needs our help. Bernice, you listen to me and listen to me good. The Bradfords are not responsible for Abby's disappearance, is that clear? I have given you your say, so now take all your photos home and throw them in the trash. They are not helping this case. And from this minute forward, I don't want to hear a peep out of you again about any of this silliness. And I swear, if I see you anywhere near the Bradfords' property, I will have you arrested for trespassing. I refuse to waste any more time on this issue. Bernice, do you understand me?"

Bernice bounced up in anger, her blue tent dress sticking between the spokes of the wooden chair causing the chair to bounce up with her. She snatched up the pictures from Honeywell's desk with her chunky fingers and squeezed them together.

"This family is evil, and un-Christian. Not only do they talk to spirits, but they are possessed of evil themselves, and goblins hide in the undergrowth of their property. And I know you found a severed arm in that house, too! And you can't deny it! It isn't safe for anyone to set foot on that land as long as they are there. Little innocent Abby went to visit, and look what became of her. Captain, if anyone is hurt out there, or another child disappears, I am holding you criminally and personally responsible!"

Bernice turned and waddled through the door, slamming it closed behind her, the breeze sending a shower of papers fluttering off Honeywell's desk and into the air.

Both Jessica and Honeywell sighed in relief, and Honeywell massaged his temples. Jessica felt as if she had been convicted of some heinous crime and then had the verdict overturned, and wasn't certain what it was she had done wrong or right to deserve any of the attention in the first place.

"Wow," Jessica said. "I have never seen anyone so worked up."

Honeywell placed his elbows on his desk and eased forward, looking Jessica in the eye. Honeywell, it appeared, had a lot more to say.

"Jessica, in my job, I come across a lot of different kinds of people. I was raised in a traditional, blue-collar household, and didn't grow up with much tolerance for those who thought differently than I did. I have to work hard, sometimes, to look beyond my own personal prejudices."

"We all have prejudices, I suppose. But I think that's what makes you a good and fair police officer."

"I like to think that, too. But this island is in chaos right now, people are afraid, and it's my job to maintain order. It's also my job to find out what the hell happened to Abby. I know my limitations, and I have already called in assistance from the state police to help resolve this case more quickly. And I don't believe for a second that Bernice will be destroying those photographs. In fact, I expect to see them on the front page of the *Manisses Times* by this time next week."

"I am sorry if I have caused any trouble."

"Well you have, and I know my limitations regarding prejudice as well. What I'm telling you is to knock off whatever it is you're doing in that house of yours. Personally, I don't care what you worship -- gods, devils, trees, water, dolls, or chickens -- it's all the same to me; I just don't give a damn. But I won't let it affect what happens in this case, my ability to help Abby or let it upset the delicate balance of peace on this island. If you folks don't find a way to keep a lower profile back there, I promise you, I will do something about it."

"With all due respect, Captain, we haven't done anything wrong!" Jessica was becoming defiant.

"A little girl went missing off your property and I am holding your vagrant father as a suspect. Your husband is a spiritual medium. And now Bernice is flashing pictures of devils, and your daughter is communicating with witches. While you are innocent in the eyes of the law, in the court of public opinion, my dear, you have already been accused, tried and convicted. You might want to reconsider a few lifestyle changes now before the same court of public opinion imposes its sentence."

Jessica sat in stunned silence, barely able to breathe. She had hoped for an opportunity to beg for leniency and her father's release, and now realized that wasn't about to happen. Honeywell's face had swollen and turned lobster red. He was even angrier at her than he had been at Bernice a few moments before. Jessica also realized she wouldn't be able to count on him or his police force to keep her family safe. Images of bricks and shards of glass hung like paintings on the walls of her memory from the incidents back in Eastbury. She had sensed back at the barn that it was all happening again, and to her dismay, she was being proven right.

It was a forty-five minute walk back to her house from the police station, and in the rain, felt much longer. As she walked, sloshing through the fresh puddles, Jessica cried. Her family's quiet, storybook existence was crumbling around her, again. Old and new memories sliced through her. She thought of her father holding her waist the first time she walked a rope thirty feet off the ground, then she thought of him languishing in the mud behind her own house, too afraid to even ask her for a simple cup of water. Her mind fumbled through arguments she could use to help him attain his release, but wondered who would be willing to consider them. She cursed the rain as it ruined her hair, and she knew that it brought with it another failed summer season for Clement, his dream of getting out from under his vocation would be another year, or two away, at best. She thought of the water she would be mopping up all night, the rain gushing through their porous roof, and assumed she would not have a chance to sleep. She grew more angry at Captain Honeywell's ultimatum, furious at the injustice of it and the clear violation of her rights. She couldn't bear to think of that busybody Bernice, except to imagine gouging her bulging eyes out in a fit of satisfying rage. She rolled through a list of towns in her mind that she enjoyed, and thought that maybe she could identify a new place to move and raise her family. Newport, she thought, was beautiful in the summer. Boston was so full of history and culture. She had once visited the Green Mountains in Vermont, and found the slower pace there so warm and inviting. She wondered how the family could afford to move, when they couldn't afford to stay. She missed her aunts, uncles and cousins and wondered if they were doing better than her father. She considered the fragile psyche of her two odd daughters, one caught up in her own steampunk version of reality, the other talking to witches and taking guidance from a handmade doll. But most of all, her heart ached for little Abby and her family. Jessica could not begin to imagine the pain Skip and Kitty were enduring, and she prayed that Abby was safe somewhere, unharmed and happy, her own amusing adventure story waiting to be told.

Jessica wiped the sloppy cascade of rain and tears from her cheeks as she reached the end of her driveway, and she looked up to the house. Her life was coming apart, and she no longer possessed the personal resolve to remain strong. And as she looked toward her home, her worst fears had started to come true, and if possible, she believed she felt her heart sink lower.

The Bradfords' home had been the victim of a vandal. Someone had shot-up the house with a paintball gun, and dozens of purple splotches now adorned the front and circled around the side. Clement stood alone in the driveway, his hands cupped on top of his head, surveying the damage in the rain.

"Jessica, what do you think?" Clement said, pointing to their home. "The three of us just got here a few minutes ago and discovered this."

"I don't know what to say." Jessica blurted, choking on her tears.

"Don't worry about it, Jess. I think they made their point. White houses are a dime a dozen around here, anyway. And you know, that's not a bad shade of purple. It's very regal. I plan to start painting this fall, right after the Labor Day rush."

Lucky materialized from the front door and stood on the deck with a can of purple spray paint in each hand. She looked back at her mother, expecting to be chastised for what they all knew she was about to do.

"Don't worry Mom, Dad said it was OK." Lucky switched on some music, and started creating, adding wide bows of purple paint, turning the ugly splotches into her own compelling, artistic rendition of a sea serpent.

"Mom! Mom! Do you see? Do you see? Look what the bad guys did to our house!" Prissy's pupils were dark and wide, and she hopped up and down. It surprised Jessica to see that Prissy wasn't upset, but rather excited.

"I'm going to take care of everything. The witch explained to Otto and me exactly how to put a curse on everybody on the island who messes with us." Abby said, smiling. "We will take care of everything. Now I know how to keep everybody safe."

Jessica glanced around at her peculiar family, and smiled. No, she was not about to give in to pressure, or give up on life like her father had done. Like it or not, this was her family, and they weren't going anywhere. This was a family that like the island itself, would endure.

Chapter 22

T his island," Horace stated to his personal servant with brash confidence, "will cement my fortune."

Horace Hunter tucked his solid gold watch into the front pocket of his gray herringbone vest and gazed with affection upon his masterpiece, the elegant International Inn. The newly constructed inn was a spectacular sight, and featured two hundred elegant guestrooms, each adorned with the finest European furnishings and linens, and a kitchen with Parisian trained chefs and a wait staff ready to pamper its guests with the highest level of hospitality and service. The bright sun reflecting off the freshly painted white wooden shingles was blinding, making the enormous structure appear temple-like, and fit only for the very rich or a head of state. There was no inn like it anywhere on the East Coast, and its somewhat sudden appearance erected on the beach of Manisses was not only a remarkable achievement, but a curiosity and, some would whisper, perhaps even a lark.

Horace Hunter had devoted the last ten years of his life, since the end of the War of the Rebellion, and exhausted his family's fortune, to the idea that Manisses could become a bustling vacation resort. Its sandy beaches, agreeable climate, and breathtaking views were as addictive as opium, and its convenient location nestled between the summer resorts of Newport and The Hamptons where the nouveau riche were already building personal, exorbitant summer cottages, guaranteed success -- at least in Horace's mind. All he needed now was for word to circulate of The International's existence, and he would attain his dream and recoup his investment ten times over.

So when word arrived by courier that President Grant was planning to visit the island, Horace worked his construction crew around the clock to ensure the inn would be complete and ready for occupancy upon the president's arrival. Horace Hunter had served with the Second Rhode Island Infantry during the war under General Ambrose Burnside, a personal friend of his father who was an investor in Burnside's rifle factory. Horace's military service was brief, lasting only a few weeks, as he broke his ankle stepping in a hole during the first charge of the rebellion's first battle, sending him back home to assume responsibility for the family's vast wealth and legacy. In Horace's eye, President Grant would always be General Grant -- the brave and brilliant field commander and defender of the Union. Horace spent many a night dreaming of the moment he would shake his hero's hand and offer him an obedient, patriotic salute.

But to make room for the grand hotel near the docks, Horace had to displace half the island's fleet of fishing boats -- an act that left him quite unpopular among the locals, devastating the island's fragile economy. After much protest, and after the fisherman had begrudgingly moved to the other side of the island, he razed their docks and supply shacks, including a believed to be inconsequential old house once owned by Mrs. Mercy Raymond, that once, for a few days a century and a half before, had sheltered and fed a cordial, yet notorious pirate.

President Grant's visit to Manisses was no arbitrary scheduling quirk. Two years earlier, Grant and his Republican supporters in Congress had approved funds to construct a grand lighthouse high above the bluffs on the same tract of land that saw so many Mohegan warriors perish centuries before. The islanders, as well as fisherman and a growing fleet of merchants, had grown weary of losing valuable cargo and lives to the ragged, dangerous coastline when lazy vessels strayed a bit too close or were washed in by unpredictable Atlantic storms. Now that construction of the state-of-the-art lighthouse was complete, one of the brightest on the Atlantic coast, the president was eager to have his name attached to it -- a savvy political move that wouldn't hurt if he chose to extend his ailing presidency into a third term.

"Shadrack, this inn may be the most beautiful sight I have ever seen." Horace said, delighted with both his work and himself. "One day, my name will be legendary here. This inn has transformed this island. Every street and every pond will one day bear my name, in my honor."

"Yes sir." Shadrack answered.

"Come, now Shadrack, why so quiet? You have lived here your whole life, have you not? Have you ever seen anything on this desolate rock so beautiful, so grand, or so elegant?"

"I suppose not, sir." Shadrack answered again.

"Perhaps... just perhaps, as I am a humble person by design you understand, it would not be too far a stretch to believe they would name this entire island after me. History, my good man, may be written by the victors, but it is immortalized by the visionaries."

"If you say so, sir."

"Today, this island is called Manisses. What is a Manisses, anyway..."

"Well, sir, Manisses is a native word that means..."

"Oh, it doesn't matter what it means, does it? Ask any of the current residents of this island and most of them won't be able to tell you who or what a Manisses is. Is it a plant? A person? Or maybe some foul disease! History has a short attention span, my good friend, that lasts a generation if you are lucky. Then all the facts, dates and moments are lost and whisked away like so much beach sand in a stiff wind."

Shadrack Brown was a native islander, part Manissean, part Black and part Dutch -- the descendant of a slave and an extraordinary, infamous survivor of the ill-fated *Princess Augusta* disaster, and one of the last remaining Manisseans. But without record-keeping beyond the notes scribbled in the margins of his family Bible, there could be no certainty, his heritage passed down to him through word of mouth and family legend. He lived alone in a shack, renovated and upgraded many times, by the great rocks off the cove where his great-grandparents had once made their home. Not only had Shadrack been born on the island a native resident, he had never set foot off the island at any point in his lifetime. Something within his genetic make-up left him deathly afraid of the seas, and no amount of bribery or coaxing could make him board a ship of any size or registry. He was content to forge a life as a servant, making a livable wage, on the island where he was born, and where he would one day pass away into anonymity, where he would proudly take his place and rejoice among the nameless specks of sand.

"Once the president arrives, we must be sure to fight the crowd and be first to welcome him to the island. I sent a wire to Washington inviting him to stay at the International free of charge, but I did not receive a response. The matters of state are quite complicated and important, so I expect it to be no more than a clerical oversight."

Shadrack nodded.

"And then, my good man, we must escort him directly to the International without delay. What an honor, and selling point, it will be to have a sitting president and national hero to be the first guest of our... Shadrack, what's wrong?"

Shadrack had turned his back on Horace and was looking out at the sea. On the horizon, he saw a ship, oddly bright and glowing, still visible even below a sky filled with a brilliant summer sun. He shivered, knowing from family legend what sighting a burning ship meant to the island.

"Shadrack, old boy it looks like you've seen a ghost!" Horace said elbowing him, attempting to raise him from his stupor. Shadrack extended his arm and hand and pointed to the east. Horace turned to look.

"Good lord!" Horace screamed.

As quickly as the burning ship had appeared, it was now gone, but in its place, a small fleet of fast-moving black ships were now cutting through the waves and heading for the island. Even at a distance, the crisp red, white and blue colors of the large American flags shone in vivid glory. President Grant and his entourage were entering the island's reticent waters as expected -- only he and his entourage were arriving several hours early.

With Shadrack in tow, Horace sprinted to the dock. He had planned to change into more formal attire, more suitable for a state visit, as his shirt and vest were soaked in sweat as a result of the unbearable August humidity. Horace looked up and down the shore, but there was no welcoming party on its way. He looked back toward the inn and the village, but the few town folk out that morning were content to ignore the incoming spectacle and just go about their regular business. When President Grant disembarked, there would be no crowd, no dignitaries, no band, and no welcoming party. Not even a reporter.

"He will think us philistines!" Horace agonized.

The ship dropped its anchor well off the coast to avoid the dangerous shallow surf, and the presidential crew lowered two oversized rowboats into the sea. The president stood erect upon one of the boat's seats like General Washington crossing the Delaware River ready to defeat the Hessians, and the crews rowed with a sharp military precision, delivering their nation's leader safely to the Manissean shore.

Grant hopped out of the boat landing knee deep in the surf, soaking his boots and trousers.

"Exhilarating!" Grant said. "My feet are killing me. These northern Atlantic waters are so much more refreshing than the sea in the south."

As Horace approached President Grant he froze, unsure if he should salute or extend his hand in friendship. Grant stopped on the beach and looked up at Horace, and Horace was surprised to see that his hero -- larger than life in his mind's eye for so many years -- was actually shorter and slimmer than himself. Grant shot him a quizzical look through his wrinkled, bearded face and stood his ground.

"And who the hell might you be?" Grant demanded.

"Horace Q. Hunter, sir. Second Rhode Island." He answered, finding the courage in his arm to execute a proper Union salute.

"Son, the war's over." Grant shot back.

"Yes sir, I know sir. I fought bravely for General Burnside at Bull Run, sir."

"Burnside, huh! Hell of a nice guy, but never should have been given command."

Grant looked up, then shot past Horace and Shadrack, as he and his advisors began their steady pace up the beach and toward the village, chatting among themselves. Included in the entourage was one of Rhode Island's United States senators, assigned by the Republican party to escort the president on his visit to the lighthouse. Horace had achieved his goal of becoming the first to welcome the president to the island, but he hadn't yet found an opportunity to invite him back to the inn.

"Welcome to Manisses, sir" Horace shouted from behind. Grant stopped and turned.

"Thank you, son. Glad to be here, but I think we covered that. Now... is there anything else? I've got a lighthouse waiting for me."

"Yes sir, I'm the proprietor of the new International Inn, just there on the beach," Horace said pointing toward his facility. "Please, sir. Do me the honor of staying the night as my guest and..."

"Thanks, son, but I've got to get myself to New York before nightfall. Looks like a hell of a place, that hotel. Best of luck with it."

Horace and Shadrack followed the entourage along the gravel road and up to the bluffs. Along the way, fisherman went about their daily tasks, weaving nets and repairing the hulls of their boats, and the farmers, preparing for the late summer harvests, sweated in their fields. Not one of them stopped working to greet the president even though they all knew who he was, the president tipping his hat to them as he passed. Grant stopped often to pluck handfuls of wild raspberries, popping them in his mouth, letting the purple juice run into and stain his graying beard.

"Reminds me of the berries around Vicksburg," Grant said. "Similar flavor, not as sweet. I fed a whole company off these damn things for a week."

As they walked, Horace couldn't take his eyes off Grant. The man appeared small, old, slightly hunched over, and walked with a limp, a mere shadow of the authoritative icon he had imagined him to be all these years. The newspapers had portrayed him to be so much larger and fierce, powerful and invincible. Yet the man before him was quiet and grim, and didn't look capable of defending himself from a single rebel soldier, never mind an entire Confederate army. Horace had dismissed the newspaper stories that talked about the corruption around Grant's administration and his ineffectiveness as a leader, considering them no more than political propaganda. Besides, Horace knew better. Grant was brilliant, and a hero.

"There it is, sir." The senator said, and the small entourage stopped to admire the stunning new lighthouse.

The structure was large and impressive, made entirely of red brick except for the marble foundation and a five-story gothic tower and glass lantern room, ringed in black iron and topped with a glistening copper roof. There wasn't a tree or shrub within a half mile, the building and property bordered by emerald green, ankle-high grass and shimmering white clover.

"The lens, sir, is the brightest in the states today," the senator began. "It was forged in Paris by some of the world's top craftsmen. The light itself burns with the intensity of ten thousand candles and..."

"Save your statistics, senator," Grant interrupted. "I must apologize. I have to admit they bore me. I will concede, however, that it's an impressive building, quite handsome, I will give it that. A fine place. But I was an infantry man, not a sailor, thank God. I wouldn't have lasted long in the military if I had to serve on the high seas. Turns my damn stomach."

"Sir, this lighthouse will save hundreds if not thousands of lives. These shores have seen at least three dozen shipwrecks in the last fifty years alone."

"A thousand lives? And I'll bet they're all Democrats." Grant walked over to the edge of the cliffs and peered down onto the rocky beach below, then glanced over at the lighthouse.

"And why did the engineers build it so close to the cliffs? Looks like it's going to fall off to me."

"The architects placed the light as high in the air and as close to the beach as it could, for maximum efficiency and distance. Erosion might one day claim the building, I suppose, but not for a hundred years or more... and sir, the election will be over by then."

The entourage chuckled, and Grant wiped his brow.

"And on that day, the lighthouse will join the bodies of many brave Mohegan warriors who were driven off and perished on those very cliffs." Shadrack interjected, uttering his first words since Grant had first set his boot on the island's beach.

The president had just lit a cigar, immediately plucking it from the corner of his mouth. He strolled over to Shadrack and squinted as he looked into his eyes. The color drained from Horace's face, fearing Shadrack's comments had somehow made Grant angry.

"What happened here?" Grant demanded of Shadrack. "Tell me."

Shadrack answered the president with pride and without hesitation.

"The native Manissean Indians of this island, of whom I consider to be some of my ancestors, were raided by a war party of Mohegan warriors here, centuries ago. The Manisseans fought with great bravery, defending their homes, and drove the invaders back to these cliffs where this lighthouse now sits. According to legend, those warriors were given a choice. They were told face starvation and perish, or take their chances jumping off the bluffs onto the jagged rocks below."

"I knew it," Grant answered, "I knew when I first set foot on this property we were setting foot on a battlefield." Grant addressed Shadrack, ignoring all the others. "Battlefields hold a particular sense about them, as if the pain and suffering of the inflicted has been absorbed into the soil and leeches out into the air. You can smell it, even taste it sometimes. Now on this field, I knew when we arrived it reeked of a siege. I knew it the moment I tasted those wild raspberries. I could taste their misery. Once you experience and are victimized by the hell of a siege, and feel the abject terror, the hopelessness and the constant starvation -- I know I would take my chances on those rocks, I assure you that."

"Yes, sir," Horace interrupted. "Like your battle at Vicksburg, it is a feeling of invincibility. It is the feeling of victory."

"No, son, war is a terrible thing, its fury to be unleashed only when it is needed to keep the peace. There are certainly winners and losers in battle, and war, but there is never victory."

"But sir, your victories over those rebel traitors saved our country!" Horace pleaded.

"Those rebel traitors are your countrymen, now. For our nation to thrive, you must make peace with that. OK, gentlemen, we've seen the damn thing. Now let's get ourselves to New York."

"Sir, please..." Horace begged. "Please follow me back to my inn. My staff is prepared to create the most tantalizing meal for each of you today. My butcher has slaughtered his best calf..."

"The sight of blood makes me ill," Grant said.

"If you can't stay this day, I understand. The important business of our country takes precedence. But stop and walk through for a visit, won't you? Just for a moment? Perhaps one day you could retire here, after your presidency. Perhaps this island would be the ideal place to one day pen your memoirs."

"My memoirs? Now you sound like that damn fool Mark Twain. That pest won't leave me alone, trying to get me to create a record of my thinking for posterity. Who the hell would want to hear about all that?"

Grant inhaled a cloud of thick, gray smoke from his cigar and held his breath, exhaling the smoke slowly into a tiny plume. He glanced up at the lighthouse, then off to the horizon. Grant waved his hand as if ordering a charge and the assembly beat a hasty retreat back along the same path toward the shore where they landed. Horace remained in tow, imploring the president to at least drop in at the inn, or take a brief detour for a quick stroll through his lobby. Shadrack turned away from the group and walked home, toward his cabin. The excitement and anticipation of the visit had been lost on him, and the day belonged to Horace and his hero anyway.

At home, Shadrack sat for a while in a rocking chair on his porch in the warm sunshine, staring across the field of high grass at the cloudless, aqua blue sky. The summer breeze was soothing and helped him think. He owned a solitary soul and had always been content to live alone, possessing no desire to take a wife or start a family. Yet, all the talk of history and legacy was eating at him. His ancestors' stories of life and survival were equally fascinating and inspiring, but as the last of his line, there was no one for him to share the stories or pass on the legacy. He thought of his great grandparents, Kattern and Hubbard, their unlikely marriage, and their even less likely survival. He felt the weight of their collective disappointment pressing on him, and wondered if his lack of an heir insulted the sacrifices they endured so he, himself, could thrive.

Shadrack went inside and opened a wooden trunk that sat at the foot of his bed. Inside was the family's collection of heirlooms, some sentimental, some valuable, and some both. He knelt before the trunk like it was an altar, and removed the items with great care, one at a time. On top were handmade quilts that his grandmother Mary had sewn during the Revolutionary War, then a wedding dress, beneath that was the family Bible -- a foot thick -- that recorded each birth, death, marriage, and transaction his small, poor family had ever made. Beneath the Bible was an ornate tin box tied in cowhide along with his father's old fiddle, and next to the fiddle lay Didier, a simple doll clutching a mortar and pestle believed to have been carved from the hull of the *Princess Augusta* itself. Shadrack brought all the items outside onto his porch and set them in a semi-circle around his rocking chair. This haphazard collection of things had intrinsic value and gave him great pleasure, as if they were his true family come to visit, representing over one hundred years of toil, love, sweat and gain. And though he believed it was too late in life for him to start a family and raise children of his own, he vowed to find a way to ensure that his family's history and its artifacts would survive years beyond the end of his own life. Whether he existed or not, they deserved immortality.

Shadrack reached down and picked up the fiddle. It felt foreign in his hands as he hadn't played it in years. After a quick attempt at tuning, he took a breath, tapped the toe of his shoe on the porch three times, and leaped into a rollicking rendition of a dance tune his father taught him, *Fire on the Mountain*, performing an impromptu concert on behalf of all the random pieces of his own unusual family legacy spread around his feet.

Deep in the thicket, Horace could hear the music. He had abandoned his attempt at cajoling President Grant into visiting his inn, and had been not-so-politely asked to get lost by both the president's chief of staff and the senator. He was now in search of his personal servant, teeming with anger, to find out why he had been so hastily abandoned.

Horace was not aware that Shadrack possessed such impressive musical talents, and the sound of the tune played with such passion and gusto, not only surprised him, but helped soothe his own bruised ego, and helped him even crack a bit of a smile. He waited unseen in the bushes for some time enjoying the music, eyes closed, letting his anger wane, and swaying his head back and forth to the festive song.

Though he was never to be believed, for the rest of his life, until he took his final breath upon his deathbed over forty years later, the details of Horace's story, explaining the bizarre scene he spied that day through the bushes, would not change.

He would swear that he watched through a holly bush as Shadrack fiddled, and a simple, wooden mortar and pestle danced a jig at his feet. And as he peered in closer, in shock and horror, he swore he saw a little doll smile, enjoying the show.

Chapter 23

"Wow, Winnie, that is some story."

Jessica sat upright, elbows perched on her dining room table, her chin resting on the backs of her hands, captivated by Winsome Q. Hunter's extraordinary tales of her famous great-great grandfather Horace, and his adventures on the island of Manisses a century and a half before.

"He even fought in the Civil War for the Second Rhode Island Infantry," Winnie explained, beaming with pride. "He fought in every major battle, from Bull Run all the way to Appomattox. He was severely wounded, and nearly lost his life. My grandmother said he personally killed a dozen Confederate soldiers, single-handed!"

"He was a true American war hero. I don't know of anyone like that in my family tree." Jessica admitted.

"After the war, when he built the International Inn, he did it in memory of his great friend, President Grant. The president came all the way from Washington just to see him, honor him for his military service, and stay at the hotel on the first night it opened."

"So what ever happened to the hotel?"

"Burned to the ground. No one ever could really explain who started the fire. Some folks said it was burned by the fishermen who were angry that their fleet had been relocated during the inn's construction, or that it was set ablaze in the night by his crazy, vindictive personal servant. Still, others insist it was doomed from the start anyway, haunted by an old island curse -- the construction workers said they saw a burning ship sailing on the horizon about once a week. The fisherman all knew that was a warning. They all knew what it meant. They knew what was coming."

"The curse! The burning ship! Prissy!"

"Don't get too excited, Jessica. It's a well-known tale, especially among the old folks here on the island. I heard the legend from my grandmother years before I ever came here. Nothing supernatural about that. You told me how much time the girls spend chatting with the old men down on Main Street. My guess is they pulled a fast one on her... impressionable minds... you know what I mean. I have staked my career on the belief that there is a logical explanation for everything."

Winnie's justification was plausible, and perhaps accurate. And with all the time Prissy and Abby played outdoors, it wouldn't be a stretch to believe the girls found that old well while out playing and exploring in the thicket all on their own.

Jessica relaxed and sipped at her cup.

"More tea, Winnie?" Jessica asked, topping off her dainty cup. Opportunities to entertain were few and far between, and even though Winnie was about to be contracted by the family as their personal attorney, Jessica found her interesting, and the two bonded.

"It's a wonder the Hunter name isn't plastered all over this island like so many of the other old family names we see every day." Jessica said.

"Oh no, old Horace would not have tolerated it. He was a very proud and modest man."

Winnie Hunter had only intended to visit the island for a few days that spring, attracted to the island by all the grand family stories and folklore, intent upon a brief, weekend getaway. Once she arrived, she fell in love with the island's charm and majesty and vowed never to leave, relocating her floundering law practice into a cramped two-room office over the noisy Captain Kidd Cafe -- which, unknown to Winnie, happened to be located in a building erected upon the ruins of the International Inn decades before. Winnie was able to sleep in the back room, and conduct business from the front. One of her first clients, the Dodge Family Trust, engaged her services to coordinate the treasure hunt at the old farm and help the estate muddle through the complicated zoning issues that were gumming up the town council meetings. Winnie was thrilled with all the new business. And thrilled she was busy enough that she could stay on the island, for a while -- hopefully for good.

And now with her father under arrest and half the island believing her family was a gang of killers, Jessica believed

Winnie's inexpensive legal representation seemed to be a wise investment. However, Jessica had no idea how she would ever pay Winnie's fees.

"I can't express to you, Winnie..." Jessica's eyes filled with tears, still battling her disorganized emotions and frayed nerves, "...how grateful I am that you have agreed to help us. I know my father had nothing to do with Abby's disappearance. He is nothing but a caring and loving man. But no one else seems to believe him."

"It would make my job easier, however, if he could perhaps be a teensy bit more cooperative with the police. I can do quite a lot to keep him here, on the island, but part of that will be up to him. As long as Abby's whereabouts remains a mystery, the police won't let him go anyway. They're going to use every trick in the book to keep him locked up. And between you and me, keeping him locked up in a cell right now might be the safest thing for him."

As the pair sipped their tea, they were interrupted by a sudden ruckus in the front yard. The loud angry voices they could hear indicated that there was some sort of argument in progress. Jessica and Winnie sprinted out the door and into the horrid weather, the rain still falling sideways in sheets, peppering and stinging their faces. In the yard, a young Manisses police officer stood behind his cruiser with one hand resting on his holster, and across the yard, Lucky stood facing him, brandishing a birch fireplace log like a sword.

"Stay away from my house, you pervert!" Lucky screamed as the officer stood his ground. "Or I swear I'll bust this over your pointed little head!"

"Lucky! What's wrong with you!" Jessica screamed and pleaded through the downpour. "Put that down! Have you lost your mind?"

"This pervert was looking in the bathroom window at me!" Lucky shouted. "And I'm going to mess up his face!"

In an effort to protect her newest client, Winnie charged into the muddy front yard to jump between them, caught her heel in the turf, and landed face first with an embarrassing thud into the squishy mud, a shoe flying in one direction, her prescription reading glasses soaring off in the other. Winnie slammed the ground with such force, both Lucky and the officer momentarily forgot about their dispute, and ran to her aid, assuming her to be injured. Winnie moaned and laid on the lawn for what seemed like an eternity, until Jessica rolled her over, and the driving rain rinsed the grass and muck off her pale face.

"Officer," Winnie gurgled, dirt and a tuft of clover protruding from between her two front teeth. "Unless you have a warrant, you have no business on this property. I am the attorney representing this family, so please relay my name to your captain. If you have a need to speak to any member of this family, please contact me first." Winnie reached into her pocket and produced a small, soggy square of cardboard bearing her phone number. The officer snatched it from her hand, and walked away in disgust. In the window above them, hanging on every dramatic moment, Prissy and Otto peered down on the scene from behind her bedroom curtain.

Jessica and Lucky helped Winnie to her feet, and escorted her back into the house out of the storm. Winnie limped into the dining room, her tan polyester suit now drenched and filthy. Jessica was half Winnie's size, but was able to rummage around in Clement's magic closet until she found an assistant's gown and a black cape for her to wrap around herself while her suit dried out.

As Winnie limped off to the bathroom to change and clean herself up, Jessica grabbed Lucky by the back of her neck and spun her around. Jessica's teeth were clenched and her face was purple with rage, and told Lucky everything she needed to know about what was coming next.

"Lucretia! What the hell is wrong with you!"

"Me? I haven't done anything wrong. That creep was peeping in our windows, what the hell was I supposed to do?"

"Maybe you would come get me? Your mother? Maybe you wouldn't decide to take matters into your own hands all the time? My God, Lucretia, your grandfather is in jail. Abby's still missing and the police are jumpy. They're grasping at any excuse they can to cause us trouble. You might have left here on a stretcher with a bullet in your skull."

"Spare me the drama, OK Mom? That cop was just one of Vance's perverted friends. He was out looking for a cheap thrill."

"From this moment on, until I tell you any different, I don't want you leaving this house, not even to step outside on the deck. I need to keep you girls safe. Do you understand me?"

"Oh, I understand, but don't bet your life on it. I'll come and go as I please, when I please. The safest place for me to be right now is anywhere on this island except here. Isn't this the house that gets shot up by paintball guns, and stalked by creepy people like Bernice Cowan and that cop? If you're trying to keep me and Prissy safe, you're doing a pretty lousy job."

"You will mind me young lady! Or I will..."

"Or you will what. Take away all my friends? Move me to some deserted island? Lock me up in my room until I'm old and gray? Haven't you done all that already? And tell me, how's that working for you?"

Lucky shoved Jessica aside and stormed up the stairs to her room, leaping over Prissy and Otto who were mesmerized, hanging on every word of the argument like they were watching the movie of the week. Jessica trailed right behind her, in hot pursuit.

When Jessica reached Lucky's room, she expected to find the door locked, and was surprised to find the door ajar. She pushed it open slowly. Inside, Lucky's giant clock sounded the top of the hour, startling her. She looked in at Lucky laying flat on her bed staring up at the chandelier hanging from her ceiling. The chandelier was exquisite, found abandoned at a junk sale and refurbished entirely by Lucky's talented hand and vision, recreating and attaching its missing components with all the skill of a seasoned craftsman.

"Leave me alone, Mom."

"I can't Lucky. I think you know that. We need to talk this out."

"So talk. But just because you're talking, don't expect me to agree with you."

"Lucky, things are tough right now. I know that. Things couldn't be any more stressful around here if we tried. But we need to stay together on this. Together, we are stronger. Your grandfather is in trouble, and we need to do everything we can to help him. We need to do what's best for the family."

"What's best for the family? Is that what we're doing? When have we ever done that before? It sounds to me like everything we do around here is what's good for Clement and Jessica."

"Lucky, that's not fair."

"Oh isn't it? I can't think of a single important decision this family ever made that was in my best interests. You treat me like I'm no more than the family pet."

"Everything your father and I do is in your best interest."

"So you lied to Hannah's mom and told her she was dead, just for me? Is that what happened in Eastbury? Thank you so much for that. Remind me to send you a card."

Lucky's words tore through Jessica's heart like a hot knife. The fiasco with Hannah and the Eastbury police was a grave mistake that they knew hit Lucky the hardest. Clement and Jessica both wished they could go back and right the wrong, change the past, make peace with everyone, and re-write history. But what was done was done, and as much as it pained them, they had to let their mistakes go and leave them behind.

"Lucky, I'm sorry. You know what happened as well as I. You know that we didn't mean for things to end up that way. It was all a mistake. But we have to move on. We can't change history."

"Oh yes. Yes I can change history. Look around my room right now. What do you see? I reject your history, and I choose to follow a record that appeals to my own sensibilities. Your world is plastic and impersonal, it's beige and hurtful, and it lacks all imagination. Mine borrows from all the great ages throughout antiquity -- the Victorians, the Edwardians, even from the Chinese and the Mayans -- and I can pick and choose the best parts from all those eras and societies and let them inspire my daily views and actions. If I choose to weld artifacts from different ages and eras together to make them fit my inspirations, then so be it. I can re-use whatever I need, and have nothing leftover to be swept aside or left behind in history's trash can. My history is fluid, alive and can change. It lives and breathes and evolves. Yours is stale and apocalyptic. It chokes on itself. It's like a ball and chain you wear around your neck everywhere you go that defines who you are and where you came from. Once a slave, always a slave. Once a king always a king. Once a clown, always a clown. It nauseates me. I refuse to be a slave to your vision of my past. I will let freedom define my future."

Jessica's heart pounded, and she paused to select her words with care before she spoke again. She had always underestimated how much pain Lucky had endured, and how much pain she still carried. She also thought of Lucky's namesake, her beloved friend Lucretia, and recognized her old traits of tenacity and stubbornness successfully channeled and now manifesting themselves in the fragile, eccentric soul of her own daughter.

Jessica paced around her daughter's room, scanning her artistic wonders, thinking of so many things she could say, and rejecting them all. Words didn't matter right now. She wanted nothing more than to reach out and hold Lucky, absorb her pain, and become part of her world once again, even if it was a foreign world she failed to understand.

Jessica decided there was only one thing that she could say to Lucky that might reach her, that might travel through from Jessica's realm into hers, that might ignite a spark within her heart that would make things matter to her again, and that she would still understand.

"Lucky, listen to me. Prissy still loves you."

Chapter 24

The island was drowning in chaos.

After two days of frantic searching, the worry that hovered in the stomachs of the islanders for Abby's safe return had transformed from a nervous flutter into a searing pain. The longer she remained missing, the more likely something horrific had occurred, and the less likely that once she was found, she would be found unharmed. No one wanted to admit it, but in the back of everyone's mind, there was a small voice asking if she would be found alive at all.

As was the case centuries earlier with the tragedy of the *Princess Augusta*, it was the fishermen who were the first to mobilize their forces on the island. Although the fleet was a mere shadow of the power it was at its height, when Horace Hunter shoved them aside to introduce tourism to the isle, the gritty, hard working men of the fleet still believed the island belonged to them and remained under their protection. Dozens of fishing boats, trawlers, yachts, and even some of the fancy charters, circled the island the minute she disappeared, casting out a protective net intended to stop any vessel thinking of escape. If a boat detained and in question had little Abby on board, the local police hoped they would receive word and reach the fishermen before the suspects had the honor of being added to someone's special bucket of chum.

And though the fishermen had provided their whole-hearted cooperation, the weather had not. In the gale and the relentless waves that pounded the island through the storm, the smaller vessels were being tossed around like Abby's favorite bath toys, and really had no business venturing from the safety of the inner harbor to begin with. Much of the crews' time was invested in keeping the vessels from becoming swamped, and though appreciated, their efforts had no practical effect on the search.

The gusty winds also prevented any effective hunt by air. The island's minimal fleet of Cessnas and Piper Cubs, mostly pleasure craft for the island's wealthy, were overmatched and wisely grounded. The police believed that had they taken flight, even in the best conditions, they would have caused more problems than they would have solved buzzing the tiny island, startling residents and wouldn't have been effective locating a four-foot tall little girl anyway.

The best and only method available to volunteers looking to help was to serve as a foot soldier in the ground search. Every inch of the Bradfords' property had been covered, but there were over a hundred other properties like it dotting the hills and dales of the island. Captain Honeywell put out a request to all officers, emergency medical technicians, firemen and other public servants, to assemble at the town hall to organize. Honeywell had supervised countless emergency management drills in the past, figuring one day they would be put into practice following a major hurricane. He considered it a personal nightmare that he had to deploy his forces to locate a little girl.

Each of the volunteers brought their own boots and raingear, and they were split into smaller groups and issued flashlights, two-way radios, and peanut butter sandwiches, packed overnight by a third-shift effort put forth by the fire department's ladies' auxiliary.

"Clement, why don't you go home?" Honeywell suggested. "I don't think your involvement here will be helpful."

"Captain, I'm just here to help... like everyone else."

A gaggle of volunteers assembled around him. Clement knew he wasn't welcome and he eyed the group with suspicion, just as they eyed him back. The longer Abby remained missing, the more people convinced themselves Clement's family had to be at the root of the problem.

"Captain, let him come with me." Skip offered. "I think Vance and I should head over and have a look around the Dodge barn one more time."

"With all due respect Skip, it might be best if you went home, too, and stayed inside with your wife." Honeywell added.

"Kitty is at the house with some of the women from the auxiliary. They're looking after things and keeping her busy, and if there's any news, she'll call me right away. There isn't anything I can do there except go out of my mind. I have to be out here looking, Captain. I don't have any other choice."

Honeywell sighed, and waved Clement over to stand with Vance and Skip.

"We went over every inch of the Dodge property again yesterday. If you think the three of you can do anything productive out there, then fine, go ahead. Please, just stay out of trouble." Honeywell tossed them a waterproof plastic bag packed with sandwiches, and the three stepped out the door and into the uncooperative weather.

For such a small island, it felt as vast as a continent to Clement when every inch of it had to be explored and scrutinized. As they slogged through the puddles and the knee high wet grass, he imagined what Manisses must have looked like when the Indians lived here and the settlers first landed, a great canopy of trees covering it from coast to coast. And he imagined how it looked after the farmers and fisherman were through with it, cutting all the available trees for wood, turning the tree-covered island into rolling farmland. He then considered how the island's landscape had been altered again later, by modern tourists, builders and landowners, planting foreign shrubs and introducing exotic new species.

A low flying Coast Guard helicopter buzzed them and instinct caused the three men to duck, and then look up.

"They're not out here to help us," Skip surmised. "I'm guessing one of those fishing boats out there went under."

And as they reached the barn, they could hear several barking dogs, and coming down the road at them was Councilman Dorry. Five of his best hunting dogs were leashed together and were pulling him toward them. Dorry had the black leather leashes wrapped up his forearm to his elbow. It was hard to tell who was leading who.

"They'll find her. Don't you worry," Dorry shouted, winking as they charged by.

"Thanks, Gavin!" Skip had just enough time to offer a friendly wave back as the dogs disappeared around the corner.

"Those are some beautiful dogs he's got there," Clement stated, "I know he's invested a lot of money in those animals, but they're hunting dogs, not bloodhounds. So what's the point?"

"He wants to feel like he's helping, that's all." Skip answered. "It won't do any harm. Plus, he'll hook up with Smyth and they'll look darn good searching, too. I'll bet they have the *Times* photographer follow them around all afternoon. Don't forget that they're both up for re-election this fall."

The excavation site at the Dodge property resembled a recent but abandoned battlefield. Piles of fresh black earth, tools and debris were scattered as far as the eye could see. Even where the ground was flat, the earth was soft where it had been repeatedly overturned, and the three men took turns sinking into the mud as they struggled to trudge through it. The three took refuge inside the barn itself, as there was still enough of the roof remaining to protect them from most of the rain, and enough of the wall to provide a modest windbreak. Clement sat on a blackened, mushy hay bale to rest, while Vance stared off across the field. Vance's signature black eye make-up had been washed away by the rain, and Clement believed that if he took off his dog collar, he might almost look human.

"I think each of us should cover a third of this field to start." Clement began. "Things are a mess out there, but we want to keep our eyes peeled for anything that might appear unusual." Clement discovered he was talking into empty space. Vance wasn't listening, and Skip had wandered off to gather up a shovel. Clement watched as Skip stood in the rain, holding the shovel high overhead, then driving it down into the ground, flipping over spade after spade of heavy loam.

"Skip, what are you doing?"

"I bought ten of these squares from that lawyer, and haven't found anything outside of a rusty old nail and a beer can. I know there is more to find out here. I just know it."

"We need to be looking for Abby right now, Skip. You can look for your treasure later."

"My luck is changing, Clem. I can feel it. Today's the day I'll find something valuable out here. I know I will."

Skip was digging with a fury, as if he was in a desperate race to locate the center of the earth. Clement had been in awe of

Skip's steely composure all morning, admiring his strength and focus in the wake of such a personal and unnerving crisis. Clement knew that if he found himself in the same position, there would be no doubt -- he would be reduced to a mass of blubbering jelly. Now he realized that Skip's outer strength and will had been an illusion from the start. Skip was holding in an emotional torrent, and there were signs that he was beginning to let it leak out. And Clement didn't blame him.

"Go ahead and dig, Skip. Vance and I will search the area." Clement offered, trying to give Skip his space and help retain his pride and dignity.

"You think I'm crazy, don't you Clem? You don't think I'll find anything here. But I will. You two stand there and just watch this!" Skip was hyperventilating, and digging faster. Rain and sweat poured from his nose. Mud flew in various directions.

"Really, Skip, it's OK. You don't have to show me anything."

"You don't understand, Clem! You can't understand!" Skip stopped digging and threw his shovel in a fit of rage, bouncing it off the side of the barn, liberating a shingle from its rusty nail. Skip fell to his hands and knees and cried out in piercing agony, cursing his luck, cursing his life and begging for the life and safe return of his daughter.

Clement allowed Skip to wail and sob in the mud for a good long time. He felt powerless, and couldn't think of anything to do that might ease Skip's grief. Then, after Skip burned out his energy, Clement collected him from the rainy field and brought him back inside the barn to dry out and re-center his thoughts. Skip sat against the barn wall, massaged his own forehead, stared at the ground, and mumbled to himself. He was now just a shell of the confident, wise-cracking guy Clement had worked to avoid around town. It was as if he had lost a friend, even if he hadn't liked him very much, and it upset him. He considered that whether Abby was found or not, Skip would never be the same.

Clement, Skip and Vance sat for an hour in the dilapidated barn in silence as the rain, in various intensities, pummeled the roof and echoed around them like millions of tiny war drums. The rasping sound of a foghorn in the distance bellowed every ten minutes, the only reminder that they were on an island at all.

"Maybe the Captain was right, Skip. Maybe you'd be best at home with Kitty. There's nothing out here to see."

"I can't go home. I already told you that. I have to keep looking. I can't look Kitty in the eye until I find out exactly what happened to our daughter."

"Is anyone going to eat those sandwiches?" Vance asked, uttering his first complete sentence of the day.

"Eat them," Clement answered tossing the bag at Vance's feet like he was one of Dorry's hounds. "Did you know, Prissy has a doll with more depth of character than you have?"

Vance shook his head, said nothing and bit into a peanut butter sandwich.

"C'mon Skip, let's walk back to town and see what Honeywell has found out. Maybe he has news, or has come up with a new lead."

Skip said nothing, but stood and gathered his belongings together. Then the three men stepped outside where the rain, at least for the moment, had stopped falling. Clement looked to the clouds and believed they might even be thinning.

For most of the stroll back, Clement enjoyed a one-sided conversation as he poked through the vegetation along the side of the road with a walking stick, staying loyal to his assigned duty. And though he addressed both Vance and Skip equally, they either didn't possess the motivation -- or intelligence -- to respond. Clement rambled on about the fall elections, the price of groceries on the island, a new novel he just checked out of the Manisses Free Library, and money-saving renovations he planned for the leaking roof of his house. The best response he could muster from either of his companions was an occasional head nod or a grunt.

After Clement grew tired of hearing himself talk, he went quiet. Their boots sloshing through the roadside puddles provided the only distraction.

"Clem, can I ask you a question?" Skip asked, breaking the long uncomfortable quiet.

"Of course."

I've been thinking. What if we never find Abby?"

Clement recoiled at the question.

"You don't need to think about that right now. Just stay positive."

"No, I mean it. What if we don't find her? Or worse, what if she's dead?"

Skip's words struck hard, and he flinched. And though Clement had thought about the same eventuality, the sound of the words spoken aloud in plain English was disquieting. But he did not want to be the one to reinforce his negativity, and vowed to stay positive.

"We'll find her. I know we will."

"But that's what I'm getting at. How do you know we'll find her? You keep saying that. In fact, you've been saying it all day long. Do you sense it, like some kind of ESP thing? Is it something in the air? Do you know already?"

"I don't know any more than you do. Since she's your daughter, maybe I can just speak with less emotion, and more objectivity."

"You know I've never believed all that hocus-pocus, talking to ghosts nonsense you dish out back at your parlor. It's all a joke, right? All for fun? But the people that come to see you, they believe. They believe every word of it. I've seen them coming back to your office over and over again, season after season, throwing down their hard earned cash, just to chat it up with old Aunt Irma and Uncle Giuseppe one last time. So I started thinking, what is it in what you do that gives them so much confidence?" Skip paused and stopped walking. "So that's my question, can you make me believe?"

"Skip, I don't understand. You're not making any sense."

"Why don't we go back to your office? We'll hold hands, chant, and do whatever it is that makes those folks believe in your channeling abilities. Then convince me my daughter is still out there. And if you don't believe she's still alive, then convince me she's happy. I need to believe it, Clem. Unleash whatever it is you do and whatever powers you have. Help me find my little girl."

Clement didn't need to believe in déjà vu, he was living it. His thoughts rolled back to Eastbury and the search for Hannah Griswold, and to his gut wrenching final session with Hannah's mother, Maria. Everything about that case was wrong, and he had let money, ambition and pride shade the delicate balance in his conscience between what was right and what was wrong. Here in front of him, to any believer in the powers of mysticism and spirituality, was another opportunity to help a friend and direct a search party to a lost little girl. It was not a road Clement would so easily follow again.

"I can't do that Skip."

"Why not? Is it the money? Name your price. I'll pay for that new roof of yours. In fact, I'll give you my whole damned house!"

"It's not the money, Skip. It's because it's just not right."

"Before you came down to the police station this morning, the other guys decided they weren't going to let you in the door. They didn't want to just run you off either, they wanted to scare you. They wanted to put the fear of God in you. Some of them think what you do is evil. They think you and your wife are responsible for this, and you know that. They don't know how, but that's what they think, and you understand how mob mentality can be. It's unyielding. There was only one voice in that room that said anything on your behalf. You know who it was? Do you? It was me, Clem. I defended you. I told them all that you didn't have anything to do with this mess, and that Kitty and I believed you had a kind heart. I told them that Kitty said all you had to do was watch how happy and well-adjusted Prissy was, and that's all you needed to know about the integrity of Prissy's parents."

"So you asked me to join your group this morning so I would lead you to Abby, didn't you? It had nothing to do with me, and everything to do with what you perceive to be my abilities as a spiritualist."

"I just thought that if that black magic stuff was true, you would have the best chance of finding her. If it wasn't true, well then, you'd be in the same boat as the rest of us. I need to be there, for Abby's sake, when she is found."

The group had reached the edge of town, and Clement was trying to decide how insulted he should feel. He didn't like the feeling of being used, or the feeling of being cheated, either. He looked out toward the docks and saw that a bright blue and yellow police speed boat had arrived in the harbor. Several of the other groups in the search party had returned ahead of them, and were standing in a circle, chatting, almost cheerful.

"What's going on?" Skip asked. "Did you find Abby?"

"No Skip, I'm sorry... not yet." Honeywell answered. But I have a small bit of good news. My requests to the State Police for immediate emergency support were granted, and they sent down one of our country's foremost experts in leading searches and finding missing children. He's taking over the investigation."

Clement gazed in horror at the familiar, tall, square-jawed man leaning against the doorframe.

"Skip, please let me introduce you to Detective Forrest Mayweather!"

Chapter 25

Bernice Cowan was a true island original. Born Bernice Varnum Brown, she was the difficult daughter of an established, struggling island dairy farmer whose roots on the island went back centuries. It didn't take long for Bernice's enterprising father to figure out that if she was ever to marry, he would need to arrange it, which he did -- to Luther Cowan, the son of the owner of the island's only hardware store. The union of the dim-witted Luther to the odious Bernice bound two old, established island families together, and provided Bernice both the lineage and the license to terrorize everyone as she saw fit.

And what made Bernice even more repulsive was her devotion to the two small businesses she owned and operated herself. One, the island's largest moped rental agency, provided throngs of tourists with the most efficient torture apparatus ever invented; a vehicle designed to torment year-round island residents by buzzing in and out of traffic, rolling through exotic flower beds and wheeling over manicured lawns. And if that wasn't enough, her part-time vacation home rental agency specialized in attracting legions of students and partiers to rent out oversized, beachfront properties, inviting public drunkenness, loud music and a colorful hodgepodge of disorderly behavior.

With her pudgy hands immersed in three different enterprises, as well as her connection to two rich family legacies, she had no need to ever run for public office. Not only did everyone on the island know who she was, she already considered herself The Lady, and considered the island Her Manor.

About once each week, Bernice would indulge her exaggerated sense of self importance and visit Water Street to check up on her obedient subjects. The town merchants knew that it was easier to nod and smile than argue with Bernice over her trivial grievances, otherwise they would risk the peril of her never-ending and annoying wrath. She would float in and out of shop after shop like a big blue, wind-driven schooner, stopping at each port to hem, haw and exert her influence upon those foolhardy enough to not willingly submit. At the grocer, she might complain about a leaky soda machine, prompting a call to the building department. At the ice cream shop, she might blow in and threaten to send a snapshot of a dirty countertop to the health inspector. Then at the liquor store, she would tongue-lash the clerk for failing to ask for her identification, even though it was quite clear she was at least thirty years over the legal drinking age. Acknowledgment of her regal superiority was all that was required to avoid her entanglements, and survive unscathed for another week.

When passing Clement's boutique, to both Jessica and Clement's delight, the schooner Bernice would give a wide berth. There was something about the aura of the place that spooked her, whether real or imagined, and she refused to place either of her round, 4E flat shoes through the door.

Jessica had left her daughters at home to run a few quick errands in town. With all the rain, Jessica feared the office might be leaking too, and with her daughters trapped in the house for so long, the food supply was running perilously thin. Jessica left strict instructions for the girls to stay inside with the doors locked until she returned, since with Abby's whereabouts still undetermined, the possibility there was a psychopath on the loose was quite real. The girls were best to remain safe and secure under lock and key.

Though she was difficult to miss, Jessica didn't notice Bernice when she first walked into the grocery store, and she plowed into her with a squishy thud as she darted around the corner of the produce aisle, not watching where she was going, her mind wandering through her own thicket of worries.

"Oh, my! Mrs. Bradford!" Bernice shouted, overreacting to the minimal physical contact. "Have we lost our ability to fly?"

"I am so, so sorry, Bernice." Jessica said, confounded by her continuing rotten luck, and trying to extract herself from the embarrassing situation with what little grace she could muster. "It was an accident. I was distracted. Please, don't be offended."

"Offended? Goodness, me no. Accidents do happen… accidents, mishaps, misunderstandings… why, I have recently learned that they happen every day. Don't they?"

"Thank you for understanding." Jessica could feel her revulsion for the woman simmering inside her, and began to back away from Bernice's sarcasm, in the direction of the cashier and the door.

"And Mrs. Bradford… you have heard the wonderful news, have you not? Our good police captain has ushered in a top-level investigator of missing children to help find that sweet little Payne girl. He's supposed to be on the case right now, pawing over the evidence. I expect we'll have an answer to this tragedy at any moment."

"That is wonderful news," Jessica answered with genuine enthusiasm.

"But we both know what he's going to find, don't we?" Bernice mocked. "His name is Mayweather. There was a very nice family of Mayweathers who once owned the property next to the Southeast Light. I will have to check and see if he is of the same upstanding pedigree."

Jessica felt faint as her simmering blood turned stone cold. There was no question that it was the same Mayweather who tormented her family in Eastbury. It had to be. Jessica's thoughts flashed to images of her father sitting in the holding cell. Old Carl didn't much like any police officer, and she already knew exactly what he thought of the devious Detective Mayweather. She needed to get a message to Winnie right away, before Mayweather decided to interrogate the only suspect in custody. And she needed to find Clement.

Back at the Bradfords' home, things were far less exciting. Prissy and Otto stared out through the rain-streamed glass of her bedroom window into the storm. From her room, Prissy could see the ocean, but it was blurred through the spray and foggy mist.

"Lucky!" Prissy shouted, running through the hallway.

"What do you want?" Lucky answered through her bedroom door, in her familiar leave-me-alone tone.

"We need to go outside!" Prissy demanded.

"Why? It's raining."

"We need to go down to the beach. It's important!"

"Mom said we have to stay locked inside."

"Yea, I know. But that's what you're for. You never listen to what Mom says."

Lucky paused.

"OK. Go get your raincoat."

Lucky and Prissy walked through the yard, past the great boulders, and strolled down the hill to the beach. Though the storm appeared to be clearing, the waves remained violent, crashing on the stones and sending a salty spray up into their eyes. Prissy ran ahead, hopping from one slippery seaweed-covered stone to the next, in a risky game of island hopscotch, waiting for her sneakers to lose their grip and send her crashing face first into the beach.

"You're going to break your neck." Lucky warned.

"I do this all the time." Prissy insisted

"Is this what we came down here to do?"

"No. I needed to see something for myself. It was hard to see from my bedroom window."

"See what?"

Prissy stopped stone hopping and placed her fists on her hips and stared out to sea.

"I wanted to see if the burning ship was still here."

Lucky rolled her eyes and sighed, and looked out to the horizon standing alongside her concerned sister.

"I don't see any burning ships, so let's go back to the house."

"Wait a minute. I want to be sure."

"Prissy, that whole burning ship thing is just a legend. It's just a story. There isn't any real ship out there. It's something some old lady made up hundreds of years ago to explain her bad luck."

"No, Lucky it's real. I saw the ship myself. And so did Otto."

Otto agreed.

"Well if you want to go ahead and think that it's out there, that's fine. I don't care."

"But it is real! The witch says that it brings bad luck to the island. If it goes away, the bad luck goes away. If we don't see the ship anymore, maybe that means they'll find Abby today and she'll be OK."

Lucky could feel Prissy's worry radiating from her in waves, and it unnerved her. History's most annoying personality trait was its capacity to repeat itself. Prissy was now heading down the same emotionally treacherous path that she had once travelled back in Eastbury, after Hannah went missing, and she knew there was no turning her around. Lucky searched for any morsel of advice she could share that would make it easier on her, and help calm her confused, young nerves.

"Abby will be alright, don't worry." Lucky said, not believing her own words, annoyed she couldn't find something more intelligent and effective to say that would help her sister.

"I think you're right. The ship is gone. The witch says..."

"You know, Prissy, it might be better if you didn't talk about that witch for a while. People think it's a little weird."

Prissy spun her head around as if it was on a pivot.

"So you don't believe me either?" Prissy shouted. "And people think you're pretty weird too, you know!"

"Listen to me Prissy, Grandpa is in a ton of trouble, mostly because of me. And Mom and Dad are going nuts. I don't want to see you get in any trouble, either. Things are crazy right now. Everybody on this island just needs to chill."

Prissy frowned and kicked at the sand and blobs of dead maroon seaweed the storm had thrown on shore. She didn't like Lucky's advice, and had hoped she would be more understanding and supportive. But as young as she was, she also knew what motivated her older sister. The gentle art of manipulation was a skill born unto the souls of little sisters for thousands of years, and knowing the precise moment to unleash it was an art in its truest form.

"Lucky, do you want to see where the old witch used to live?"

Lucky was intrigued, and powerless to resist.

The pair trudged back up the hill past the great stones to the frog pond, where over two centuries earlier, Kattern and Hubbard made their home, and where Shadrack played his fiddle. The fields Hubbard cleared to grow their vegetables and Kattern's herbs had long overgrown, and were now choked with dense shrubs and tall weeds. The area in the corner by the stone wall where Prissy had revealed the old well was the only spot that appeared disturbed, decorated by footprints in the black loam and uprooted vegetation created by Abby's search party. Prissy stood and scanned the area like a docent preparing a presentation to a group of students. Lucky waited, unable to imagine what she had come up with this time.

"The witch and her husband had a well, and it was back by the stone walls."

"Yes, I know. You already told us all that."

"That stone wall there that leads up to it isn't just a stone wall; it was part of the wall to their kitchen. They moved the house because they wanted the well to be as close to their house as possible. The witch's' first house was in the pond."

"The witch lived in the pond?"

"No, stupid! They moved the house when they needed a place to make a pond. They wanted a pond because they had a bunch of thirsty goats. The witch wanted to raise goats to make chccsc. So thcy put the pond there where all the Indians were, and moved the house next to the well."

"Indians lived with the witch?"

"No, the Indians were dead. That's why they are under the pond, silly!"

"Prissy, you are totally freaking me out right now."

With her arms wrapped around her sides, Lucky strolled to where Prissy had pointed out the house. With the toe of her black boot, Lucky kicked at the ground. As she followed the jagged stones along the ground with her eyes, she could see they formed somewhat of a straight line through the undergrowth, a line that bent at four perfect angles into a square. It was obvious to her now that many years ago, a house very well could have stood here on this property. A small brown and green frog jumped into the pond behind her breaking the silence, making a splash and causing the usually stoic Lucky to emit a piercing shriek.

"OK, I admit it. I'm spooked. And we need to go back inside before Mom gets home and kills us." Lucky said. "I want to get back in my room where it's safe."

"Why are you always in your room, and not outside? I hate being locked up inside all day."

"I don't know. Maybe I feel like I can control things better in there, and work on my projects."

"I hate art." Prissy said with confidence. "It's stupid."

"Art is not stupid!" Lucky shot back. "What do you know about art? Art is beautiful. It can be a reflection of your soul, or your feelings. It can represent the world around you as you see it, from deep inside your imagination."

"And art keeps you from playing with me."

Lucky paused, and looked around at the rocks scattered along the ground near the stone wall. The stones were of a variety of sizes, all carried up from the beach by someone generations before, and all shaped and carved flat and soft by thousands of years of tides, wind and the persistent lapping of the waves. Lucky reached down and picked up a few as if weighing them, rubbed them clean, then laid them out on top of the flattest rock on top of the stone wall.

"Prissy, come over here and help me. Another thing that art can do is preserve a memory."

Lucky placed a large, smooth flat stone on the wall, then balanced another upon it. With great care, Prissy would select other stones and Lucky would stack and balance them on top of each other. On the first few attempts, the pile came crashing down, and Lucky would have to start over again. After some time, Prissy helped balance the stones, too, and the girls worked for an hour selecting and balancing them in ideal positions. Lucky showed her how by selecting rocks with certain colors or features, you could create pretty patterns within the primitive sculpture, and how the sculpture would look different from various angles, giving off differing effects. Once finished, the impromptu sculpture featuring the girls' balancing stones stood three feet tall.

"A stack of rocks like this is called a cairn. In olden times, Indians used to put these in the woods. Old farmers would put them in their fields, too. They didn't have street signs like we have today, so the cairn might tell them that this was a place where food was stored, or it would be a marker telling a traveler which direction to go, or it might help identify a grave, or a very special, even sacred, place."

Prissy nodded, captivated by Lucky's explanation.

"This cairn sculpture we just made -- this little piece of art -- commemorates our walk on the beach today." Lucky declared. "Most people who walk by this pile of rocks won't even notice them. A few other people might think it's strange that someone went to the trouble to stack them up in the first place. But whenever you or I walk by this pile, from now on, we will remember this afternoon that we spent together."

"They're just like the great, giant rocks next to the beach. I wonder what those rocks help people remember?" Prissy asked.

"The difference is nature placed those rocks like that. We created this pile ourselves."

"But our cairn is just sitting there. Shouldn't we take it home? What if somebody knocks them over!"

"So let them knock them over, or even steal them. It doesn't matter. They can't change the fact that we already did it once. We will then have the choice of rebuilding it, or just building another one somewhere else."

"Uh, oh..."

As Prissy and Lucky stood and examined their handiwork, they both heard Jessica's car screaming up the driveway of the house off in the distance. Prissy started to panic; she wasn't used to being in this sort of trouble.

"Don't worry about anything." Lucky said, easing her fears. "We can get in the house through the basement window around back behind the rhododendron."

"But that window is broken and it doesn't open!"

"Oh yea? That's what you think. Then from the basement, we can go up the back staircase and get into my room before Mom catches us."

As the girls ran at full gallop toward the house, Jessica unloaded and carried her groceries and packages from the car into the kitchen. The clock ticked its countdown for the girls as Jessica stored her milk in the refrigerator, then hung her damp raincoat out on the porch to dry. She shouted after her daughters who she presumed were going about their usual business upstairs, but neither child answered her call. After a few moments of spontaneous tidying, and urgent rain bucket emptying, she called out again, and then began her slow march up the creaking wooden stairs.

At the top, Jessica pushed open the door to Prissy's bedroom only to find the room quiet and unoccupied. She strolled further down the hall and pushed open the door to Lucky's room. Inside, Lucky was lying across her bed on her stomach, thumbing through the pages of a magazine. Next to the bed was Prissy, standing at full attention, eyes as wide and black as Jessica had ever seen them.

"Is everything OK? You two didn't answer me when I called you." Jessica asked, appearing concerned.

"Yea, everything's boring." Lucky answered. Prissy forced a grin and said nothing, but the growing puddle around Prissy's soggy socks and shoes told Jessica another tale. It was obvious something had been going on.

"You're sure there aren't any problems? Nothing is wrong?" Jessica prodded deeper.

"Aww, c'mon, Mom. Stop bugging us. We told you nothing was going on." Lucky answered again, her eyes riveted, never gazing up from the pages of her magazine.

Seeing that they were OK, Jessica didn't pursue the issue and allowed the girls to retain their secret -- whatever it was. Jessica shut Lucky's door and returned downstairs. Prissy flopped herself down on the bare floor at the foot of Lucky's bed and pulled her knees up under her chin.

"Lucky?" Prissy's voice still quivered from fear of being caught, her hands shook, and she was still panting from their wind sprint across the yard. She found it difficult to talk.

"What is it?" Lucky answered.

"That was fun."

"Now don't go telling Mom or Dad about that basement window. Mom and Dad are pretty easy to fool, but I don't want to take any chances. Do you hear me?'

"Yes Lucky, I can keep a secret. I promise."

Prissy hopped back up and sailed for the door. It was unusual for Lucky to allow her to stay in her room for more than a minute or two, and she anticipated receiving her usual terse eviction notice at any moment. As Prissy turned the brass door knob to let herself out, Lucky called to her.

"Prissy, wait a minute." Lucky sat up on her bed. "Stay here for a minute."

"What is it Lucky?"

"Listen to me. I know it's hard, but don't worry about Abby too much, OK? I don't know what they're going to find out, but remember, no matter what happens, you have me and Mom and Dad -- and you will always be OK."

Prissy paused to consider her sister's advice, then dismissed it.

"I didn't see the burning ship today. That means Abby will be alright. The witch says..."

"And about your witch, Prissy. Can you tell me about her?"

Prissy lowered her head, shrugged her bony shoulders and stared at her soggy shoes. She held Otto by one leg and swung him back and forth in front of her like a pendulum.

"OK, I'll tell you Lucky. But if I can't tell Mom and Dad about the window, you can't tell Mom and Dad about the witch."

"I swear to you Prissy, I will never tell a living soul."

Chapter 26

If the library was the island's busiest building on rainy summer days, the Manisses Heritage Society wasn't far behind. When tourists trapped in the over-priced (though the proprietors preferred the term "seasonally adjusted") hotel rooms near the ferry landing grew tired of shopping in the same handful of stores, and dining at the same overpriced restaurants, they would eventually find their way to the steps of the Heritage Society to temper their boredom and learn about the island's founding and its factual history. Inside the small yet austere structure, visitors were able to watch brief film presentations, tour through several rooms filled with antique fishing gear and obscure sailing apparatus, and listen to a presentation by one of several volunteer hoopskirt clad docents trained less in teaching history than they were in entertaining elderly know-it-alls and bored, disobedient children.

On such days, Brenda McMahon would be summoned to provide lectures between her waitressing shifts at the Captain Kidd Cafe and her duties overseeing the island's Preservation Commission. Brenda was well-versed in the black and white facts of the island's founding and took pleasure in speaking to groups and dazzling the uninformed with her superior intellect. Brenda was always one of the busiest people on the island; her meals were usually consumed in a single bite between a can of diet soda and a long inhale of smoke from a cigarette plucked by her thin lips from a green box of Newport Menthols, as she jogged with haste from one responsibility to the other.

Brenda glided into the main hall within seconds of the start of the presentation, cigarette smoke thick on her breath and blue jeans plainly visible under the hem of her ill-fitting, hastily lashed hoop skirt. As her audience looked on, she clapped her hands and launched into her well rehearsed, smoky-throated production.

"You folks made your way down to Cow Cove just yet?" She asked, but none of the glossy-eyed visitors answered. "Well, let me tell you all about Cow Cove. You see, right around 1636, there was this white trader who was brutally murdered by a local Indian here on the island. Well, nobody knows exactly how many Indians lived here before that day, but after the settlers got through either slaughtering or chasing the rest of them off in revenge, it only left a few hundred hearty souls behind. At that point, the way was clear for settlers to move in, and in 1661 a bunch of them left settlements in Massachusetts to make their permanent home here on Manisses. Now, when they got over to the beach at the cove, the water was too shallow for their boats to make it all the way to the shore, meaning they were going to have to swim their way here. Now that was fine for the settlers, but not so good for all the big milking cows they had on board. So as the Indians watched from the beach, the settlers spent the afternoon struggling to push their cows into the water, forcing them to swim all the way to the island. Legend has it that the sight of the settlers pushing their cows into the ocean, and the sight of the big ugly animals splashing for shore, was enough to send all three hundred Indians to the ground in a fit of hysterical laughter. It is a little known fact that the last tribe of poor, old Manisseans laughed themselves to death."

The crowd nodded in a polite silence.

"In their honor, Cow Cove was named after those cows. And many years later, they installed a rock out there with a plaque that has the first settlers' names on it, in their honor. Without them, none of this would be here."

Brenda's presentation droned on for about fifteen minutes, and the visitors, like the island's first cattle, were pushed into the next room for a fascinating presentation about the swordfishing industry. As Brenda rummaged through her handbag searching for her smokes, she realized one of her audience members had stayed behind.

"May I have a word with you, Mrs. McMahon?"

"Of course," she answered, assuming she was addressing a tourist. "Are you staying on the island, or are you just here off the ferry for the day?"

"I am staying on the island, but if all goes well, it will be only for a short time," Mayweather answered.

"I think I know who you are. You're that police detective Captain Honeywell brought in to help find Abby Payne."

"Yes, ma'am," he answered with a respectful tone. "I am. And I was hoping you could give me a little help with that."

"Of course I will." Brenda agreed with enthusiasm. "Just let me know what you need. Anything at all."

"Well, thank you for being so cooperative."

"Oh, you're welcome! You came to the right person... there isn't anyone who knows more about this island than I do. You'll find that here on Manisses, most of the permanent residents are typically generous and cooperative to a fault. We are the products of quaint New England upbringings, and we're all pretty even tempered. I must tell you that this is a very safe place, too, not a place you'll find murders and knife fights. The only crime around here happens when folks drink a little too much... or when those fool tourists on their mopeds trespass on private property. I think that's why this awful situation with little Abby has everyone so unnerved. It doesn't fit in. It doesn't make sense. I mean, sure, we have hundreds of strangers getting off the ferry every day, and if one of them happens to be an insane kidnapper, there isn't much we can do about it. On Manisses, we have our share of eccentrics, a few misfits, an oddball here or there, and even a few loners. The island naturally attracts retirees, naturalists, artists, writers, and performers of all kinds. Aww, hell, we even have our own psychic now. But I find it hard to suspect anyone who actually lives on this island of committing such a heinous crime."

"You're very perceptive, Mrs. McMahon."

"Oh please, call me Brenda!" She swooned.

"Well, Brenda, here's what troubles me. Most abductions of children are not committed by psychopathic strangers. They are committed by relatives and friends -- or neighbors. They are committed by people that the child knows and trusts, often for a long time. Abby and her family knew many people on Manisses, and many of those citizens possessed the ability to take advantage of her trust."

"Oh my! I never thought of it like that."

"Most people don't."

"So how can I help?"

"Captain Honeywell believed you would be the best person to fill me in on what's been happening over at the Dodge property, around the barn."

Brenda ushered Mayweather into a side room that at one time served as the old farm house's oversized pantry. Unlike the rest of the structure, the room had never been restored, and stepping through its threshold was like stepping back into another time. The walls were shedding flecks of flat green paint, and the room's only light swung like a metronome from a long, exposed cord attached to the peak of the vaulted ceiling. The furniture was rickety and worn, revealing its age and decades of overuse. Across the countertops, Brenda had arranged several old bed sheets, and on top of the sheets, laid dozens of items -- artifacts now being maintained under the care of the Preservation Commission. Many of the items were recognizable and included thimbles, silver buttons, shoe buckles, hairpins, bottles, shards of pottery and other mundane flotsam and jetsam from hundreds of years of ordinary life. Other items were less familiar and mysterious, random bits of rusted metal that could have begun life as part of a bucket, a bridle or a coffee pot. Each article was affixed with a white tag and a white bit of string that identified where, when and who found it.

"The treasure hunters over at the barn have been letting us borrow their finds." Brenda began. "We can't make them do it, but most have been cooperative and respect what we are trying to accomplish here. Here we can clean them up, take photographs and keep a detailed record of what was found. In that grassy acre, we have been able to catalog and identify three hundred different artifacts so far, some of them going back over ten generations. I think we will be able to create a wonderful exhibit from this someday."

"Fascinating." Mayweather paced through the room and fingered several items. He picked up a small piece of copper, about twice the size of a thimble which resembled a small cup.

"That," Brenda explained, "is the tip of an old cane, perhaps used by someone who was blind. The wooden part of the cane has long rotted away, but you can see small wooden fragments still attached."

"And this? What have we here? Kind of an odd item to find in a field on an island with such a peaceful populace."

"That's a pistol found by old Mr. Sumner." Brenda said. "We have it dated to the late nineteen-twenties, snatched right out of the heart of Prohibition."

"It's a classic. If this was in better shape, I bet it would fetch quite a lot of money." Bits of rust chipped off and fell to the floor, and Mayweather cringed as his palms turned a dull, rusty orange.

"Manisses was quite the hotspot back in the Roaring Twenties -- during the Prohibition Era -- we were New England's capital of rum-running. We were just far enough out to sea, and just close enough to shore, to benefit the smugglers and the kingpins, and thwart the authorities. There was no better spot anywhere along the Eastern Seaboard to dock your boat, hide out and count your money."

"This island is quite the paradox."

"People think nothing ever happens here. They say it all the time. But I know better. So tell me, why all this interest in this excavation? What does this have to do with Abby?"

"Maybe nothing." Mayweather glanced out of the pantry into the larger part of the museum. A new gaggle of tourists had waddled into the presentation room, waiting for their turn at rainy day entertainment. From his pocket, he had produced a pad, and Mayweather began scribbling notes.

"On an island where nothing changes, a few days ago, something did change. Something significant. Valuables were discovered in an abandoned barn under so much mud and hay. And shortly after that, a little girl goes missing. So now you tell me, Brenda. You have spoken to all the treasure hunters. Do you think any of them have been acting unusual?"

"Unusual? In what way?" Brenda hesitated.

"Treasure changes people, Brenda. Gold fever. For most it's a harmless source of entertainment I suppose, but to others, it transforms them and their personalities much the way gambling does. They see fortune as the solution to all their problems, and it's always just outside their grasp. They have that need to be in control, and it eludes them. When they don't find what they are looking for, they can become... let's just say... unpredictable."

"I don't believe anyone has acted too strange at all. There has been some harmless bickering, and maybe a scuffle or two, but most people seem to be having fun with it, except..."

Brenda paused once again.

"Except who, Brenda?"

"I hate to say it. It's not fair. I feel like I am accusing someone of something horrid."

"It's alright. No one is accusing anyone of anything here. I'm just gathering facts."

"No. It isn't right."

"My only interest in this issue is finding Abby. We need to maintain her interests in this well above everyone's, even if it means hurting a few feelings or bruising a few egos."

"Skip Payne!" Brenda shouted his name loud enough to cause the clamoring visitors in the other room to fall quiet. "There, I said it. He has been acting with almost an obsession about finding something around that stupid old barn since that first gold coin turned up. But I have known Skip for years, there is no possible way he had anything to do with his daughter's disappearance. That's just crazy. I know he can be a real wiener sometimes, but I also know he loves his daughter more than he loves life itself. I know he had nothing to do with this. I just know it"

"I'm sure you are right." Mayweather answered, but Brenda didn't find his tone comforting. He slipped his notepad back into his pocket.

"What about that bum they found out in the thicket... wasn't that Jessica Bradford's whacko father? I thought he was the number one suspect? And what about that Bradford family? Now there's a strange kettle of fish. Weren't they the first to find something out there in that barn?"

"An excellent point, Brenda. What about the Bradford family?"

Mayweather thanked Brenda and started his walk back across the village toward the police station. He hadn't come to Manisses with his eyes closed. Honeywell had been able to provide electronic copies of all his reports before he left the mainland, and he was able to quickly familiarize himself with both the particulars and the people surrounding the case. Before he spoke to Brenda, he already knew about Skip Payne, the Bradford's and Jessica's vagabond father. He carried a brash confidence like General Grant once carried a side sword, and like Grant, he wasn't afraid to brandish it when he felt it was his duty.

When Mayweather arrived, the police station was under a siege of activity. As the command center for the investigation, the building welcomed citizens and search parties who darted in and out, exchanged updated plans, and reported on results. As he marched into the crowd of volunteers, their chatter abruptly went silent, and the citizens parted, creating a clear path up the steps and into the station. Once inside, he walked past the dispatcher and past Honeywell's office door. Just as he reached out to unlock the secured latch of Carl's cell, a tall, blonde woman in a polyester suit, threw herself between him and the solid door.

"Sir, my name is Attorney Winsome Q. Hunter, and I represent Mr. Johnson. Unless you plan to charge him, I must insist upon his immediate release."

"Stand aside."

Mayweather swept Winnie aside with his cold, muscular forearm, like he was dislodging an annoying mosquito, and unlatched the door to the cell. Carl had been sitting against the wall asleep, but was roused awake by the unexpected activity.

"You!" he shouted, jumping to his feet in a half-dazed stupor.

"A pleasure to see you again Mr. Johnson," Mayweather mocked, arms folded across his chest.

As Winnie danced between them, Carl unleashed a vile and unrelenting, depraved verbal assault on Mayweather that startled everyone in the building, permeating the station's thin walls, and providing unexpected entertainment for the mob out in the street. Winnie pleaded with her client to relax, quiet down and let her do the talking, but Carl would have none of it. Winnie later admitted that she wasn't familiar with many of the obscenities Carl was spewing, and after several minutes, Winnie believed he was simply running syllables of well-worn obscenities together in random strings, creating whole, new swear words on the spot, in an angry, almost poetic stream of consciousness style that even the most jaded beat poet would have admired.

Mayweather never blinked. And when Carl finally stopped shouting to catch his breath, Winnie intervened again to plead on her client's behalf.

"Sir, I am so sorry. You have to understand. My client is under a lot of stress, he has been homeless and..."

"Release him." Mayweather said.

"What? I'm sorry, could you repeat that?" Winnie was stunned. She did not believe she had heard the detective correctly.

"I said, release Mr. Johnson."

Honeywell was incensed, and he galloped in from his office next door. He didn't believe what he had heard either.

"Detective? We can legally hold him for another day. He could be dangerous. Are you sure you want to do this?" Honeywell was beside himself in confusion.

Mayweather nodded. "Counsel, Mr. Johnson here can go, but I want your word that he won't leave this island without checking with me first. Is that acceptable to your client?"

"Of course!" Winnie responded, still trying to figure out if his release was secured by something she had done. "He'll stay under the care and watch of his daughter."

Outside, a commotion was building in the village. Angry voices were being volleyed back and forth across the street, and the voyeurs who had rushed inside to watch the battle unfold, rushed back outdoors to watch the new skirmish churning up the sidewalk like a nor'easter coming up the coast. A couple of Honeywell's officers had arrested three men, all in their forties, for raucous behavior and public drunkenness. Two of the three were singing a barely recognizable, out of tune rendition of *Margaritaville*, while the third stomped and thrashed around trying to free his hands from the handcuffs secured behind his back.

"What the hell is this all about?" Honeywell demanded to know.

"Bernice Cowan rented one of the Moondust Beach Houses to these miscreants last night," one of the officers explained.

"Bernice? Again?" Honeywell sighed and lamented.

"I think someone from every house in that neighborhood called to complain," the dispatcher affirmed.

"Two of the perpetrators were able to hop on mopeds, race down the beach and get away. The ones here who had drank too much to run were apprehended without too much effort."

Honeywell sighed. "Fine. Just toss them in the holding cell until they come back to their better senses. And somebody please shut them up and give them a damned bucket!"

As the troublemakers were led through the building, the police staff began to whistle along to the drunkards' tune, that is, until Honeywell shot them each their own personal evil-eyed glare. When the hooligans reached the holding cell, Winnie and Carl passed by them on their way out. Without warning, one of the new prisoners lunged forward capturing Carl in a bear hug, causing him to moan aloud.

"Boys, look! It's Uncle Carl!"

Farther down Main Street, Clement had started a steady, determined march to the police station to confront Detective Mayweather. He hadn't seen him since the disaster in Eastbury, and unlike Carl, he had to think and carefully plan each and every word he wanted to say before he could say it. He spoke aloud to himself as he walked, waving his hands, rehearsing his tone and demeanor, much like he did rehearsing his magic tricks in front of his mirror at home as a teen. But now, Clement had to struggle to even look at himself in a mirror. Though he carried so much rage and hatred toward Mayweather for how he had been duped and how his family had been treated, he also carried equal doses of guilt and self-loathing. As he walked, he felt his anger pique, and also felt his courage begin to flutter and wane. So when he approached town, instead of turning left toward the police station to confront his nemesis and extract his long overdue revenge, he instead turned right down a narrow gravel path that led to the beach to confront himself first.

The path was lined with tall, dark green rhododendrons at first, but gave way to the shorter spartina beach grasses as he passed through a marsh. Just before the beach, the marsh disappeared, and the ground arched up and turned back to a raised platform of solid earth. On top, a single stone grave marker protruded from a knoll of fluttering yellow grass. Clement approached, then stood in front of the marker for several minutes swaying in a raging storm of his own thoughts. The marker simply read, *Palatine Graves 1738*, and marked the place where the islanders had hastily buried the victims of the *Princess Augusta* almost three hundred years before.

As he reflected on the lonely grave, Clement believed he could sense the anguish emanating up from the salty ground beneath his shoes, and swore he could feel it tickling the arches of his feet as it rose through him. In the distance, he thought he heard the echo of a cry from a frightened girl, or perhaps he rationalized, it was simply a hungry seagull. He hung his head low, then spun around to gaze upon the horizon. Prissy insisted that her sighting of a burning ship was true, and Clement squinted at the horizon until his head ached, to see it. He wanted to see it. He wanted Prissy to be right. He wanted to believe so badly that something or someone was in control of his destiny, good or bad, other than himself. He wanted to believe, like Prissy wanted to believe, like Skip Payne wanted to believe, like Maria Griswold wanted to believe, and like all the lonely visitors who found their way into his shop for a good old Victorian dose of fortune-telling wanted to believe.

Clement knew he needed to confront Mayweather, if not to extract revenge, then to do nothing more than retain his own self-respect. And if he did it, what would he gain? What would change? Clement could no more change the past than he could raise these Palatine victims from their graves.

He thought about what a strange day it had been.

And he thought about Manisses. He wondered how an idyllic place could attract so many weird people.

He stared at the horizon one last time. The storm was passing, and the clouds were breaking. With luck, that day's sunset would smear the sky with brilliant hues of purples, pinks and reds. And since there was still no burning ship, just like the witch told Prissy, it meant everything was going to be OK.

Chapter 27

Make no mistake, my friends, we are at war!"
Reverend Lloyd slammed his open palm on the Bible that lay open before him on the podium. Beads of sweat circled his round, pink, wrinkled face and dribbled into his white beard then disappeared. He gnashed his teeth, closed his eyes and tightened his cheeks, then raised his hand back over his head once again.

"We are at war with a bottle! My friends, the consumption of alcohol has placed the inhabitants of our island into the regretful shackles of human bondage. These shackles are tightened each day by a devil that takes delight in turning the screws and enslaving human will with his loathsome instrument of miscry. Men no longer pray to God, but now kneel and pray to their barrels of drink instead. They consume their beer and their rum with glee, and become slaves to its demonic abilities. With their bellies full of wine, they set upon their children and wives with violence, out of their minds, ripping at the very flesh they have sworn before God to love and protect. They empty their hearts to fill their cups, choosing the evils of liquor over the comfort of their trade and love for their families. They bear witness to their allegiance to the bottle, not to God, as they lie as drunkards in the streets, writhing in the filth among the worms and the rats."

Shadrack Brown sat in the front row of the First Congregational Church of Manisses hanging on each of Rev. Lloyd's words. About once per month, the good reverend would ramble on about Temperance -- a growing and popular movement among religious congregations nationwide, as the feeling that public drunkenness had become such a nuisance that drinking alcohol not only needed to be curtailed, it needed to be banned and made outright illegal. Drunkenness was a growing problem on tiny Manisses, too. The crews of men brought to the island to construct hotels and cottages to support the booming local economy found little else in the way of entertainment. And President Grant's recent visit to the island had reinvigorated Rev. Lloyd's commitment to the cause, as he believed the country's ills began and ended with the drunken, corrupt fool who occupied the White House in Washington.

Shadrack never missed a Sunday service, though he did not consider himself a serious believer. He enjoyed the sermons, Bible stories and the rituals as a welcomed respite from his own boredom of everyday work and drudgery, but centered his own spirituality and confidence in the old stories his family had brought to the island from Holland a century and a half before. However, he didn't come to the services to satisfy his own need for personal entertainment -- he participated as a favor to his neighbor, Reverend Lloyd, and for three very dear and unusual friends -- Nelson, Henry and Varnum.

None of the three brothers were able to see, speak or hear.

Throughout the sermon, the four well-dressed men would sit upright and attentive in the front row. Shadrack would hold Nelson's right hand and would pantomime Reverend Lloyd's sermon for him. For example, when Shadrack placed Nelson's hand over his own heart it meant love, a hand across his throat meant evil, a fist meant to stop doing something, and a fist raised to his lips meant to drink. Nelson, who was also holding Henry's hand, would help him act out the same signal repeating it to his brother, and Henry would then do the same for Varnum. Altogether, the group had developed and rehearsed over one hundred hand signals, and they would sit and perform the entire sermon every week in an offbeat, yet pious ballet.

New parishioners were often startled by the sight, shielding their children from the bizarre scene, believing that by staring, they too could somehow catch the affliction. The regular weekly attendees to the service, however, had not only become accustomed to the sight, they enjoyed the curious Sunday performance, and privately cheered them each time the brothers would smile and nod, acknowledging an understanding of the message within the day's teachings.

The three brothers were not born afflicted, but lost their physical senses sometime late in childhood, and the root cause was a mystery to even their own family. Some believed it was brought on by an exotic disease transported to the island by a passing merchant sailor. Others believed it was caused by tainted well water or some unknown poison the children had inadvertently consumed. And others believed it was a curse placed on the family, punishing them for some heinous unknown sin and lack of faith in the Lord.

Whatever its cause, Nelson, Henry and Varnum were highly intelligent, hard-working devout Christians who accepted their fates and whatever help they were offered, but desired more than anything to be masters of their own lives and were driven to support themselves. It was not unusual to see any one of the brothers out on an island stroll -- many believed they knew the nooks and crannies of the island better than the sighted. And on occasion, Henry would even stand along the ridge of the treacherous Mohegan Bluffs where so many warriors had once perished, to enjoy the warm sunshine and cooling summer breezes, with nothing except a well-placed copper tipped cane to keep him from plunging to his death upon the jagged rocks below.

Henry was the showman of the family, enjoying the presence of others, and was easily the most jovial. The townsfolk in the growing village considered him a sort of honorary, unofficial mayor, and Henry would greet everyone with a smile and handshake each morning as they made their way into the village to conduct their business. Those from out of town saw him as no more than a fancy beggar, as each handshake typically provided Henry with a coin or two that would help finance the brothers' meager existence. The islanders saw it as much more. With each donation to his cause, Henry would place his fingers upon the face of his donor, and upon feeling their cheeks stiffen into a smile, he would smile back, and bow a sincere thank you. In their honor, he would call upon his instinctive talents as a showman, offering a brief dance or a bit of improvisational slapstick theater. Islanders were amazed by his ability to read thoughts from the muscles in people's faces, and be able to communicate them back. It was as if he was channeling into their very own minds.

Nelson shared his brother's sense of humor and pleasant personality, but he was far more private and reticent. Nelson found his comfort in the words of the Bible and spent his free time following and harassing Shadrack to act out Bible verses and phrases for him. When Shadrack didn't have time, or when he had grown frustrated by the persistent requests, Nelson would wander over to the First Congregational Church to lose himself in prayer, or to persuade Reverend Lloyd to act out the verses on his behalf. Early on, it was Nelson who had convinced the Reverend, through a series of clever hand signals, that he and his brothers needed to be baptized, and the Reverend agreed, arranging a special ceremony just for that purpose. The whole congregation was invited and attended, and many not only found the ceremony inspiring and spiritually fulfilling, but would later ask Reverend Lloyd for Nelson's assistance and participation in the baptism ceremonies for members of their own families. Reverend Lloyd gladly provided modest compensation to Nelson for his invaluable service to God and the church.

Varnum was a businessman. Less motivated by scripture than Nelson, and unable to bring himself to beg like Henry, Varnum endeavored to follow in his family's business by trawling the seas for fish from one of the many fishing vessels moored on the island. But despite many attempts by the island's kinder-hearted fishermen to find him a functional trade, attempts that often sent poor Varnum tumbling over the rail and into the sea, Varnum was forced to rely upon himself and improvise, leaving him to find his own calling within the various industries of the sea.

The industrious Varnum had an idea. The island surf was rich and crawling with lobsters, and demand for the ugly creatures was fast on the rise. Once considered food for the downtrodden or to be used as simple fish bait, lobsters were now in demand in the better restaurants in Boston, Philadelphia and New York. Varnum decided that if his affliction prevented him from catching the lobsters, perhaps he could devise a way for the lobsters to catch him instead.

Each morning, Varnum would meet Shadrack in his root cellar, where Varnum was allowed to store his lobster baskets and supplies. Shadrack would help Varnum wrap his feet and toes tight with rags, secure the baskets to his back, then guide him and his gear out to the beach. Varnum would wade out into the cove until the water was up to his chin, and then, he would insert and wiggle his toes under the abundant stones along the sea floor. Every few minutes, as Shadrack watched Varnum's head bob up and down between the waves, the mute Varnum would let out an ear piercing screech -- a sure sign that a lobster had caught him as planned. Varnum would then disappear beneath the water, seize the unsuspecting assailant from his toe, and toss it with proud accomplishment into the bushel basket that floated behind him.

During the hot summer months, Shadrack would often entertain the three brothers with music in the root cellar where Varnum stored his supplies, and where Shadrack kept his stock of vegetables and preserves from spoiling. Beneath the ground, the temperature maintained a pleasant coolness and with the aid of a few candles, was a delightful place to spend a humid summer's evening. Shadrack taught Varnum to keep a consistent rhythm by banging on the wine barrels he had stowed away in the cellar, and if he banged hard enough, he would create a beat that Henry could feel resonate in the dirt floor. At first, the brothers had a terrible time coordinating their efforts, and each song they attempted to play decayed into inevitable chaos. Each brother would then blame the other for the misstep, creating a violent dispute that would end in a comical slapping and kicking quarrel among the three that only they could understand, allowing them to vent their pent-up frustrations. The men were genuinely patient, and with time and practice, they improved. So as Henry danced, and Varnum drummed, Shadrack would strum his beloved fiddle into the wee hours of the morning. And Nelson would sit and laugh with Didier on his lap, clapping his hands to the steady pulse.

Across the whole of the island, new construction projects seemed to be blossoming like yellow summer daisies. Now that the breakwaters were complete for the harbor and ships could more easily access and dock, Horace Hunter's vision of Manisses as a resort was coming into sharper focus. Each day it seemed, a new ship would arrive at the island's shores delivering a new collection of strange and unusual people to join the strange and unusual people already there, and each day, a new project would begin -- either a fancy hotel would go up assembled in the elegant Victorian style of the day, or a new home would be built by a member of New England's nouveau riche. In the afternoon, Shadrack would watch from his front porch as one summer cottage was being built on a hill just across from his, and he would reflect on Reverend Lloyd's sermon about the evils of alcohol as he watched half-drunken laborers create the home that would one day, nearly a century and a half later, be purchased by Clement and Jessica Bradford. Shadrack wondered how a roof built under the craftsmanship of drunkards wouldn't be prone to constant leaks.

And as activity and populations increased, so did the drinking. Nelson had taken the Temperance message to heart, and refused to participate in any more merriment with Shadrack until he agreed to empty his evil wine barrels. Shadrack, a mild-mannered soul self-disciplined to drink no more than two glasses of wine each day, flatly refused. In response, a furious Nelson devoted his days to gathering assistance from volunteers at the church and distributing biblical verses, hand-written on small white cards, among the townspeople, alerting everyone to the perils of drinking. Those who knew him, including his fellow Congregationalists, were inspired by Nelson's resolve. But the patrons of the newest tavern on Main Street, The Skulduggery, were not as enthused.

The Skulduggery was one of many drinking establishments that had popped up on the island seemingly overnight, designed to separate tired, bored construction laborers from their miniscule wages with the enticement of a bottle of harmless inebriation. The tavern featured a broad selection of wines and whiskeys, but it was the cheap flowing ale and its vibrant, raucous and wild reputation that filled its seats night after night. To Nelson, The Skulduggery represented a classic target of the Temperance movement, and to bear witness to God, he vowed to make contact with, and attempt to persuade, every patron.

Once Nelson walked inside, it didn't take long for the boisterous, drunken customers to turn on him, bullying him with every cruel trick they could devise. They would steal his hat and cane, douse him with beer, then spin him around to make him dizzy, and laugh as he staggered and struggled to find his way back to the door. They treated Nelson like an untrained animal, poking and prodding him, abusing him at every chance, all to feed their own sadistic, drunken amusement. But the stubborn and devout Nelson would not yield, until that is, the inebriated patrons picked him up by the back of his trousers and threw him like a bale of straw into the hard, dusty street.

It would be a hundred years before it changed its name to the Captain Kid Cafe and replaced its spirits with ice cream.

Nelson's heroics were not lost on Henry and Varnum. At first, they admired and supported their obstinate brother's passion, though they didn't understand why he would insist upon submitting himself to the painful, ritual abuse. Nelson would return home each night covered in scrapes and bruises and soaked in all manner of foul-smelling liquids. As time wore on, and it became evident that Nelson had no plans to give in to the constant cruelty at any cost, his brothers became concerned not only for his physical health and well-being, but also for their own.

During the day, Henry and Varnum suffered from guilt by association. To the drinkers, one deaf, dumb and blind zealot was as good or bad as any another, and all three brothers became targets of habitual retribution. As they walked about on their distinctive island strolls, it became common for any one of them to be struck by stones and sticks, to be tripped up, or to be intentionally spun around and left confused. When one perpetrator tried to push Henry to knock him down, Henry lost his balance and fell back on top of the man by mistake. Henry's hands and fingertips scuttled across his attacker's face like spiders, and he was horrified to read and absorb a man's feelings of true hatred and anger for the very first time.

Ritual abuse of the three brothers lasted all summer long without a pause and by September, the men spent more time seeking asylum in Shadrack's root cellar than they did meandering around the village they considered home. Only

Varnum would venture out each morning on schedule, feet wrapped in rags and lobster baskets strapped to his back, prepared to pay tribute to his Protestant work ethic and maintain some semblance of steady income for their struggling family. Besides, he thought, out among the peaceful, lapping waves, he was isolated and immune from the mounting abuse he received from the humans on shore.

Shadrack had once believed he was too old to start a family of his own, preferring to live a quiet and meek existence. But that next winter, he married a woman half his age -- the daughter of the bartender of The Skulduggery. She had become enamored with Shadrack's sense of charity and his calm, kind heart, and stood by his side the day he had to mime the heart-wrenching news of Varnum's drowning and death to his disbelieving, inconsolable brothers.

Varnum's full basket and severed lines washed up on shore in front of the great rocks, where William Kidd once hid his leaky skiff and where Hubbard knelt to collect Kattern from the icy ground. The tide dutifully delivered Varnum's lifeless, bloated corpse the next day.

Some on the island believed that Varnum's death was inevitable. A blind, deaf and dumb man had no business trying to overcome the unrelenting surf and unpredictable undertow pushed into the island by the ever-present, massive and dangerous ocean storms. Other rumors persisted that he had succumbed to the evils of alcohol himself, nipping at Shadrack's stores of wine in secret to ease his mind before venturing out to undertake his difficult, daily duties. But what no one was willing to admit aloud was that Varnum's demise may have been caused by the hand of another -- possibly ordered by a greedy and vengeful tavern owner seeking to maximize profit.

Shadrack's decision to marry was a direct result of Varnum's untimely passing. Death, he now realized, was too absolute. The incident inspired a need within his heart to pass his name and legacy on to a new generation, to preserve the good things from his era, and preserve the vital lessons he had learned from his past. He believed he had learned the secret to immortality, and he viewed it as his duty to raise his own children in his own image and return the favor his generous ancestors had provided him.

And he and his new bride had already agreed to name their first born son Varnum in honor of their most dear and unusual friend.

Decades later, before he died himself, Shadrack invested the few dollars he had been able to save into preserving and restoring his family heirlooms. The heirlooms had always been dear to him and a day did not pass where he wouldn't caress them between his fingers, hold them to the light, reflect on their meaning and channel their previous owners. He was careful to leave a detailed will that bequeathed his most prized possessions into the hands of his most trusted and reliable heirs. Unfortunately, his heirs didn't share the same vision or see the same intrinsic value in his treasures.

Following his death, Shadrack's beloved fiddle was given as a gift to his grandchild, used as a toy, and was summarily destroyed. His grandmother's Revolutionary War quilts were donated to the local poor house where they warmed the shoeless feet of the unfortunate until they became worn, infested with bed bugs, and were burned. And the old family Bible, crammed with centuries of detailed notations and family secrets, was water damaged in a heavy rain storm and thrown mindlessly into the fireplace. His ornate tin box, its maroon ribbon and its contents, remained in the family until Prohibition when it was carted off by a burglar during a robbery.

Shadrack's joyful mortar and pestle, carved from the hull of the *Princess Augusta,* that Horace Hunter swore he saw dancing at Shadrack's feet, fared better. It's indescribable charm captured the interest of an antique dealer and it made its way to the proud display shelves of an exclusive university museum far off the island.

And Didier, the faithful and resilient doll that survived the tragic wreck of the *Princess Augusta,* was handed down several generations until it reached Shadrack's great-great granddaughter Bernice Varnum Brown, and sadly, could not survive one of Bernice's fits of mundane spring cleaning. Bernice tossed Didier into a trash barrel one afternoon that was collected dutifully by a Manisses Department of Public Works garbage truck and hauled away.

However, had the hauler not been driving too fast when he swerved to avoid a tourist on a moped, Didier might never have been ejected from his barrel and would not have landed on the perimeter of a deserted beach. And had the seagulls and ants not pecked and eaten away at his ancient fabrics so quickly, his metal and wire frame would not have been exposed and would not have caught the eye of Jessica Bradford on her stroll around the island, and would never have had the opportunity to be reincarnated as Prissy's new doll and to be renamed as Otto.

Chapter 28

A welcome ray of golden, summer sunshine ricocheted through the leaded glass of Prissy's bedroom window and exploded on the wall in a burst of vivid color. The storm that terrorized the merchants and residents of Manisses for the past two days had marched north, leaving in its wake the delightful summer sunshine that was so prized among the merchants and vacationers and fueled the island's furnace of activity.

Prissy sat on her bed cross-legged clutching a tin box, struggling with a tight knot folded into an old maroon ribbon that held the box closed. It was evident that the box had once been beautiful, but years of exposure had faded its color, leaving behind black grime and sticky tarnish. Lucky stood by the door with her arms folded.

"Is this like a genie in a lantern? If you rub the box, will the witch pop out?" Lucky asked, in her usual snarky tone.

"I can't get this stupid thing untied. Otto tied it too tight. Help me." Prissy asked.

In one motion, Lucky produced a candy apple red pocket knife from a garter belt hidden beneath the white lace of her thigh-high leather dress, and she sliced the ribbon in half. The ribbon fluttered to the bed, and the tin box fell open, releasing the leather bound book that was concealed inside.

Lucky sat on the corner of Prissy's bed and picked the book up off her comforter. The spine cracked as it opened, and its pages were so yellowed and brittle that flecks of dried paper showered from it. Lucky gently thumbed through its pages, one at a time, fascinated by its contents.

"Is this your witch?" Lucky asked.

"It's written by a witch. Her name is Kattern. She used to live here a long time ago. Inside, she explains all about her curse, and all about the ghost ship. And she explains about her well, and her husband, and her goats, and..."

"Where did you get this? This should be in a library somewhere, or maybe in a museum."

"I found it in that barn behind a pile of paint cans."

"Does anyone know you have this?"

"Just Abby and Otto. Abby said it was a stinky old book and I should throw it away."

Lucky opened to a random page and read aloud.

Very pleasant, it was, the weather of this morn, yet I am drowsed. Hubbard hath gone fishing, that I deem a folly, yet I miss his pleasant talk. I shall not boil roots for our supper, for fear I insult the poor man, if his basket were to return unfilled with the codfish...

"Prissy, some of this is really hard to understand."

"Yca, I know. Otto reads the harder parts to me."

Lucky rumpled her brow and stared at Otto with doubt and hesitation. Not intimidated, Otto stared right back. Lucky opened and read from another random page.

A wretch dog disturb my visit, last evening, of home. Amsterdam had bloomed, and thither come the children to the garden, and my nose fills with the bribe of roasting hens and biscuits and creame. Father says a boatfull of Spaniards are singing by the dyke, and we must take the coach with haste...

"This is incredible. It's like having a time machine that goes back three hundred years." Lucky was spellbound. "Why don't you want anyone to know that you have this?"

"Because of what happened when I found the coin! Everyone got stupid. I wish I never found that stupid pirate treasure, and I wish I never found this stupid witch's book, either. That's why I didn't want to treasure hunt with Abby anymore. Please don't tell anybody." Prissy begged, and Lucky continued to read.

The traitors shall see the rigging and sails aflame, and the courage will be drained from each rogue and toad on the isle. A curse hereby levied upon all that they have in hand, fear shall fill their bellies, and they shall suffer. Erewhile the Palatines make revenge to clear the account of their debt, for all times...

Lucky continued to turn the brittle, crumbling pages one by one. Not only was she holding a diary by the island's first alleged witch known as Dutch Kattern, she was holding much more. Inside were recipes, spells, incantations, and prayers, lists of ingredients, sayings and even short original poems. The writing was in multiple languages and though legend implied that Kattern was uneducated and lowbred, it was clear from this journal that she was far more intelligent, sly, worldly and even sophisticated.

About halfway through the book, Lucky realized the quality of the paper had changed. It was still brown and yellowed, but slightly thicker and she noticed that someone had repaired and re-glued the fragile binding. The handwriting changed, too, to a darker ink and a heavier hand. The first entry in this new style was dated July 9, 1876.

I am called by the name Shadrack. It was a Bible name that my mother had bestowed upon myself with the hope I would be raised with firm resolve. I reside upon Manisses Island in the Atlantic Ocean. I feel well and it is a pleasant day.

"Well this guy is a ball of fire," Lucky complained.

Shadrack's half of the diary contained far fewer handwritten entries, but instead, included drawings, charts and maps. There were also stories about Henry, Nelson and Varnum and even what appeared to be a song Shadrack had written for him and his friends to perform. One page mapped an entire beach in such detail that it documented the location of each and every stone larger than a pumpkin. Another map sketched the location of all the island's pre-paved, dirt roads, still nearly the same a century and a half later, and each building on the island was marked with a small square and an arrow that identified the owner. It was a wealth of genealogical as well as priceless historical data. The back pages included a map of the Bradford's current property, the stone walls, the old well and a curious rectangle marked simply, "root cellar." Lucky noticed that the stone walls that zigzagged the property, as viewed from above, formed two perfect arrows pointing at one another.

Lucky dropped the book on Prissy's bed as if it had burned her hands.

"Lucky, what's wrong?"

"The shape of those stone walls. I've seen this map once before."

"Seen it where?"

"Follow me."

Prissy chased Lucky down the stairs to the dining room, jumping over every other step along the way. Upset and not feeling well from the heavy drama of the day, Jessica had retired to her room to rest and soothe her pounding forehead and the house had fallen quiet. Lucky wasted no time and started to feverishly offload all the breakable items from the hutch in the corner.

"Help me." Lucky insisted.

With the hutch emptied, together, the girls were able to slide the heavy piece of furniture away from the wall just enough to expose its back. On the back of the hutch was a crudely drawn design. Lucky held the image in the old diary up against it to compare the two.

"This hutch was here when we moved in, remember? The people who sold us the house said it was too heavy and expensive to move, so we were welcome to just keep it. Mom was thrilled to own an original island antique. I remember staring at this design for a while wondering what it could be. Mom said it was just an old scribble, but I could tell it was more than that. I just couldn't figure out what the heck it was supposed to be."

"It's a map!"

"It's a map alright, but a map to what?" Lucky's eyes flashed back and forth between the hutch and the diary.

"Look over here... the stone walls out back form arrows. One starts at the giant rocks near the beach and points to a place just past where the witch's old well used to be. The other arrow starts at the house and points to the same spot. But here in the diary, there is a small rectangle labeled "root cellar" where the arrow tips point. But on the hutch, the rectangle is a lot bigger, over twice the size."

"Why would anyone care about a root cellar?" Prissy asked. "And what is a root cellar?"

"In the old days, before people had refrigerators, they could keep things cool by putting them in a room dug into a hill or underground. Food would last longer that way and wouldn't spoil so fast."

"Oh." Prissy responded, disappointed the answer wasn't more exciting.

Lucky and Prissy flew through the front door and dashed through the yard on their way back to the thicket. Both girls had been blessed with their mother's natural athletic abilities and moved with both speed and grace. The diary was tucked firmly under Lucky's right arm as she ran, and the heels from her black biker boots were sticking out from under her left. But Prissy's shorter legs struggled to keep up with her older, faster sister, and she soon fell far behind.

"Slow down!" Prissy hollered as the top of Lucky's head disappeared over the hill.

Lucky stopped and sat on the stone wall and waited for Prissy to catch up. She opened the diary again and started reading. The content captivated her, much as it had Prissy, as it came alive in her mind's eye and she almost couldn't bear to put it down. Lucky's view of history as a formal subject was considered odd and perverse, but that didn't mean she didn't respect it and relish it when it was authentic and raw, unmolested by the interpretations of politicians, historians and social scientists pushing their theories and veiled agendas.

"Why are you reading again?" Prissy demanded to know. "I thought we were exploring."

"We are exploring. It's just that this is so darned interesting."

"Otto said you'd like it."

"I have to tell you, Prissy... this Otto thing is getting on my nerves. Why is it he talks to you but not anyone else?"

"I dunno. Maybe you should ask him yourself?"

"Prissy, why don't you just leave him in the house next time we come out? He'll stay cleaner and happier that way, I'll bet. He's been looking a little grungy lately."

"No, I can't leave Otto by himself. He's in danger."

Lucky knew she had to ask, but really didn't want to know the answer. She sighed and rolled her eyes up to the clearing blue sky, and asked anyway.

"So, Prissy, why do you think Otto is in danger?"

"Because Mrs. Cowan wants to kill him. She wants to throw him in a fire."

"You know Mom and Dad will never let that happen. And don't let that fat old Bernice intimidate you one bit. She's just a big harmless windbag."

"Otto is afraid of her. He said she tried to kill him once before."

"Really, Prissy, Otto isn't in any danger. I swear. Look at me... I promise I will do everything I can to help you and keep Otto safe. The well-being of her favorite doll is not something a little girl should ever need to worry about. OK? Now, follow me."

The girls followed the stone wall just as it was drawn in the pages of Kattern and Shadrack's diary until they reached the point where the two stone wall arrows met. The area was a non-descript place that both Lucky and Prissy had crossed through many times before without offering it much thought. The vines and shrubs were overgrown and miniature dogwood trees dotted the perimeter. The area had been well trampled by the police and the search parties, and debris from the discovery of the witch's old well was evident. With the diary in hand, Lucky paced off the edges of what she believed to be the location of the shack that Hubbard had built and Shadrack had improved into a cabin decades later. From there, Lucky paced off where the map told her the old root cellar had once been located, and she imagined a door that would be lifted to gain entrance. She noticed a few large stones protruding up from the undergrowth, and assumed they were some sort of marker. But under her feet, she felt no door -- only rock solid ground.

But the other map -- the map scrawled on the back of the hutch -- was burned sharp into Lucky's memory. She closed her eyes and moved forward, estimating that the map on the hutch was about two hundred percent larger than the map illustrated in the diary. Lucky used her design skills and artistic talents to pace off the distance with her eyes closed, and her arms stretched out to her sides for balance. She counted and walked slowly, offering an uncanny resemblance to her mother in her younger days balancing with elegance along a tightrope high above a boisterous crowd. Lucky counted each footstep as she walked, and lost her count when her forehead smacked into the low hanging branch of a dogwood tree sending her sprawling to the ground in an ungraceful, awkward flop.

Prissy giggled aloud.

"Don't ask me if I'm OK or anything," Lucky snarled, sitting herself up then leaning back on her hands. "Do me a favor though... if I kill myself out here, don't forget to tell Mom and Dad."

As she continued to chastise Prissy for the perceived lack of empathy, the girls heard what they thought sounded like a child's cry, a sound eerily similar to what Clement had heard standing over the Palatine grave marker on the other side of the island. It was followed by a sharper crack that echoed around them like thunder and one of Lucky's arms suddenly disappeared into the quivering ground as if some unknown demon from the bowels of hell had reached up, grasped her wrist, and pulled it down inside. Lucky screamed and Prissy shot to her feet, gasping for air, terror racing up her spine.

"Run! Prissy! Run as fast as you can! Go get help! Now!"

As Prissy raced for home, behind her, Lucky emitted a horrifying, bloodcurdling scream.

Chapter 29

On the faithful pine bench under the familiar, faded dusty awning on Water Street, the three old men -- Guilfoyle, Sumner and Jude -- had retaken their well-known and honored positions. Their personal quarrel over the future of the Dodge barn and property felt both trivial and meaningless to them now, considering that their little friend Abby's whereabouts continued to remain a sad and disturbing mystery. Now that the storm had passed, and too old to search any more than they already had, the men returned to their duties as official gargoyles monitoring the daily comings and goings of the island's visitors, their eyes tearing at any mention or passing thought of their dear, little missing friend.

Clement had left the Palatine grave and was marching with a determined focus toward the police station. Skip had already gone ahead to find Mayweather to seek an update on any progress the search teams may have been making. As Clement reached Water Street and passed by the three old sentinels, he honored them with a sharp, customary New England head nod. But rather than return the time-honored gesture, Sumner called out, and waved him over to their side of the street.

"Mr. Bradford.., if you have a moment?" Sumner inquired, stopping Clement dead in his tracks. The three old men didn't approve of the Bradfords' choice of business, and it was rare that they would elect to initiate a conversation with him at all. Clement found the three men brash and intimidating, and if he couldn't avoid them, he always approached the men with caution and suspicion.

"I want to ask you," Sumner began, "how is little Priscilla coping with all this trouble? Is she OK?"

Clement relaxed his posture a bit and smiled. "Yes, Prissy is fine. Thank you for asking."

"I can't tell you how those two little girls brighten our days," Guilfoyle said. "The most important things in Abigail and

Priscilla's world are ice cream and gumballs. I can't remember ever being that young or that carefree."

"That's because you're half senile." Sumner shot back. Guilfoyle feigned deafness and ignored the insult.

"Those girls mean the world to us," Guilfoyle continued, "always so happy and excited, the highlight of our day. They seem as if they have the whole world figured out. I have to give you credit, Mr. Bradford, you are raising a wonderful, charming daughter."

"Thank you, sir. Jessica and I are quite proud of her. Abby's disappearance has torn the heart right out of me -- out of all of us I suppose -- but Prissy seems to be coping with it better than all of us. It's inspiring. For some reason, she has complete confidence that we are going to find Abby, and that she'll be just fine."

"We helped search for Abby for a while," Jude added, pointing at the sky with the damp toothpick he dislodged from the corner of his mouth, "but we're just too old anymore for that kind of physical activity. It's killing me that we can't do more out there. I had hip replacement surgery last August and don't walk so good. And Sumner, here, has terrible sciatica from dragging those fishing nets off that trawler for thirty years. And Guilfoyle? Well, his eyesight is so bad the only way he's going to find anything is if he trips over it."

"I see everything I need to see!" Guilfoyle crabbed, widening and pointing his wrinkled finger at his pinkish, bloodshot eyes.

"Sometimes," Jude interrupted, "I believe old geezers like us can provide more help by just sitting here. We see things and we hear things most other people don't notice. We've been around a long time, and we just blend into the scenery after a while. Folks just walk on by and pay us no attention. That lets us pick up and stow away little bits of information about everyone and everything in town that interests us."

Clement was intrigued. "So what have you heard? Is there news?"

The men had hoped he would ask.

"Well for one thing, your friend Skip might be in for a bit of trouble," Sumner answered. "The detective fellow that

Honeywell called in from stateside has been nosing around, asking a lot of questions about him. I think he's questioned just about everybody I can think of who might know him."

"But why would Skip be arousing suspicion? He's working harder than anyone else out there searching for his little girl."

"We ain't going off gossiping, now." Jude jumped in. "It ain't our place. But I'll tell you this... Skip and Kitty moved to this island just before Abigail was born. At the time, it felt to me like they were running away from something. I'm guessing it ain't the first time Skip has had run-ins with the law."

Clement didn't respond right away. He knew little about Skip and Kitty Payne's family background, but found it impossible to believe Skip could be involved in anything disreputable -- it just wasn't in his personality. Skip was smug and pompous for sure, and enjoyed flaunting his wealth, but he appeared harmless, even naive, to the core and Clement didn't believe he possessed the gumption to hurt a fly. Then Clement reflected on Mayweather and what he knew firsthand about his unethical, despicable methods of investigation. If Skip was called in for an interrogation, he would be shucked like a fresh clam at a raw bar.

"No." Clement finally stated with authority. "No. Skip isn't capable of doing this. You're wrong."

"Maybe so, but this island has a way of attracting the strangest characters. Always has." Jude said. "But let me ask you this. When you moved to Manisses last year, what were you running away from?"

Clement excused himself from the conversation and sprinted toward the station. Hundreds of day trippers with overstuffed backpacks, waiting for the final ferry excursion of the afternoon to the mainland, were gathering at the dock, and he zigged and zagged his way around and through them. Handmade posters with Abby's photograph and description seemed to be plastered on every available surface -- buildings, telephone poles, windows -- some even blowing like autumn leaves through the street. As he ran, Clement tried to rehearse in his mind what he wanted to say to Mayweather and Skip once he reached them, but the words were still elusive. All he could seem to focus upon was Jude's question. How arrogant, he thought, for Jude to pose such a presumptive and insulting question about him without knowing any of the facts, even if it might be true.

Clement wasn't prepared for the sight of Jessica's half inebriated family huddled together on the lawn of the station when he arrived. And to Clement's surprise, he was as thrilled to see each one of them as they were thrilled to see him. The cousins let out a celebrative cheer as soon as they saw him charge up the walkway, and greeted him with a round of bear hugs and friendly, good-old-boy back-slapping. Though he was surprised, Clement savored it, as he considered his time on the road with Jessica and the Flying Zalenkos clan as the most fun, exhilarating and carefree of his life. It was the only time he every remembered being accepted. They had become as much his true family as his own biological parents were back in Connecticut, if not more.

"Quiet down!" Honeywell's voice blared from an open window. "Or I'll reconsider my decision to let you idiots go home."

"Sorry sir," Winnie answered. "I promise it won't happen again."

"What the heck is going on? Does Jessica know you're all here?" Clement asked, coming back to his senses.

"Not yet, the boys here wanted to surprise her!" Winnie explained.

Clement recoiled. "Things have been a little high-strung around here the last few days. I really think it would be a good idea if you call first."

Winnie agreed and nodded. "The boys here were picked up on a disturbing the peace complaint, but the police decided to let them all go, including Mr. Johnson. I can fill you in on the details later. However, they only let them go under the condition that they stay with you and your wife.., and that they stay out of trouble."

"Of course, of course they can stay with us. Jessica and the girls will be thrilled. How did you get in trouble? And what brings you all out to the island in the first place?"

"They were looking for me," Carl answered, an apologetic tone fluttered through his voice, still embarrassed by his own unbecoming predicament. "It's my fault."

"We were worried about old Uncle Carl, here. We hadn't heard from him in a long time and knew he had been down on his luck. We chased him up the coast from Florida this spring, lost him in Baltimore for a while, then found him again in Newark. We guessed he was on his way up here to visit with you folks. Looks like we were right on about that." One of the cousins said, his arm wrapped tight around Carl's shoulders.

"And to check out the clubs. You all got some nice bars here on this island." Said another.

Winnie could read the concern scrawling across Clement's face.

"Don't worry, Mr. Bradford, the Captain insisted I escort them to your home myself. I won't let them leave my sight. They won't get themselves into any more trouble." Winnie insisted.

Standing on the lawn, they could all hear the distinctive echoes and patterns from a volley of angry voices emanating from inside, though they couldn't quite make out what was being said or who was saying it. For a moment, Clement had nearly forgotten why he was at the police station to begin with, and part of him wanted more than anything to lock arms with Jessica's cousins and march home, ignoring the uncomfortable spectacle that awaited him inside. Yet, the sudden presence of Jessica's family had roused an intensity of confidence deep inside him that he had been seeking for days and had not felt in years.

"I'll catch up with all of you guys later on."

As the jovial gang disappeared around the bend, Clement swallowed hard and flipped open the door to the station. The building appeared empty at first, eerily so, as the commotion and activity that had dominated the past few days seemed to have vanished without warning. The warming humid air felt oppressive, and beads of sweat were accumulating on his forehead and neck. As he walked slowly through the station, the floor creaked beneath his shoes announcing his presence. Clement noticed Captain Honeywell standing in the shadows, arms folded, staring out the window.

"You don't belong here, Bradford."

"Neither does Skip."

"That's not your problem."

"This isn't right."

Honeywell was angry. "What is it with you people? Half this island thinks you or someone from your lunatic family is responsible for Abby's disappearance... that you turned her into a frog or something. You'd be smart to take your family, and your wife's family, and go away. Stay quiet. Hide somewhere until this blows over. I warned your wife about keeping a low profile. But I can't seem to go more than five minutes without turning around and seeing one of you people in my damned police station!"

Clement struggled to maintain his confidence, but held his ground. "You need to let Skip go home to Kitty. You know that."

"That's not my decision to make. It's out of my hands."

The station's spooky quiet was replaced by more angry shouting, reverberating through the door of the interrogation room. Skip and Mayweather were inside alright, and it was obvious from Skip's high-pitched squealing that he was being grilled, and it wasn't going well. Clement reached for the door handle.

"I wouldn't do that, Bradford. I swear I will lock you up."

Clement paused. "What am I supposed to do then, just walk away?"

"You would if you were smart." Honeywell answered. He had turned, and his body was now poised to strike at Clement. "I'm not going to say it again. Get the hell out of my police station."

Both Clement and Honeywell could hear every word, with perfect clarity, coming at them through the closed door. Clement didn't move, except to hold his head low and focus on the drama playing out inside.

"I don't know what else I could say that will make any difference!" Skip begged.

"Let's just forget I've already asked the question a dozen times already. Tell me, Mr. Payne, where is your daughter." Mayweather refused to cave in.

"I don't know! I told you I don't know!"

"And why don't you know? Do you often let your nine year-old daughter wander around an island all by herself?"

"I told you, she was out playing with her friends. That's what nine year-olds do... they play outside!"

"But you let her out of your sight. Just like you let Lucy out of your sight."

"No!"

"Isn't that what you told me when Lucy disappeared? That she was playing by herself and then suddenly, she wasn't there anymore? That she just... vanished? Tell me how this is any different?"

"She fell overboard off the side of the yacht and drowned. It was an accident. You know that."

"At least that's what you told me when it happened. You told me it was an accident then, too. Was I a fool to believe you then, or am I fool to believe you now?"

Clement wanted to fling the door open, but his arm and wrist were paralyzed in fright. He did not know that Skip and Kitty once had another daughter, and that she had also fallen victim to some unexpected, horrific fate. The news stunned him, while confusing judgments and emotions flew like a warrior's angry arrows through his chest. His already broken heart now ached even more for Skip and Kitty's loss, but then he considered for a moment that Mayweather could be right. Could Mayweather be on to something? Could Skip be guilty of not one but two heinous crimes or was he just profoundly ill-fated, caught up in some cruel, satanic game of déjà vu? With Mayweather poised to pounce on Skip and tear out his throat, Clement made his decision, called Honeywell's bluff, and swung the door open wide, nearly dislodging it from its hinges.

Honeywell did not budge. Inside, Skip was sitting cross legged on the floor, eyes and face red from steady bouts of crying, one of his boat shoes was missing, and his clothes were disheveled and twisted around him as if he had been wrestling. Mayweather stood over him, and he spun around on his heels at the sound of the opening door. Mayweather was furious at the interruption and clenched his hands into large, white-knuckled muscular fists. Mayweather shouted, "Bradford! Get the hell out of here!"

"Leave him alone, Mayweather."

"Who are you to tell me what to do? You're impeding an official investigation! I could have you locked up!"

Clement thought it odd that Honeywell, who had made the same idle threat just seconds before and was standing just a few feet behind him, still hadn't taken a single step in his direction. Clement sensed, for some reason, that Honeywell just might be on his side.

"Come on, Mayweather. End this. You know Skip didn't do it."

"Oh and how do I know that? Do you think this is some casual discussion here? That I snagged him at random off the street? Or maybe you think I have some sixth sense? ESP perhaps? Do you think there is a little voice in my head making my decisions, guiding my actions, telling me what to do? Well here's a newsflash Bradford. Unlike some self-proclaimed professionals in the room, I don't simply make things up to suit me. I rely on experience, evidence and hard facts to earn my paycheck."

"You have evidence? What evidence? No one knows what happened to Abby..." Clement began.

"Except the person who had something to do with it." Mayweather shot back.

"I didn't do anything!" Skip shouted. "I swear it!"

"It seems that Mr. Payne here has a problem misplacing his children." Mayweather jabbed, trying to incite both Clement and Skip at the same time. But Clement remained calm and focused.

"Don't worry about anything, Skip. Ignore him. I know you are innocent. And I don't think you should say anything else before you get your lawyer in here."

"Are you able to channel legal advice now Bradford? Quite impressive."

"Please, Clement! You have to help me!" Skip rocked back and forth on the floor and sobbed.

"You want his help? Ask him how he helped Maria Griswold find her daughter? I'll bet that changes your mind. It's one hell of a story."

"Mayweather, you're nothing but a fraud. You have no integrity or conscience. You don't care who you destroy or what the costs are to get what you want."

"So I'm a fraud, am I? I have no integrity? I find missing children and I am damn good at it. That's what this is all about. I wouldn't even be on this armpit of an island if it wasn't for this missing persons case. Now tell us, what do you do for a living, Mr. Bradford, other than separate lonely old women from their government checks? Hey Skip, have you ever heard the phrase 'gaff the games?' An old carnie like Clement here knows what it means, don't you now? It's how a con-artist describes using little bits of science or physics to steal your money. The best swindlers can not only pull off the stunt, but get their victims to return with cash in hand and a smile across their face to get ripped-off again and again and again."

"I don't care what you think of me or what you think about what I do. But you have no right to violate the innocent. You have no right to devastate people, destroy their sense of self and leave their souls for dead just to satisfy your thirst for glory. Lucretia had nothing to do with Hannah Griswold's disappearance, and the case almost destroyed her. It could have killed her. Jessica and I will never forgive you for that." Clement's eyes bugged from his brow and beads of sweat rolled down his reddened cheeks. Skip retreated into a corner and rolled into a ball fearing a fight was about to break out.

"Interesting. So now let me ask you a question, Mr. Bradford. Am I responsible for your daughter's destruction? Or are you?"

Throughout the argument, Clement never heard the telephone ring in the next room, nor did he hear Honeywell run off to answer it. He also didn't hear Honeywell dashing around the office, fumbling for his keys, collecting his weapon, or calling out on his radio for support from his officers. So when Honeywell burst into the room and inserted himself between the two men, Clement raised his fist to strike him and Honeywell grabbed it.

"Listen to me... we just received a call in from your wife, Clement. Something is up. I think they found Abby."

Chapter 30

loyd opened his lunch pail and removed a hastily wrapped bacon salad sandwich that included two pieces of stale white bread, lightly toasted, a bit of mayonnaise, a thick slice of red onion, and two slices of cold, broiled bacon leftover from breakfast. Two sweet gherkins and a bottle of soda pop finished out as perfect a lunch as any unemployed working man could hope to enjoy on an island as depressed as Manisses.

Floyd was renting a room in the dilapidated Herringbone Inn for just a few dollars per week. The Herringbone had once been an upscale, exclusive resort that catered to the whims and fancies of the rich and privileged, but at the onset of the Great War, the rich tourists abandoned the idyllic little isle taking their discretionary income with them, and had yet to return. The Herringbone was one of the few great hotels not boarded up, its owners surviving on the random, casual laborers the struggling fisherman hired to maintain their fleet. In between odd jobs, Floyd washed dishes and swept the floor at a bar near Water Street called The Skulduggery -- a popular restaurant and drinking establishment open on the island for better than fifty years. The Skulduggery was one of the few successful, busy and profitable businesses remaining, since it sold its liquor illegally as the island's only speakeasy and had done so since the passage of Prohibition a few years before.

The bacon salad sandwich yielded with a satisfying crunch when Floyd's front teeth tore through it, sending two identical trails of mayonnaise bubbling out from the corners of his mouth. He reached into his lunch pail and produced a page from a newspaper that he spread between his shoes on the beach in front of him, using his toes to hold down the corners so they wouldn't flutter in the sea breeze. As he ate, he looked down at the B. Altman Department Store advertisement that featured an assortment of pearls and fine jewelry, including an elegant selection of beautiful, but expensive engagement rings. The page had been torn from the *New York Times* and mailed to Floyd by his on again, off again girlfriend Trixie who lived in Brooklyn. Trixie had worked at a myriad of part-time jobs but didn't seem to ever be able to hold one down for more than a few months at a time. Whenever Floyd could gather up enough money to travel to New York to visit her, she would only talk of her dreams of wealth and marriage as the ticket out of her own poor, depressing neighborhood. She told Floyd that if he could find a real good job, she would marry him. But so far, Floyd's journey to career and riches had been mired in drinking, gambling and a string of other questionable decisions. Yet the mere thought of starting a life with the beautiful, young Trixie kept him motivated each morning to wake up, comb his thinning hair, and set out to try again.

On the horizon, Floyd saw what he thought were the flickering flames of a small fire. As he stared into the haze a small but lightening fast boat appeared, tearing through the waves and coming toward him like a rocket. He recognized right away that the boat was the *Black Duck* and that it was carrying, no doubt, as many as 400 cases and barrels of illegal liquor -- sometimes champagne, sometimes fine Canadian whisky, and sometimes freshly-distilled Caribbean rum. But whatever the boat was carrying on this day, he knew the proprietor of The Skulduggery was ready to pay as much as a dollar for every bottle the boat could bring to shore. And that was motivation enough for the captain of the *Black Duck* to brave occasional gunfire from slower Coast Guard patrol ships that were forever on the lookout for the infamous, artful bootleggers.

The same geography Horace Hunter recognized as an ideal location for tourism, and that 17th Century pirates recognized as an ideal location to hide treasure, also made for an ideal environment in which bootleggers could thrive. As a home base, Manisses was perfectly situated to not only supply the liquor needs of The Skulduggery, but also to feed the insatiable appetites of speakeasies in cities from New York to Boston and all the smaller communities in between, and to support the burgeoning organized crime syndicates that dominated all of them. The overwhelmed and understaffed police forces, including the Coast Guard, were no match for the rich, powerful and wildly popular bootleggers.

About twelve miles off the mainland, just outside the invisible line that identified international waters, fleets of ships waited in what the islanders called "rum row." Here, the ships laden with enormous stocks of liquor sailed in from all over the globe would wait for the moonlighting fishermen and entrepreneurs in their speed boats to pull up alongside and conduct business. The speed boats would then bring their wares ashore to a never-ending and delighted collection of thirsty and inebriated consumers.

Next to the same great rocks where Varnum once fished for lobster, and Verrazano's cabin boy Bissette once rested among a gaggle of native maidens, and where Wequai sang to her newborn child, Floyd finished his lunch and threw the final crust of his bread into the air for the voracious seagulls to fight over. Floyd was jealous. He had spent all thirty-five years of his adult life seeking honest pay for honest wages and barely had two-bits in his pocket on any given day. He had even served his country in the Great War, contracting the flu and barely escaping death, spending a long year in a depressing army hospital that left him thin and weaker than many of his friends. He watched the *Black Duck* speed by him parallel to the shore, angering dozens of hermit crabs with the sudden break of the waves it left in its wake. He looked again at the fine jewelry in the department store ad he now held in his hands and wondered if there was room in the burgeoning rum-running industry for him to share in the wealth and to also rescue Trixie from her own misery in Brooklyn.

As he walked back to town for his shift at The Skulduggery, he made the decision that it was time he went into business for himself. He rationalized that since he had nothing to begin with, he had nothing to lose.

His first executive decision as a businessman was to satisfy his two most immediate needs: acquire a gun and acquire a boat. He considered his current wages, and determined that it would take him a century to afford either, and there wasn't a soul who would trust him with a loan to start an illegal business operation. He wondered how the great mobsters of the day like Al Capone, Legs Diamond or Dutch Schultz would deal with a problem of severe undercapitalization. Across the street, he noticed the well-kept residence of Henry Brown -- the great-grandfather of the future Bernice Cowan who lived in a home the Bradford family would one day purchase -- and he stopped dead in his tracks. Floyd had never stolen a thing in his life, except maybe a few pieces of penny candy from the general store in Providence's Federal Hill neighborhood where he grew up, and he wondered what Mr. Brown might have inside his lovely house that he could part with, and help a down-on-his-luck entrepreneur along the way on his own road to riches.

Floyd was not a religious man, but he knew stealing was wrong. He felt a bubble of guilt building in his gut, and he swallowed to fight it off. Before he could think any more about what he was about to do next, he charged toward the house and peered into a window. The house was dark inside and quiet, and it was clear the Brown family was not at home. Floyd tugged at the window and discovered that Mr. Brown, the trusting gentleman and neighbor that he was, had left the window unlatched.

Floyd raised the window and wiggled his skinny body through the frame, landing on his stomach in the Brown's dining room, striking his head on a new, beautiful wooden hutch. As he laid on the floor, his heart pounded in his chest with a rhythmic force. When he heard a sudden, unexplained creek in the next room, he stopped breathing altogether. Before he passed out, he slowly raised himself to his feet, resumed breathing and scanned the dark room. He saw nothing of any particular value, surrounded by the familiar, unremarkable trappings of any of the island homes -- furniture, family photographs, lanterns, books -- nothing he thought would help him in his endeavor. He shuttled back and forth through all the rooms, snatching up only a bit of loose change and a handful of Mr. Brown's favorite imported cigars. Next, Floyd dashed up the stairs and pushed open the door to the Brown's master bedroom. The room was quaint and clean, and decorated with a good dose of Mrs. Brown's Yankee modesty in mind. However, across the room on a dresser, Floyd's eye spied what was a large jewelry box. He rushed toward it and flung it open, only to find it empty, except for a few random articles, obituaries and recipes clipped from a variety of newspapers. Undiscouraged, Floyd next approached the bedroom closet and heaved open its doors. He rifled through all manner of neatly folded jackets, shirts, pants, shoes and other random bits of cloth until his eyes fell upon something of keen interest -- an ornate tin box.

The box was a long-kept family heirloom, once owned by the late Shadrack Brown, and contained an amazing diary from an original island witch who was an unlikely survivor of a great maritime disaster. Floyd, of course, knew none of this, and rummaged around for the key that would release the lock and expose its mysterious contents. As he searched for the elusive key, he saw something else of much greater value to him and his eyes widened. It was a new .38 caliber, double-action revolver and was exactly what Floyd had been hoping to purchase once he fenced the stolen goods. After shaking the pillow free from the pillow case he had grabbed off the bed, sending its contents tumbling, he dropped both the revolver and the tin box inside.

With gun in hand, he elected to not press his luck any further and chose to leave before he was discovered. He also decided that he did not want to be seen running, or even walking, up the street toward town just after a burglary, so he chose instead to travel overland, through the thickets, across the fields, and over the many stone walls that crisscrossed the island. Behind the Brown's house, he passed the frog pond, the remains of Shadrack's cabin, and the opening to an old root cellar, its door torn from its hinges and left rotting in a jungle of weeds.

The farther he ran, the harder he breathed, and the more guilty he felt. He was ashamed of himself for robbing poor Mr. Brown, and knew that the police would certainly investigate. Mr. Brown was not only a gentle man, but a prominent man at that -- someone who was even being courted to run for office. A burglary of his residence, above anyone else's in the community, would sound an alarm and warrant a thorough investigation.

Then Floyd thought about the Herringbone Inn where he boarded, and how many different rooms had been searched and how many scoundrels had been dragged out by the island police department just in the short time he had lived there. In fact, after almost every significant crime on the island, the Herringbone was where the police made their first stop, and not a surprise to many, their last. The clientele of the Herringbone included many unsavory characters, criminals, rogues and addicts -- and many who were simply escaping something heinous on the mainland. His room was the last place he could stow his bounty.

As he jumped over a stone wall and inched closer to the village and the docks, he spied a red barn on the Dodge property up ahead. The barn was old and looked abandoned, and as he approached it, he noticed that the pungent smell of manure and rotting trash perfumed the air. The Dodge family used the old barn as a trash dump and it was no longer fit for human or even animal habitation, although he could see and smell evidence that a couple of hogs had recently been rooting around in the mess. Unbeknownst to Floyd, the Dodge family had received so many complaints about the stench, the town fathers had ordered them to clean it up or risk a fine. Floyd considered that the old barn, disgusting, abandoned, and far from the Dodge farmhouse, might be a great place to stash his loot until the heat was off and he knew it was safe to transport it back to his room.

Floyd climbed over the trash heap and set his stolen pillow case on a work bench. A shovel with a broken handle leaned against a wall, and he used it to push away dirt, leaves and decay from the corner. Floyd dug down about three feet into the same parched earth that Prissy and Abby would dig into almost a century later, when Floyd's shovel struck something bizarre. He paused. It appeared to be some sort of sack, sealed with a leather strap, with a big rusty buckle latched across its top.

But when Floyd dropped to his knees to pull the sack up out of the ground, the old rotted leather gave way in his grasp, spilling its contents of dirty, stained gold coins across his shoes. The legendary bag of treasure that Captain Kidd had never had the opportunity to recover, hidden two hundred years before, had been found.

Floyd was stunned and he fell back against the barn's wooden wall, striking the back of his head. He sat in silence for several minutes with his arms crossed, listening to the sparrows chirp on the roof of the barn above him while he stared at the pile of gold in disbelief. He reviewed the garbage heap in front of him and was repulsed by some of the disgusting things protruding from the pile, including some things he couldn't begin to identify that were festering with maggots and teeming with flies. Then he looked back down at all the gold coins, and he played with them. Floyd's confusion was profound.

And then he laughed. What kind of god, he thought, would reward a thief like him by leading him to a buried treasure? Floyd fell on his side and laughed again, louder, and held his aching ribs as he rolled around in the swill.

Floyd leaped up and grabbed his pillow case, dumping its contents with recklessness on a shelf above the workbench that was already filled with other abandoned tools, paint cans and supplies. The gun and tin box were far less important now, even a distraction. He dropped to his knees again and reloaded the sack with the gold coins, one grubby handful at a time. He was careful to be diligent and thorough, and he spent considerable time rooting around in the dirt just like one of the Dodge's prized hogs, for fear he might miss something. The truth was that Floyd had recovered almost every one of Captain Kidd's doubloons that afternoon -- except for one. Prissy would recover that coin herself many decades later.

After the bag was full, Floyd threw it over his back and carried it into a thick grove of nearby trees to hide until nightfall. He knew it would raise an eyebrow if he were to be seen carrying a heavy bag of gold around town in the middle of the afternoon. As he sat on a stump in the woods alone, he daydreamed. He fantasized about the grand house he could now buy for himself and Trixie, his beautiful bride-to-be, and thought about how much fun it would be to have his own new automobile. He wanted to travel, eat in all the fanciest restaurants, and stay at the most elegant inns and hotels. He dreamed about living the life of an aristocrat, of having servants, and of having every one of his needs fulfilled with the snap of his fingertips. He thought of buying a ship, maybe a sailboat, and of being transported up and down the east coast carried by nothing but the grace and whim of the wind.

Then he was struck by reality.

If he feared bringing a tin box and gun back to his room in the flophouse, what might the police think if they discovered a bag full of gold coins under his bed? And on an island as small as Manisses, exactly where and how was he going to spend this treasure? He knew few people, and trusted none of them. He considered taking his riches and leaving the island but could neither afford a pass on one of the ferries, nor a private charter, without raising suspicion. And if he did make it back to the mainland, where exactly would he take a million dollars worth of gold with complete anonymity?

Floyd knew it was late, and he decided to bury the gold there in the woods until he figured things out, but not before he removed two coins from the bounty and tucked them into the pocket of his trousers. It was also time to go to work, and if he didn't want to raise attention to himself, he had better stay on his usual schedule and get himself to The Skulduggery before anyone became suspicious.

He hurried into town as darkness fell, and made his way through the crowd of locals who were venturing out for their customary evening nightcap. Once at the bar, Floyd snuck in the back door, tied on his apron, and dove into the pyramid of dirty beer glasses that had already stacked up in his absence, acting as if he had been there all along.

"Why does this kitchen smell like a pig pen?" Duke, Floyd's bartender and manager asked. "Floyd, you smell like a whole boatload of manure."

"Sorry, Duke. I was out at the farm before I came to work and lost track of time. I didn't get a chance to go home and clean up."

"You do whatever you have to do to clean yourself up right there. This place is hopping tonight, and we need those glasses straight-up. You got that?"

"You betcha, Duke. I'll take care of it."

It was a warm night, so Floyd kicked off his sludge-caked shoes and yanked off his shirt, throwing them into the alley behind the bar. He washed and cleaned his dishes at a frantic pace to catch-up, as Duke was right -- the bar was as busy as he had ever seen it. Within the hour, patrons were starting to complain, but not about Floyd's putrid clothing. It appeared that the bar was running out of alcohol. The patrons had drunk the place dry.

"We got problems, Floyd. Big problems." Duke admitted as he came back to the kitchen for a fresh supply of glasses. "This is the third night this week we have run out of beer. We can't go on like this. The *Black Duck* has stopped delivering to the island. The captain says he's making a bigger dime selling to the hoods in New York than to us. I told him we'd be willing to pay a lot more, but he won't listen. I'm going to have to figure something out."

Floyd nodded. He didn't have much of an education, but he was smart enough to know that there was an opportunity here to make a fortune.

"You know, Duke. I have an idea. I think I know how to get us more product. I'll look into it tomorrow."

"You be careful now, Floyd. These boys ain't playing games."

"I know. I'll be careful."

"And hey.... the police were in here earlier tonight asking about what I knew about a break-in out at the Browns' place. I gave them a bottle of Canadian whiskey and they went away. You haven't heard anything, have you?"

"Nope. I haven't heard a thing."

It was late when Floyd got back to his room, but with the all the excitement of the day, he was alert, wide awake and barely able to contain himself. The police had been in earlier and searched through his room and all the other rooms in the inn while he was at work, arrested two of his neighbors, and left a mess behind, but they found nothing that could incriminate him. He removed the two gold coins from his pocket and sat them on the rickety table in the middle of his room. From the trunk under his bed, he produced paper, a pen and ink. He was not one to write many letters, but when he was motivated to do so, he could fill an encyclopedia.

Oh Trixie, my dearest, my love. It is too long. How I miss you so. I have tremendous news that I cannot dare to express on paper, as I must tell you in person. I beg you to come see me. Travel out to the island on the next ferry. Drop everything. When you arrive I will make your wildest dreams and wishes come true. All of them. I promise. I cannot wait to see your eyes and smile, and watch your face light up when I tell you of our tremendous good fortune. With deepest love, from my heart to yours, Floyd.

Floyd tossed, turned and didn't sleep more than a minute all night, and was up and pacing about his tiny room long before dawn. At first light, he flew out of the inn and made a beeline to the secluded dock along the inner harbor where it was a badly-kept secret that the *Black Duck* was moored. Even the Coast Guard and federal agents feared sailing in too close as the dock was fortified with arms and manpower, and the hard-nosed crew was in a constant state of unease.

The *Black Duck* itself was a wondrous vehicle, a converted luxury yacht retrofitted with twin engines rumored to have been taken from an airplane. Its hull had room for 400 cases of the best imports in the world, and its deck was fitted with guns that were poised to fire in any direction. No one was sure who the skipper of the craft was, as it was a well-protected secret, but members of the crew changed often and were infamous and regular patrons of The Skulduggery. The person most assumed to be the first mate, an Irishman called Obie, was a wretched excuse of a man, his face burned and disfigured in the war. His left arm was missing -- caught in and yanked clean off by a fast-moving, snarled length of rope when his fishing boat's nets were flung overboard by an impetuous greenhorn.

Floyd was terrified. Obie was guarding the dock, his one hand on a gun concealed in his baggy gray trousers. As Floyd approached, he knew if he wasn't recognized within a few seconds, Obie would probably shoot him.

"What do you want, Floyd? You got no business being out here."

"I want to talk to someone. Duke says the bar isn't getting enough product."

"That's too bad, mate." Obie said, "You tell your boss he's got to open up his wallet a little wider."

"I know, he's cheap."

"Cheap? That nitwit Duke wants to buy one case at a time, and he wants to pick and choose. Do we look like a damned

Fifth Avenue department store to you? Why should we risk coming into the Old Harbor to sell to him if we can sell the whole hull to the big boys in New London. It ain't worth the money or the risk."

"I know, but what if..." Floyd stuttered. "What if I made it worth the risk?"

"You?" It appeared Obie was pointing at him with an arm and hand that didn't exist. "I know you're broke, so what could you possibly have that would interest us?"

Floyd reached into his trousers and produced one of his gold coins, kissed it, and threw it at Obie who snatched it out of the air.

"This is solid gold!" Obie declared, rolling it back and forth between his fingers. "Very nice. Where did you get this?"

"Does that matter?"

"I suppose it doesn't. In fact, I don't want to know and I really don't care a lick."

"How many of those would it take to buy a four-hundred case shipment?"

"Between you and me Floyd, I'll tell you this. The ships we do business with come from all corners of the Earth. The Canadians bring the whiskey, the French bring the wine and champagne, and the Spanish come up from Cuba and the Caribbean with rum. And they all bring some of the most hideous beer you've ever had in your gut. But they're all picky when it comes to which currency they'll take, and the exchange rates change every day. But if our captain trades in solid gold, he's going to make a lot more friends out there. You have more of these?" Obie held the coin out as if to give it back, then slipped into his shirt pocket.

"As many as you need to make the deal."

"Let me talk to the captain. I'll get back to you. Now get out of here before someone sees you."

Floyd spun on his heels and hustled away from the dock. The morning fog was dense, and he could hear the guttural moan of the horn from the Southeast Light in the distance, warning approaching ships of the perilous shoreline. Though stressful, the first half of his plan had come together with comparative ease. Now he needed to receive one more stroke of good fortune to make his plan come to life.

As Floyd walked up the steps to Henry Brown's front door, he believed he was more afraid of Mr. Brown than he had been of Obie. Less than one day earlier, he had robbed the old man, and now, he was about to knock on the door and ask for a favor. It was a bold risk, maybe even foolish.

Mr. Brown answered the door after one knock wearing a bright and well-known handsome smile, startling the already edgy Floyd. Floyd swayed from one foot to the other, and clenched his hands behind his back to keep himself from biting his nails.

"May I help you, son?" Mr. Brown asked, scanning and evaluating Floyd from head to toe.

"Yes, sir... good morning. My name is..."

"You're that Floyd fellow who works at that bar in town. I've seen you eating lunch on my rocks down at the beach." Mr. Brown said, smiling as if he had recognized a long lost friend.

"Yes, sir. I am pleased to make your formal acquaintance. I am here today to ask a favor."

"A favor? What sort of favor?"

"Well, sir, I have a dire need to rent some space, for storage. I have come into a large collection of expensive fishing supplies... inherited them, actually. My uncle has died. Nets, ropes, barrels..."

"Fishing supplies?" Mr. Brown continued to smile, but was suspicious.

"As I have walked past your home many times... and admired it from afar, of course, I could not help but notice that on the lower portion of your property there is an old root cellar."

"The old root cellar?"

"Yes, sir. Down near the pond. Your root cellar would make a splendid place to store my fishing supplies."

"Why wouldn't you store your fishing supplies where you could use them, down by the fleet?"

"An excellent question... I spend much time by those docks, and unfortunately, there are some rather unsavory characters who frequent the island these days. What a world it has become... so sad, so dangerous. I want to keep these supplies safe. They mean so much to me."

"So you want me to give you my root cellar?"

"No sir. You are a fair and honest man, and I propose to pay a fair and honest rent. Name your price, sir, and I will see to it that I will pay that rent, whatever it will be, on the first day of every month."

Mr. Brown smiled again, and rubbed the back of his hairy, wrinkled neck, and even let out a slight, pleasant chuckle.

"Well, Floyd, that is some offer. But I do have a question."

"Yes, Mr. Brown?"

"Do you take me to be a complete idiot?"

Floyd gasped. "Sir?" Mr. Brown's face had turned a cold, steel gray.

"You rum-running hooligan bastards have ruined this island. Twenty years ago, this was the nicest place anywhere on the east coast to bring your family and enjoy a nice holiday. Now look around you. Half the buildings have closed up and people are afraid to set foot on the beach for fear someone will run them off with a rifle. It's shameful."

"I'm sorry, but I wasn't here twenty years ago. I've never seen this island as anything but what it is right now -- a community where the rich run rum and the poor starve in the street. I'm just looking to make ends meet."

"Is that what you call it? Making ends meet? In my day, the only living was an honest living."

"So I suppose, Mr. Brown, that would leave you the last honest man on Manisses not profiting from the trade?" Floyd pulled the second gold coin from the pocket of his trousers and threw it at Mr. Brown, who pinned it against his chest, over his heart.

"Here's my down payment. I'll give you ten dollars on the first of every month, just to rent that stinking hole in the ground... to store my... fishing supplies."

Mr. Brown fingered the coin much the way Obie had, and looked Floyd in the eye.

"Here are the conditions. On the first day of every month, you put a sealed envelope with the rent in my mailbox. If it's even one day late, I will take those...fishing supplies... for my own. You don't talk to me, you don't ever come looking for me. If the police or anyone ever asks me, I will tell them I have no idea who or what is down in that hole and I will tell them they can take and keep whatever they find. If I do see you come up the walkway to this house, I just might fire a slug through your scrawny little neck. Do we have an understanding?"

Floyd nodded his tacit agreement, then turned his back to Mr. Brown without uttering a sound, and walked back down the slate footpath to the road as if he had been issued an order.

"I think you forgot something," Mr. Brown called out, and before Floyd could turn around again, the lunch pail he had been carrying when he broke into the house the day before, and had left behind, struck him square in the back of the neck. Floyd winced as a trickle of blood ran into his collar, but he dared not turn around or acknowledge the insult. He now knew that if Mr. Brown understood he was the burglar, yet let him rent the root cellar anyway, it meant he was somehow involved in this business, too. Mr. Brown was part of the syndicate. He was on the payroll.

Floyd made his way right over to the old root cellar, and it was in even worse shape than he had feared. Inside, the air hung heavy with the stench of dead rodents. Several seasons of fallen leaves had blown in and rotted against the earthen walls, cobwebs hung like ghoulish Christmas garland from the dehydrated ceiling beams, and mounds of broken, abandoned preserve jars filled the room's corners. There were also four handmade but broken wooden chairs, once enjoyed by the property's previous tenant and his three strange friends that were used to sit upon while they would sing, laugh and hide from the summer heat and the cruel realities of their less-enlightened age.

Floyd exhaled hard and scanned the dark room. He had some serious work to do. And he grinned.

The *Black Duck's* first shipment of beer and spirits arrived just a few days later, right on time at three in the morning, as Obie promised, and was left stacked on the beach in the soft glow of a full moon for Floyd to carry through the thicket and deposit with great secrecy into his hiding place. He chose to endure all the back-breaking work alone as he trusted no one, for fear his enterprise would be discovered. He accepted that the secret must remain all his own. He hustled back and forth through the night without a moment's rest, and as the sun rose at six that first morning, without an ounce of energy remaining in his weary back, he fell asleep in the cellar draped across a barrel of prized Canadian whiskey. Three days of cleaning, making emergency repairs and loading-in his product had knocked him out cold. But it also proved it could be done.

Floyd enjoyed every back-breaking second of that busy summer. For the first time in his life, he felt like he had a purpose -- even if the enterprise was illegal, and he was making more money than he had ever dreamed. His sack of gold coins was half gone, replaced by a stack of cool, crisp paper greenbacks. He had worked out a deal with Duke to serve as The Skulduggery's exclusive supplier, and relished in the fact that he no longer had to wash dishes to eat. Duke was thrilled with the new arrangement, and by September, Duke opened a second bar in the abandoned restaurant of the Herringbone Inn that turned out to be so popular that by Christmas, he would open yet a third.

So while Duke was expanding his business, Floyd was perfecting his own. When he wasn't sleeping or loading in the new shipments that arrived twice each week, he was making dramatic structural improvements to the old root cellar. The first problem was that the confined space was just too small, and he spent week after week burrowing like a common shrew into the island's soft underbelly to triple the room's original, constricted size. Each of the walls needed to be reinforced with new timber, and the tightly-spaced beams and planks that provided the ceiling were replaced with care, one piece at a time, to keep the underground hovel from caving in on his head. He rarely visited his former room at the Herringbone, often sleeping across stacks of crates in the cellar, returning once every few days to keep up appearances, take a hot bath and check on his mail. Other than the liquor, it was the mail that kept the coals hot in Floyd's belly and the fire lit in his heart.

About once each week, usually after a particularly hard and arduous day's labor, he would nip at a bottle of old Kentucky bourbon, quiet his soul, and sit and write to Trixie. He found the escape into the dank cellar, much the way Shadrack had years before, somehow comforting. Floyd guessed he would receive one handwritten letter from his beloved for every ten he sent to her -- but he didn't care. When he did receive the rare dispatch from his Trixie, it was confirmation that she was receiving and reading all the letters he had been sending.

Dear Floyd: Sorry I don't write as often as I should. Glad you are doing so well on that island. I want to come see you, but I work two jobs now. I took a gig as a waitress in this new club right next to Ebbets Field in Flatbush. The ballplayers come in sometimes, even though they aren't supposed to. My momma's not doing too well, either. She's got an awful case of dropsy. I hate to leave her side. You should come to see me in the city. With all my heart, Trix.

By the end of Floyd's first year in business as the island's only and most popular wholesale distributor, he had amassed an incredible selection of beer, wine and exotic spirits. Dozens of cases, kegs, casks and barrels were neatly stacked, stored and organized in the cellar, maintained near a delightful fifty three degrees year round to preserve all the unique flavors and integrity of the collection. He built himself a subterranean apartment, too, complete with a comfortable bed, lanterns, a few books and a desk where he kept track of his accounts with both Duke and Obie -- but there was no electricity or running water. Had Floyd ever received a visitor, they would have been most surprised by his collection of firearms that included over twenty handguns, rifles and shotguns, and enough ammunition to hold off the Spanish Armada; though it never occurred to Floyd he could only fire one weapon at a time. As Floyd amassed more wealth and more product, his paranoia grew right along with them.

But much of his paranoia was well placed. The Rhode Island State Police had assigned two officers to the island, to be assisted by permanent federal agents, charged to investigate the growing presence of rum-runners and bootleggers populating the state's waterways. Rhode Island had been only one of two states to refuse to ratify Prohibition, thumbing its tiny, upturned, bulbous red nose at Washington, but was obliged to enforce the law nonetheless. As the alcohol trade grew, so did the violence between the underworld gangs throughout New England, and had it not been for the increasing complaints of honest fishermen who grew tired of pulling human skulls from out of their fishing nets, the authorities would have just bellied up to the bar along with the rest of the drunkards. And the infamous *Black Duck* was on the top of their hit list.

As police presence on the island increased, Floyd shifted his attention from improving the cellar to better concealing it. Once the site of Hubbard's shanty and Shadrack's much improved cabin, natural decay and undergrowth had already started to help Mother Nature reclaim the remains of the parcel. All Floyd needed to do was help things along a bit.

First, Floyd surrounded the above ground area with new plantings of dogwood and crabapple trees, then he dragged in broken branches and heaps of dead leaves to cover the ground, and then he lifted boulders the size of watermelons from the top of the stone walls and scattered them around in a random, natural-looking pattern. His ability to camouflage was so astonishing that in the dark of night, he would often need to root around himself to locate the hidden rope handle to the doorway tucked beneath the frenzy of tangled wild grape vines. Random passersby, including the property's rightful owner Mr. Brown, had no chance of finding it.

"Impressive, Floyd, I must admit it." Mr. Brown said, his trademark smile bending up from one ear to the other. Floyd jumped back as if someone had jabbed him in the ribs with a hot poker. "I've lived on this land my entire life and I don't believe I could even find the door to your cellar."

"What are you doing here!" Floyd shouted. "I paid my rent!" Floyd had been careful. He had not uttered a single word to Mr. Brown since the day his lunch pail hit him in the back of the neck.

"Relax, son... I'm not here to scold you."

"Then what do you want?"

"I have good news. This efficient little operation you have built for yourself has got itself some attention. A man by the name of Dutch Schultz, who runs a growing syndicate in the

Bronx and Brooklyn, needs somebody to run his warehouses in the city. He asked to see you."

"But how does he know about me?"

"Don't be so naive, Floyd. You have amassed a small fortune out here; you pay in pure gold and have a year's supply of liquor in secret storage. Don't you think the boys onboard the *Black Duck* talk to the ships waiting on Rum Row? Don't you think Duke talks to the other bar owners on the mainland? You have drawn a lot of attention to yourself without knowing it. And you have impressed some big people."

Floyd thought a moment about what Mr. Brown said, and then his well-honed paranoid tendencies kicked-in.

"Why are you telling me this? What's in this for you?"

"I'm just a messenger, Floyd, that's all. Remember that fishing tackle you told me you inherited? Well, let's just say that I inherited a whole lot of that... fishing tackle... too."

Floyd has assumed as much. "So when will this guy Dutch be out here to see me?" he asked.

Mr. Brown chuckled. "Oh, no... Mr. Schultz won't be coming to Manisses. You'll be travelling to see him in New York. You have been booked for special passage aboard the *Black Duck*. They will pick you up on the beach first thing Saturday morning. Mr. Schultz will be expecting you."

Floyd was speechless. Was this the lucky break he had waited his whole life to find? Had he tapped into the big time? He mulled over what it would be like to live and work in New York, and when the realization hit him that he could reunite with his dear Trixie, he threw caution into the persistent, salty wind.

"I'll be there. Thank you, sir. Thank you!"

"And by the way, Floyd. Do yourself a favor and clean yourself up before you go? Go into town and buy yourself a new suit, and a hat. And shave that sparrow's nest off your chin. Mr. Schultz is a very important person. When you meet him, you will want to make a good impression."

Floyd had been given three days to get ready for his voyage, and discover the promise of a rich, exciting life. Everything seemed right with the world. His coffee tasted richer, the air smelled cleaner and he even found himself whistling a Duke Ellington tune that had caught his ear. Floyd never remembered whistling before. When he reached the island's only tailor, a shop owned and operated by Reuben Cowan who also owned an adjoining hardware store off Water Street, he glided through the door with the swagger of a gangster, shoulders back, head held high. After he selected a nice brown pin-striped suit off the rack, and a fedora, he was surprised to find that the nervous Cowan refused to let him pay.

"Just have a safe trip." Cowan advised.

After cleaning himself up, Floyd went to the Herringbone Inn to organize his personal effects, all the while, thinking of nothing but Trixie. She flooded his mind and his soul, and his hands were shaking when he pulled out his pen and paper to write her. The mail currier was leaving within the hour, and if he was quick, he thought he might have a shot at getting the news into her hands before he arrived in New York himself. Floyd scribbled fast, his handwriting had never been that great before and it was even worse now, barely legible. In the letter, he admitted everything. He explained to Trixie about the gold, and the *Black Duck*, and the liquor. And he explained just how large his personal bankroll had grown and that he had been summoned to meet with Schultz, a known mob boss. But more important, he revealed to Trixie precisely where the door to the cellar was hidden, and even included a tiny map of the island. In the back of Floyd's mind, he knew the trip was fraught with danger and felt a need that he didn't begin to understand, to tell someone about his operation. Only there was no one else he dared trust.

Mr. Brown met Floyd on the beach at four in the morning as planned, well-dressed, a single bag hung over his shoulder. Floyd was surprised to hear that Mr. Brown was travelling to the city with him, having been ordered by one of Schultz's underlings to guarantee Floyd's safe delivery. Floyd wasn't in much of a position to object, and he didn't care anyway. He was focused on something more. By nightfall, he would be having a romantic, candlelit dinner with Trixie.

The two men waited, but the *Black Duck* was nowhere to be seen. The sea was calm, and the waters were quiet and Floyd and Mr. Brown said little to one another as they sat on the rocks and stared into the blackness. Then as the night conceded to dawn, the distinctive gurgling sound of the boat's large motors could be heard approaching from the south. Once it arrived, a few yards off the beach, Obie hopped off, waded through the surf, and walked ashore to greet Mr. Brown.

"What the hell is going on, Obie? You're two hours late." Mr. Brown was furious.

"There were complications last night with a delivery."

"That's no excuse. You know what's at stake here. Now help me get Floyd aboard."

"Nothin' doin'." Obie held the flat palm of his one hand out to stop them. "The Coast Guard is everywhere; they chased us up and down Narragansett Bay all night. There are a lot more of them out there all of a sudden. It's too risky to travel now in the daylight."

"You don't have a choice, Obie." Mr. Brown insisted. "Schultz is waiting for us. We can't keep that man waiting."

"Heading out right now might get us killed."

"And so will delaying the trip. If I were you, I'd take my chances with the Coast Guard. They won't yank out your fingernails when they catch you. I'd think you'd be more protective of your only remaining hand."

With a great sigh of reluctance, Obie conceded and the three men climbed aboard the *Black Duck*. The boat's powerful engines roared as it turned to the west at full steam, leaving a thick rooster tail of white spray in its wake.

Floyd sat in the middle of the vessel, knees squeezed together and hands folded on the lap of his pinstriped suit. He hated boat rides of any kind, as he was prone to seasickness, and the speed of the *Black Duck* was impressive but upsetting to his stomach. Obie and Mr. Brown scuttled themselves to the front of the boat to talk, the screaming engines making it difficult for either of them to hear the other.

"Obie, after you drop us in New York, are you sure you know what to do?"

"Yes. I will take care of everything. But why don't you just take care of this yourself?"

"Because I might not be coming back for a while. Schultz isn't too happy with me at the moment because I was supposed to deliver this patsy to him a month ago. So I need every bottle removed from that cellar before nightfall tomorrow. Then, fill it in with rocks. There can't be any trace left behind of that cellar ever existing."

"Did you bring a map? The only thing I need to know is where the cellar is located."

"It's at the back of my property, in the field. It's very well hidden. I left a map for you back at my house."

"With who, your wife?"

"No... no, she doesn't know anything about this operation, or the location of the cellar. We have this bulky, old hutch in our dining room. I told her to expect some men to come to the house tomorrow and get rid of thc hideous thing. I drew a map on the back of it and it will point you to the exact location of the cellar. When you're finished, just bury the hutch in the empty hole and be done with it."

"Aye, sir."

As the boat passed Montauk, the crew of seven and their two passengers overtook a fleet of fishing trawlers that were heading out on their day's run, and the boats saluted the *Black Duck* as it passed by. A few sailboats and pleasure craft were out, too, that morning, sitting still atop the flat, serene horizon as if a child had glued them there. Without warning, Obie sprinted across the boat and pointed his finger ahead of them.

"There!" He shouted. "Look!"

In the haze, a Coast Guard patrol boat was heading right for them. The boat appeared to be new, and a bit quicker than the others the crew was used to evading, but Obie was still confident they could outrun it. The crew scrambled for arms, took their defensive positions and turned up the engines. As the patrol boat made its first pass, its captain ordered the *Black Duck* to stop, which as expected, the crew ignored. Obie was concerned by the size of the gun mounted to the patrol boat's bow, and ordered both Mr. Brown and Floyd to lie on the deck just in case, which they eagerly obeyed.

"Don't worry," Obie said. "Most of the time, they just harass us a little. They rarely fire."

The patrol boat struggled to keep up, but was able to make a second pass at the *Black Duck*, except this time, despite Obie's assurances, they did open fire.

A strafe of bullets peppered the hull of the boat, one of them entering and exiting Obie's throat, sending him tumbling overboard like a lobster trap into the sea. Obie would likely have been the only casualty of the attack had Floyd, terrified and too embarrassed to throw-up on the shoes of the crewman, not jumped up at the wrong moment to vomit over the rail into the sea, taking a bullet to his chest, puncturing his heart. And had Mr. Brown not elected to try to stop him and pull him back down, he would not have been struck by his own fatal shot to the temple.

The *Black Duck* performed a sharp u-turn, and headed with force to the east, as the patrol boat, its own engines now smoking from brash overuse, gave up the pursuit. The enraged and stunned crewmen tossed the lifeless, well-dressed bodies of both Floyd and Mr. Brown overboard to join Obie, along with Floyd's bag, keeping only Floyd's new fedora as a morbid memento of the awful incident. Floyd's body and the last handful of Captain Kidd's gold coins came to a gentle, peaceful rest on the bottom of the cruel Atlantic, at the welcoming mouth of Long Island Sound.

The only three people who had any direct knowledge of the precise location of Floyd's stock of liquor in the old root cellar were now dead. The letter that Floyd sent Trixie before his voyage was now the only remaining record of the great enterprise.

Had Floyd's heart not stopped beating at the instant that the bullet tore through it, his heart would have stopped anyway had he ever completed his journey to Trixie's apartment. The letter he wrote just before he left Manisses did, in fact, arrive on time in Brooklyn, and joined about a dozen other unopened letters he had sent that were stacked on Trixie's nightstand. On the evening of Floyd's demise, Trixie's new fiancé -- a small-time hoodlum in the local numbers racket -- had come to take her out on a date. As they left her apartment, Trixie snatched up all of Floyd's letters in one handful and dropped them down the incinerator shoot in the hallway of the apartment as they made their way out on the town for dinner.

The intense flames burned the paper in an instant sending Floyd and Trixie's hopes and dreams into the air as bits of ash and smoke, drifting like Manisses' milkweed into the smog-filled Brooklyn sky.

The location of the old cellar would remain a secret for almost one hundred years, its treasures not re-discovered until a little girl named Abby Payne fell through Floyd's hidden, reinforced roof while on a mission to find her own treasure.

Chapter 31

lement, Mayweather, Honeywell and Skip were among the last to arrive at the chaotic scene. On the left, seated on the ground was Lucky, a handsome young EMT doing his best to flirt with the moody teen while he bandaged her elbow, and on the right was Abby, alert, awake and being cared for by a team of paramedics while she endured a tearful bear hug from her mother, Kitty. Friends and neighbors were arriving from all corners, some gasping, some pointing and some were even crying though many of them didn't seem to know why.

When Lucky's arm broke through the roof of the old cellar and became trapped, she was startled. But what caused her horrific, primordial scream was the chilling sensation of the little hand that reached up to grasp her dangling fingers. Prissy ran like the wind home to get Jessica, who called for help, and then followed her back to the site. From there, news spread like wildfire around the island that something big was happening at the Bradfords' house, and the whole neighborhood, some on foot, some on bicycle and some on moped, poured in. They knew that if it was happening at the Bradfords' house, it was going to be one heck of a show.

After Jessica released Lucky's arm, she peeled back the remains of the rotting doorway to reveal Abby seated on the corner of Floyd's bed, blanket wrapped tight around her, blinded by the day's bright sunshine. Abby was bruised, hungry, sprained and scared, but otherwise looked to be alright. Jessica carried her from the cellar, and she and Prissy hugged her until Kitty dashed to them -- one of the first to arrive.

When he first caught a glimpse of his daughter, Skip bolted like lightening through the brush to join Kitty in the family bear hug. Tears flowed, and the growing swarm of onlookers wept and cheered the emotional reunion. Jessica wiped tears from her own cheeks and greeted Clement with his own sappy hug.

"Jessica... Is Lucky alright?" Clement asked.

"Yes, she's fine. Just a few scratches on her elbow. Though that EMT might not recover."

"So what happened here?" Clement was baffled, his eyes and head jerking from side to side trying to interpret the weird scene.

"Abby has been out here all along, she fell through the roof of an old storage cellar. Lucky and Prissy found her. And the best news is that she looks like she wasn't hurt."

"Thank God she's OK. What a relief." Clement's eyes welled with tears along with the rest of the crowd.

Jessica lips parted to say something else, but stopped.

"Is something wrong?" Clement asked, sensing his wife's apprehension.

"You are not going to believe what's in that cellar."

Honeywell, Mayweather and his officers ushered the crowd back away from the scene, and started stringing yellow caution tape between the trees. From the perspective of public safety, the area could be dangerous. If a little girl could fall into the ground, so could a whole crowd of nosy neighbors.

"Let's go, folks. Everyone please step back out of the way." Honeywell ordered. "This is a potential crime scene."

"A crime scene?" Clement gasped. "What crime?"

Honeywell shot Clement an irritated stare. "Well, first I have to wrap-up a missing persons case, then I have to figure out how and why these two girls got hurt. I'll let you know if we believe a crime has been committed once we conclude a proper investigation."

"Man, we've got the greatest cousin ever!" A voice reverberated from beneath the ground, coming up through the doorway. One of Jessica's cousins popped his head out of the ground like a prairie dog, and held up a bottle of hundred year-old Spanish wine.

"Jessica, did you know they..." Clement began to ask.

"Yes, I knew..." Jessica answered.

"Why didn't I predict," Honeywell said, "that I would run into you idiots again today. Now put that down and get out of my crime scene!"

After shooing everyone away, Honeywell peeled more of the decomposing doorway from the entrance to the cellar and walked down its steps. Clement followed closely behind. Honeywell shined his flashlight into the darkness, and the light ricocheted and glistened like little diamonds off the hundreds of undisturbed bottles. The cellar had remained untouched, in the same pristine condition that Floyd had left it in his haste to leave the island back in 1927. The room resembled a Hollywood movie set, or a panoramic display plucked from a room at the Smithsonian Museum. There was a rack on the wall that displayed all of Floyd's impressive firearms. A chair was in the corner with Floyd's old work clothes still flopped over it, and his desk, complete with writing pen and dried ink was still poised, waiting for Floyd to compose his next letter. Clement reached his hand into the sack that leaned against the bed.

"Oh my!" Clement exclaimed, producing a three inch roll of twenty dollar bills. "This sack is full of money!"

"This is an old rum-runner's den," Honeywell surmised, peering around the room. "It was probably built here during the Twenties and Prohibition. The islands off New England's coast were heavily involved in smuggling product in for the speakeasies back then. Not many people realize how deep Manisses was in that business. Wow. This is one extraordinary find. Even historic I would think."

One hundred years of New England blizzards, hurricanes, nor'easters and blazing sunshine had almost no effect on the condition of the cellar, a nod to Floyd's superior attention and craftsmanship. And had it not been for the recent flooding rainstorm that saturated and weakened the old door just before Abby stepped on it, the location of Floyd's cellar would have remained a mystery, no doubt, for many decades to come.

Outside, Skip and Kitty had released their loving vice grip on their daughter so she was able to breathe again and explain to everyone what had happened. As Abby sat on the ground holding court, Prissy fastened to her side, Mayweather stood over them scribbling in his notepad, the setting sun making his imposing and intimidating shadow appear to be ten feet tall.

"I was just running between the bushes," Abby began, "on my way to the barn to go treasure hunting, and I fell through the ground and landed on my back. It hurt a little bit, but I was OK. I was really scared at first because it was dark, and I screamed and I screamed, but nobody could hear me. I was also really mad at Prissy, because I thought she could hear me screaming, but was ignoring me because she was mad at me."

"I was not!" Prissy insisted. "Tell her, Otto!"

"Oh, not that ghastly doll again!" Bernice complained, having just waddled up from the street, camera swinging from her neck like a pendulum. Prissy grimaced and stuffed Otto up under her shirt.

"Then I cried by myself for a while. It was cold down there, and I was lonely, and I was so happy when I crawled around and found some blankets. When the sun came out, it shined just a little bit through the hole I fell through and I could see all the bottles. They were really hard to open, but I was hungry and very thirsty, and I figured out that I could break them open by banging their tops on the end of the bed. The square ones tasted really icky, but the tall ones were sweeter and tasted pretty good after a while."

"I think the square ones are bourbon," Clement explained, rising up the stairs from the cellar. "And it looks like she polished off a couple of bottles of vintage champagne, and sampled a bottle of Cuban rum, too."

"Way to go, Abby!" One of Jessica's cousins shouted from among the onlookers.

"All the drinks made me sleepy. Mom said you guys kept looking for me and shouting out my name, but I never heard anything. It felt like I was down there forever, and I didn't think you were ever going to rescue me. The next thing I remember was hearing a noise and seeing Lucky's hand reaching down for me. I grabbed it and didn't want to let go!"

The sense of relief emblazoned on the spirits of both Kitty and Skip was inspiring, and the jovial crowd shared in their abject joy. As the EMT's prepared to take Abby back to the island medical center for a more thorough check-up, everyone was in the mood to celebrate -- except, that is, for Mayweather.

"OK, Bradford. I think you and your wife need to come with me down to the station."

Clement's back stiffened. And despite the great news about Abby, he hadn't forgotten his fury or his argument with Mayweather at the station. He was still incensed. "Us? For heaven's sake why? What did we do?"

"This is all too suspicious if you ask me. It's just too darned convenient. The moment I turned up the heat, on you and your family, the girl turns up in a hole on your property, bruised, and showing obvious signs of being drugged. I have a few questions..."

"No. We are not going anywhere! I've had enough of your self-serving lies, your innuendo and your harassment." The crowd that moments before had been so filled with bubbling joy had fallen quiet as if preparing for the next act of the show. Spasms of mumbles waved through them. Images of the purple splotches that vandals shot at their home were still fresh in Clement's mind, as was the public ridicule they endured from their days in Eastbury. Clement and Jessica were well aware of how the anonymous, fickle court of public opinion could turn nasty on the back of a single thought or unsubstantiated rumor.

"You can come with me voluntarily," Mayweather threatened, "Or I can have you taken away in handcuffs, if that's what you prefer."

"Come on now, Detective, do you really believe this is all necessary?" Honeywell asked, trying to inject some common sense into the dispute, also fed up with Mayweather's overreactions and grandstanding.

"If you lay one hand on my daughter, I will break it off!" Carl shouted from within the crowd, fist raised, as his nephews and Winnie launched into action to subdue him.

"I, for one, agree with the detective." Bernice interrupted, snapping a photo of Carl's angry, waving fist as she spoke. "And I know I'm not the only one here who thinks that, too. Everything that happens with this family is a threat to our public safety. It wouldn't surprise me if Mr. Bradford plied that poor girl with alcohol and threw her in that hole just so he could find her later and be a hero. Only the good Lord knows what that girl has been through at his unclean hands." The crowd groaned, and someone volleyed an offensive, obscene catcall at Jessica.

"But I didn't find Abby. Lucky did!" Clement shouted back at Bernice. And the moment the words left his lips, he wished he could have sucked them all back in. He and Jessica had worked hard to shield their daughters from the biases and perils of the outside world, and from the natural prejudices his line of work seemed to attract. He did not intend to drag Lucky into this. If he had his wish, both Lucky and Prissy would remain invisible, forever.

"Yes, Miss Bradford, tell us please... exactly how did you come to find Abby." Mayweather's tone was snide and sarcastic. "Tell us how after a dozen search parties walked across this very square of land, you were able to sashay to this very spot, poke your hand into the ground and pluck out the little, lost girl like you were picking a potato?"

"Lucky didn't do anything wrong!' Prissy had sprung to her feet and was pointing Otto at Mayweather like he was a loaded weapon. Otto was not comfortable when everyone was staring at him. "The witch showed Lucky where to find Abby!"

Some of the crowd gasped, a few others released uncomfortable giggles, and a few more mumbled under their breath. Winnie had all she could do to hold back the angry Johnson clan from jumping the detective, pounding his face, and inciting an all out riot.

"So, Miss Bradford, did the witch fly in on her broom and draw you a map?" Mayweather smirked and taunted, drawing a few more snickers.

"Lucky, you don't have to answer him," Winnie advised. "Please let me handle this."

All eyes turned now to Lucky who was sitting on the ground, alone, cross legged. She had not yet answered any of Mayweather's discourteous questions. Her black dress with a metallic silver fringe was reminiscent of what a flapper would have worn in Floyd's day, but her leather biker boots the fringe rested upon were not. Lucky's arms were outstretched from her body, her palms turned up to the sky, and her eyes were closed. Jessica had never known her daughter to meditate and started to wonder if something was wrong -- maybe the stress and pressure of the moment had disturbed her in some way. Memories from the aftermath of Hannah's discovery haunted them all.

"Lucky? Is everything alright?" Jessica asked, reaching out to her troubled daughter.

With all the grace of a seasoned midway performer balancing high above the center ring, Lucky rose with a smooth elegance to her feet. Her hands came together in front of her face as if she were in deep, thoughtful prayer, except her fingers were spread wide apart. She placed her index fingers on the tip of her nose, opened her dark eyes wide, and stared straight ahead through the crowd as if they were transparent. Lucky took a long, slow, deep breath and began to shout.

"For three hundred years, you and all who have populated this island have lived under the spell of a vengeful and angry witch named Kattern." Lucky began, now spreading her arms out wide as if she was attempting to hug the crowd all at once. "The spell was cast to avenge the deaths of many loving and innocent souls lost at the hands of your prejudiced, self-indulgent ancestors. This witch, who chose to reveal herself to me, shared her innermost thoughts, loves, dreams and fears, as well as the hopes and dreams of her children and her children's children, and through her remarkable vision and boundless grace, she did, in fact, guide me to this very spot, where I found Abby."

Prissy sat on the ground with her knees tucked up under her chin as if she was watching her favorite television show. She looked down and whispered to Otto.

"Why wouldn't they listen to us when we told them about the witch?"

Otto did not have a good answer.

The crowd stood silent and remained confused, not sure what to make of Lucky's bizarre spectacle, but entranced nonetheless. Jessica and Clement stood silent as well, except their mouths hung half open in shock. They had never seen their daughter act so out of character.

Lucky and Jessica's eyes locked for a quick and fleeting instant. Lucky wiped her brow with her wrist, then touched her left ear. To the crowd, they were innocuous movements, intended perhaps to swat away a pesty mosquito. But to Jessica they held great meaning. Now she understood what Lucky was doing. Lucky's gestures weren't random hand movements at all, but signals -- they were the same signals Clement used in his parlor during channeling sessions to communicate with Jessica. Lucky knew them all as well as she did, and there was no question what she was trying to communicate. Lucky was in trouble and asking for help. Jessica stepped forward to assist, and accepted her rightful place to perform in the next act of the day's family play. As Mayweather once put it to Clement, there was a game to be gaffed.

"From the moment Abby went missing, the good people of this island pledged their skills and industry to find her. Our fishermen patrolled the shores, our police organized search parties, and we as a family of spiritualists, used our natural-born talents to do what we were trained and destined to do. Like you all, we pledged our soul and skills to help our friends, neighbors and fellow islanders. For the past three days, we have held a vigil of our own, relying on our well-honed senses to help identify the powerful indigo aura of this beautiful lost child."

Clement had also seen the signals, figured out what was happening, and could not have been any more proud of his wife and daughter. He then enjoyed a momentary flashback to a time in his youth, on a hot carnival midway, when a beautiful girl rescued him from the threats of a bully. Funny, he thought, how history cycled to repeat itself. But this was not the time for reminiscing.

Jessica relayed a secret signal to Clement who stepped forward and took control of the impromptu weed-filled stage. Clement then signaled to both Lucky and Jessica who stepped toward him and dropped to one knee, closed their eyes, and hummed a quiet chant. Jessica's cousins recognized the bit, looked at one another, then pushed their way through the crowd and obediently did the same, and even Prissy and Otto rushed over to join them. It was part of a routine that Jessica's old mentor Lucretia had taught Clement in her tent on the midway many years before, a routine he rarely had the opportunity to use. It was a routine borrowed from the "mesmerists" of the 19th Century, stolen from Russian Gypsies, with elements even utilized by stage hypnotists to this very day. Jessica wondered if

Clement might even be channeling old Lucretia to guide the family through the routine. Many of the casual spectators were intimidated by the unusual moment and stepped away. But others, including Winnie, Smyth and even Luther Cowan -- to Bernice's infinite fury -- rallied and joined them. In fact, at least a dozen other islanders dropped to one knee and joined their unplanned, impromptu vigil.

But as they all had anticipated, it was an interesting show.

"I ask you all to close your eyes and relax your souls," Clement began, pacing around. "With your permission and cooperation, I request only your trust and positive thoughts. If everyone here is willing to assist, I may be able to channel this witch, and bring her here now, to reveal herself to all of us."

The gathering, now about fifty people strong, either stood or knelt in polite silence. The breeze fluttered the leaves of the dogwoods and the calm summer quiet was disturbed only by the throaty call of a distant cormorant.

"Everyone, please... concentrate only upon the sound of my voice. Focus all your helpful thoughts, good feelings and positive emotions like a beam of energy upon me. If you are a non-believer, if you harbor negativity, or if you consider yourself a skeptic, kindly step back so that you do no harm to the intent of your neighbors and friends."

Clement extended his arms and bent his neck back to face the sky. And he waited.

"I feel no presence. Please, focus! The earth at this site is rich with the triumphs and disappointments of many. I can feel the presence of native Manissean maidens and warriors, of white settlers, pirates, farmers, and fisherman. I feel the hopes and dreams of immigrants, businessmen, great leaders and bootleggers. I feel the warmth of children, the old, and the unfortunate. But I do not feel the presence of our witch, Kattern. Witch Kattern, are you with us here? Please reveal yourself to me."

After a few seconds of silence, Lucky leaped up to her feet.

"The witch. She has joined us. I feel her spirit and her presence."

Just as Lucky finished speaking, a sharp, terrifying, muffled scream emerged from beneath the brush in the field many yards behind them that startled everyone, and as fifty heads turned, it appeared that no one -- or at least no one of this world -- was there. Jessica, Clement and Lucky exchanged quick glances, each trying to determine which one of them was responsible for that portion of the gaff. No one took credit, and the audience was now on edge. Their senses were focused, prepped and right where Clement needed them to be.

Clement continued.

"I now feel your presence Kattern, I know you are here. Speak to us!" Clement signaled Lucky.

"I feel you, Kattern! My hands are tingling!" Lucky responded.

Jessica answered next, speaking as if her breath had been taken away. "I feel it! Yes! My hands and arms are tingling, too."

The same breeze that had massaged and soothed the summer air all day blew through the crowd, as if on cue.

"I feel it! I feel it!" Kitty announced, surprised and glancing down at her trembling fingers. Then someone in the back agreed, and another, and then another.

"Wow, wicked cool!" Vance exclaimed.

The entire group was mumbling and looking around for the source of the supernatural interference, as if comparing notes, and finding only one another's astonished stares. Even the most ardent skeptics seemed confused and were taken back a bit.

"The spirit tells me she no longer has a quarrel with the residents of this island," Lucky proclaimed, her eyes closed and her head tilted to one side. "She says the work we have done, the love we have shown for the children of our island, releases us all -- from this time now and forever -- from the evil in her curse."

"What about the ship! Tell her to get rid of the burning ship!" Prissy demanded, staring up at Lucky. Lucky opened one eye to look down at her, and if she could have kicked her in the rear-end and told her to get lost, she would have.

"With the curse released, the ship shall appear no more."

Mayweather had stood by and watched the drama unfold with curious amusement, but had now seen enough. He knew

Clement to be a fraud, and none of these theatrics or this sudden collection of new fans made any difference to him. He strolled into the scene like an angry stage manager, and grasped Clement's wrist.

"That's enough of this nonsense, now let's go."

"I'm not going anywhere!" Clement remained defiant, and the crowd moved in.

"You may have some of these people fooled, but not me."

Clement tried to stay in character as he was being pulled away. "It's dangerous to interrupt a session in progress, you know. It disrupts the spirit world."

"I'm terrified." Mayweather joked. "And I guess you'll just have to take your chances. No one asked you to do this."

"That's not true!" Skip had jumped in front of Mayweather, impeding his progress towards his squad car. "I asked Clement to do this!"

"Step out of the way, Skip. I don't have any quarrel with you."

"Well you did an hour ago now, didn't you? And who was it that came to help me then? The other day, I asked Clement and his family for help.... no, I begged for it. I asked him to do anything he could to help find my daughter. I offered him anything he wanted... anything... I offered him everything I owned in exchange for even the slightest chance that his talents could help. I don't know what he did, but my God, look at the result. And what did the police do while the Bradfords were looking for Abby? You were interrogating... me! You were accusing me of murdering my own daughter. Clement, I owe you everything. Thank you."

Skip lunged forward and threw his arms around Clement's skinny neck, and Kitty followed suit, planting a wet kiss on his unprepared, pale cheek. Honeywell took Mayweather by the elbow and led him away from the scene. If by some chance the police believed Clement was guilty of something, there wouldn't be a jury on the planet that would convict a suspect being hugged and kissed by the victim's parents. Hugs and kisses and even a bit of light applause enveloped everyone. It was a happy day. The burning ship had been exorcised, and was gone forever.

As the crowd broke up to go home, comparing eerie stories about how they, too, felt Kattern's presence, an officer stayed behind to guard the cellar and its valuable cache. Kitty and Skip joined Abby for an ambulance ride to the medical center, and Jessica collected phone numbers from the crowd to book future private channeling sessions. As the last of the onlookers meandered away, the Bradford clan regrouped to head for home.

"That was amazing," Clement declared. "Lucky, I am so impressed."

"It looked like you needed someone to rattle the chandelier a bit. That's all." Lucky answered, then paused, falling back into her usual, irascible mood, "...and don't think I'd do it again!"

Jessica was distracted, and instead of celebrating with her family, she had turned around and was wandering back to the cellar.

"Jessica, where are you going? What's wrong?"

"My father... has anyone seen Dad?"

But before anyone had a chance to become too concerned, Carl appeared heading toward them, taking his time walking and balancing himself along the top of the stone wall that led to the house. He hopped off the wall and wrapped his arm around his daughter. Bits of green leaves fell off his shoulder and stuck in her hair.

"What happened to you?" Jessica asked, brushing the debris from his clothing. "You're a mess."

"You didn't think I would stand by and do nothing, did you?"

"That scream! Clement declared. "That was you!"

"I almost didn't try it. Once I burrowed under the vines on the hill, I almost changed my mind. I wasn't sure if I could get my voice to project in an octave that high. Then I suppose you were all able to hear me alright?"

"Perfectly."

Through the centuries, the thicket had proved to be a safe and efficient cover for rabbits, deer, birds and even a native maiden hiding from possible island invaders. Carl was only its most recent guest.

Carl stroked the front of his wrinkled neck. "I strained my vocal chords. My throat is killing me."

On cue, the cousins produced a vintage bottle of 1926 Dom Perignon in one hand, and a bottle of cognac in the other. No doubt, they were worth thousands.

"Let's see if this eases the pain," he said.

There hadn't been much time for celebration in the Bradford household, but Clement didn't need any extrasensory help to know that tonight, things were going to be very different.

Chapter 32

A month had passed since Abby had been found, and the short attention spans of most islanders had turned to more pressing issues, coming crises and new problems. Merchants turned their attention to the rapidly approaching Labor Day Weekend, which was one of the busiest and most important weeks on the island all year long. Tourists saw the holiday as one last opportunity to crowd aboard the ferry to celebrate summer, worship the sun, and absorb all the island's charm and splendor, while merchants saw one last opportunity to fill their coffers by separating their visitors from their vacation budgets with a tip of the hat and a friendly, Yankee smile.

As Prissy and Abby skipped their way up Water Street, more than once they had to hop into the gutter to avoid being trampled by tourists who were barreling ahead without looking where they were going. The girls' mission that afternoon was to survive their perilous journey from the safety of Clement's busy office to the treasures of the Captain Kidd Cafe next door, with a goal to pirate themselves each a serving of yummy strawberry ice cream.

"Oh no!" Abby exclaimed.

The line at the door to the cafe extended deep into the street, and disappeared around the corner. The girls' chance at charming a snack from the now frantic waiters was near zero.

"Oh no!" Prissy exclaimed. "Look!"

Their three old friends -- Guilfoyle, Sumner and Jude were, once again, not sitting together. Like before, Guilfoyle had been banished to a bench in front of the candle store to sit alone.

He uncrossed his arms to offer a cordial wave at the girls from his lonesome seat on the corner.

"Prissy! Abby!" Jude shouted, removing his new straw hat. "What a wonderful surprise. It's so nice to see you ladies again. And Abby, how are you feeling?'"

"I'm all better, sir." Abby answered.

"That is wonderful, just wonderful news. We are so happy you came out of that awful ordeal with such good spirits." Sumner giggled under his breath at the unintended pun.

"Mr. Jude, why is Mr. Guilfoyle sitting way over there... again?" Prissy asked.

Jude sighed, and delivered a careful answer laden with political correctness. "Sometimes, Abby, adults don't get along so good. And spending a little while apart like this can be a good thing for everyone."

"Don't listen to him. It's because he's a blithering idiot!" Sumner interrupted.

"I heard that!" Guilfoyle shouted from down the block. "I have new hearing aids, remember?"

"You see, ladies, Mr. Guilfoyle supports that new windmill project. A new company is coming to the island, and they want to install dozens of these fancy, new windmills out in the ocean to make electricity for all of us."

"That sounds cool!' Prissy said. "I like windmills."

"Yes, it is a pretty good idea, but Sumner and I have our worries. We don't want to have Manisses' beautiful view ruined by a bunch of windmills, and we're not sure what would happen to all the fish -- the windmills might scare them away and then all our fishermen would go out of business."

"Alarmists!" Guilfoyle shouted from down the street.

"Well, whatever he thinks, it will be on the agenda tonight at the town meeting... and oh, that's right, it will be a big night for your dad, too. I'm looking forward to that."

"So is he." Prissy complained. "That's all he talks about... all... day... long."

Later that evening, like the swallows returning to Capistrano, the islanders fluttered in from all corners of Manisses and landed upon their usual perches in the cramped town hall chambers. Anyone who was anyone was there, chattering and fidgeting in their uncomfortable wooden folding chairs, waiting for the meeting to begin and refresh their need for unsullied news and juicy gossip. Smyth had thought ahead and seen to it that the neighboring club's blaring techno music would remain unplugged until the conclusion of the meeting, or the owner would risk a hostile review hearing of his liquor license.

Like many of the meetings in recent months, significant controversies abounded. Not only was there this new hullabaloo surrounding the proposed windmill project, but a final decision on the fate of the Dodge barn was at the top of the agenda, and on the tip of everyone's tongues. Because of the discovery of the Prohibition-era wine cellar behind the Bradford's home, things had changed. Clement, to his delight, had unintentionally become a key player in the historic preservation of critical pieces of island history.

Smyth pounded his gavel once on the solid table.

"Let's go folks, quiet down. We have a lot to do, I haven't had my dinner yet, and I want to get home early."

The council began its proceedings as Bernice arrived, squeezing her way up the narrow aisle, then depositing herself in the last remaining empty seat in the room -- square in front of Prissy and Abby -- creating an impenetrable wall that blinded their view of the meeting. Bernice's wooden chair cried out in agony, and she turned to scowl at the girls.

Prissy hugged Otto very tight.

"Mr. Dorry," Smyth asked, "Would you please present your proposal."

"Of course. First I would like to ask Clement Bradford and Brenda McMahon from the Preservation Commission, to join me up here. As you all know, we have been ringing our hands over what to do about the old barn. At our last meeting, I proposed razing it, which I know wasn't the most popular idea I ever had. But the good news is that there have been some recent, new developments." He explained.

Clement and Brenda stood idly by.

Dorry continued, addressing the crowd. "So first, please allow me to introduce you to Mr. Walton Redstone!"

A middle-aged, well-dressed stranger stood, smiled, turned, waved and returned to his seat in mere seconds as if he had been rehearsing.

"Mr. Redstone is an executive vice president with Atlantic Wind Industries. They are the company, as most of you know, who have proposed to build the wind farm off the coast."

The room grumbled.

"Mr. Redstone has also signed a purchase and sales agreement to acquire not only the barn, but the entire Dodge property to be used as a permanent residence for himself and his family."

The room exploded in chatter and sharp conversation. Some reached out to shake Redstone's hand and pat him on the back to welcome him, others shunned him with a cool disdain.

"So, what about the barn?" Jude shouted from the gallery. "Is he going to save it, or burn it down?"

"Well that's where we come in," Clement interrupted, bubbling with enthusiasm. "Since we discovered the old cellar a month ago, Jessica and I have been debating what we should do with it and all its contents. We've talked to a lot of people, and done a lot of research, and we believe the right thing to do would be to preserve the site as much as possible and maintain it as an historic landmark here on the island."

Jude interrupted again, "...but what about the barn?"

"Mr. Redstone has agreed to pay for the restoration of the barn as long as we agree to move it off his property," Brenda added. "And Clement has offered to donate a small parcel of his property large enough to accommodate a new foundation for the barn. With the barn moved within proximity of the cellar, the Preservation Commission will then be able to not only oversee the construction and restoration process ensuring its historic accuracy, but also operate tours and incorporate the site as part of our regular interpretational programming."

"Hey Clement, where on your property are you planning to put that moldy, old, beat-up thing?" Guilfoyle asked.

"As near to the beach as we can," he answered, "without violating any right-of-ways or freshwater restrictions. It will make for an incredible picture-postcard photo if we find the right place.

We have this outcropping of rocks by the shore..; I'm thinking if we just blast those out of the way, we might have something..."

"The council voted in executive session this afternoon to contract the services of Attorney Winsome Hunter to walk us through the minefield of grant writing, permitting and zoning ordinances that are going to be needed to make this all happen," Smyth said.

The chamber burst into another round of spontaneous chatter, discussion and arm waving. Bernice's chair expressed a grateful sigh of relief as Bernice rose to speak, her shrill voice cutting through the racket like a referee's whistle.

"I for one think we owe Mr. Redstone here tremendous thanks for his warm and generous offer," she said.

"Sounds like Bernice can smell the money," Jessica whispered to Lucky.

"I think that's what she does just before she eats it," Lucky whispered back.

Sumner rose to speak next. "Well now, I'm so glad this sounds so hunky-dory to everyone, but it sounds fishy to me. Does this guy think that by paying to relocate that barn, one board at a time, we're going to let him waltz right in and have us hand over our hallowed waters for his stupid windmills? This sounds like nothing more than a fancy bribe to me!"

Redstone stood.

"Why yes," Redstone answered tongue-in-cheek," that's exactly what it is."

The chamber burst into laughter, causing the veins on Smyth's forehead to pulse and his face to turn red as he pounded the table in front of him, again and again, in a futile attempt to locate the elusive order he required to keep the meeting moving forward. It was becoming clear to everyone that this meeting was going to take a while. It would be a very long night.

And it was well past midnight before the meeting mercifully adjourned and the Bradford family offered their cordial good-nights and embarked on their long stroll home. The night was warm and the breeze was still, as the rhythmic, soothing chirp from armies of crickets and peepers guided each step of their path. Clement was on cloud nine, arm in arm with Jessica, and they paced well ahead of their bored drowsy daughters, who lagged in the shadows.

"Lucky?" Prissy whispered so her parents couldn't hear. "When we get home, can I borrow your blowtorch?"

"What? No!" Lucky responded surprised she would make such an outlandish request.

"Pleeeeeeease?" Prissy whined.

"Are you nuts? It's dangerous. You'll burn the house down. And why do you want my blowtorch, anyway?"

"Because."

"That's not an answer."

Prissy stomped her foot. "You have to help me, Lucky, please!"

"Oh, whatever. I don't want to talk about it right now. I'm too tired to argue with you. Come see me in the morning and explain it to me then."

And Prissy did exactly what her sister advised. A few hours later, just minutes after the sky brightened, but before the morning sun dared peek above the horizon, Prissy was slapping her palm against Lucky's bedroom door. And as Prissy had anticipated, Lucky had no intention of answering.

Prissy pried open the door, wandered in, and stood by Lucky's bed. Lucky was buried beneath an avalanche of black and silver comforters, and Prissy was curious how she was even able to breathe, never mind sleep tangled up in the chaos. She stood for a while by the bed and said nothing, considering her options, and then with a sharp burst of surprising vocal strength, she shouted her name.

"Lucky!"

The interruption was met with a barrage of pillows fired in Prissy's direction. The volley was well aimed but caused no physical harm. Prissy refused to yield or surrender.

"I hate you, you pest!" Lucky hollered. "Why won't you leave me alone and let me sleep?"

"You said to come see you in the morning. That's what you said."

"Come back later."

"No, Lucky... I need you to help me now!"

Lucky raised herself from within her cocoon and sat on the edge of her bed. She yawned, stretched and rubbed her eyes that were swollen and sore from lack of sleep. She hadn't bothered to clean the make-up from her face before she went to bed the previous night, and to Prissy, the smeared black eye shadow gave her the look of a confused raccoon. If Prissy had been feeling like herself and not so focused at the serious task at hand, she would have laughed herself silly.

"Alright now, what is so darned important?"

"This!"

Prissy pulled Kattern's tin box from a sack she had tucked under her arm, and held it out into the unwelcome, rays of golden sunshine that were now streaming in the window.

"The box? What about it?"

"I need to get rid of it. I need you to use your blowtorch and seal it up."

Lucky shook her head. "No, you're nuts. That box and the diary are important historical artifacts. If you don't want it anymore, you should take it down after breakfast and give it to Mrs. McMahon for the museum."

"Please, Lucky... you have to help me get rid of this. I need to get rid of this right away. You don't understand! It's very important."

"Why is it so important?"

"Because Otto says it is! He insisted!"

Lucky dropped her face into her hands and sighed, rubbing the black make-up onto her palms, then smearing it off onto her pajamas.

"Prissy, listen to me. You're getting to be a big girl now. I know how much you love Otto, but you're old enough to make decisions for yourself. You don't have to listen to everything he tells you."

Lucky looked into Prissy's eyes, and was frightened by the size of her black pupils and the depth of her resolve. Prissy's motives and interests always baffled Lucky -- the two girls were different in nearly every conceivable way -- but Lucky could tell when Prissy was dead serious. She knew if she didn't help accomplish whatever it was that was occupying Prissy's obsessed mind, Prissy would end up burning her own fingers off on the blowtorch on her own. Lucky had little choice except to concede.

"Fine, then. What is it you want me to do?"

"You need to seal up this box so nothing can get inside like water or rain or even air... with your blowtorch."

"Well first, I don't think we need a blowtorch. I think a soldering gun will do the trick. And second, don't you worry, I can seal this box up so tight it will last more than a hundred years...if that's what you want."

Lucky hopped up from her bed and gathered her tools. She was a masterful craftsman, cleaning the old box with a gentle hand, then going to work sealing it for good. When she was through, Prissy dropped it back into her sack and bolted outside without saying a word, or even a thank you. Curious, Lucky followed well behind.

Prissy marched through the yard with long strides like a determined soldier off to battle, and reached the great rocks by the beach. With the bag clutched tight in one hand, Prissy began her careful ascent to the top as Lucky stood on the ground and watched her weird, almost possessed sister from below. The great rocks that had stood for hundreds of thousands of years had been sentenced to demolition. Prissy would be the last to ever climb them. Once she reached the top, Prissy swung the sack over her head in circles like an Olympian would prepare for the hammer throw, then she released the bag sending it high into the air, landing in the ocean waves with a heavy kerplunk, sinking fast, and disappearing out of sight into the shallow, green sea.

"Do you feel better now?" Lucky asked once Prissy had returned to the ground.

"Yes. Yes I do." She said.

It wasn't until the following April that the sentence levied upon the great mound of rocks was carried out. Executioners in the form of four bulldozers and a professional demolition team arrived at the Bradfords' home early one Monday morning and went right to work preparing for the blast. Prissy had even been given special permission to stay home from school to watch the spectacle, as the newspaper, photographers, politicians and curious onlookers all gathered on the Bradfords' lawn for a brief ceremony to celebrate what would become the location for the future, relocated Dodge barn and historic site.

But before the blasting and destruction was set to begin, Smyth and Dorry set up a rickety podium, poked a flag into the ground behind it, and read a prepared speech. About fifty people gathered and milled about, motivated more to watch the rocks explode than to celebrate a profound historical moment. Clement stood beside the podium with his hands folded with pride and smiled for the flashbulbs, but Jessica and her daughters elected to stay far behind, preferring to stand on the porch to watch the production from a safe distance, instead. From their vantage point, they couldn't hear what was being said, but were able to distinguish sporadic moments of polite laughter and the occasional round of applause that would bound and echo across the yard.

An enormous flock of seagulls appeared overhead, circling the crowd, assuming as seagulls often did, that a collection of people in one place suggested an easy meal. The white birds provided a majestic backdrop to the modest event, circling in wide, elegant arches against the gray, overcast sky behind them. That was, until one of Jessica's cousins selected a leftover clam cake from the bag he was holding and tossed it in Bernice's direction. The cold, rubbery clam cake bounced and rolled up behind her flat shoes, not escaping the notice of about fifteen of the majestic, aggressive, and infinitely hungry birds.

Clement watched the sudden commotion from his position next to Smyth and didn't have any idea what had caused it, but the site of big, round Bernice bounding across the yard with her hands flapping over her head and a squadron of hungry seagulls on her tail, delivered the best laugh he had enjoyed in months. Clement was so distracted by Bernice and her amusing antics, he didn't see the taxi arrive in his driveway, nor did he see a young female figure exit the car and walk up onto the porch.

Smyth and Dorry ended their presentation with an urgent, direct order for everyone to clear the area. The flag was plucked from the ground, and two volunteers hustled the podium away. Honeywell and his police officers ushered everyone back to a distance they had deemed to be safe to watch from, and he flashed a hand signal to the demolition team instructing them to begin their final preparations.

Clement made his way to the porch to join his family, and gave Prissy a peck on top of the head as he jogged up the stairs. Clement felt like he was a little boy again playing with his train set, waiting in childlike anticipation for it to appear around the next bend.

"Watch this, Prissy. This is going to be awesome!"

It was then that Clement noticed Jessica was crying. As he instinctively reached out to console her, he saw that she wasn't upset at all, but was smiling, shedding tears of joy. Jessica wiggled her finger and pointed across the yard where Lucky was standing on the lawn hugging a girl. The two girls were also crying. Clement couldn't see the other girl's face, but felt he knew her. She felt somehow familiar.

"Who is that?" Clement asked.

"It's Hannah."

Clement was stunned.

"Hannah? What? How!"

"She stepped out of that taxi about five minutes ago."

Clement peered into the taxi's window and could see someone else inside, a tall male passenger sitting in the shadows in the back seat. Clement recognized the square-jawed silhouette right away. There was no doubt who it was.

"Mayweather!"

"Please, Clement, ignore him... don't go over there. He brought Hannah over to the island this morning just to see Lucky. I'm not sure how it all happened, but I think he's trying to make things right."

The ground shook, the crowd gasped and a deafening, vicious explosion of rock filled the morning sky, sending the great pile of stones tumbling and falling upon one another in a violent ballet. Prissy covered her ears and screamed, and the onlookers waved and cheered. Boulders the size of the Bradfords' home rolled over and cracked in two, while bits of others fell and crashed across the beach and into the sea. The great spire stood no more. Wequai had been the first to stand upon its peak, and Priscilla Bradford the last.

Manisses

The place where Wequai had given birth to Manisses; where a native boy first spied Verrazano's *La Dauphine;* where Hubbard witnessed the sinking of the *Princess Augusta*; where William Kidd warmed himself in the sunshine; where Shadrack watched the remarkable blind Varnum fish for lobster; and where Floyd waited for the *Black Duck* to bring him to his beloved Trixie, was now gone forever, cleared away to make room for a restored barn that had been used to shelter hogs and human refuse.

Chapter 33

I t is the noble birthright of every New England Yankee to complain about something whether it be the weather, taxes or the skyrocketing price of a pound of lobster. But no people hold that legacy and duty any more dear than the residents of the island of Manisses. From April until October, as thousands of visitors each day invade, swarm and stomp over the adored isle, grumbling about the noise, litter, traffic and crowds is universal. But as the last sweaty tourist steps aboard the ferry for the return trip to the mainland, the nine hundred permanent residents complain of nothing except the inflexible, ever-present boredom that hangs over the island like a thick autumn fog.

It had been over a year since work crews obliterated the once-majestic and surreptitiously historic boulders to make way for the barn reconstruction project, and a team of egg-headed university preservationists had now erected a tower of scaffolding on the site to manage the fine details of the plan, right down to the placement of each individual hand-forged nail. The Bradfords' home, too, was undergoing a renewal. Part of the money Clement received from auctioning off Floyd's gun collection, rum and wine to serious collectors and aficionados was invested in a new roof. And to pay off a year's worth of rent, the Johnson clan was hard at work providing the complimentary labor. And as his nephews bellowed song after song from the peak of the roof into the chilling November air, Carl kept his feet on the ground pushing a paintbrush, covering the last remaining bits of purple on the exterior with a stately, cold, New England white and a robin's egg blue trim.

By autumn, Clement's appointments had become fewer and farther between, and he spent more of his time hanging around the house conducting research, rehearsing new routines, or working at what Jessica referred to as, "goofing off." But if Clement invested his boring, shortening days into lounging around in his pajamas, Jessica felt it was his due. Ever since the afternoon Abby was recovered, like the great rocks, business had exploded. He had been working around the clock for months.

"Clement!" Jessica called from the living room. "Come here! You need to see this."

Clement ran into the room like an oversized toddler and slid across the wooden floor in his stocking feet, pecking Jessica on the cheek as he glided by.

"Look at the television."

"Is that Mayweather?" Clement asked, scratching his head through a mess of uncombed hair.

It appeared one of the local news channels was covering the recent election of Connecticut's newest Attorney General, a former police detective named Forrest Mayweather. Clement and Jessica knew he had finally declared for the office he had so dearly sought, but since they didn't tend to watch much television, it had been easy to avoid the coverage. It appeared that since the moment he had been declared victorious, certain allegations about his conduct as an investigator had emerged. One former suspect was accusing him of brutality, another of committing fraud, and a third of luring him with a shocking entrapment scheme. As the investigative reporter grilled him, and Mayweather defended himself, touting his faultless record, the screen flashed an old picture of Hannah -- the picture plastered all around the village of Eastbury the day after she went missing -- causing Jessica to gasp.

"I guess that dog has had his day." Carl said, wiping paint smudges from his forearms. "And it's about time."

"I made peace with it. It doesn't bother me anymore." Clement insisted. "You can learn from the past, but you cannot live as a slave to it."

Clement expected Carl to respond with a wise-crack about his sappy, sentimental philosophy or with another dig at their nemesis who continued to sweat it out on TV. But instead, Carl heaved a sigh and threw his paint stained towel into a trash barrel at the other side of the room.

"You're right, you know." He began. "I have been living as a slave to my past. I've been living under your roof, eating your food and feeling sorry for myself. And those jokers up on the roof aren't any different. We've all been talking about this among ourselves for a few months now.... but I think it's time we move on and let your family have its old life back."

"Carl, I wasn't talking about you, I was talking about me and..."

"I know, I know. But what's the difference? You became the better man and were able to see beyond your jealousies and anger. Yet I wallow in them. I'm still useful. I still have a lot of life left in me... I'm not ready for the grave just yet. Tell me, Clement, where do you see me in three years? Five years? Ten years? Still living in your basement, trimming your arborvitae and playing hide and seek with Prissy?"

"She loves that, you know."

"And so do I. But that's not a life for a grown man. Besides, I don't think I can survive another of these long, boring winters on this island."

Jessica had hung on every word of the discussion, and had waited to speak. She knew this day was coming, but she wasn't upset. Instead, she smiled.

"Having you here the last year has been a blessing for all of us. But I know you better than anyone. After Lucky found you out back, I told Clement that I didn't expect you to hang around for more than a day or two. You have wanderlust in your genes. It's part of who you are. You aren't a Bradford, or a Johnson. You are a Zalenko!"

"No... a Flying Zalenko!" Carl pounded his chest with his right fist.

"But what will you do?" Clement asked.

"There's a small traveling carnival in Texas that works the Bible Belt during the winter months. They have some rides, games and even exhibit a few animals. They tend to visit churches, community centers and private schools -- that sort of thing. I worked for them for a little while a few years ago keeping their new carnies off the bottle. It was kind of fun, to a point, kicking those sad sacks around. I have an open invitation to return whenever I want, and I plan to take the boys with me this time. The winter tour picks up the weekend after Thanksgiving. They are a nice group. They remind me a lot of our old outfit."

"Do they ever travel back up north?" Clement asked.

"If there's a paycheck in it... they'll show up on a glacier."

The doorbell rang and Lucky, who was expecting Vance to arrive with his daily delivery of cream-filled pastry from the village's new French confectioner, dashed off to answer it. Jessica was proud of her father -- an unconventional character, but loving and committed to his family to the end -- and knew that even if he went back on the road, he would return. She hadn't seen the last of him.

"Dad? You have a delivery. And it's huge."

Clement had not been expecting a shipment of any kind, and because of its size, it was too big to bring in the front door. So the four of them circled the appliance-sized crate on the porch like it was a Martian landing craft, daring one of the others to touch it first. Then Carl reached out and tore the shipping label off the top.

"Who the heck do we know in Hartford?"

"My mother and father? Could this be from my parents?" Clement wondered. He had not heard from his mom and dad in over a year. He had accepted long ago that they would never forgive him for eloping with Jessica, joining a carnival, and embarking on a lifestyle that crashed into their conservative religious beliefs, and in their minds, bordered on immoral. Clement reserved his contact with them to logistical matters of birth, death, marriage and anything that might pop up on television that could prove embarrassing to the family. Clement ripped open the box's heavy lid and plunged his hands and forearms into the vat of fluffy, white foam peanuts.

"Oh my God!" Clement said as he fished around in the box. "Oh my God!" He repeated.

Clement's right hand emerged from the box clutching a red 1935 Lionel Hiawatha locomotive. Hank and Edith Bradford had shipped his entire antique toy train collection to Manisses.

"I suppose," Jessica said with a sheepish grin, "I had better come clean."

"What are you talking about? Did you have something to do with this?"

"I called your parents a couple of weeks ago."

"Why on Earth did you do something like that? You hate my parents."

"No, that's never been true. You always told me I was supposed to, but I never did though they did drive me crazy sometimes. I don't know what it was that made me call, but I thought it was time. I believed they needed to know about what an important man you had become in this community, about all you have accomplished, and how proud they should be of you and their brilliant grandchildren. I hope you are not too upset."

As Jessica spoke, Clement and Carl dropped to their hands and knees on the porch and snapped train track segments together like little boys. Jessica assumed her earnest confession was being ignored by everyone except the curious sparrow that landed on the porch railing.

"Upset, no. I'm not upset." Clement answered after an embarrassing delay.

"That's great," Jessica replied, "because I also invited them to Thanksgiving dinner."

Chapter 34

Prissy and Abby were under strict orders to always walk directly home from school. On days when they ignored the order and wandered off to explore, they might not turn up until well after dark, riling the anger and anxieties of their loving, snake-bitten parents. As the autumn calendar marched forward, darkness arrived with a stern impatience, and the girls' opportunities for mischief decreased with each shortening day.

Abby stood in the circular driveway of the small red brick school, tapping the toe of her sneaker on the curb, waiting for Prissy who was late. Her dearest friend was always the last kid to leave the building, yucking it up with her favorite teachers, darting in and out of abandoned classrooms, and Abby knew the clock was ticking like a time bomb, set to expire, setting off an explosion that would leave her in a heap of trouble. When Prissy finally did arrive, she zipped right past her, turned right into the street, and left Abby in the dust. Abby squawked.

"Hey! Where are you going! We're already late."

"I'm going to the library."

"But we have to go home."

"But I have to go to the library."

"If we go to the library, we're going to be in big trouble."

"If you don't want to go, that's fine with me. You can just go home."

"Why do we have to go to the library right now?"

"Because..."

Abby stopped in the street to ponder her options. She had not wandered off alone, on her own, in two years, and on that last eventful day that she did, she found herself swallowed up by a hole in the ground. She sighed, and decided that it would be better to just stay with Prissy and take her chances with her parents later at home. Abby also recognized the same stubbornness and resolve in Prissy that frustrated Lucky, and knew that once Prissy's mind was focused on something, it wouldn't easily be changed. In fact, there wasn't any chance it would be changed at all.

The girls scampered into town, turned up the well-worn cobblestone path and pushed open the heavy, glass double doors of the Manisses Free Library. The small building was quiet, the only sound being the clackety-clack of a handful of high school students peppered around the room who were typing out homework assignments on strategically placed computer terminals.

"C'mon, Prissy. Just get the book you need and let's go home! Hurry up!" Abby pleaded.

"Excuse me, ma'am." Prissy asked in her most polite manner. "Where would I find books on local history?"

The librarian pointed her pencil at a darkened corner partially hidden by a potted palm tree. Once there, Prissy scanned titles about the native Manisseans, early settlers, sword fishermen and legendary pirates. There were photographic essays, town meeting records, and books about famous New England hurricanes. Abby was impatient, and as she stood by the door ready to burst, Prissy scanned one last shelf and found an old diary from a Civil War widow who had lived on the island until after the First World War. Prissy nodded to herself that she had located the correct spot, reached into her backpack, and pulled out Kattern's tattered, historic diary, and slid it into place.

The old diary had been hidden under the mattress of her bed since the day she shared its secrets with Lucky. But as time passed, the book came to haunt her. Prissy decided all on her own that the historic reference belonged someplace where it could be cared for and read. And was there a better place for that to happen than a library? What a tragedy, she thought, that the book could someday find itself behind a glass case in a museum display where no one would ever be allowed to touch it again. Kattern had become somewhat of a friend. She believed her secrets, wisdom and insights should be shared and read until Kattern's very words faded and fell from its pages.

It was several months before one of the librarians discovered the rogue volume among a pile of random items discarded on a table waiting to be re-shelved. They had no explanation for its sudden appearance, and assumed someone conducting research had the unfortunate luck to carry the priceless treasure in but leave it behind.

However, it was much more fun to believe that the old witch Kattern had dropped by and placed it among the stacks herself -- and even left a tarnished gold coin taped inside the front cover to pay the 300 year-old late fee.

Chapter 35

rissy rounded the corner by the candle store on Water
Street, with a hop in her step, and headed down the
sidewalk carrying two heavy bags. At first, the three old
men didn't notice her, their failing eyesight dismissing her as just
one of the other dreary, baggage-laden tourists stepping off the
ferry for their holiday on the island. Prissy stopped in front of the
cragged men and dropped her bags with a heavy harrumph,
annoyed that she hadn't been recognized, startling them all.

Without uttering a sound, the first of the men jumped to
his feet and embraced her, and she hugged him back with all the
affection a daughter could offer a loving father she had not seen
in some time, and she planted a tender wet kiss on his wind-
burned, pink cheek.

"Oh my goodness... is that our little Prissy?" Mr. Cowan
asked.

"It is! It is!" Skip Payne rose from his seat with much more
care than Clement had, balancing on his cane, the victim of
multiple back surgeries over recent years, to greet her himself. As
the years pressed on, she had become almost a second daughter
to him. Prissy hugged Skip and he smiled.

"Oh, Mr. Payne, how is Abby? I don't talk to her anywhere
near as often as I want to."

"She is wonderful. Just wonderful. She brought the family
out here to the island just last month. She and her husband
opened their second restaurant in Boston last summer, and
they've been working around the clock to make it work out."

"I wish I could have been here to see her. I miss her so
much!"

"How long will you be able to stay?" Skip asked.

"She's staying the whole week!" Clement announced,
hopping with pride. "I have my little girl all to myself for a whole

week!" The spring in Clement's step was that of a man half his age.

"My husband was called away to Los Angeles on business," Prissy explained, "and our son Jack went off to Greece for some site work he needed to finish up his master's degree in archaeology. I discovered I suddenly had this whole week with nothing to do. So, I asked the firm to give me some time off and I decided to spend it here."

"And how is Winnie?" Mr. Cowan asked. "I haven't seen her in ages.

"She's getting on in years I guess, but you'd never know it. She still bounces around the office tripping over things like she did when she started her practice here on the island. The first thing I learned when she made me a full partner was that as partners, we were responsible for keeping an eye on her, keeping her from injuring herself and out of trouble."

"Some things never change." Mr. Cowan laughed.

"Some things don't ever change, do they? Like the air. The air, here, smells so good. I think I've missed that the most."

"It's low tide, and it's warm today." Skip added. "And I don't believe municipal services emptied Captain Kidd's dumpster this morning."

"The air here is always so heavy and clean, and just smells to me like home." Prissy closed her eyes and inhaled deeply. "Oh, how I've missed it. In one breath, I can see the crabs scuttle in the seaweed along the shoreline, a platter of hot clam cakes at the cafe, and a lobster boat pulling into the dock. The images of everyone I have ever known, and everything I have ever done here, just come flooding back in one breath. It's like taking a ride in a time machine. It's wonderful."

Prissy and Clement left her bags behind with the others for a few minutes, and they strolled together through the streets of the old village. So much had changed over the years, yet so much had stayed the same. Seagulls circled the ferry as it prepared for its return journey to the mainland, and passengers dressed in splashes of gaudy color lined up to board, just like they had for decades.

The ferry's piercing horn sounded, frightening a group of toddlers, each with their own strawberry ice cream cone, who now wailed together in an annoying concert. The opportunistic seagulls paid careful attention, as they always did.

"Lucky will be so excited to see you, Prissy. She has been looking forward to this."

"I can't wait to see her and her family, too." Prissy paused. "You know, Dad, it's funny to hear people call me Prissy again. That only happens here on Manisses. My name is Priscilla to the rest of the world."

"Well then, I would venture to say the rest of the world is wrong. You are part of this island; you are Prissy -- a nine year-old girl who likes climbing rocks near the beach."

As they sauntered along the sidewalk, Clement pointed out all the comings and goings of the merchants their family had grown to know so well through the years. He explained how the family who had owned the liquor store had moved to New York, how the old man who ran the candle shop had developed a gambling problem and gone bankrupt, and how the woman in the t-shirt shop ran off with the husband of the woman who ran the convenience store. Prissy rolled her eyes at each passing tale. And Prissy swore the island was shrinking -- everything looked so much smaller than it had since her last visit, and as she recalled it being in her childhood.

"Oh look! It's your toy store! Let's go inside."

Clement bristled at the suggestion. "No, you can go inside if you want to, but I'll wait out here. I ran that shop for thirty years, and when I sold it to Luther's son, I promised myself to let it go -- to let all of it go. The smartest decision your mother and I ever made was to reinvest the proceeds we received from the contents of that wine cellar into a real business. I had always wanted to run a toy store. It was a dream. So I didn't shed a tear when we shut down the old office, but I think your mother missed the performance and drama of it all. Theater was in her blood -- I think she would have made a great actress if she had chosen that path for herself."

"That's your train set still inside, isn't it?"

"I didn't have the heart to take it with me when I retired. The boys and girls love that thing. Every summer, when the kids come to the island with their parents, it's their first stop -- the second they step off the ferry they want some ice cream and want to see the trains. They look forward to it. I just couldn't disassemble it, bury it in a box and take it home to waste away in a basement. Luther Junior promised to take good care of it if I left it installed. It belongs to the kids now."

"That was sweet. I know how much those old trains meant to you."

"They were the connection to my own childhood. But it means more to me when I see all the bug-eyed kids staring at them through the window. In this day and age of technology, it's refreshing to see the old toys bring them the same joy they did for me."

"Does the store still sponsor the carnival you and Grandpa brought here?"

"Yes it does! Maybe that will be my greatest legacy to the island. I'm not involved anymore, but the troupe still comes every August. The town has added a concert and a craft show to the event now, and it draws thousands in from the mainland. Your mother adored that chance to perform with her father and family again, even if it wasn't on a high wire, and even if it was only for a few seasons. I think the experience re-ignited her sense of purpose, and it's what inspired her to open that little gymnastics and dance academy over the toy store when she got older. The sound of all those little girls jumping around up there used to drive me bonkers, and the vibration could even knock the train off its tracks when they really got going, but she loved everything about it. I didn't have the courage to complain."

"So how are you doing... without Mom? Is everything still alright?" Prissy asked, needing to know but not wanting to ruin her father's happy mood. Jessica had been dead for over five years, passing in the night in her sleep without warning, succumbing to an affliction she never told anyone she even had, not unlike the stubborn, fortune-telling mentor who helped raise her. The whole family was stunned by the untimely news, but Clement took the shocking reality even harder than Prissy, or anyone, expected.

"It gets easier every day. Lucky takes good care of me -- keeps meals on the table and makes sure I take all my daily meds. I walk on the beach a lot alone now, often at sunrise, and I can still feel your mother's presence there with me, her hair and breath on my neck. If the waves are quiet, I can even hear her whispering."

Prissy walked and peered into each window along the way, wide-eyed as if it were her first visit to the town, until they arrived at the old storefront where her mother and father had spent their early years on the island channeling spirits. The sign above the door now read, "Fine Art by Lucretia" and the shop was filled with both the whimsical and serious sculptures, and modern art, of her talented older sister and select local artisans, including old friend Hannah Griswold. It was a popular stop for many island visitors, with a reputation that extended to collectors and art galleries all over the world.

"Do you think she's here?" Prissy asked.

"Oh no, she never comes out to the shop. She tried that when she first opened, but as you know, helpful interpersonal skills were never Lucky's strong suit. Positively not good for business. She is a smart kid. She leaves the retailing to the hired help."

"Look through the window, I think that's the same Victorian table and chairs that were here when I was little. Did you know that I used to hide under that table with my doll when you were interviewing new clients? I used to love to spy on you and Mom."

"You mean with Otto?"

"You... remember Otto?"

"Are you kidding? How could I forget, Otto! The two of you were inseparable. When I flip through our family photo albums, it's hard to find a picture of you when you were little without him squeezed under your arm or clenched in your fist. I wonder whatever happened to that old doll."

Prissy paused, and looked down at her shoes, took a deep breath, and avoided any appearance of sadness.

"I don't recall. I guess that day came where I grew up and didn't need a doll anymore, and he just went away when Mom cleaned out all the other old clothes, trinkets and toys."

"Such happy memories," Clement said. "All those birthday parties and cookouts on the beach. I wish I could relive them all over again. Which was your favorite?

"Oh, that's easy. I think about it often. It was the Thanksgiving that Grampa Carl and Grampa Hank and Gramma Edith all came to share Thanksgiving dinner with us. There were a dozen of us seated at the table at the same time -- our whole family in one place. There was food, singing, dancing and games... I remember enjoying the feeling of being part of something bigger, a big family, with everyone there, all together. That weekend was so much fun."

Clement grimaced. "I'd almost forgotten about that. I believe that was the single, most stressful weekend of my life. Everything was going along great until my father accused Carl of making a pass at my mother. Captain Honeywell was furious we interrupted his own Thanksgiving dinner on a disturbing the peace call. I found pieces of that train set in the yard and shrubs for months after that weekend."

They walked further and stopped in front of Island Convenience. Prissy placed her head on her father's shoulder and squeezed his hand. "It's getting late, Dad, and I can't wait to see the house and Lucky, too. Come on... let's go get my bags and go home."

"Oh wait... before we go there's one more thing."

"What is it?" Prissy looked concerned.

"You didn't get your gumball yet."

"Why would I want a gumball?"

"The little girl I knew never walked down Water Street without stopping in the convenience store for a visit to the gumball machine."

"I can't believe they still have that old thing in there."

Clement stepped back from his daughter and raised his arms to each side as if in performance. His arms weren't as straight as they had been in the days on the carnival midway when he would produce rabbits magically from thin air, and his back was now hunched over and he was forced to stand mostly on one foot to maintain his dubious balance. But there was no disputing the power and radiance of this performance as he waved his hands above his head, snapped his fingers twice, and produced a single quarter from out of nowhere. He presented it to his daughter, who applauded and laughed aloud. It was as if the thin fabric of time had been punctured for a single flash, and

Clement was in his early thirties again, and his daughter just nine.

"Thanks, Dad... but I think I'll pass on that gumball."

"Well that's just too bad." Clement performed an awkward pirouette, and this time instead of a quarter, produced the gumball itself.

Prissy smiled again and accepted the gift with a polite bow.

"You've been practicing again, haven't you?"

"A little. I do tricks for the kids when they walk through the village sometimes. Why... am I not getting better? You look disappointed."

"Actually.., I was hoping for strawberry ice cream."

Chapter 36

"W
ell we made it, finally... here it is. What do you think?"
Chaz Whistler stood with pride in the front yard
of his new home -- a meticulously restored, three
hundred fifty year-old farmhouse with a spectacular ocean view,
nestled upon an idyllic New England island -- that he had
purchased for his family.

"This is it?" Chaz's ten year-old daughter Luna whined. "It
looks boring."

"I think it's adorable," Chaz's wife Ivy commented, trying
to maintain her enthusiasm. "It's a house like the people used to
have in olden times. But you have to wonder how they were able
to survive in a house like this without modern conveniences."

"According to the real estate agent," Chaz explained, "this
house was built in the eighteen fifties, during the presidency of
Ulysses Grant. That's over three hundred and fifty years ago. It's
quite impressive and historic."

The Whistler family had arrived by high-speed hover ferry
that morning, and strolled from the bustling village to the house,
taking in all the unique vistas, sandy beaches and wild life the
isolated island offered them. Chaz had been named the new vice
president for Atlantic Wind Industries, the largest windmill power
company in the world. And Chaz's territory -- the forest of wind
turbines just off Manisses' coast that fed the growing demand for
electricity to all New England -- would now be just minutes away,
visible from his own dining room window. For Chaz, the move
was a dream -- he could work from home, take his own
hovercraft out to the windmills to supervise maintenance as
needed, and be home for dinner just minutes later. His daughter
Luna was not happy with being separated from her school and
friends back near the wind fields of New Orleans so many miles

away. And Ivy wasn't thrilled by the prospect of life on a dull island either.

"What's so historic about this place," Luna grouched. "It doesn't look all that special to me."

"Well let's see if there's any information about this property on The Feed." Ivy depressed a small switch on the side of her wristwatch, and the image of a screen appeared in the air in front of her. She manipulated a few holographic buttons, and whispered a few instructions. A moment later, a three-dimensional hologram of a man appeared standing next to them. The man had inherited Lucky's deep, dark eyes and Vance's protruding forehead.

"This is Vice President Bradford Asher. He served during President Galway's administration during the Great Oil War. It says here, he was born in this house about a hundred and fifty years ago. It also says his mother Lucretia was a critically acclaimed artist of the day, and his father Vance was a fisherman. According to this article, he has been credited with creating the Hawking Program that sent the first manned spacecraft to Jupiter. How exciting is that!"

Luna shrugged, and didn't appear impressed.

"That's it? Is there anything else?" She whined.

"No, it looks like he was the only person who ever lived here that made any difference in the world. Besides, I think it's refreshing to live some place quiet where nothing ever happened," her mother added.

Luna squinted up at the address on the street sign planted at the end of the driveway, which read, "Bernice Lane."

"Who was Bernice?" She asked.

"I have no idea." Chaz answered.

"No one named Bernice comes up on The Feed." Ivy added, switching off her connection with the wave of her wrist like a carnival magician would make a rabbit disappear.

Chaz continued. "But it was customary to honor famous and important people by naming streets or buildings after them. My guess is that whoever this Bernice person was, she must have been an extremely important person to the island many years ago to warrant such an honor."

Chaz might have developed a different opinion had he known that the road was named by Luther Cowan who installed the sign himself, upon the order of his wife, and that no one on the island possessed the courage to take it down.

The sun was warm, the breeze was fresh, and the cormorants and gulls were dancing and swooping in the sky, so Chaz, Ivy, and Luna set out to enjoy the pleasant weather while strolling and exploring the property before touring through the cozy confines of their new home. Chaz knew Manisses didn't have the excitement, hustle or bustle of the city, or the technology and entertainment available anywhere on the mainland, but he hoped that the beautiful setting might convince Ivy and Luna that this move would be good for all of them.

The family strolled across the green lawn where Lucky had once hugged Hannah, and where Clement once recovered pieces of his beloved train set after Hank threw them through the window. They glanced up at the roof where Jessica once performed her impromptu high wire act for Prissy and Abby, and passed by the spot where Bernice surreptitiously gathered her snapshots. They trundled over to the place where Smyth set up his podium, where Prissy played tag with Abby, and where Vance Asher, a man of very few words, dropped to one knee in a pair of torn black jeans one afternoon and proposed to Lucretia Bradford. But all these moments and memories were fleeting, and had taken their place alongside the ghosts and adventures of Wequai, Manisses, Shadrack, Hubbard, Kattern, Varnum, Floyd and all the others who called this single spot on the small island home. A singular place where nothing ever happened.

"What's this?" Luna asked.

"It looks like it was once an old cellar of some kind." Chaz answered.

The wine cellar that Shadrack had built, Floyd had improved, and Abby had crashed through so many years ago, had fallen into shocking disrepair. The program that the Preservation Commission once operated, providing guided tours, lost its funding after a sharp economic downturn during the early part of the century, and was never reinstated. Across from the cellar stood the charred foundation of the old Dodge barn, which survived many years more than the cellar, but eventually succumbed to the ravages of time, neglect and the thoughtless acts of vandals.

"It's a real mess back here, isn't it? But don't worry about that. I'll get a truck back here to bury that debris and fill in this hole. We wouldn't want anyone falling in and hurting themselves."

The family walked down to the beach, and Luna slipped off her shoes and stomped into the surf. The foam and bubbles tickled her toes as she wiggled them around, and she pointed and smiled at a crab that scampered in terror to hide itself under the nearest rock. She reached down and picked up a stone the size of a softball and heaved it with both hands into the sea, releasing a great splash of water as it landed.

As their daughter played and splashed around in the water, Chaz and Ivy sat on an enormous stone that had rolled onto the beach following Clement's explosion, where Wequai had once leaned to rest and nurse her newborn son. All around them, stacks of small stones were balanced in dozens of little piles as far as the eye could see, just as Prissy and Lucky had first created together so many years ago.

"How strange," Ivy said, "someone would go to the trouble to stack all these stones like this."

"The real estate agent told me these cairns are spread all over the island, and building them is a tradition that goes back many decades. No one knows who built the first one, but they are stacked by their creator to memorialize a special moment."

"Do you mean like the first time a family visits its new home?" Ivy asked. Chaz felt she might be warming up to the island.

"Exactly!' He responded with enthusiasm.

Chaz and Ivy went about gathering up as many round, flat stones as they could find to make their own cairn. At first, the piles toppled over, but they quickly got better at arranging them, and in a matter of a few minutes, working together, they had created their own stack of ten well-balanced stones to add to all the others.

"There," Chaz said, "it's official. Let it be known that the Whistler family now resides on the island of Manisses."

As they worked to improve the balance of their pile, Luna approached them, carrying an old tin box covered in seaweed.

"Yuck. Where did you find this?" Ivy asked.

"It was stuck between those rocks over there. I followed a crab and he led me right to it."

Luna had found Kattern's tin box that Prissy had pitched into the sea over a hundred and fifty years ago. Over a century of Atlantic storms had pitched it back.

"What do you think it is, Chaz?"

"It is very old, and in terrible condition. Just some piece of trash, I suppose, that fell off a fishing boat. That would be my best guess."

"It used to have a lock." Luna pointed out, "See? And if you shake it, you can tell something is inside. Is there some way we can open it up? Maybe it's full of treasure!"

Chaz reached into his pocket and produced a small laser pocket knife. The high-tech knife could cut through anything, and he aimed the laser with great care so as to not slice off his finger tip, or damage the box's mysterious contents. After a few minutes of searing through Lucky's old weld and solder job, the box flipped opened and its contents sprang free, landing with a plop in the salty beach sand.

Otto looked up at the blue sky and felt the sea wind brush against his face. It felt good to be able to stretch his legs after such a very long time in confinement.

"Oh my! It's a doll!" Luna exclaimed. "Look, it's a doll."

Luna snatched Otto up from the sand and brushed him off, spinning around, analyzing every inch of him.

"How peculiar that someone would box up a doll like that." Ivy said.

"The seal on that box was meant to last and preserved that doll perfectly. Whoever put him in there expected he would be in there for a very long time."

"Please, can I keep him, Mom?" Luna begged.

Ivy took the doll from Luna's hands and looked him over.

"A doll is a wonderful thing to help prepare a little girl for her future. But he's going to need some work, and I think I can repair him for you. Sprucing him up might be a fun little craft project. His eyes look a little loose to me, and he's very fragile. Be gentle with him."

Otto appreciated the advice.

"But I don't see any reason you couldn't keep him if you want to."

"Thanks, Mom!" Luna was thrilled.

"Your new doll is going to need a name," Chaz pointed out. "What do you want to call him?"

"First of all, he's not a boy...he's a girl. I can tell."

"But he doesn't look anything like a girl." Ivy said.

"He just needs some long hair and girl clothes. And I already know what her name is -- her name is Priscilla!"

"Priscilla? That's very original! A nice old New England name for an old New England doll. What an imagination! Where did you come up with a name like that?"

Luna paused and considered the question. It seemed like a reasonable inquiry, she just didn't know how to answer it.

"I... don't know... it's just what her name is... that's all. I could tell right away when I looked at her."

"Very well. Welcome to our family, Priscilla!"

It had been many ages since he had been considered female, and he thought it was a good time for a change of pace. Besides, the wardrobes and the pampering tended to be much better.

Before he had been named Otto, he went by the name of Didier. Through the ages, Otto had always taken on the name of his previous owner if they had offered him any great love or sacrifice. While he was called Didier, he was brought to Manisses by a young boy named Otto, who sacrificed his own life to do nothing more than honor a promise he made to a dying girl aboard the *Princess Augusta*. During his time as the doll named Otto, his owner Prissy believed he was in grave danger from Bernice Cowan who was out to destroy him. So, she sealed up the one thing in the world she loved more than anything else, applied tremendous love and care, then threw him into the sea where he would be safe, sensing that one day, he would be found again. She had sacrificed a part of herself to ensure his survival.

He would be grateful to carry the name, Priscilla, in her honor.

Otto had taken several names through the ages. Before he was Didier, Otto spent time in Norway during the famine where he went by the name of Gregoris. Before that, his name had been Sophia during a Russian war with the Ottomans over access to the ocean. Before that he had traveled with a servant of Marco Polo, visited Greece when it was overrun by Slavs, and was in Athens when it was sacked by the Goths. He also spent time in India, Mongolia and with various members of the royal court during the Shang Dynasty in China.

If he existed, Otto, and his kind, went by different names in different societies -- angels, spirits, ghosts, jengu, sprites, yakshis, fairies, nymphs, spirit guides -- and in some cultures, simply demons or devils. He had only ever been exorcised once, and he didn't enjoy it.

If he did not exist, then he was no more than an inanimate doll, providing harmless comfort to children, satisfying the fancy of creative minds and providing amusement to the spiritually misdirected.

But whether he existed or not, it was true that he was quite real in the minds of those who thought he was. And Otto had a habit of turning up for those people, just at the moment he was needed most. He was not a being that could be channeled. He was obliged by birthright to conduct the channeling himself.

"All your windmills look impressive from the beach," Ivy told Chaz, "but I think one of them is on fire."

Chaz's eyes widened and he spun his head around like it was on a pivot. He glared out across the blue waves, stared at his windmill forest, and exhaled a sigh of relief.

"That's not one of mine, thank goodness. I would guess that's just the setting sun reflecting off the mast of someone's sailboat."

"Are you sure? It looks like a fire on the horizon to me."

Otto was pleased he had been found, just in time. It was going to be a very busy summer.

AUTHOR'S NOTE

I have always enjoyed the work of artist Jean Leon Gerome Ferris (1863-1930) who is best known for creating *The Pageant of a Nation* – 78 individual, epic paintings that romanticize famous moments in American history. Though few know his name, anyone with a typical American grade school education would recognize some of his more well-known creations from the pages of almost every middle and high school textbook. One of his more notable works, *The First Thanksgiving*, that inaccurately portrays the native Wampanoag's sitting on the ground being served bread from a Pilgrim's platter, is iconic.

What I find most fascinating about Ferris' work isn't the over-the-top patriotism or his classical painting style (of which I admit minimal critiquing skill) but his uncanny ability to use unconventional moments to capture landmark historical achievements. For example, rather than paint Washington sitting atop his horse on the battlefield (as the more famous painter John Trumbull did) to depict the American victory at Yorktown, Ferris painted the portrait of a simple courier, letter in hand, delivering it to Washington's own mother, while an eager crowd of friends, neighbors and even slaves hold their breath in anticipation of the letter's message.

In my mind, Ferris' work is infinitely more poignant. Did the war end when Cornwallis surrendered and laid down his arms, or did the war end, in the minds of average citizens, when they heard the official news days later? Ferris' ability to capture the emotion of that instant, in my mind, is genius.

Above my desk hangs a print of my favorite Ferris painting, *Drafting the Declaration of Independence*. The painting portrays Benjamin Franklin reading the legendary document for the first time as John Adams and Thomas Jefferson, quill in hand, look on. The three iconic statesmen are alone together in a disheveled room, open books and crumpled papers litter the table and floor -- hardly a scene worthy of such American demigods. Ferris' work argues that history was not created when the official document was voted and adopted, but rather, in that magical nanosecond that it was conceived. Imagine what it would have been like to be standing among these three illustrious founders at the instant in time when their eyes met and they realized, *"wow... I think we have something here."* And if that instant is the more valuable historic moment, perhaps to better understand our country, we should be touring the messy bedrooms of our nation's founding fathers, and not immaculately restored historic places like Monticello or Independence Hall. Consider which would offer us the deeper insight.

And somewhere in this hodgepodge of philosophy of history, the idea for *Manisses* was conceived. For those who may read this who are not from New England, *Manisses* is based on the real-life island of Block Island which sits 13 miles south of the Rhode Island coastline. While formulating the plot and themes behind this book, I happened to visit and read about the island's unique history – and its role in everything from the War of 1812, to World War II when a German U-boat was sunk in its waters. Yet anyone traveling to the Northeast looking to learn about New England's rich history would never have Block Island on their radar – the island's proud history dwarfed by the better-known, immortalized, history-book moments that happened in New York, Boston, Hartford and even Providence.

But *Manisses* is not meant to be a history book anyway. It is a fictional locale only, created to symbolize all those small, insignificant, profound moments that Ferris devoted his life's work to immortalize. Besides, the island's real history is far more interesting. Although many of the characters and events exist in the true historic record, such as Captain William Kidd, Witch Kattern, the *Princess Augusta*, and the *Black Duck*, many others do not, including Horace Hunter, Shadrack, Floyd and The Skulduggery – and exist in my mind only to represent a specific era in history and move the tale along.

If I had to select a favorite character from these pages, it would easily be the great, epic pile of rocks on the beach that participated in all Manisses' rich historic moments, only to be denied its stay of execution in the end. It truly represents what this story is all about and how, as Americans, we so often miss the point, message and majesty of our own collective past.

And I know Otto would agree.

Steven R. Porter
Harmony, Rhode Island

ACKNOWLEDGEMENTS

First, I would thank the good people of Block Island for allowing me to portray them as greedy, impatient, callous, trivial, caring, dedicated, helpful, loving and compassionate -- and a host of other characteristics weaved and embedded throughout the novel. I know of no one who has ever visited the island and not left feeling as if they were leaving a dear friend behind.

Samuel Truedale Livermore's book, *A History of Block Island*, (1876), was a continual inspiration and fascinating source of tasty morsels of historic detail.

Howard S. Russell's book, *Indian New England Before the Mayflower*, (University Press of New England, 1980) was a valuable source of information about how the native Manisseans may have lived and perceived the world in the era before European influence. And I would also like to acknowledge Roger Williams' classic *A Key Into the Language of America*, first published in 1643, for the same reason.

And finally, as with my last novel, this book would not exist without the continual support, critiques, edits and labors of my dear wife, Dawn.

A B O U T   T H E   A U T H O R

The Author at Settler's Rock at Cow Cove
Block Island, Rhode Island
Summer, 2011

Steven R. Porter author of the critically acclaimed debut novel, *Confessions of the Meek and the Valiant,* is a writer, marketing consultant and former Director of Advertising and Public Relations for Lauriat's Bookstores, Inc. Steven is also a frequent speaker and lecturer on Internet technologies and emerging publishing techniques. In September 2011, he founded the *Association of Rhode Island Authors* **www.RIAuthors.org** and served as its first president. He and his wife Dawn are active volunteers in their local community and reside in the village of Harmony, Rhode Island with their two children Thomas and Susannah.

For updates and information about forthcoming and new releases, visit:
Website: **http://www.StevenPorter.com**
Blog: **http://AlongtheVillageGreen.wordpress.com/**
LinkedIn: **http://www.linkedin.com/in/stevenporter**
Facebook: **http://www.facebook.com/people/Steven-R-Porter/554283413**
Twitter -- **http://twitter.com/stevenrporter**
Email: **Steve@StevenPorter.com**

Also from

STEVEN R. PORTER

Confessions of the Meek and the Valiant is not your father's --
or Godfather's -- mob story.

The notorious underworld gangs of South Boston are gone,
but loyal men still meet to glorify them in the backrooms of the
raucous neighborhood pubs. So when Riley Lynch, a shy, bright and
likable Irish-Catholic kid from Southie is accepted to a prestigious
college in New York, his proud family and their old connections rally
to support him. But in doing so, they inadvertently expose
disturbing secrets from his family's past that cause Riley to question
everything he was raised to believe. And it is only through the
passion of a pure and innocent heart that he and those he loves can
be rescued from his family's dark legacy, and from the control of a
rising, new and ambitious mob kingpin.

Confessions of the Meek and the Valiant is a fast-paced
chronicle of love, family, adventure and redemption. It is a story of a
young man's quest to discover who he is, who he wants to be, and
whether he can accept what the world believes he has become.

ISBN-10: 1463542003 / ISBN-13: 978-1463542009

Also from

STEVEN R. PORTER

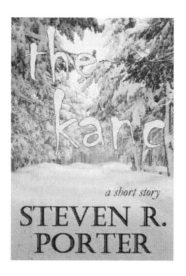

When Rick and Annie Waldron, a bitter elderly couple, turn onto New Hampshire's legendary Kancamagus Highway in a dangerous snowstorm, they are unaware that their fate may lie with an ancient forest alive with a vengeful spirit.

Amazon Kindle: **ASIN: B0070A8K1Y**
Barnes & Noble Nook: **BN ID: 2940014103152**

Made in the USA
Columbia, SC
15 February 2018